PRAISE FOR *L*

'Former publisher Giles O'Bryen clearly knows which buttons
to press in this his first thriller. The unusual main location –
the Western Sahara – is described in all its terrible beauty and
political complexity, thus adding depth to a standard twisty tale of
duplicitous spooks and greedy crooks. More please.'
—*London Evening Standard*

'Featuring spies, black humour and suspense, it's a novel that is
almost impossible to put down... It's dark, tense, and the politics
of the Western Sahara are fascinating.'
—*Pure M magazine*

SAY A
LITTLE
PRAYER

ALSO BY GILES O'BRYEN

Little Sister

SAY A LITTLE PRAYER

A JAMES PALATINE NOVEL

GILES O'BRYEN

fTHOMAS & MERCER

Published by Thomas & Mercer, Seattle

www.apub.com

Amazon, the Amazon logo, and Thomas & Mercer are trademarks of Amazon.com, Inc., or its affiliates.

ISBN-13: 9781503937123
ISBN-10: 1503937127

Cover design by Mark Swan

Printed in the United States of America

To Nell

'Because there's everything and nothing to be said'
—Craig Raine, 'The Onion, Memory'

Prologue

From: Dr Eleni Asllani [eleni_a@uni-pr.edu]
Sent: 09 April 2002 21:41
To: james.palatine@hotmail.com
Subject: K

Dear James,

I have to tell you something terrible. Katarina has been arrested. A man tried to grope her at a bus stop so she struck him and he fell backwards into the street. His head was hit by the wing mirror of a van which was rushing past, and now he is in a coma. They say he is not in immediate danger, but anyway he may still die, or suffer brain damage, which could be worse. She stood at the bus stop until the police came to arrest her.

When Anna and I arrived at the police station, we were told that Katarina had hit the man with a knuckleduster. That knuckleduster, yes. Anna thought she had thrown it away, or that you had taken it. But no, Katarina has been carrying it round with her all this time.

Of course, Katarina refused to answer any questions or even give her name. The police thought she was being obstructive, so then we explained what happened to her three years ago and how she has not said a word to anyone since. Poor Anna, she hates having to admit that her own daughter will not speak to her.

We thought things were getting better, but this is a truly frightening setback. James, we here in Pristina are feeling so sad that we can hardly get through the day.

Love,

Eleni

James

(Kosovo, January 1999)

1

We reached the crest of the hill and a break in the trees gave us an uninterrupted view down the icy, rutted track that led to the farm. TJ gestured for us to take cover and we moved to the periphery of the clearing. Frost-curled leaves crunched beneath our boots, our exhalations boiled briefly in the air. We settled down to wait. If in doubt, wait. It was one of TJ's maxims. A cow coughed from a shed. A thread of smoke slanted from the chimney of the farmhouse and frayed against the hard blue sky. The stillness had a peculiar quality, as if the village had been temporarily switched off. TJ was always very intent at such moments: displays of caution on his part were not to be taken lightly.

'I don't like this,' he said eventually. 'You sure it's here?'

The question was for me, and I'd already checked half a dozen times. This was the spot where the satellite had lost track of the Serbian anti-aircraft unit. Looking at the steep-sided valley and the huge oak trees that overhung the road beyond the village, it was easy to see why.

The pristine silence was abruptly torn open by a long, high-pitched wail. I flinched, then looked over at Azza for reassurance that it wasn't just me who'd been unnerved by the sudden cry. My appeal was met only by an expanse of shorn, gingery scalp: he was leaning over to inspect at close quarters a large mole on his calf, which – as he told us several times a day – was almost certainly on the point of turning cancerous. He sensed me watching him and looked up. The wailing sound came scything through the air again, shockingly loud. Pretty much anything could inspire a witticism in Azza, but he was silent. We all knew that what we'd heard was the sound of a woman in mortal distress.

'Fuck it,' said TJ. 'In we go.'

We moved down parallel with the track in relays: two on the move; two covering them; two protecting our flanks. And me staying close to whoever was covering the advancing men and trying not to make the inane mistake they expected of me. In the gaps of silence between the woman's cries, I found myself in a state of unbearable apprehensiveness, like a man who has glimpsed a tray of instruments he believes will be used to torture him.

We followed a worn trail that led to the pasture lower down the valley, then crossed a stream and circled round to the rear of the farmstead, peering into the sheds and coops and yards at its fringes. Nobody had done much farming here for a while: there were bales of rotting straw and bits of machinery scattered about like discarded bones. The woman's keening flayed the air, ever louder, ever more insistent. TJ would report that we were searching for evidence that might help us work out which way the Serbian AA unit had gone, but really we entered the farmhouse because we were compelled to by the siren call of her suffering.

TJ cupped his hands downwards, then pulled them apart – his sign for a booby trap. It was the custom for Serb militia to ensure that returning to a Kosovar village they had emptied would be a hazardous business, and traps were expected: tripwires set across gates; doors that exploded when you turned the latch; and, I'd heard, plastic mineral water bottles filled with a solution of caustic soda, then sealed to make them look like new. But this place was different: no burnt-out buildings, no belongings abandoned in flight, no stubborn old men shaking with rage and humiliation. TJ pointed to Big Phil and Ollie in turn, beckoned them to join him. They ran along the wall of a ramshackle cowshed and entered the yard by a gate alongside the farmhouse. Azza, Peanut, Zeb and I formed a protective cordon around them. We watched them search for traps, like blind men feeling their way across unfamiliar ground. After a few minutes, TJ waved us forward.

'I don't like this,' he repeated. 'Slime, hide in that.'

That was me. Green slime – the Regimental term of endearment for officers of the Army Intelligence Corps. TJ was indicating a galvanised rubbish hopper by the entrance to the yard. I declined to climb inside, but crouched behind it obediently enough, only to be startled by a clunk behind me. I slipped in a patch of ice and ended up on hands and knees looking at a bony cow that had stuck its head through the door of its shed. TJ waited pointedly until I was settled, then gestured to Ollie to enter the farmhouse through an open window to the left of the door.

Ollie was half way through the window when a door banged open on the other side of the house. Suddenly the men around me were on full alert, absolutely still, weapons raised. TJ signalled: *stay hidden, do not fire.* Two rough-looking men ran out from the corner of the farmhouse, splashed across the stream and started to scramble up through the steep woodland on the far side. They climbed fast, reaching for handholds in the undergrowth, lumps of dislodged earth cascading beneath their feet. A moment later, they reached the top and disappeared.

We waited. The keening stopped and the woman spoke, a piteous, babbling grief that tumbled around the yard like a wounded bird. TJ nodded at Ollie and gave him the thumbs-up, then followed him through the window. I heard them moving around inside, kicking doors and shouting 'Clear!' as they checked each room in turn. After three minutes, Ollie stuck his head round the edge of the bin and told me to come inside. I went, a feeling of dread churning in my stomach.

I couldn't help but meet her eyes. She was sitting in a low chair beside a TV set that was flickering and murmuring into the gloom. Her slippered feet stood in a puddle of pink fluid. Her dress had been ripped open and her breasts hung sad and ungainly in a beige-coloured bra. Nor could I prevent my eyes from glancing over the mess below, or snatch them away quickly enough afterwards. The woman had been eviscerated.

'Priest.'

She was holding up a cellphone in one hand. Amid the reek of slaughter was another smell I couldn't identify. I retreated to the doorway, gulping at the column of vomit in my throat.

'Priest,' she said again.

'Not there, for fuck's sake,' said TJ. 'Outside.'

I wish I could have expelled the horror from my head as easily as I did the food from my stomach. I went back inside. The floor was strewn with broken glass and dozens of small peeled onions. That was the other smell: vinegar.

Someone had used the dying woman's blood to daub a cross on the wall opposite the door, along with the legend ЈЕБЕМО УЦК. *We fuck KLA.*

'Priest,' the woman moaned. She swallowed and spoke again, louder: 'Priest. Kill me.'

She'd dropped the phone while I was vomiting in the yard, and now it lay in the pool of blood below her dangling hand. I was aware of the others moving around behind me. Why was no one tending to her? The ashy shadow of a Road Runner cartoon cavorted across the TV screen beside her head. I avoided looking into the woman's eyes and answering her plea. She was begging for a priest to help her die in peace. Could I not even manage that?

I walked quickly to her side and picked up the phone. There was a number on the screen. I pressed call and held it to my ear. I heard the connection, then the familiar droning Morse of a handset demanding to be answered. The woman was nodding. 'Priest, priest...' she said, over and over again. The priest did not answer. The connection went dead but I could not bring myself to take the phone from my ear and admit that I had failed her. Perhaps she saw the vacillation in my eyes, or heard the hum of the disconnected line, because she started to wail again.

'Priest. Kill me.'

I placed my hand on her shoulder and held it there – a poor gesture but it was all I could manage.

'She wants us to kill her,' I said.

'Your call,' said TJ without turning round.

Azza was climbing a rickety ladder that led to a hatch in the ceiling.

'Where's Ollie?' said TJ.

He never lost track of his men – especially not Ollie, his second-in-command. The brazen savagery of the scene had disrupted the rhythm of a group of fighting men who were considered elite even within the SAS; now, for a moment, they were just six people trying to cocoon themselves from the contagion of the woman's suffering, even as she moaned and bled in their midst.

Azza pushed the hatch-cover aside.

'No no no...'

Her voice found a new pitch, wild and swooping. She was shivering, so hard the chair clattered beneath her. I realised I still had the phone pressed to my ear and put it hurriedly in my pocket. Azza was pushing his head up through the hatch. No soldier of his experience would normally do such a thing, and no leader of TJ's calibre would normally let him. We were in thrall to circumstance, going through the motions, like men climbing to the gallows.

7

'No,' the woman said. She tried to speak again but her voice failed and she could only mouth the words and stare at me, a look of desperate entreaty in her eyes.

I felt dizzy. I was drowning in the sick-smelling air. A square of sunlight fell on the brick-tiled floor, the shadow of Azza's body swayed across it. I started up the ladder after him. An automatic rifle blurted out and a body thumped against the joists above my head.

'Stop!'

TJ, yelling at me. Azza was slumped in the eaves, his upper body shielded by a large wooden crate. One leg was stretched out awkwardly in front of him, illuminated by a lattice of sunlight slanting in between the roof tiles. Another three-bullet burst. Shredded canvas flapping from his shin, a spatter of blood gleaming on the toecap of his boot. His hands reached out to drag the limb to safety and a splinter of light fell across his shorn scalp.

An unearthly rage consumed me and I drove myself up over the lip of the hatch and into the loft. I saw him then, the gunman, crouched by the end wall, rods of white sunlight sliding over the barrel of his rifle as it arced up towards my stomach. I did not even break stride, but launched myself at the gunman. Bullets slammed into the planked floor. My forearm effortlessly rolled the muzzle aside. My head impacted his solar plexus and the air guffed from his lungs. He crashed to the floor and I had him pinned, disarmed, breathless, his slight body motionless and his heart palpitating in my ear.

Then I did something I can't explain. Something I wish I had not done. I seized a handful of his shirt and levered him upright. I swung him round till his head lolled back and exposed his neck, white skin drawn tight over his voice box. I sank down on my haunches, pivoted at the waist and drew my shoulder back, then hurled my fist into that angular, undefended throat. I felt the cartilage crumple. He croaked once, a harsh, mechanical noise. His legs sagged and I let him drop to the floor.

I turned and saw TJ kneeling beside Azza.

'Medi-pack?'

'Downstairs.'

'Get it. And press something to that ear or your fucking brains'll fall out.'

I reached up and found my neck was slick with blood. I stared down at the victim of my assault and saw that he was barely more than a boy. His eyes still showed the shock and loneliness he had felt at the point of death.

Ollie had come up to help with Azza.

'See what Slime did,' he said to TJ, nodding at the corpse. 'Reckon he's one of us.'

2

We manoeuvred Azza back down through the hatchway and out into the yard. The woman had bled out. TJ was all over us, dispensing orders in his flat-vowelled but oddly tuneful West Midlands accent, and the men were grateful to be told what to do. Our position was serious. Azza had a bullet lodged in his shoulder and his breathing was thick and spluttery, which meant he was probably bleeding into his lung. The wound in his calf was flecked with splinters of bone – the kind of injury that ends in amputation. We were twenty-three kilometres from the border and no chance of an evac – we weren't even supposed to be in Kosovo.

Ollie cut Azza's shirt away and cleaned up the shoulder, while Big Phil worked on his leg. Then they lashed him to a makeshift stretcher, most of which was hidden by his pillar-box of a torso and cruiserweight thighs.

'Good news,' said Phil. 'The lead's taken out that mole you're so arsed about.'

Azza smiled. He had enough morphine in his veins to smile without the good news.

'Bad news is, Slime saved your friggin' life.'

TJ glanced up from the GPS on which he was plotting our

route to the border and saw that I was still holding a handkerchief to my head.

'Peanut, patch him up,' he said. 'Phil, Zeb, back up the track and recce. We move out in two minutes.'

Peanut was a lugubrious, knobbly jointed Scot, the oldest of the six and the one who seemed to derive most enjoyment from taunting me. He picked a gauze from the pile by Azza's stretcher, then yanked my hand away from my ear.

'Earlobe's gone,' he said. 'Bleeding like my nan's piles after a night on the ginger wine.'

He slapped on the gauze and I held it in place while he bound my head in an unnecessarily long swathe of bandage. He meant this as a kind of insult, but I hardly noticed. I was in shock. My mind was flashing up images of the bleeding woman, the exposed throat of the boy I'd killed. Who were they? What happened?

'Out we go,' said TJ.

We made our way up the hill to the clearing, then doubled back along a track that followed the ridge where we had seen the two men fleeing the farmhouse. With Azza to bear to safety, we didn't have time to work our way along stream-beds or weave through the undergrowth as we normally would, and as soon as the track levelled out, TJ ordered us to up the pace.

After a few hundred yards we came to a path which led up past a copse of birch trees to a gloomy church, improbably grand for its remote locality, with a pair of squat, octagonal towers either side of an arched doorway. A little further on we found a Mitsubishi camper van parked in a lay-by; the track led on to a single-storey building of painted breeze blocks with a pitched roof of tarred felt. The metal window frames had leaked trickles of rust down the walls, and several broken panes had been replaced with squares of warped plywood. The front door was served by a short set of steel steps and a railed platform. A green wheelie bin stood at one corner, surrounded by sodden cardboard boxes and black plastic bags. Leaning against the bin was a child's bicycle, its chain drooping in the dirt.

We crouched low by the Mitsubishi while TJ sent Ollie and Zeb ahead to see if there was a quick way of skirting the building in our path. Shadows moved across the dingy yellow light behind the front door. Azza coughed and a little pink foam appeared at the corner of his mouth. The scouting party returned. It seemed that to the right of the track was dense undergrowth, while to the left the way was barred by the building itself. I watched TJ think it through, fingers tapping on a rung of the aluminium ladder mounted on the rear of the camper van. He'd already announced that he planned to make the border in four hours, and what TJ announced he liked to bring about. Dusk was falling. Azza's condition was dangerous, and might worsen if he got slung around as we negotiated the steep slope below the building.

'Stick to the track. Eyes down. No talking.'

As TJ spoke, I felt the Mitsubishi shift on its springs. I looked up and saw the distorted reflection of a child's face in an oblong of scratched, convex glass – large black eyes and a curved fringe of hair. The face disappeared and again I felt the merest rocking from the body of the vehicle. I was too astonished to move or speak. I focused on the oblong in which I had seen the face and realised it was a reversing mirror mounted on a stalk that projected from the upper rear corner of the vehicle. There was a child inside.

The mirror was blotted out by TJ's head. 'You with us, Captain Palatine?'

I stood up. It was disturbing to think that there was a child inside the camper van, so close to the scene of slaughter in the farmhouse, but I resisted the urge to investigate further in case I frightened her. Zeb and Peanut were already in position on the far side of the building. Phil and Ollie set off with Azza. We watched them carry him away into the gloom, then TJ beckoned me to follow. As we approached, I saw a figure moving behind the ribbed glass of the door.

'Don't even look up,' said TJ quietly.

I couldn't help it. The door opened and a man of about my height stepped onto the platform at the top of the steps. It was dusk and there was a light behind him so he was really no more than a silhouette, but I had the impression we were very similar in appearance, though he must have been ten years older. He held out his arm in greeting and said something in Albanian. He was dressed in a clean black suit and grey tunic topped by a white clerical collar. TJ muttered at me and quickened his pace. The man spoke again.

'Can you please look out for one of my children?'

He spoke English with a regional accent I couldn't place – mainly I noticed that his voice was somewhat toneless and dispirited. I stopped. TJ glared back at me, without breaking stride. The priest walked down the steps and came over.

'A girl – she ran away about an hour ago, we think. She can't have got far.'

'There's a girl hiding in the camper van back there.'

'Not her. She likes to sit in there – in hope of going somewhere, I suppose,' he said, in his despondent voice. 'My name is Father Daniel.' He held out his hand and I shook it. 'Daniel Cady.'

He looked back over his shoulder at the open door, then turned and met my gaze. There was something strange in his eyes: *You see how wretched I am,* they seemed to say, *but I cannot tell you why.*

'The girl who ran off is twelve or thirteen. An orphan – people leave them here at our refuge. If you find her, will you please bring her back to us?'

'The woman down there was asking for you.'

'Down there… You were at the farmhouse? Is she all right?'

'No, she's not.'

'Dear God. I must go to her.'

'I called you on her phone. You didn't answer.'

It wasn't meant as a reproach, but the priest's eyes went hollow and his face as white as ash. I wondered whether he'd heard the gunshots. He opened his mouth to speak, but before the words could form themselves he was running down the track towards the farmhouse. I turned to look for TJ and the others, but they had gone.

* * *

I was ignored when I caught up with them ten minutes later. I had undermined TJ's authority and he would exact his price in due course, but the priority was to get Azza to safety and I was an irritating distraction. I didn't care. The cold lost its bite and it started to rain, a pattern of stippled grey swirling down the track between the trees. We stripped off our outer clothes and stowed them in drysacs, covered Azza with a square of tarp, and marched on.

The rain became heavy, hissing and clattering in the branches overhead, numbing our hands and making the stones shine beneath our boots. Azza stared up into the darkening sky, raindrops exploding in his eyes and streaming down the creases in his face. TJ scrutinised his route, studied the landscape wherever we broke cover, counted yards. The GPS signal was cutting in and out and the map was cursory: this was a place to get lost in.

Half an hour later, we took a smaller path that led off the ridge and down into the next valley to the south and found ourselves plunging through sucking, slippery mud, six inches deep and cluttered with fallen branches. Peanut put his foot on a lump of rotten wood that imploded and slid sideways. He grabbed for a handhold in the undergrowth and ended up face down in a thicket of hazel stems.

That was how we found her.

It was like coming across a defenceless little woodland animal. Huddled amongst the tree roots, hugging her knees, jet-black hair clinging to her face. So drenched and dirty it was impossible to see what she was wearing, but her feet were bare. She had not reacted at all to the sudden arrival of Peanut's bony shoulder at her side, but simply stared from wide, blank eyes at the two panting, mud-slicked giants who'd suddenly appeared in front of her.

TJ ran back up the path to find out what was holding us up. He saw the girl, took her by the arm and pulled her out onto the path. She was so stiff with cold that her legs did not uncurl and he ended up dragging her across the mud on her knees. She was clutching a white plastic bag that contained something about the size and shape of a box of chocolates.

'Go back,' said TJ. He pointed up the path to the refuge. 'Back! And be quick about it.'

I put my hand between her shoulder blades. She was bone cold, beyond shivering. I knew what exposure was. Disorientation. Exhaustion. She'd be lucky to get two hundred yards. In a couple of hours' time, her wet clothes would start to freeze.

'I'll carry her,' I said.

'Carry her where?' asked TJ.

They weren't going to wait while I went back to the refuge. I'd have to find my own way to the border, in darkness, with no map and only intermittent GPS. I wasn't much of an orienteer even in broad daylight.

'With us,' I said. 'She's an orphan, anyway.'

I started to lift her up, then realised she couldn't hook her arms round my neck while still holding the white plastic bag. I tried to take it from her, but she wouldn't let go. Her large, dark eyes, so unnervingly empty until that point, filled with panic.

'What's this, pass the fucking parcel?' said Peanut.

I picked her up and folded my arms around her small, cold body, trapping the object in the plastic bag between us. She extracted one arm and laid it weakly on my shoulder.

'We lost contact with Captain Palatine at—' TJ checked his watch. 'Seventeen forty-three. In view of the urgent requirement to evacuate Corporal Harrington, we were unable to mount a search. I knew he had the skills and equipment necessary to find his way to the border and therefore ordered my unit to continue on our route. It is my opinion that Captain Palatine does not have the levels of fitness and discipline necessary for further assignments with the Regiment. You get my drift?'

I nodded. This got all of us off the hook. The men of TJ's unit were immaculately cold-blooded, hand-picked for their aptitude for doling out violent death without experiencing the slightest frisson of distracting emotion; but they also cherished the idea that they were, paradoxically, softies at heart – especially where children were concerned. And perhaps the scene in the farmhouse had left some kind of mark on their leathery psyches. Either way, no one wanted to leave the girl to die alone at night on this mud-drenched hillside. TJ had steered them through the unexpected moral crisis with unerring nous – and rounded out his solution with a soldierly insult. Everything was just as it should be: the girl would be saved and TJ had settled his score.

3

The rain turned to sleet as darkness furled itself around us. I stumbled, slipped and jolted down the steepening path, worrying about the girl in my arms. I wanted to feel her flex and shift and cling, but her limbs were brittle, her breathing weak. I wanted to stop and find something to wrap her in, but TJ wouldn't wait and if she and I got detached then we were both in trouble. Zeb and Peanut were carrying Azza now, and the others held torches to light the way. I followed the little cones of sleet-streaked light as they danced through the darkness, and the flying slush bit into my face and arms like lashes from a whip. The trees roared around us, and whenever a little moonlight broke through the cloud, I saw branches rearing and shying like terrified horses.

I kept thinking TJ must call a halt, get us under tarps, at least until the storm blew out. But the survival of a comrade was at stake, and SAS men don't stop for a little rain. We plunged on down the path, brambles fishing at our faces, icy water sluicing over the tops of our boots. I began to dread that when we finally reached our forward operations base, I would unpick a dead body from my arms. But at last we arrived at the cleft of the valley and turned onto a wider track.

As soon as I was sure I could see far enough ahead to follow the weaving torch beams for a hundred yards or so, I put the girl down and pulled out a survival bag. I tucked it round her shoulders, put a watch cap on her head, then took the plastic-wrapped package from her hands. I stowed it in my Bergen and she was too far gone to protest. I offered her chocolate, but she couldn't even take it into her mouth, so I swung the rucksack onto my back and took her up again. It was as well she was so small and my Bergen was only half full, because I guessed I was carrying around forty-five kilos, which was more than I was used to. But I was fit and strong as I'd ever been and, as countless training instructors had told me, the body could perform miracles if only the mind would let it. I held her close and started to run after the others.

We gained quickly, and when we caught up I kept running, but with shortened strides, pumping my knees, willing myself to work harder and harder, channelling all the strength in my body to the task of generating enough heat to save the life of the creature in my arms. We pounded along the track behind the rest and I felt warmth from my chest begin to seep into her, I felt her arms around my neck pulling herself closer to me, I felt her head lose its awful rigid, lifeless pose. She began to shudder, great spasms that convulsed her slight frame. I shivered too. I wrapped my arms even tighter around her. Then her head fell into the crook of my neck and she sighed.

I'd saved her from death, and the emotion was like nothing I had known before – proud and primitive and full of joy. It wasn't just the feeling of being her saviour that so overwhelmed me. Does it sound fanciful to say that the act of carrying her scrunched in my arms through that terrible night released me from the horror I had witnessed in the farmhouse? To me it does not.

She rested her head on my shoulder and her breaths came soft in my ear, and the images that lay strewn across my mind loosened their baleful hold. A twenty-five-year-old Englishman, rendered insensate by his first experience of the trauma of violent combat, and a desperate, dying Kosovan child had found each other at just the necessary moment and bestowed on each other just the necessary form of salvation. Our fates had interlocked: a coincidence not so much of time or place, but of need.

I ran and ran and I knew my body would not fail and my mind would find rest and the girl would live. We held each other close as the forest snapped and howled around us and the sleet glittered like flecks of silver against the billowing velvet blackness of the sky.

* * *

We crossed two more ridges, the second ascent so steep that after twenty yards we had to stop and rope up – the unencumbered men anchoring themselves to trees before hauling the stretcher-bearers up behind them. They offered me the rope but I declined. I didn't need it. I was superhuman, all powerful. With one arm I held the girl I had rescued and with the other reached out into the darkness to grab handfuls of sodden undergrowth and drag us up the next few slippery yards. She clung on, bare feet curled into the gap between my hips and my ribcage. I heard Azza cry out as his porters slipped, heard TJ urge us on like a demented muleteer with a pack of exhausted beasts.

I don't know how long it took us, but we were way off the schedule TJ had demanded; and I don't know what would have happened if, on finally reaching the brow of the second hill, we had not seen the road to Skopje in the valley ahead – dots of streetlight jinking between the dwindling hills and then, in the narrow plain beyond, the steel and tarmac sprawl of the border post at Blace, glowing like an electrical circuit in a cube of bluish, arc-lit air.

Our FOB was six kilometres beyond Blace, but we couldn't cross here: the border to the west of the road was fenced and, in theory at least, patrolled. We turned south, following a rutted trail along the fringe of the forested hills, then entered an area of close-shorn uplands that would take us down into Macedonia without too much risk of detection. Out on these exposed slopes the raw, burly wind sucked the breath from our lungs and we couldn't see more than ten yards ahead for the driving sleet.

After twenty minutes of this, the storm blew out, the cloud rolling back and the sleet rattling away down the valley. A low, bulbous moon appeared, casting shadows alongside us and turning the wet plains to the colour of polished slate. Water that had puddled in ruts and potholes became oily and viscous as it started to ice. We halted and got out our dry clothes, and I sat the girl on my Bergen, dragged a pair of socks over her feet and wrapped her up in a spare shirt beneath the survival bag. I gave her water to drink and chocolate, which this time she ate. She'd recovered enough to inspect me, the look in her eyes wavering between wariness and astonishment.

We made good progress from there, skirting the wash of dim light from the border post until finally it lay to the north-east and we knew we must have crossed the unmarked border and entered Macedonia.

Big Phil got on the radio and called for transport. We hit a dirt track, walked south for ten minutes, and arrived at the spot where we'd been left by a Mercedes people carrier with blacked-out windows two days previously. And there it was again, the yellow cones of its headlights nodding and swaying as it lumbered along the track to fetch us. I checked my watch: five hours and thirty-five minutes since we'd left the farmhouse.

Zeb bent over Azza, dabbing blood from his lips.

'All right, fella. Nearly home.'

The injured man didn't respond. His eyes were open very wide, as if transfixed by something he'd seen high up in the black sky.

Nobody spoke for a few moments, then TJ said to me: 'Get

yourself out of sight. Wait for an hour, then make the call. We go back in tomorrow at eight hundred. RV at the mess. What you going to do with her?'

'Take her into town, I guess.'

'Get a good price for her in Skopje,' said Peanut, 'if yer not that way inclined yerself.'

I would have broken his jaw if I hadn't had her in my arms. Peanut was hard as they come, but I had a reputation, too. I might defer to my Regimental buddies in all-round field skills, but put me one-on-one with any of them – TJ excepted – and I'd like my chances. It was one of the reasons (a fractious relationship with authority and general restlessness being the others) why I was skulking around with an SAS unit in Kosovo rather than swapping bogus secrets with Pakistani army colonels in Lahore.

'Stow it, Corporal, or you'll be shitting teeth,' said TJ.

'Jesus H. Christ,' grumbled Peanut. 'Joke, right?'

I took the girl into the shelter of a depression fifty yards off the track and watched the others march down to meet the transport, outsize frames silhouetted by the approaching headlights. What had my foundling made of the angry voices she had just heard – and the fact that we seemed to have been abandoned? I shifted her weight and found her an oatmeal bar in the pocket of my Bergen.

They loaded Azza, climbed in after, and the Mercedes performed a laborious turn before lurching off towards the base. When they had gone, I carried her back to the track and started to walk, just to keep us both warm. But before I'd taken even a couple of paces I felt her detach herself from my arms and drop to the ground. She hobbled over to my Bergen and sat down beside it, arranging the crumpled shroud of survival bag beneath her.

'We have to wait for a bit, then we'll get a ride into Skopje, OK?'

It seemed unlikely that she would understand, but I talked to her anyway, about how well she'd done and how I would take care of her. The sky had clouded over again and it was too dark to make out the expression on her face, but her eyes shone like an owl's beneath her tangled black hair. I checked between her shoulder blades again and there was some warmth there, so I thought it would be OK for her to sleep for a while.

Now that she was no longer in imminent danger of dying from the cold, her wider misfortune came into focus and I felt a surge of pity. I would get her back to the refuge, but then what? She had run away – she was old enough to understand the consequences of getting lost on such a night, but still she had run. She must have had a plan, a destination in mind. Perhaps she believed her mother and father were still alive. She was brave. And there was something about the way she had removed herself from my arms – a gesture of independence, determined and even a little impatient. I didn't know much about twelve-year-old girls, but I was beginning to sense that she was stronger than she looked. Now she was tapping my Bergen where the oatmeal bars were stowed. I gave her another one, and found a torch. I showed her the switch and she shone it at her feet and started to remove the wet socks. Her feet were bone white. I rubbed them with my hands, alarmed at how hard and stiff they were, then pulled off my boots and gave her my socks, which were scarcely any drier, but at least warm from my feet.

I didn't wait the full hour before making the call; and we didn't get the Mercedes, but an old Land Rover with an ill-fitting hard-top.

'What the fuck is that?' said the driver, catching sight of the girl.

'Refugee,' I explained, helping her into the rear of the Land Rover. 'I have to get her to the UNHCR – know where it is?'

'No, sir,' said the sergeant. 'Hope she's not going to piss on the seat.'

He threw the Land Rover into gear and we bounced off down the track. He drove carelessly and fast, and I put my arm round the girl to stop her being flung about. Once or twice I caught him inspecting us in the rear-view mirror. The speculative look in his eye was irritating.

'Hear you got left behind by TJ Farah's lot,' he said after a few minutes. 'Sets a wicked pace, they say.'

TJ hadn't lost any time turning his version of events into a morsel of Regimental gossip. What had happened at the farmhouse was going to get him in trouble with the Ruperts, as the officer class was known. Not that he wasn't used to it. TJ was a rogue and a maverick who regarded orders and rules of engagement as restrictions invented by officers to make their lives easier and his more difficult. The objective was what counted – and, one way or another, TJ always achieved his objective. He was such an effective soldier that the Ruperts overlooked his excesses and let him get on with it. His reports were said to be masterpieces of obfuscation.

Still, this time he'd led his men into contact, got one of them wounded, and been forced to pull out before the op was complete. The story about some puffing idiot of an Int Corps officer getting lost along the way would be a useful distraction.

We hit the main road into Skopje a few kilometres south of the border post. They were setting up a refugee camp there: bulldozers had already flattened thirty or forty acres of floodlit ground into a frozen black quagmire, and container-loads of supplies were stacked up beside the access road, along with enough fencing panels to hem in the entire population of Kosovo. A little further on, the NATO base sprawled before us, the tents, flatpacks and prefabs of a dozen different nations arranged either side of a spine of rollaway track, lorries and four-wheel drives squeezed into narrow grids, double-skinned ammunition warehouses hunched in far corners – and the whole apparition rendered fuzzy by the millions of tiny interlocking squares that made up the perimeter fence. We drove past the front gates, and twenty minutes later were hurtling along the empty boulevards on the outskirts of the Macedonian capital.

We passed the UNHCR building anyway – it was easy to spot because there was a densely packed line of perhaps six or seven hundred people camped out along the pavement from the main entrance. Most were lying down; but perhaps it was too cold for sleep because as we cruised by I saw eyes staring out from among the bundles of belongings, shining weakly in the streetlight as if their batteries were failing. A long, knotted braid of humanity, spewed out by the conflict that had descended over their lives, and now washed up here on a pavement in Skopje. I felt a prickle of shame. These people had fled their homes because they feared the bombing campaign I'd been helping to prepare.

The apartment I had taken when stationed in Skopje two months earlier was on the third floor of a narrow, modern building sandwiched between a café and an ironmongery store. I thanked the driver and gave him a twenty-dollar bill for his trouble, then led the girl up the six flights, unlocked the door and set her down on a cream vinyl sofa, where she lay and regarded me with an apprehensive expression. The apartment consisted of two tiny rooms and a bathroom with leaky pipes and patches of mildew and bare cement where the tiles had fallen off. It was at least served by a central-heating system of heroic proportions: the huge iron radiators were hot to the touch, and the poor girl had already cast aside the survival bag and seemed ready to pass out under this luxurious onslaught. I threw open all the windows and went through my cupboards to see what I had to eat.

On first moving in, I had bought a few supplies in a woeful attempt to make the place seem homely – and of course they were all still there because I disliked cooking for myself and didn't have anyone else in Skopje to cook for. The girl was, in fact, my first guest. I put on pasta and a bottle of sauce, then found her a can of Coke in the fridge, which she took with an expression of relief on her face, as if this was a sign that, no matter how extraordinary and unexpected her present circumstances, normality might still be within reach.

I had no experience of children whatsoever, but a common-sensical dictum kept running through my head: *she needs to get out of those wet clothes.* The problem was, I didn't have anything else for her to wear. I was friendly with the woman who ran the café downstairs and knew she would lend me clothes in the morning; but for the time being all I could come up with was a towelling dressing gown which, though it could have accommodated three or four of her, was at least clean and dry. I went and turned on the shower, then came back and pointed to the bathroom.

'You need to get out of those wet clothes,' I said.

I reached out and tugged at the damp cotton of her T-shirt, then did a brief shivering mime and handed her the dressing gown. But her only response to my encouragements was to shake her head.

'It's OK,' I said. 'You don't have to. So long as you're warm.'

She opened her mouth and I thought I saw the word 'Mama' on her lips, but then instead of speaking she burst into tears. Yes, Mama, I thought. Mama is needed. Captain James Palatine really won't do. I put my arm round her skinny shoulders, but she shrank away from me. I didn't even know how to comfort her. She wiped her tears away, but more spilled from her eyes, and I felt overwhelmed by her tragedy. She was trying to recover from her outpouring of grief, to be sensible and behave as a grown-up would. But she had not even the vaguest idea who I was or where she was or what would happen to her next. I wanted to tell her that the trials she had been through that day would have reduced even the most sensible grown-up to tears, that I was sure her mother would have wanted her to wash and get out of her wet clothes, that I would take care of her and she mustn't worry at all. But I thought my scant Albanian would only make matters worse; and in any case her immediate future, both with me and then without me, was so uncertain that there was not much I could truthfully say to console her.

I'd forgotten to time the pasta and it had gone sticky, but I divided it between two plates, spooned the sauce on top and set the food on the coffee table between us. She watched me twirl the spaghetti onto my fork before conveying it to my mouth, then she copied me, scratching the fork-tines against the plate and coaxing the awkward strands into a manageable mouthful. Her slender fingers were clumsy from tiredness. Again my heart went out to her.

Now that she had warmed up properly and eaten hot food, a little pinkness had come into her cheeks and I could see what a pretty child she was, with her black hair, oval face and delicate mouth. I had taken her large eyes for mournful, but I saw now that I'd been wrong: even at the end of that wild day, they were full of vigour and intelligence, darting round the room and glancing surreptitiously into mine. I wondered what she saw there. Of course, I was exhausted, too, and traumatised in ways I hadn't even begun to understand.

We finished eating and there was nothing else to do but sleep – and not nearly enough time for that. I eyed my Bergen with dislike, decided there was no point unpacking it, then went into the bedroom and got her a pillow. I placed it at the end of the sofa and mimed sleep. She lay down and I threw the dressing gown over her and turned out the light.

I went into the bathroom and unwound Peanut's insultingly elaborate bandaging from my ear. The lobe was split and started bleeding the moment I pulled off the gauze. I needed to get a fresh dressing so I padded back into the darkened room and unbuckled the Bergen, and there was the white plastic bag with its oblong box inside. I laid it on the coffee table beside the girl and her eyes flicked shut as I looked over. I found the medi-pack, tended to my silly little wound, then went through to my bedroom, leaving the bathroom door open so she wouldn't be in the dark. I set the alarm on my cellphone, lay down and slept.

This was what my mind had been waiting for. The dreams reared up and danced. The downy throat of the dead boy, his limp arms and desolate eyes, the legs of the woman's chair standing in the glazed pink puddle, her heavy breasts in their beige bra. Sticky cellphone, vinegar stink, Road Runners plunging down chasms of rock. She was begging me to help her and I did not. Fear dragged at my heart like an ice-cold undertow, a fear that refused to make itself known.

4

The alarm went but time struggled to reassert itself. When I finally realised the frantic, muddled night was over, my body relaxed and my hands unclenched as if I had only just lain down to rest.

Six a.m. I had two hours to get the girl sorted out and rejoin TJ and company back at the NATO base by the border with Kosovo. The UNHCR wouldn't be open yet. I got up and dressed, and there was the dead woman's cellphone in the pocket of my shirt, the screen obscured by a film of brownish red. I still had Father Daniel's number – perhaps he had contacts in Skopje who could take the girl in.

I went into the sitting room. She was still asleep, one delicate wrist crooked beneath her chin, face very pale. She should sleep there all day, I thought. And then all night if need be. What did she have to wake to?

I went downstairs and found Maria sweeping the corners of her restaurant on the ground floor. Over the months I'd been based in Skopje, I had eaten exclusively at her place, and we had struck up an easy friendship, one that was pleasantly free of expectation or obligation on either side – apart, that is, from the obligation to remain loyal to Café Pogboriza. Maria had a low opinion of the rival establishments in her neighbourhood.

Leonard Cohen was playing over the restaurant speakers, Maria crooning a practised accompaniment to his weighty lament.

'James! Wait one minute.'

She went behind the counter and turned Leonard Cohen off. I explained what had happened.

'James, you are not a sensible man, no,' she said. 'You bring this orphan girl out of Kosovo? Now she is your responsible. You must look after her,' she went on sternly. 'This is how God wishes it.'

'I'll do my best – you have any clothes I could give her?'

'Sure. She is twelve, you say?'

I nodded and Maria went up the stairs at the rear, while I wondered what else God might be wishing for me. Despite Maria's decree and the emotional bond the girl and I had forged the previous night, my priority now was not looking after her but rejoining TJ's unit and going back into Kosovo.

At twenty-five, I still had a young man's restless uncertainty about who I really was and what I was really for. I'd never expected to become a soldier – by training I was a computer scientist. I'd completed a PhD in data-processing and chip design which had caught the eye of the intelligence establishment. GCHQ and their ilk were already beginning to struggle with the volume of data to which they had granted themselves access, and my work held out the promise of actually being able to sift through the bits and bytes faster than they could accumulate them. I'd toiled round the conference and consultancy circuit for a year, fending off unctuous cyber-surveillance executives who wanted to sweet-talk me into selling them my life's work – past, present and future. To me their corporate objectives seemed immoral at best. The phrase 'exceptional remuneration package' kept coming up, and I felt I was being invited to join some conspiracy. So when the Army Intelligence Corps made their cack-handed yet oddly charming approach, it looked like an honourable way out.

Now I was thinking that perhaps I was a soldier after all. What was it Ollie had said? *Reckon he's one of us.*

Maria returned with jeans, a T-shirt and hoodie, and a pair of bleached canvas trainers.

'What will you do? Take her back to Kosovo?'

'I can't. I thought I'd leave her with the UNHCR, though she deserves better after what she's been through. And there are queues a mile long.'

I searched Maria's eyes for some indication that she either approved or disapproved of this idea, but she only shrugged and looked away. I should have asked her to take care of the girl. I should have begged her. Just for a few days. Something held me back. Reticence about asking such a favour from a woman I knew only because I ate at her restaurant? Or perhaps it was in my mind that my heroism would be compromised if I didn't finish the job myself. I don't know. All I told myself at the time was that I should speak to the priest before deciding what to do.

'Bring her here to eat,' Maria said as I left. 'I don't want you giving her soldier's food, out of a packet. Ugh!'

The girl hadn't moved when I got back. I touched her guiltily on the shoulder. She came awake instantly, sat upright and drew the dressing gown I'd covered her with up to her chin. She seemed frozen with terror. I pointed to the neatly folded clothes.

'For you.'

She kept her eyes fixed on me, and pressed herself back into the arm of the sofa. Why was she frightened of me? I was finding her difficult to read. I picked the clothes up and placed them on her lap. Cautiously, she lifted the T-shirt and inspected the hoodie and canvas trainers beneath. Then she looked up at me and solemnly nodded her head, as if to say that she accepted these clothes as a sign that everything was going to be all right.

I went and opened the bathroom door for her. 'You want to put them on?'

She scooted past me and I shut the door and left her to change, while I called the priest on the dead woman's cellphone. The connection rang out. It was a mobile number – switched off or out of battery, perhaps. I thumbed through the contacts list to see if there was a landline. The entries were in Albanian and it took several frustrating minutes with a dictionary before I found a number for the refuge.

'*A flisni anglisht?*' I asked. The connection was poor and I wasn't sure it was the priest who had answered.

'Yes,' came the reply. 'Who am I speaking to?'

'Is this Father Daniel? We spoke yesterday, outside the refuge.'

The line cut out briefly, then he said: 'I remember, yes.'

'I found the girl. She's with me now, in Skopje. I would take her to the UNHCR, but I don't have time. Is there anyone I can leave her with?'

'The girl?' The priest's voice was faint.

'Yes. Where shall I take her?'

There was a long, exasperating pause.

'Can you bring her here?'

'No, I'm in Skopje,' I shouted.

The line cut out again and I was about to hang up and redial when the priest said: 'I thank the Lord you have her safe.' The bad line still muffled his voice, but at least it was audible. 'Did she have any belongings with her?'

'I got her some dry clothes. Hers are filthy.'

'Oh dear.' He made a matronly *tsk-tsk* noise.

'And something inside a plastic bag – a box maybe.' I couldn't see why we were discussing this.

'The poor things get so attached to their few treasures,' he said, as if reading my mind.

'Is there anywhere in Skopje I can take her?' I repeated.

'There's a place the children sometimes stay overnight. Seventy-seven Ulitsa Syrna.' He spelled it out for me. 'Ulitsa means street.'

'OK, seventy-seven Syrna Street. I'll be there inside an hour.'

'That's very good, I'll let them know. Thank you.'

'Do you want to speak to her?'

'No, no… It might unsettle her. May I know your name, please?'

'It isn't necessary,' I said, and hung up.

Father Daniel had seemed distracted – but given the scene he would have found in the farmhouse the previous night, he could be forgiven that. The main thing was, I had somewhere safe to deliver the girl. I could drop her off and still make my rendezvous with TJ. In a day or two she'd be back at the refuge – much better for her than spending the next few months being shunted round Skopje by various agents of international welfare. I'd borne her to safety, given her a decent meal, dry clothes and a warm bed for the night, and arranged for her return to the refuge. I congratulated myself on discharging my responsibilities in full.

The bathroom door opened and the girl stepped out. As well as the clean clothes, she had tidied her hair and washed the vestiges of mud from her face, and she looked quite pleased, I thought, if a little sheepish. Seeing her transformed liked this, from the forlorn subject of my heroic rescue to an ordinary girl in hoodie and jeans, had a curious effect on me: I felt that some distance had come between us. The wild emotions of the previous night had receded, and we two were, after all, a twenty-five-year-old English soldier and a twelve-year-old orphan from Kosovo who had nothing in common at all.

There wasn't time to feed her at Maria's. I boiled the kettle and soon had toast and a mug of tea in front of her. She sat on the sofa and I stood impatiently while she ate. A hank of unruly black hair fell down over her face and she reached and coiled it carefully behind her ear, finishing with a little flicking movement of her head, and then she took a sip of tea and it was too hot so she set it down again and looked apologetically up at me. My mood swung again and I felt guilty that I was so keen to get this poor girl out of my life, this girl who was trying so hard to get things right and who had no choice but to believe or hope that I would do the same.

Six thirty-five. I wanted a shower but already it was too late. I went into the bathroom for a pee. She'd have friends at the refuge, and be looked after in her own country by a man who obviously cared about her. I pulled the plug and heard the plunger rattle in the cistern. Empty. The damn thing leaked and I had tied the ballcock up with a rubber band to stop it filling. No time to tinker with the plumbing. I picked up my Bergen and led her down the stairs and out into the street.

My neighbourhood was an ill-assorted collection of cut-price apartment blocks like mine, a few tatty older houses set back from the road behind iron railings, and a car park occupying a row of vacant lots. Usually, you could look to the east from my door and enjoy an uplifting view of snow-capped mountains, but today they were smothered in a miasma of polluted brown air. The sun was up, but had managed only to smear a little dingy light across the lower fringes of the sky. It was raining again, a settled, drenching kind of rain that left a taint of burnt diesel on the lips.

We didn't have to wait long for a taxi. Skopje was the new home for legions of government and government-sponsored employees from all the concerned nations of the West, and the people of the city were milking them accordingly – via a parallel economy of impromptu restaurants, bars, hotels, nightclubs and taxicabs. I flagged one down and handed over the scrap of paper on which I'd written the address.

'There first, then I'm going on to the NATO base just south of Blace.'

The girl got into the back seat and I climbed in after her, while the driver lit a cigarette and examined the paper. He was about fifty, with a wrinkled, stubbly face and profuse grey hair, rather dressily combed and stained a treacly brown by the suspension of tobacco smoke inside the car.

He turned and studied the girl. 'I look after her now, OK?'

'No. Take us to that address.'

'I drive girl here—' he tapped the paper, showering ash onto the passenger seat. 'My friend drive you to base. Good, yes?'

'Just drive,' I said, meeting his eyes in the rear-view mirror.

'Sorry, I take you, please, no problem. Sorry.'

I was in full-blown heroic mode again, my impatience to get back to war set aside while I kept my young charge safe from predatory taxi drivers. After driving for ten minutes through a district of rundown tenements on the eastern edge of town, we pulled up outside a ramshackle two-storey villa.

I wiped the condensation off the window and looked out. It didn't look like the right place to leave a child. There were black hoppers surrounded by knotted rubbish bags and a motorbike with its entrails spread across the pavement. The house had a green-tiled roof patched with plastic sheeting where the tiles had fallen off. The porch had sheared away from the front door and lay on its side across a row of beer crates. A huge satellite dish was set up in the back of a pickup parked in the yard alongside the building. Beyond it I saw a line of corrugated-iron shacks with padlocked doors and a skip covered with a tattered blue tarpaulin. A large, brindled dog with pendulous ears and emaciated hindquarters stood shivering in the lee of the pickup.

This wasn't what I'd expected… But then, as I told myself briskly, this is Skopje, not some well-to-do Surrey suburb. People who helped the Church in its charitable endeavours didn't have to live in well-kept homes. We got out of the taxi and made our way up to the front door. I knocked on the glass and the dog emitted a series of croaky barks which suggested it regarded its custodial duties with a mixture of reluctance and terror. I knocked again, and finally the door was opened by a girl in her early twenties with startlingly blonde hair and sleepy eyes. There was a faintly resentful cast to her mouth, but when she saw us she smiled cheerfully enough, and I had the impression of a good-natured person. She spoke to the girl beside me, who looked hopefully up at her.

'Thank you, mister,' the young woman was saying to me. A smell of hot fat wafted out from the passage behind her. She reached out to put her arm round the girl's shoulders and the lapel of her dressing gown fell forward, revealing a triangle of soft, pale skin at the upslope of her breast. She saw me looking at her and smiled again. The floor of the passage was covered with newspaper, and there was no bulb in the light fitting. I was in a state of confusion, you must understand, my mind bouncing and skittering, my feelings blunted and swollen like beaten limbs.

'Look after her, OK?'

The hair was dyed, I saw now. Was this how it ended? No officials with ID tags and practised smiles, no rigmarole of forms, databases, stamps and numbers – just this plump-breasted young woman in a seedy house on Syrna Street. Should I ask for a receipt, like a courier delivering a parcel?

I turned to the girl and held out my hand. She took it solemnly and we looked into each other's eyes... And then the dyed-blonde was guiding her away down the passage and closing the door behind her, and the moment to turn back had passed.

5

I climbed into the passenger seat of the taxi, because I am six foot four and there wasn't much legroom in the back. I didn't notice that the girl had left her white plastic bag behind until I was paying off the driver outside the gates to the NATO base. I was tempted to leave it there, but the priest's words came back to me: *The poor things get so attached to their few treasures.* I took it to the guardpost and, when I'd shown my ID and sat down opposite the desk to wait for the duty sergeant to check that I was who I said I was, opened it and looked inside.

Not a box, but a book. And not just any old book but a leather-bound volume, extensively tooled in gold leaf and secured with a brass lock on a thick leather hasp. The words *Book of Prayer* were stamped on the front, and beneath them, *A spiritual record.* It was a treasure all right, but it belonged to the priest, not the girl. It was heavy and as thick as a Bible. I tried the lock and the book fell open in my hands. Quite a few pages had been torn from the back, suggesting the priest didn't treat this object with quite the veneration its ceremonial appearance seemed to demand. Maybe he'd used the thick, powdery vellum to write a note to the cleaner or amuse the children with paper darts. I liked him for that irreverence.

Father Daniel had showy handwriting, even and upright but the shapes bold and full and the serifs adorned with neat flourishes. The page I was looking at was covered with it, all set out inside boxes and margins he'd drawn to divide up the big white space. *Lord, I have delivered myself unto Thee*, I read. *Nothing I do but I do it at Thy bidding and in Thy name.* I turned the page. *Today I considered the text given us by your servant St Anthony: Do not question your Lord, but be sure that he who is pure in heart and <u>true to his calling in God</u> cannot stray far from the path set out for him.*

I was educated at a succession of Catholic boarding schools, and this sort of meandering self-reinforcement was very familiar to me. I turned to the front of the book to see if there was anything like a table of contents, but instead I found a poem typed out on a sheet of paper and folded inside the cover:

> The sea spits ice, the masthead swipes the sky,
> The bulging hull leans drunken on the swell,
> And creaking braids weep bitter tears of brine.
>
> Braced in the hold, I hear the net clump down,
> The load of writhing slides across the deck,
> A flow of gleaming stink, a slapping stream
>
> Of mouthing jaws and gills blown open wide,
> Torn scales, pink slime, a thousand drowning eyes.
> I hook my elbow to the rung and shovel ice.
>
> *Watch if the load shifts...* The cord at my waist
> Sounds a bell on deck. I can call for help. I do.
> But it's God who hears, and He's a fisherman, too.

I couldn't square this weird poem with the routine pieties elsewhere in the book. Jesus offered to make his disciples Simon Peter and

Andrew 'fishers of men', and the symbolism would resonate with any Christian minister. So why the resignation, the disappointment, the sense that the cry for help is heard but goes unanswered? At the foot of the page was a note, handwritten in that showy script of his: *Weakness. A terror that will not relax its grip.*

I was about to flip through and see if there were any more of these unsettling poems – or prayers or laments or whatever you wanted to call this one – when I saw the following edict printed inside the front cover:

> All members of the Order of St Hugh are bound by their vows to keep a private record of their spiritual development. Any person into whose hands this book may fall is earnestly requested to respect the special nature of its confidentiality by refraining from perusal of its pages, and further to return it care of the Rector-General of the Order of St Hugh, The Old Rectory, Huddlestone Road, Northampton NN10 0AE, so that it may be restored to its owner.

I shut the book quickly, feeling as if at any moment a bony-fingered monk might catch me by the shoulder and tell me how I had sinned and what would be the consequence. I pressed home the latch at the end of the hasp and found that it wasn't in fact unlocked. It was broken. The sergeant was tapping on the desk and I looked up.

'You're with TJ Farah, right? He's expecting you. Know where to go?'

'Yes. There a BFPO on site?'

He gave me directions. I found the post office and the grunt at the counter handed me a form to fill in – an army classic: name, rank, ID, DOB, destination, return address, contents… Then it cost me ten dollars to persuade him to perform the arduous task of putting Father Daniel's Book of Prayer in a padded bag and stapling it shut. At last I was free to go in search of my unit. I found them already sitting in the Mercedes people carrier with blacked-out windows.

'Captain Jimmy Palatine,' said Peanut, his voice gritty with spite. 'No one knows what he's for, but he tags along anyway, sure as a hair on a Dundee tart's backside.'

The atmosphere inside the van was grim. No one looked at me as I climbed in.

'Morning, comrades,' I said, somewhat aggrieved by the cold shouldering. 'I got the girl safe. How's Azza?'

'Azza's dead,' said TJ.

6

We were driven down the bumpy track to the place where we'd been picked up the previous night – our regular crossing point into Kosovo. No one spoke. There was so much anger compressed inside the van it felt as if the windows might blow out. At least we didn't have to go back to the farmhouse – the AA unit we were after had gone east. Back on the remote plains above the border we moved fast, as if to demonstrate what we could do when released from the burden of stray children and wounded comrades, and because TJ understood the cathartic power of motion – of running the body up to peak capacity and keeping it there until everything else gets stripped away, everything except the mechanical challenge of supplying energy to muscle and the mental challenge of trying not to stumble or lose heart. By the time TJ called a halt at the crest of a long ridge, we'd made twenty-seven kilometres over awkward terrain in three hours flat. We got off the track, dropped our Bergens and stood stretching and panting in the cold air.

A sharp wind hummed in the trees, and the air up here smelled clean and sweet as peeled bark. Southern Kosovo is a beautiful place. The cloud had lifted and it was as if a different dimension had yawned open above our heads, miles and miles of pale, scoured blue, thin as tracing paper where the sun's corona filtered out from the east. The wet hillside opposite gleamed like hammered silver beneath a far horizon soft as still-warm ash. A heron cranked its way across the sky, legs trailing like broken struts, head disparagingly cocked.

Our mission was to locate the Serbian anti-aircraft units positioned across Kosovo so they could be taken out by JDAMs in the prelude to a NATO bombing campaign. Satellite imagery gave us intermittent snapshots of the emplacements, but the tree cover was dense and it was easy enough to move them by night; and the Serbs had been constructing dummy guns to confuse us further. So it had been decided that a number of joint SAS/Int Corps teams should be sent in to firm up the intel on the ground. In due course, the guided missiles would do their work and the bombers could cruise by unmolested.

We were hampered by the fact that the public line was that there wasn't going to be any bombing campaign: the Serbs would be persuaded – at a grand peace conference near Paris – to leave Kosovo to the Kosovar-Albanian majority without having their hand forced by thousands of tons of high explosives. The UK government was privately sceptical; but still, our operation had to be carried out under conditions of strictest secrecy. Even requesting intel from KLA sympathisers in the region was forbidden.

Eager to test myself in the field, I'd volunteered for the role – and my CO, Colonel Andy Hillson, had agreed to let me go. I was a source of vexation to Hillson: I was supposed to be the Int Corps' shiny new tech, and he'd been boasting about the extraordinary potential of a hacking device I'd been working on; but so far I'd shown more interest in learning how to blow things up. I'd declined a technical consultancy and liaison role at GCHQ and threatened to take a job in the private sector if they didn't find me something more interesting to do. Evidently someone had decided I ought to be humoured, and when I found out I'd be joining TJ Farah in Kosovo, I thought my little campaign could not have turned out better.

What evidence I had suggested that our current target was roughly five kilometres to the north-east. TJ took Zeb off to get eyes-on – he should have taken me, from which I inferred that I hadn't been entirely forgiven. We settled in to wait. It seemed that our exhilarating dash through the hills was going to be followed by a long period of frigid inactivity, and I started to brood on the events of the previous twenty-four hours. It was astonishing to find that it was only this time yesterday that we'd stopped above the village and heard the woman's wailing cries. But what I thought about most were Ollie's words after I'd killed the boy in the loft. *He's one of us.* I couldn't get that phrase out of my head. Ollie's tone had been grudging, yet also faintly gleeful. Why? He was a steadfast, taciturn man and not one for opinions or conjecture. His observation was matter of fact – as if he'd just noticed I was missing a little finger or couldn't tell my left from my right.

Nor was it the first time someone had made a discomfiting observation about my character. At school I'd been friends with a Nigerian boy called Faisal. Just before supper one day, I'd been summoned to the infirmary. Faisal lay in bed, his right arm in a sling. The powdery smell of clean bandages hung in the air. His face was swollen and purple around both eyes, his mouth bloody.

I didn't have to ask Faisal who had done this. Boys from the local village often hung around in the lanes bordering the school and yelled insults at the 'ponces' as they walked up to the playing fields; two in particular picked on any Africans they could find. After leaving Faisal's bedside, I climbed the wall that surrounded the school grounds and crossed a field to the bus shelter. There were six of them there. I crouched by a gate a couple of hundred yards up the road and waited. Eventually, the two I was after detached themselves and headed towards me. One was heavily built with a baseball cap pulled down over his doughy forehead; the other was half the size but hard-faced and wiry. I showed myself and watched them approach.

The wiry one got to me first and swung a fist at my jaw. I dodged the blow, seized him by the hair, yanked his head down so that his throat was crushed against the top bar of the gate, and punched him three times in the temple. After the third punch, the boy's head lolled against the bar. I let him fall and started after the other boy, who was pounding back down the road and would have made it to safety if he hadn't slipped in a patch of grit. He rolled onto his back and kicked out ineffectually as I ran up. I dropped knees-first into his gut, then drove the point of my elbow into his nose.

The local paper described the attack as 'brutal' and the police said they wished to find the 'perpetrators' as a matter of urgency – the boys were saying they'd been beaten up by four ponces from the private school, rather than just the one. It saved me from being found out, though my housemaster guessed the truth.

'This is something you have to watch, James Palatine,' he told me, a hint of admiration in his eyes. 'It could get you into very serious trouble.'

Perhaps I'd always been *one of us*. My head had been so scrambled at the time that Ollie's words had hardly registered; now, I was eager to show that I was. My actions had been driven not by an involuntary rush of blood, but by some predilection within me that the events of the day had brought to light. I could do it again and again. I was that kind of man.

* * *

TJ and Zeb came back and announced that they'd found the anti-aircraft gun. I sent in the coordinates. Mission accomplished. I felt obscurely annoyed that I hadn't been allowed to take part.

43

'In, out, quick as a fuck in a convent,' said TJ. 'Any more pop-guns parked up round here, Jimmy? Those bomber-boys do hate to be shot at.'

He knew there weren't because he'd asked several times already that day.

'I'll check again,' I said, thinking gloomily that I'd probably be back in my stuffy little apartment in Skopje by dawn. I sent over the coded prompt on my handset and the confirmation came back: no other Serbian units in our area of operation.

'So, we have time on our hands,' said TJ. 'And a little damage needs doing. You with us, Jimmy?'

The green slime epithet had dropped out of their lexicon since I'd rejoined them at the base, but that didn't mean they trusted me. I looked round and saw I was being closely observed by five men whose eyes were dull with a hunger such as you would not readily volunteer to see sated.

'What kind of damage?'

'You wouldn't know anything about this if I had my way,' said TJ, 'but the girls here reckon you've got the right, seeing as you saved Azza's life – albeit he didn't live long afterwards.'

'And seeing as yer up to yer neck in it anyway,' said Big Phil.

I looked round at *the girls*, feeling as much astonishment as pride. My eyes came to rest on Peanut; he stared right back at me without saying a word, but without obvious hostility, either – the Peanut equivalent of a warm hug.

'Feel free to get lost again, if you don't fancy it,' said TJ.

'I'm in,' I said.

'What did I tell you?' said Ollie.

'It's like this,' said TJ. 'The gang from the farmhouse, they did for our boy Azza, insulted the Regiment and showed a general disregard for human decency. We don't like them.'

'One of them's already dead,' I said. 'And the others ran off. How're we going to find them?'

'The one that croaked on the end of your fist was but a kid,' said Peanut. 'No disrespect.'

'We reckon they sent him up to the loft to look for stuff to nick,' said Big Phil. 'We turned up, they left him there and legged it. Cunts.'

'Remember what was on the wall?' said Zeb. 'Anti-KLA stuff. Means they're Serb militia, right?'

'According to the brief,' said TJ, 'the big dogs round here are a gang called Bura. Means *tempest*. They operate out of the police station in a town called Kric.'

'About seven k that way,' said Zeb, pointing north.

TJ snapped his fingers. 'See what I mean, Jimmy? It's pure chance. We didn't move that AA unit, we didn't ask it to move, but we came after it and here we are, seven kilometres away from some fuckers we don't like. To turn round and walk away would be just plain wrong.'

As a piece of ethical logic, this was as about as lame as it gets, but they didn't care and neither did I. The muscles in my shoulders twitched and my mouth filled with saliva that tasted of salt and iron. Anyway, the bare facts were true. The Serbian militia who'd been plundering Kosovo with increasing brutality for the previous twelve months were often based at local police stations – hardly surprising, since most of them were commanded by local police chiefs. These pillars of the community swelled their ranks with itinerant ex-cons released from jails further north – many of them veterans of a life of thievery and violence in Bosnia. They dressed up in military gear, armed themselves to a level of extravagance that would have made an SAS armourer blanch and, under the guise of preserving law and order amongst the Kosovar militants, terrorised the countryside.

It was a fair bet that the three men responsible for the slaughter at the farmhouse had at least some connection with the nearest police station – or so TJ and his men had convinced themselves. And I was more than ready to join them.

We cleaned our weapons, ate and rested, then set off north at midnight. A three-quarter moon dangled above the trees like a huge, misshapen pearl, its smooth light making the faces of my fellow soldiers look pensive and gaunt. We moved silently so that our breaths were the loudest noise to be heard. A bird lost its nerve as we passed, flopping from its roost on heavy wings. I felt exhilarated, full of courage and purpose. Flitting through the black trees under the polished grey dome of the sky, I believed that I had at last discovered who I was and what I was for.

We came in close to Kric and the track dropped steeply down into a series of meadows, crossed by a river that wound its way towards the fringes of town. A low mist drifted over the grass, thick as fleece in the grey moonlight. The valley was studded with farmsteads and there were pens and livestock sheds, and dogs to guard them, no doubt. At the sight of these habitations, it entered my mind for a brief, unpleasant moment that the people we did not like might be asleep with their families in this house or that, and it was at least conceivable that Kric Police Station was a model of probity and restraint.

This is not how soldiers think, I told myself, as we left the track and crept through the mist towards the river. It was only ten or twelve yards across, but running high and fast, its black surface milling with glassy swirls. There was a bridge a little way up, and the land on the far side did not seem to be farmed or inhabited. We squelched along the bank, clambering over tatty fences and tumbledown walls, listening to the water sluicing through the reeds.

As we approached the bridge, TJ stopped frequently to check the way ahead. We were very exposed here, with the river to our right and the open plain behind, and my eagerness for the night's work revived. It was thrilling to be out on this illicit and dangerous mission under the leadership of the notorious TJ Farah, stalking towards an unknown place where the honour of the Regiment would be satisfied.

The bridge was an old stone hump-backed affair with a rowboat moored in the lee of its pillars. We crossed one by one, then continued along the far bank, under cover of a sparse fringe of undergrowth. The reason no one farmed here was obvious now: the ground was swampy and we were soon slopping around up to our shins. The ooze stank of decay and the twigs and branches we pushed aside were slimy to the touch. We laboured on until we reached the lower slopes on the far side of the valley. The going became easier and in ten minutes we had circled round to a vantage point just to the west of town, which is where TJ's map suggested the police station was located.

We were in a playground – a square of rough tarmac with a lopsided swing and an obstacle course made of rotting tyres. The town below us had a main street with low iron lamps and a square with a large church flanked by a pair of sycamore trees. Two or three ranks of houses were arrayed parallel with the main street, their rooftops receding into the dark hillside behind. The police station was not going to advertise its presence, since such places were obvious targets for KLA raids. TJ decided to send someone down to recce.

'You lot are good at sloping around on the sly,' he told me. 'Go and find out where it is.'

When it came to sloping around on the sly, TJ was a hundred times slopier and slyer than I could ever be, and as I crept off towards the town square it occurred to me that I might have been set up. I'd find the police station and, assuming I evaded detection, return to an empty playground. My comrades would already be half way to Macedonia, their progress hindered only by the hilarity they were enjoying at my expense. The Regiment was known for its thunderous sense of humour and hearty appetite for the practical joke. This one would run and run.

I put these mutinous thoughts aside and moved on towards the centre of Kric, keeping to the shadows and checking behind me at every turn. The wind that had rasped steadily over the higher ground was gusty and capricious down here in the valley. An empty plastic bottle skittered and popped along the gutter ahead of me, and somewhere on the other side of town I heard the clang of a dustbin overturning. Out of the silence that followed there came voices, singing, shouting. I crouched behind a shed and watched three teenage boys roll along the main street, brazen and fisty with drink. They'd set off a couple of dogs with their racket, but the barks were merely dutiful and soon subsided. Once they had passed, I stepped to the corner and watched. They swayed on for a hundred yards or so until they were about to enter the darkness beyond the last of Kric's iron streetlamps.

A door to their right banged open and a man swaggered out. He was wearing a cowboy hat and, judging by the way its huge shadow was lurching across the wall behind him, he too was drunk. The boys fell silent and he summoned them over. They assembled themselves before him. He said something and made a peremptory gesture. They each went through their pockets and one of them came up with a flask-shaped bottle. He handed it over to the man in the cowboy hat, who spun off the lid and took a swig, then waved the teenagers away. Two of them moved off, but the other held out his hand for the bottle. The cowboy tipped back the brim of his hat, leaned over and spat in the boy's outstretched palm. The boy backed away, rubbing his hand on his trousers. Cowboy hat watched him go, then went back into the house, slamming the door behind him.

What kind of man confronts three drunken teenage boys at dead of night, steals their drink and spits at them? A man with authority. A man who commands fear. These boys had pointed out the police station as surely as an illuminated sign above the door. Even the cowboy hat fitted in: they were popular among Serb militia, the gun-slinging, every-man-for-himself-on-the-wild-frontier motif bolstering the pretence that there was more to their activities than various categories of crime. Still, I decided I'd better go and make sure: if I led TJ and co to the wrong house, I'd never hear the end of it.

I took an alley that ran parallel with the main street and soon reached the house where I had seen the cowboy-hatted man. It was a utilitarian building in whitewashed render, much like any large family house except that it lacked the usual signs of domestic cheer: no curtains, just Venetian blinds over the ground-floor windows, no pot plants or ornaments on the window sills, no bikes or toys... It reminded me of the single men's barracks in some desolate army town – the sort of place I had slept far too many nights over the last few years. At the back was a large yard with a high wall and double gates topped with barbed wire. I pulled myself up and looked over. Parked up against the house was a gleaming black double-cabbed Toyota pickup, its jacked-up haunches bulging over fat, white-lettered tyres, its snout dipped crossly like a mastiff at its meat. The perfect wheels for a man who wears cowboy hats, I thought, though he'd have to be doing well for himself to pay for it. Next to it was a dark red Skoda estate.

I carried on round the house until I came to a window at the front where one corner of the blind had got jammed up, releasing a wedge of yellowish light into the street. I crouched down and looked through. He was stretched out on one of a pair of battered black leather sofas set either side of an electric fire, cowboy hat on the floor beside him. The room was littered with crushed beer cans, their tops smeared with cigarette ash, empty half-bottles of vodka, old newspapers and discarded clothes – jeans, T-shirts, socks, boots. There were half a dozen wooden chairs, a grey steel cupboard and a large wooden table bearing two crash helmets and a stack of dirty plates.

As I watched, the man put the bottle to his mouth and drank, then studied the contents against the light. A few more dregs. He finished them, swung his arm down and let the bottle drop to the floor. He sank back again, and I could tell from the way he twisted his big girth and rearranged his arms that he was about to fall asleep.

I completed my circuit of the house, but most of the other rooms were dark, with just a little light filtering through from the hallways. There was no sign that anyone else was in, and when I got back to the room where the man lay, he had his eyes shut and his mouth open.

I went round to the yard, climbed the wall and took a set of steel steps to the back door. It was locked, but someone had propped open a small, square window and I squirmed through into a foul-smelling toilet cubicle. I went to the back door and pulled back the bolts, found and pocketed the key, then drew the Browning Hi-Power handgun I carried and padded upstairs. Six rooms, strewn with mattresses and sleeping bags and more evidence that the regulars here were fond of a drink and a smoke. I went back down and, obedient to procedure, checked each room in turn, though it was already obvious that the men who based themselves here were out for the night and had left the drunken cowboy to hold fort.

At the back of the house was a room which looked like the boss's lair: a high-backed chrome and leather chair behind a desk with a half-empty bottle of tequila and a collection of shot glasses, a deck of playing cards and a crucifix mounted on a plinth. The waxy-hued body of Christ faced out into the room, reproachful splotches of red adorning its hands, feet and ribcage. A blue military cap hung on the corner of the chair: uniform of the Special Police Force of the Serbian Interior Ministry – *special* because, unlike the regular police who occasionally dealt with regular crimes, they devoted themselves full time to the persecution of Kosovars.

In front of the desk was a wicker chair with the seat cut out. There was a cupboard against the far wall. I opened it and found girly pics glued to the inside of the doors. Why the inside? This wasn't a school locker room. Who wasn't supposed to see the pink curves and dark cracks – Jesus on his cross? The girls looked back over their smooth shoulders at stacked cartons of ammunition in half a dozen different calibres and, on the lower shelves, a galvanised steel bear trap and a petrol-engined chainsaw. In a cardboard box on the floor beside the cupboard there were two baseball bats and a collection of knuckledusters with stained grips. I picked a set from the box, worked my fingers into the holes and closed my fist over the grip. Tools of the trade for the men who worked here, at once utilitarian and savage. I pressed the business end against my cheek, feeling how easily the ridge of brass could pulp skin and shatter bone.

I put the thing in my pocket and went to the room where the man slept. I leaned against the table and watched him snuffling on his couch. I no longer cared whether he heard me or not. If he started to make an arse of himself, I would kill him, because I was *one of us* and we didn't like him. He didn't stir.

There was a notice board above the table, displaying schedules or rotas of some sort, names and days of the week and places, though I couldn't make them out. In the centre of the board was a photo of a dozen men posing against a felled tree. They had cigarettes slanting from their mouths and shotguns or automatic rifles dangling from their fists, and wore combat gear, military boots and black bandannas or cowboy hats. A spent fire smouldered in the foreground. Some were big, cheerful-looking types who could have been local farmers out on a Sunday shoot, jolly uncles with guns and a sack full of dead rabbits; but there were also several dark-eyed, scrawny characters with shaven heads and the sour, chippy expressions of people who think they've been hard done by. One of these was stripped to the waist, revealing a triangle of hairless torso above high-waisted black trousers. A gold cross on a thick chain swung from his neck and his chest was tattooed with an image of what looked like a corpse with a knife protruding from its ribs.

I unpinned the photo and folded it into my breast pocket, then went back to the passage that led to the rear of the house. It was lined with tall filing cabinets and I pulled open a drawer at random. It was so jam-packed with paperwork that the top edges of the folders made a tut-tutting noise as they flipped against the frame. I opened a few more drawers and found a carved wooden crest of a two-headed eagle, a plastic wallet full of official certificates and accreditations, and two pink teddy bears in cellophane wrappers.

I left the house and jogged back up to the playground. My comrades hadn't deserted me but were sheltering behind a stack of tyres. As I approached, Zeb crept up behind me, poked me in the ribs and whispered 'Gotcha!' in my ear. Just to remind me how much I still had to learn.

'Key to the back door,' I said, handing it to TJ. 'And a picture of our Bura friends.'

TJ studied the photo. 'What category of cunt gets a tattoo of his dead self all over his own fucking ribs?'

'I don't think it's supposed to be him,' I said.

'It's him all right,' said TJ. 'I can prove it.'

He handed the photo back and pulled out his map. 'How soon can they ride to the rescue, I ask myself. They haven't gone out for a frolic in the woods, so – the nearest Kosovar village is here, maybe ten or eleven k…' He mused for a while, and his men watched in a kind of awe, because when TJ frowned over his map and muttered, it was a ritual that seemed as mysterious and infallible as the summoning of some supernatural force. He was arranging a future in which the men of his unit took on the Serbian militia known as Bura and destroyed them, and it didn't pay to interrupt.

I stuffed my hands in my pockets and felt the knuckleduster. Why had I taken it? It seemed a dirty thing, out of kilter with the honourable nature of our mission. When no one was looking, I dropped it into the trough of a tractor tyre.

8

We went down to the police station and in through the back door. TJ ran to the front room, slapped the sleeping man hard in the face, then seized him by the throat and levered him upright.

'Fallen asleep on the job, cowboy? What a fuck-up.'

He slapped him again. The man saw that he'd been attacked by someone just about half his size – TJ is small, five-eight and probably seventy-five kilos, and big men always find it humiliating that he can dominate them physically by dint of speed, balance and ferocity alone. This one decided to fight back. He swung a fist up towards the little pest's jaw – must have thought it was the perfect shot until the fist was half an inch from his assailant's chin. TJ brought one hand up beneath the cowboy's upswinging elbow while simultaneously pressing the other against the outside of his wrist. The cowboy's knotted fist shot past TJ's nose and smashed into his own. The weight of the punch sent him sprawling across the sofa and he lay there, stunned.

'Smartass,' said Peanut, searching the prone man and pulling a fat Makarov pistol from a holster under his arm. 'I'm dreaming of the day when your block is late.'

'Not a block, a guide,' said TJ. 'Zeb, get the toy truck up and running. Jimmy, have the Lone Ranger here call his friends for help.'

I pulled the cowboy back to his feet and found his cellphone in the breast pocket of his shirt. I pointed at the man in the photo who'd decorated himself with a tattoo of a corpse and held out the phone. The cowboy looked flabbergasted that I should want to bring this particular character down on our heads. I jabbed him in the gut by way of encouragement and he took the phone.

'He's going to tell them we're here,' I said, watching the cowboy call up the number with fingers made clumsy by fear and drink. As the trained spook amongst us, I felt obliged to make this obvious point.

'No shit,' said TJ. 'Let him talk for five seconds max, then bring him out back.'

The cowboy started to yammer into the cellphone. His eyes wandered over mine. How long before I realised how foolish we had been? I counted to five, then pulled the phone away from his ear and cut the call.

I hustled him out to the yard. Zeb had the bonnet of the fancy pickup raised and was admiring the monstrous V8 engine, which was grumbling away like it had a throat full of phlegm to clear. Toyota Invincible it said on the tailgate.

'The Lone Ranger drives. Zeb, get the gates open. Phil, four of those in the back.' He pointed to a trailer full of jerrycans in a corner of the yard. People were already hoarding petrol, especially those who could bully others into parting with it for free.

I bundled the cowboy into the driver's seat, thinking that TJ was taking a risk by putting a drunk behind the steering wheel. But what with being slapped awake by some kind of diminutive tyrant and then punching himself in the face, the cowboy seemed to have sobered up. TJ climbed into the passenger seat, I sat in the row of seats behind him and Zeb, Phil, Peanut and Ollie rode in the rear. The interior was upholstered in black leather and the courtesy lights had been kitted out with red bulbs, making TJ's face look unnervingly fiendish. The cowboy manoeuvred the pickup through the gates and we rolled down to the main road.

'Tell him to go after his Bura brothers,' said TJ. 'He won't object.'

I pulled out the photo again and thrust it in front of the cowboy's face. 'Which way?' I said, pointing left then right. He nodded eagerly and pointed right. We headed west out of town, accompanied by a frustrated burbling from the Toyota's V8 – frustrated because TJ wouldn't let the Lone Ranger drive any faster than thirty. As soon as we left the streetlights behind, he started watching the road ahead intently, tapping the cowboy's arm when he wanted to slow further so he could inspect the dense woodland that hemmed us in on either side. The road climbed out of the valley. After a few minutes, TJ spotted a logger's track and made the cowboy pull over.

'Drive,' he said, pointing up the steep track into the black depths of the forest.

The cowboy looked frightened now: no doubt he had experience of the kind of things that may get done in dark woods at dead of night. But he did as he was told. After a couple of hundred yards we came to a clearing. There was a stack of corded timber, a mound of sawdust and a small truck equipped with a heavy-duty block and chain swinging from a steel gantry.

'Perfect,' said TJ. 'Out we get.'

We assembled at the front of the Toyota.

'Jimmy's our bait. He waits at the roadside with the pimpwagon. Soon as the mighty Bura see him, up the track he flies with the mad dogs on his tail like he's a bitch on heat.' He turned to me. 'Soon as it's on, radio in. Keep the lights on and the engine running. You're driving the big chief's wheels, so they won't shoot you up. Bring it up close to that timber-stack, then bail out. Work your way round to the sawdust pile. I want you there in less than ten seconds, so no standing around stroking your chin.'

I nodded. I'd probably have nodded if he'd told me to stand in the road and see off the Bura dog-pack with a handful of well-aimed stones. I was in a state of bristling delirium, surges of blood pounding through the arteries of my neck. I felt as if I could uproot a tree and fight with that.

'Peanut, you're with me. Phil, find an RV point three hundred yards uphill from here. Ollie, Zeb, set yourselves up at the neck of the track. This fucking well ought to be regular army business but it isn't. Anyone got anything that can ID them?'

No one did. The three last-named stepped out of the brilliant cones of light from the Toyota's headlights and disappeared.

'Jimmy, get the fuck out of it,' said TJ. 'They'll be here in ten.'

* * *

How did he know? I swung myself into the cab and powered the big pickup in a wide semi-circle, leaving the clearing in darkness. Because he'd consulted his map, of course, worked out what villages they might be looting and how quickly they could get back from the one nearest to Kric. The Toyota handled badly: its bloated tyres were too wide for the axle so the front wheels fought each other at the slightest turn, and the automatic gearing was too low to keep the ridiculous power of the V8 in check. I slithered and bucked down to the road, then backed up and turned so the vehicle was facing up the track.

After a few minutes alone, I began to feel nervous. I was sitting in the Bura chief's pride and joy, lit up like a funfair ride. The words TJ had used came back to me. *Bait. Bitch on heat.* Well, hadn't I predicted the previous night, when I'd insisted on rescuing the frozen girl, that he'd find a way of getting his own back? Filing a report that declared me unfit for SAS assignments evidently wasn't enough.

The engine fan came on, a loud, hectic whirr. I turned the

aircon off and the cab thermostat up full to help draw the heat from the engine. Why did TJ think the Bura were going to fall for this? They weren't callow criminals but men who'd chosen violence as a way of life. TJ had gambled that when the Lone Ranger had made the call to his boss, he'd have had time to say only that he'd been attacked – and not that his attackers had ordered him to make the call, nor how many there were, nor that this was a trap. Well, TJ was probably right: the cowboy was drunk and in a state of shock. If he was wrong, I'd be the one to pay for it.

Focus, I told myself sternly. I stepped out of the cab and took several deep breaths of the cold, pine-scented air. They might see me before I saw them and approach on foot, surprise me. I pictured them in the photograph, the hunter's poses and death tattoos. Christ on his cross and a cupboard full of tools. Did having Jesus on your desk make it OK to dangle your victim's balls over the jaws of a sprung bear trap? Was that why they'd cut the seat out of the chair? I got back into the cab and locked the door. Adrenalin scratched at my armpits and I felt afraid – afraid for my life, afraid that the jolly farmers and their Bura mates would get me into the boss's room and torture me in some way I hadn't even thought of.

Hot air was belting through the heating vents. Maybe this was the trick I'd been anticipating: TJ and the rest had already gone, up over the hill and half way to the border... A test, an initiation. Could I survive the Bura strike and make it back to base without them? I trusted them even less than they trusted me, I realised. I had no idea how far the act of going to Azza's aid in the farmhouse loft had overcome either their institutional prejudice against officers in general and intelligence officers in particular, or their instinctive hostility to outsiders. I was pinned here, the means by which two gangs of habitually violent men would be drawn into combat.

I sat in the hot, trembling vehicle, my mood oscillating between wild bravado and sickening fear – and I will never know whether the next few minutes would have seen me run away or stay and fight, because the rear window of the Toyota gave a sudden flash and a sequence of curved shadows slid slowly around the interior of the car like revolving blades.

Headlights. Two vehicles. They dropped out of sight, and a pale, silvery evanescence crept like a cold flush over the undersides of the trees. Twin shafts of light poked at the sky as the lead vehicle climbed out of the dip, then flipped down as it crested the rise.

I thumbed the call button and TJ was there.

Report.

'I see them. Two vehicles. Four hundred yards, closing fast. Over.'

Sure it's them?

'No. Over.'

Stay on. Keep talking.

'Stopped, less than fifty yards away. A pickup and a small truck. Two men are out, doing something to the front of the truck.'

Can they cut you off? Can they get past you onto the track? Over.

He was right, they could. I put the Toyota into gear and eased it a few yards up the track.

'Not now.'

I looked back over my shoulder. The shadowy mass of the unlit truck was moving towards me and I thought I saw men running beside it.

Stay on, Jimmy. Talk to me.

'Looks like we're on.'

Just be sure they've taken the bait, Jimmy. Don't let me down. Out.

The truck was suddenly at my rear fender, smoking and shuddering in the red haze of the tail lights. The driver gunned the engine hard, holding it on full for a few seconds. I heard a bang from my tailgate and in the side mirror saw three or four men coming my way. Time to go. The door handle rattled beside me and I turned to see the muzzle of a handgun aimed at my face – behind it, a shaven head, staring eyes and a mouth stretched open, screaming abuse.

I hit the throttle harder than I'd meant to and the wheels spun viciously, clumps of earth flying from the tyres. The Toyota rocked sideways and the man stepped back from the window. Then the huge wheels gripped and the vehicle shot forward.

I got twenty yards up the track and slammed to a halt as if I'd hit a brick wall. The axle must have snagged on something. I let the Toyota roll back before stamping on the accelerator again. The great brute leapt forward, then rocked to a standstill.

I hammered the revs. The V8 howled, bonnet weaving from side to side. I got about two feet before the wheels lost grip and the engine whizzed up into the red zone. Ease off, check the rear-view mirror. They were climbing up the muddy track, gun barrels gleaming. One of them stepped gingerly over something directly behind the vehicle.

Hawser. Taut, vibrating. They'd got me hooked up to their truck and I was held fast.

I hit the throttle again, but the Toyota was going nowhere. Diff lock? I stared down at the transmission controls, but if there was one I couldn't see it, and I didn't have time to consult the handbook. The Toyota's V8 should have been able to outmuscle the truck, even on an uphill track, but when I turned and peered into the gloom I saw that they'd jammed one of its front wheels up against a tree stump. The hawser would be braided steel, it wasn't going to snap.

The guy with the shaven head was back at my window. He wasn't screaming now, he was leering, sticking his tongue out and waggling it from side to side, making like the savage after his blood-feast. Below his jaw was a tattoo of a snake, pulsing like a huge distended vein. There was a thump above my head and then another face hung down over the windscreen – one of the farmer types, pressing his cheek against the glass so it looked like a stubbled pancake.

One thing in my favour: TJ was right, no one was going to shoot up the boss's toy or smash the glass with the butt of a shotgun. Why do that when, anyway, they had me cold?

I flipped into reverse and sent the Toyota bouncing back through the deep ruts left by my wheelspins. The guy on the roof slid down to the bonnet and tumbled off. I picked up speed and careered towards the truck at the foot of the track. The driver bailed out just as the Toyota's rear bull bars crashed into the winch mounted on the front of the truck. I pumped the throttle and powered on, shunting the truck back off the tree stump in a cacophony of scraping steel. Once clear of the neck of the track, I swung hard round and reversed down the road.

The hawser now ran forward from the Toyota's rear axle and along the length of the chassis, emerging beneath the front bumper. As it tautened, my front wheels lifted, making the big vehicle impossible to steer. There wasn't enough space to turn it round, so I straightened up and tried again. Eventually I managed to wrestle the truck out into the road and drag it another hundred yards downhill, tyres squealing in protest. Finally, the old truck tipped ponderously into the ditch. I drove forward a couple of yards to release the tension in the hawser, then threw myself out of the door and rolled under the back of the Toyota.

It was hot and dark down there, the exhaust sizzling from the high-revving battle with the hawser and the mud. I took it step by step, following the cable with my hands, feeling for the hook that must be latched onto the rear axle. The steel braids were twisted and chewed and my knuckles were getting barked and burned and I couldn't see a thing. The voices of my pursuers were stifled by the grumble of the engine and sounded far away, but when I heard boots on tarmac, I'd have five seconds to get back in the cab or make a run for it. There! A lump of forged steel, hooked over the axle just by the diff. I gave it a bang and worked it from side to side.

It shifted a little, but wouldn't come free. I worked it into a position that would let me get a boot to it, then rolled onto my back and spun round, felt for the block with my heel, drew back, braced...

I gave it a kick so violent it would have broken every bone in my leg if it hadn't at last dislodged the steel hook that was making such a desperate farce of TJ's best-laid plan. I heard it clunk onto the tarmac just before the first shotgun blast came booming down the road between the trees.

Another blast, pellets skittering along the tarmac. I pulled the Browning and loosed off four rounds in an attempt to persuade them to keep their heads down. It worked for just about long enough to get me to the driver's door. I pulled it open and reached across the seat to yank the gear lever into drive. The glass shattered above my head, little gritty cubes of the stuff cascading down the back of my neck. I'd written off the boss's pride and joy and it was open season now. Keeping tucked in behind the open door, one hand on the bottom edge of the window frame, the other on the steering wheel, I swung my leg into the footwell and rammed my boot against the accelerator pedal.

The Toyota belted up the road. I rode the running board and felt glad that the thing was so grossly overpowered. I liked the fact that the treads on its tyres were four inches deep. I liked it that the truck had slid into the ditch, because I didn't have to steer past it. And I wish I could say I'd planned it so the Buras would be shooting at me from the wrong side of the vehicle, but that was just good luck.

When I judged I was close to the logger's track, I hauled myself into the driver's seat. Shotgun lead and rifle rounds clanged into the vehicle's once-smooth flanks. One headlight was out and I almost drove straight up the bank as I swung hard into the turn, but I got round without rolling or having to do an ungainly and probably fatal three-point turn. The headrest on the passenger seat abruptly disintegrated, leaving only two steel prongs as clean as picked bones. I ducked down and pressed on blind. Both tyres on the passenger side had been shot out and I might have been steering a brick mounted on slices of Swiss roll. A thump behind me and I felt the chassis jolt. They'd burst the other rear, too. But there was so much rubber on those tyres that they still found traction and the Toyota powered uphill at an impressive lick.

The gunshots died away. I picked the radio off the floor and called TJ.

'On my way up, twenty seconds.'

You taking fire?

'Plenty. Out.'

What he really wanted to ask was, *What the fuck have you been doing, you shit-eating motherfucker, why did I trust...* And so on. But TJ was a pro and it could wait. I rumbled into the clearing and manoeuvred the stricken Toyota alongside the wood-stack as accurately as its shredded tyres would allow. As I ran for cover, my nostrils filled with the thin, corrosive smell of evaporating petrol.

TJ was waiting for me.

'How many?' he asked, handing me a rifle and spare clip. 'And why aren't they following you?'

'At least eight. I took out one of their vehicles. Rest are in a pickup, maybe some on foot.'

He radioed the others and told them, then flicked on a torch and pointed out our positions on a diagram he'd drawn: Zeb and Ollie covering the exit track, Big Phil and Peanut in the undergrowth on the far side of the clearing. 'Any that head this way have got my name on them. Or yours, if you're quick. RV is a cave at the eastern end of an escarpment, here, just over half a k south. Where's your radio?'

'Shit...'

'Your problem. We leave at two-twenty sharp.'

I heard the grinding of the Bura pickup now, saw its lights sweeping the track. Despite having air in all four tyres, it was making heavy weather of the hill.

'What's the plan?' I asked, and immediately regretted voicing such a naive question. Anything I needed to know, TJ had already told me.

'It's like this, Jimmy,' he said, in the phlegmatic tone of voice he had made his trademark. 'There's a gang of Serb militia who call themselves Bura, and we're going to kill them.'

The pickup bounced into view at the neck of the track. I put the rifle to my shoulder. TJ pushed the barrel down. 'No one fires until I do.'

The pickup stopped. Two men in front, their hunched forms picked out by the cab lights. They were suspicious now. No one was getting out to reclaim the Toyota. The driver killed the lights but left the engine running. I looked for TJ, but he had gone. I inched round behind the mountain of sawdust and saw— How had I missed it? The Lone Ranger, trussed up and hanging by the ankles from the winch on the back of the logger's truck, mouth open improbably wide... No, it wasn't his mouth, but his neck, the gaping lips of the wound pale above the treacly red mask of his face. His body spun slowly, one way, then the other.

I looked over at the pickup. By now they must have known they'd been ambushed, yet they seemed transfixed. Six or seven of them in the back, moving around uneasily, readying their weapons and staring into the dark undergrowth. The old diesel clattered away. A pocket of life, surrounded by purveyors of death. At last the driver threw open his door and dived out, did a neat roll and came up running for the cover of the wood-stack. The man who'd been sitting beside him followed, but he was fatter and not so agile or quick. A single shot rang out and his head jerked back.

I turned and there was TJ standing in the middle of the clearing, sideways on to the Bura pickup, rifle at his shoulder. The men in the back were piling out. One went for the wood-stack, three got down behind their pickup, two more sprinted for the far side of the clearing. Rifle fire erupted from the undergrowth ahead of them. The first staggered on for a few paces, veered away from the place where Phil and Peanut were concealed, then collapsed at the edge of the clearing. The other sprawled face down in the dirt, then curled in on himself and lay still.

TJ hadn't moved from centre stage. The barrel of his rifle swung round and three shots cuffed the base of the wood-stack. An unexpected clang, then the whump of oxygen being sucked from the air and a roaring, sooty flame slashed thirty feet into the sky, smoke boiling from its core. The man who had just run there doubled over behind the Toyota, hands shielding his head from the air-crumpling heat. The Toyota blew up and he tumbled backwards, rolled into a flailing ball by the flash of exploding gas.

The men by the pickup had cover from TJ's rifle, but were taking crossfire from our positions at either end of the clearing instead. They didn't stand a chance. The wood-stack popped and spat and flame-light snaked over the clearing, as if Beelzebub himself had turned up to claim his kin. Then I remembered the man who'd run first. He'd scrambled for safety behind the wood-stack and probably got away before it went up. Less than twenty seconds since TJ had fired his first shot…

I sprinted up into the woods behind the clearing. It was a plantation, the conifers arrayed in straight lines and not much growing away from the fringes. I quickly made two hundred yards, then stopped and listened. More gunshots: Zeb and Ollie rounding up the latecomers. The Bura pickup coughed into silence. The stench of burnt petrol streamed up between the black columns of the trees. I ran another two hundred, now angling away to the left, then stopped again and listened to the wind whirring through the high branches. I checked my watch: 01:53. I ran on and reached the escarpment half a minute later.

The tree canopy was looser up here, and the low moonlight threw branch shadows on the sheer face of the granite ridge ahead of me. Between the rock wall and the first line of trees was a fringe of bracken and bramble that looked like the perfect place to hide from a pursuer. Browning in hand, I followed the line of the escarpment, keeping a little way into the forest where the going was easier. A steady stream of chaff blew off the bracken, catching the moonlight like flecks of ash from a bonfire. I studied the undergrowth for signs of movement, but saw only bouncing hoops of bramble, blackthorn bushes shuddering in the wind. After thirty yards, a fox cantered up from the woods. It paused and looked my way, then sloped off into the undergrowth. I jogged to the point where it had disappeared and peered into the darkness. When I turned round, TJ was watching me from five yards away.

'You fucked up again there, Jimmy Palatine. I don't trust you.'

His eyes had the flat stare of a cobra pinning its prey.

'I got the Bura up here for you,' I said. 'I could've been killed. Was that what you wanted?'

'You for telling tales, Jimmy, like they taught you in slime school?'

'I told you, no.'

I looked off along the escarpment in an effort to communicate to TJ that I didn't think this conversation amounted to much.

'Your sort always find something.'

'I'm part of this, TJ. I killed the one who shot Azza, right?'

'You keeping tabs on me?'

'No.'

I was beginning to see how badly this might end. We were alone, in Serb militia territory. And, QED, Captain Palatine was inclined to get lost.

'One of them ran this way,' I said. 'I came after him. Why would I do that if I was spying on you?'

His gaze did not waver.

'He's holed up somewhere round here. The longer we leave it to get after him...' I shrugged.

'Down there.'

He pointed diagonally across the wooded slope. I looked through the fanned ranks of tree trunks and their counterpointing network of shadows. It felt as if I were being ushered into some elaborate exercise in perspective: step into those receding triangles of moonlight, and you traverse them for all eternity.

'Don't fucking think, Jimmy. Walk.'

I stepped past him and the springy crust of pine needles seemed to propel me down the slope. The darkness opened ahead of me and closed in behind. I counted the trees, ten, fifteen, twenty... I could not hear TJ behind me, but knew he was there. Then I saw what looked like some pale, fleshy fungus sprouting from a tree at waist height. TJ walked past me, past the tree, spun round. The noise of the wind receded and I heard a grunting, gurgling sound. I moved to the side and stepped closer. Not a fungus but hands... The hands of the man I'd been pursuing, arms stretched round the tree at his back and zip-tied by the wrists. His head was pressed tight to the bark, held there by a cord lashed round his throat.

'Left his mates to die and legged it, just like the cunts at the farmhouse.'

The man was in shock, his eyes unfocused. One of his knees was slightly cocked and the bottom half of the trouser leg was dark with blood. TJ went up and unzipped the bound man's jacket, then pulled out his knife and sliced through his T-shirt. The man snorted sharply and a strand of drool swayed from his lips.

TJ shone a flashlight on his shaven torso and I saw the tattoo of the dead man, leaning backwards, a knife in his chest. The Bura's lean belly pumped in and out, and the tattoo of the corpse writhed in time with his panic-stricken breaths.

'See how bad he wants it, Jimmy?' TJ said. 'He's fucking gagging for it. You going to give it to him?' He lined up the tip of his knife with the wound in the ribs of the tattoo corpse and pressed. 'Just here is where he wants it to go.'

He stepped back and gestured at me to take over. It wasn't how I wanted to prove myself. It wasn't heroic or brave. It wasn't just or dignified. Neither passionate nor dispassionate. It was thick with ulterior motive and slippery with hidden meaning. It was confused and devious. It lacked integrity. I did not understand why it was happening, nor what its consequences would be. And yet the hand that drew the honed steel blade was dry and calm, and I did not shirk the Bura chief's eyes as I stepped up to face him.

I put my knife where TJ's had been and leaned in on the hilt and felt the give as the blade pierced the cartilage and entered the muscular chambers of his heart. The grip pulsed in my palm as he gave up his life to me, and I felt a thrill so strong and cold that I sometimes long to feel it again, and often pray fervently that I never will.

Even as his body convulsed, I did not avert my eyes from his gaze. Whatever TJ said, he did not *want it*. He was not *fucking gagging for it*. He'd done bad things in his life, and now he was frightened and lonely, just like the boy I had killed in the loft thirty-six hours ago.

Are they all like this? Is this how I will be?

If you study the photo TJ took at the moment when I pulled my knife from the Bura chief's heart, you see it in my eyes, too. Fear. Loneliness. Nothing else.

9

After the clean, cold mountain air, my apartment in Skopje was cramped and filthy hot and I festered in it. You rescued a girl from certain death, I kept telling myself. I didn't feel like a hero, but a man in a dark cell reaching for a chink of kindly light from a barred window. I was haunted by memories of my forty-eight hours with TJ's unit, and I wasn't sure that I wanted to be rid of them. A soldier who could put such things from his mind was irrevocably *one of us*. After the night in the woods with the Bura, Ollie's words seemed less like an accolade and more like a curse.

Clean your kit, I ordered myself. Feed yourself. Write a report for Hillson.

Colonel Andy Hillson was my CO, a career intelligence officer with whom I had a lopsided relationship: I liked him for his well-meaning sincerity, while he detested me for an arrogant clever clogs (this from a mathematician with a PhD in an excessively abstract branch of formal logic). In consequence, I was always being friendly and trying not to cause him trouble, while he was always trying to take me down a peg or two – an objective for which this report would provide plenty of ammunition. I keyed in the formulaic offi-cialese, taking care to incorporate the face-losing lie concocted by

TJ – that I had become detached from my SAS escorts and made it back across the border into Macedonia without them. Reviewing the few paragraphs that would go on the record, I was dismayed. The gap between the bland assertion, *mission accomplished*, and the churning, feverish violence which made up the actual truth was like the disconnect between a supermarket display of shrink-wrapped meat and the squeals and gore of the slaughterhouse. How much bloody mayhem lay bagged up and buried beneath the sanitary circumlocutions of the official reports that occupied so many miles of shelf-space in the annals of war?

I was supposed to file my report in time for a four o'clock debrief at the Army Intelligence office – three desks in the stuffy basement of the British Consulate a few minutes' walk from my apartment. Then a message came through that the meeting was postponed until the following day. This was a familiar pattern: on past evidence, the debrief would be postponed several more times, then I'd be summoned back to London for a bout of mutual frowning. Until they decided what to do with me next, I was in limbo.

I pulled on a tracksuit and went out for a run. I hadn't gone fifty yards before having to swerve into the road to avoid a detachment of pie-eyed KFOR outside the Bar Vodno – big, slab-sided Dutch soldiers who had reached that stage of inebriation where anything on two legs must be addressed – either amorously or aggressively, depending on gender. I heard their spluttering jeers and turned to see one of them jogging after me, chest puffed out, arms flapping, knees splayed. The joker of the pack, and how his comrades roared.

I was in the mood for a fight, and came within an ace of burying my fist in the comedy corporal's gut. But, fortunately for everyone, I brought myself to heel in time and ran on – only to cannon into a knot of KVM huddled round the menu of a restaurant that, according to an indignant Maria, had only recently elected to describe itself as French.

KFOR was NATO's Kosovo Force and the KVM was the Kosovo Verification Mission, a team of official EU observers there to oversee Serbian compliance with an agreement which the Serbs hadn't in fact agreed to, let alone signed. In recognition of the high likelihood that they would get themselves into trouble on one of their forays into Kosovo, these observers were shadowed by a 1,500-strong NATO force tasked with performing a timely rescue. Meanwhile, their predecessors from the OSCE (Organization for Security and Co-operation in Europe) were still hanging around in Skopje, composing their debriefs and taking ersatz girlfriends to dine in ersatz French restaurants before being summoned home.

And that was how Skopje was in those days. When the concerned world rides to the rescue, it must first divide itself into a panoply of overlapping military and bureaucratic units, each with its own acronym, its own command structure, its own mission statement, and its own sense of its own importance. These executors of *concerted international action* jockeyed for desk space in Skopje's modest administrative centres, then set about their grand endeavours by issuing unfulfillable contracts to the commercial operations that scurried in their wake: contracts for transport and logistics, catering, accommodation, legal and translation services, administrative assistance... Lines of authority zigzagged across this landscape of officially sanctioned chaos, contradicting each other wherever they met and causing fist fights at one end and diplomatic incidents at the other.

I don't say these things are easy, but some sense that the right hand even knew that the left hand existed would have been helpful. And I haven't yet mentioned the countless special-interest NGOs – nor (of course) the unknown number of infiltrators like myself, representatives of organisations which preferred to remain invisible. The list went on and on and on, and then on some more, and the foreigners poured into Skopje, bringing their strange tastes and

habits, their burly, well-fed arrogance, their astonishing wealth, and
– most baffling of all – their uniforms, a babel of sartorial hiero-
glyphs which signified, to the un-uniformed, nothing more precise
than that those who sported them had the power to take a life or, in
the case of the bureaucrats, to ruin one.

I ran on until I came to the UNHCR mission. The sight of
the drab building with the densely braided line of refugees camped
outside brought a horrible flush of unease. This is where I should
have brought the girl, queue or no queue. Why hadn't I? The house
where I'd left her... What was it? The home of someone who helped
the priest? Why had I not yet called Father Daniel to find out if the
girl had made it back to the orphanage?

Because I was terribly afraid she had not. I sprinted back to the
apartment. Shopkeepers watched me askance, arms folded. Who
does he think he is? I didn't know who I thought I was, but Sergeant
TJ Farah had a photo of me sliding a blade between the ribs of a
man tied to a tree in a dark wood. What kind of man would do that
kind of thing? The kind who kills a boy with a punch to the throat.
That kind. Self-pity welled in my throat. I hadn't meant to do anything wrong. I'd wanted to prove myself, that was all. I'd rescued a
girl from certain death and carried her to safety. So why were these
recriminations manoeuvring in my head like a cohort of leathery-
faced military police?

Back in my apartment, I stomped around hunting for the
phone I'd taken from the eviscerated woman in the farmhouse. I'd
hidden it – from myself, because of the grim way it had come into
my possession. It was ten minutes before I found it – pushed to the
back of the top shelf above the stove, behind a row of empty storage tins. That I couldn't remember putting it there was a measure
of how distracted I'd become, how hemmed in by bad memories
and a nebulous sense of dread. I found Father Daniel in the call
list and pressed the green button, but after a few rings I got his

answerphone. I left a message. *The girl who ran away – I dropped her off at seventy-seven Syrna Street yesterday morning, as agreed. I need to know if she got back to you.*

I thumbed through the entries in the call list on the dead woman's phone: female friends, Theresa, Alana, Safina; her doctor; a long call to the UNHCR in Skopje. Maybe she'd been helping Father Daniel with the business of transferring children into their care. I scrolled to the UNHCR number and pressed call.

'I need to find out if the UNHCR has a house in Syrna Street where refugees stay,' I said to the woman who answered.

'Please say again. My English is not so good.'

I repeated the question.

'Oh, I don't know. I am only just arriving in Skopje. I will ask. Wait please.'

I waited. She came back on the line and said she didn't think so, but why did I want to know? I hung up and tried the refuge landline. It rang out.

I sat down and found that my hands were trembling. The eggs and toast I'd had for breakfast liquefied in my gut. How could you be fit enough to run half a mile flat out and then feel like this fifteen minutes later? The heat from my hand was making the dried blood on the cellphone case tacky. I dropped it on the table. The chink of kindly light was fading. I was falling apart. I stumbled to my bed and slept.

* * *

It was six when I woke. I felt as if I'd fought my way free of a fever. I was possessed by a desperate thirst, and when I hauled myself to the kitchen tap and drank three glasses of water, the thirst was replaced by hunger. I changed out of the rumpled tracksuit and went down to the café.

'You don't look well,' Maria declared, seating me at a table by the counter at the rear. 'We have a saying here in Macedonia: we say, you look like you have seen a ghost.'

'Thanks for that, Maria,' I said, a touch disappointed that the local vernacular couldn't furnish anything more original. 'It's just that I'm starving.'

'You will have to wait,' she said gleefully. 'The usual?'

She shouted the order into the kitchen, then juggled two bread rolls onto a plate and plonked them down in front of me. 'Eat this bread so you do not die before the food comes.'

I did so, and she brought me a dish of olives and cubes of salty goat's cheese to keep me alive some more. It was good to sit at the little formica-topped table with the gentle hubbub of human conviviality for company. To Maria's disappointment, I was the only foreign newcomer who had taken to patronising her establishment; but in any case the place was full. Most of the customers were men having something to eat or drink on their way back from work, and there was a whiff of naughtiness in the air – everyone knew they should really be at home, which made the bottle of beer and the plate of kofta even more delicious. At the table next to me were four old men – bus or lorry drivers, judging by their humped backs and hooped arms. They were wheedling and joshing each other in turn, their conversation a series of elaborate insults whose crescendo was a triumphant thump on the arm and an eruption of crackly laughter.

Over by the window were two young women wearing pale grey cardigans embroidered with the logo of the Coincasa Italian department store. They were leaning close to each other to whisper, then pulling back and looking quickly around them, their eyes bright with mischief. One of them saw me watching and a lengthy confabulation ensued, interspersed with several fits of giggles hidden behind a token hand.

I felt like an alien in this enclave of normality, a tolerable intrusion; but it was reassuring to find that such places still existed – that, outside my head at least, life went on as it always had. Maria must have taken pity on me, for my food arrived inside five minutes: three skewers of chicken, rice, stewed tomato and aubergine, and a heap of salad, along with a carafe of oily purple wine. I ate quickly. A plate of honey and pistachio pastries followed, then sweet, grainy coffee. Finally, with the early evening rush over, Maria sat down opposite me and poured herself a glass of wine.

'You look better, James. But not happy, no. What happened to the girl?'

I shrugged. 'She's on her way back to the refuge in Kosovo. At least, I hope she is.'

'Poor kid. Why she run away?'

'I don't really know. There are terrible things happening out there, Maria.'

'War is coming. So now the bad people come out to play.'

She sighed and summoned one of her children to bring her cigarettes. The boy came running over to our table. Maria lit up while the boy, who must have been about the age of the girl I'd rescued, grinned at me.

'You have gun, mister?'

Maria directed a brisk volley of orders, which the boy ignored.

'I see gun?'

Maria aimed a blow at his backside. He dodged it and scampered off.

'Tomasz thinks it is exciting, all these soldiers and guns.'

'If the peace conference works out, then we'll be going home, guns and all.'

'*Peace* conference? The one near Paris? Ha! I don't think they are planning for peace. People who are powerful, they like war. They have armies and they want to show how they are big and strong.

What is Milošević without a war? I will tell you: an old fool who ruined his country.'

Her eyes, cocked behind the glass of her black-framed spectacles, challenged me to disagree. Since I'd been helping to prepare for war myself, I decided it would be disingenuous now to argue that peace was nigh.

'You know of the Battle of Kosovo?' Maria went on. 'It took place in the year 1389. They have stories and songs about it. The earth is red with the blood of Serbian men, they sing, it is wet with the tears of Serbian wives, tra-la. Kosmet is the heart and soul of Serbia and they will defend it until they are all dead.'

'I heard you should expect twenty thousand refugees here in Macedonia.'

'There are already twenty thousand refugees in Macedonia, and the war has not started. But what is a number to the kings and queens in Paris? You should go and get drunk, James. It will make you to forget your troubles for a time.'

10

I ignored Maria's advice and went back to my apartment, read a technical journal I'd brought with me in case my chronic enervation hit a new low, then lay down for another night with my nasty dreams. Next morning, I called Father Daniel again, but got no answer. I went out into the street and took a cab to 77 Syrna Street. I wanted to see the place again, judge if my misgivings were justified. And I had an image of the sleepy-eyed young woman who'd opened the door, of my hands reaching for her warm, plump waist inside the folds of her dressing gown.

It was a beautiful day, the sun slanting between clumps of wind-blown cloud, but the house still looked forlorn. A gust caught the plastic sheeting on the roof and it clattered and flapped, then I heard a shout from the yard and the brindled dog slunk round a concrete gatepost and scuttled down the street for twenty yards before turning to look back over its shoulder. I knocked on the front door. No answer, so I knocked again.

A heavily built man in filthy blue overalls appeared from behind a grey VW Passat saloon parked in the yard.

'I left a girl here the other day,' I said. 'I want to know if she's OK.'

He gave me a blank stare. He didn't understand me – or if he did, he wasn't going to say so. He had a scar down one cheek, a ridge of pale skin that cut across the black stubble. I had the impression he was expecting me to back away.

'A girl,' I said again, taking a step towards him.

'No girl.' He made a shooing gesture with his hand.

'Yes, a girl,' I said hotly. 'About twelve. From Father Daniel's refuge in Kosovo.'

He recognised the name and I saw calculation in his eyes. The taxi that had brought me here accelerated away down the street. I'd told the driver to wait. He hadn't even collected his fare.

'No girl. Fuck off.'

'Think I'll wait here.'

I sat down on a section of the broken porch. The big man continued to stare at me, his hard face betraying nothing. Then he stumped off round the corner of the house.

I pulled out the cellphone and dialled Father Daniel. This time, he answered.

'Father Daniel – you got my message?'

'Your message?'

His voice was faint and he sounded even more dispirited than I remembered.

'About the girl. I wanted to know if she's back with you.'

'Oh... I don't... I don't think so, no.'

'What do you mean, you don't think so?' I said. 'The place where I left her, seventy-seven Syrna Street – what is it exactly?'

'I don't understand what you are asking.'

'The house on Syrna Street,' I repeated. 'It doesn't look like it has anything to do with the UNHCR. Or a Catholic refuge for that matter.'

'I can't help you,' he said. 'I'm sorry.'

'I'm not looking for help,' I replied angrily. 'Do you follow up what happens to the children after they've been left there?'

'There's all the UNHCR paperwork – at the refuge.'

'And you've spoken to the children themselves, once they're settled?'

'No. I have to—'

I never heard the rest of his sentence. A shadow moved in fast from my left. I wouldn't have seen it if the sun hadn't been so low in the sky, and the iron bar would have crumpled the back of my skull. I rolled sideways, felt the timbers of the fallen porch shiver as the bar landed. I rolled again, sprang to my feet, then hurled myself backwards as the second blow swung towards my ribcage. A thick iron bar with a rusty cog attached to the business end.

He was wielding it one-handed. A man of great strength, going at me deliberately, no malice in his eyes, just plain intent. I crabbed backwards over the rubble of a broken-down wall. He stepped in, drawing the iron bar back. A chunk of mortar came into my left hand. I flung it as hard as I could and it grazed his cheek – enough to make him hesitate. By the time the lump of iron hammered into the broken wall, I was on my feet and driving my fist into his temple. The weight of the swinging bar had pulled him down into a half-crouch, and the blow took him off balance. I saw his knees wobble as he heaved his weapon from the pile of brickwork. His arm was out straight, braced with the effort. I kicked hard, the crook of my ankle impacting the underside of his elbow. The joint popped up. He let out a grunt of shock, then went for the iron bar with his other hand. I picked up a lump of brick the size of a grapefruit and steadied myself to ram it into his mouth.

If he'd been full of heat and fury, I would have killed him. I was eager to kill him. But I needed the excuse and he knew it. He straightened up, arm dangling, temple red and beginning to swell, and surveyed me as a churlish man might survey a small child who has spilled milk on his shoes. The top buttons of his boiler suit had got torn off and I saw a small blue cross roughly tattooed on the pale skin of his upper chest. His mouth formed a sneer of contempt, then he turned his back on me and walked away, disappearing round the side of the house where his brindled dog sat anxiously sweeping the dirt with its long tail.

The cellphone had been crushed when I'd fallen into the broken wall, so I couldn't call Father Daniel and tell him that his UNHCR liaison's halfway house was in fact the den of a murderous troll. I didn't hang around for the troll to fetch a gun, either, but ran back down the street and round the first corner, then on another few hundred yards until my way was blocked by a railway track behind a high steel fence.

There were no turnings off this street. I was about to retrace my steps when I heard a vehicle approaching from the direction of Syrna Street. I dropped down behind a white van. A car was idling at the corner – the grey Passat I'd seen at the house. Two men got out and the Passat pulled away. I heard it revving hard for a hundred yards or so, then the engine dropped to an idle again and doors banged. The troll, organising a pursuit… I tucked myself in behind the rear wheel of the van and looked along the kerb.

One of the men was walking along the pavement towards me, a phone clamped to his ear. He stopped alongside a black rubbish hopper, placed his hand over a bulge at his waistband, then shoved the hopper aside with the sole of his foot so it teetered off along the pavement.

I checked the other side and saw a second man. There was a garage next to the house across the pavement from me, not twenty yards away, but nowhere obvious to run for cover next. Anyway, this was their patch: once they'd seen me, they'd know how and where to hunt me down. I crouched helplessly in the narrow oblong of gritty, pockmarked road behind the van, visualising their methodical progress as they worked their way along the street towards me.

I could handle one of these men, armed or not, but if the other had time to call for help... I looked back at the chain-link fence. Run for it, then. An urban fence like that is always holed somewhere. But it was still a couple of hundred yards away. My shoulder brushed the handle of the van's rear doors. It felt loose. I gave it an experimental tug. Something scraped noisily against the inside of the doors. I stopped and checked the street again. They didn't seem to have heard. It was clear that the lock was broken. I eased the doors apart, but after three inches they held firm – wired shut with a length of galvanised steel cable. I braced my knee against one door and pulled the other open as far as I could, then thrust my hand in and tried to work out how it was fastened.

I had an image of my pursuer stepping level with the back of the van and finding his quarry with his arm jammed in the rear door. The stupidity of it made me suddenly furious, and I pushed hard, ignoring the creaks from the hinges. My fingers found the place where the ends of the cable had been twisted round the door bolts, but the stiff braids would not yield to the clumsy pressure of my fingertips. I needed a few more inches of reach to get any purchase. There! I felt the wire braids slacken. Then I heard a voice. Thirty yards away, maybe less. The man on my side of the street, talking on his cellphone. I had just a few seconds to prise apart the last kinks in the cable, open the doors, climb in, close the doors, hide. Silently.

I got the cable off. That was it.

I started to whistle. A jaunty whistle. The whistle of a man attending to some workaday task in the back of his van. The whistle of a man who thinks he's alone but doesn't care if he isn't. It wasn't easy. I crashed open the van doors, cleared my throat and spat. Then I whistled some more.

He stepped round the edge of the door and I was right there, my face in his face, my knee thudding into his groin. He doubled up with a sickly moan. I wrapped his throat in the cable and dragged him into the van. He lashed out and his foot banged against the door, which swung back and crunched against his shin. His body jack-knifed and we lurched backwards into the dark space, flailing around in a clutter of hard-edged lumps and lengths of things that scraped along the van's sides as they fell. He had one hand plucking at the wire pinching the flesh of his neck, the other reaching for his gun. But he wasn't a big man and I rolled him over easily, then drove my knee into his spine and yanked back on both ends of the cable.

I meant to choke him until he blacked out, expected to feel furious resistance from the muscles of his neck and shoulders. But I used too much force. Far too much force. There was a dull crack and his head tilted back at an impossible angle. The twisted wire caught under his jawbone and before I could slacken my grip I'd ripped one end of his jaw clear of his skull. He made a retching noise and his body slumped.

I had time now. It was easy. I pulled the gun from his waist-band. Registered the dark shadow as it moved across the bonnet of the car parked behind the van. Watched the shadow hesitate. Noted how the squeals and clanks from the goods train grinding along the track at the end of the street would muffle the snap of the gunshot. Took aim at the face now framed in a rhombus of pale sky. Pulled the trigger. Recorded in my mind a picture of a man bringing his hands up to his shattered face and stammering some words I did not understand. Reeling sideways into the van door. The door bouncing against its hinges, folding him into the gutter. The soft thump as he fell.

I loaded the dead man into the van with his dead mate and wired the doors shut again, then climbed out through the front, wiping my fingerprints off everything as I went. I jogged to the steel fence alongside the railway track and soon found a place where it had been peeled back. I crawled through into a ribbon of waste ground at the foot of an embankment and set off towards the centre of town, picking my way through pockets of dense, spiny undergrowth and ragged drifts of garbage – rotting cardboard, plastic crates, rubbish bags torn open by scavenging teeth. I heard no shouts or speeding vehicles. I wasn't going to report this to the police. The troll wasn't going to, either, being the sort who would have killed the two men himself if he'd discovered how they'd fouled up. The street had been deserted – and if anyone had heard the gunshot, they'd probably already thought better of it.

After walking for twenty minutes, I found a pile of dried grass and leaves arranged in the shape of a bed under a spray of wiry bramble. I lay down on it. There didn't seem to be any reason to hurry back to my apartment. Nor to hurry on to anywhere else.

I lay in that desolate place for an indeterminate length of time, staring up through the trembling lattice of thorns as the sun inscribed its feeble arc across the wind-scoured sky. A week ago, I'd been a callow, arrogant Army Intelligence officer with a brilliant career ahead of him. What was I now? I thought about what I had done and how I might rescue the girl from the house on Syrna Street, which I could not pretend to myself had anything whatsoever to do with the UNHCR. Then I thought about the man with his jaw hanging off, and the one with his hands held up to his bloodied face, stammering. Then I managed not to think at all, until I realised I wasn't alone.

An old woman was squatting at my feet, muttering and prodding at my boots with a twig. As soon as I saw her, I felt that I must kill her.

I sat bolt upright, shocked that this thought had taken hold of my mind with such force and clarity, even for an instant. She must have seen how dangerous I'd become, for she got quickly to her feet and scrambled away into the bushes. I climbed out of her lair and walked on until the embankment levelled out and I saw a signal box ahead. I dropped down to the chain-link fence and looked for a way out. The fence adjoined the back wall of a warehouse covered with soot and graffiti, its cracked windows too high to reach. A smell of paraffin drifted on the air and I heard bangs and the grinding of a big diesel engine.

The warehouse gave way to a low-built workshop, beyond which there was a fork in the line, with a section of track leading off to the front of the warehouse. There were double gates on the far side of a concrete yard. All I had to do was cross the track, then walk to the gates. There were men operating a hoist to unload wire cages of stone from a line of trucks into a pair of lorries parked alongside the track. I experienced again that sense of distance from the ordinary run of humanity which had beset me in Maria's café the evening before – only this time the gap was more like a gulf, the comfort and security on the far side quite out of reach. I would have to fight again. I would have to run.

I crouched there for a long time, studying in turn the bulging worms of cement between the breeze blocks of the workshop wall and the knot of muddy weeds embedded in the earth at my feet. I'd killed four people in the last three days, and delivered an innocent girl into the hands of evil men. How had this come about? The memories looped through my head, a giddy parade which I could not find the strength of mind to stop.

Eventually I emerged from this trance sufficiently to realise that there was no choice to be made. I walked up to the track, looked left and right, as any sensible man would, stepped over the rails, and carried on across the yard. A few of the workers stopped to watch my progress, but no one came after me, and the man in the hut by the gates merely grimaced. It was some relief to be back on the streets. I had an address and I was going there, that was all.

11

I don't drink often, a failing which invokes equal measures of incomprehension and contempt in my Regimental colleagues. But Maria had said it would help me to forget, and the prospect of forgetting was enough to take me down to the Bar Vodno that night.

The Dutch KFOR had been replaced by a unit of Swedes embarking on the same ritual of steady effacement, the breaking down of consciousness into a state of myopic fixation and chaotic impulse. This was the state I craved, the world very small and very close, a gaudy swirl of eyes, hair, cheeks, mouths, hands, glasses, bottles, bulges and curves. Everything else could be elbowed away to the margins, a fog of things ignored or denied.

I sat at the bar and drank cold lager and wondered if cold lager always tasted of ash. Men came and stood next to me to buy drinks and made convivial noises in my ear and I raised my glass in gestures of bonhomie; but nothing like a conversation ensued. A fat woman with melancholy eyes put her arm around my shoulders and wriggled herself against me in a coquettish manner, and I remember smiling and taking her by the waist. But she disengaged herself and walked away, giving me a solicitous look as she went. I don't know how many beers I drank, but though I forgot everything else, my mind would not release the memories I needed to shut out.

The Swedish soldiers started to include me in their rounds of shots, and the memories became lurid, looming up at me from pools of glossy darkness. I took the hard little glasses that were full of some fierce spirit and clinked them with my new friends, grinned when they grinned and slapped their heavy backs and roared at jokes I didn't understand. Then one of them asked me who I was and what I was doing in Skopje, and I couldn't reply but only stammered, and then I brought my hands up to my face like the man I had shot. They didn't like that. I had something to hide. I was taking the piss. I was a fucking weirdo. The mood turned evil and I had to leave.

'You buy drinks now, English shit!' one of them shouted after me.

I started walking and didn't look back. It wasn't raining, but the air was heavy and cold, the pavements damp. It was about eleven and the streets were full of people, hundreds and hundreds of them in pairs or little knots or gangs – some hurrying along in a modest, fearful way, some wrapped in each other's arms, some smart and out to impress, some singing or shouting or dangling their fists. I bought a hamburger and stood under a shop awning to eat it. I thought I must be drunk by now, though all I really felt was a sense of being hollowed out. A taxi rolled by and the driver leaned from his window.

'You want I take you good place? Have a drink, nice girls, OK?'

I climbed in and the taxi sped away.

'Four clubs you like in town,' said the driver. 'Best is Vegas Lounge. Nice young girls, fresh. OK?'

'Whatever you say.'

His face leered at me from his rear-view mirror. 'You American, boss? English?'

I stared out of the window. Maybe I should tell him to turn round and take me back to my apartment. But another image I hadn't succeeded in obliterating yet was of the young woman at the house, the triangle of soft, rosy skin between the lapels of her dressing gown, her dyed blonde hair and languid eyes. I did want a girl. I wanted her. But any girl would do. You're an off-duty soldier, I told myself, and this is how it goes: you get rat-arsed, fuck a whore, *then* go home. If you still can.

* * *

The Vegas Lounge was a low-built box with a flat roof sprouting a satellite dish and a pair of air-conditioning units. The windows were whitewashed over and covered with chicken wire. As I got out of the taxi, a man in a puffa jacket strolled over and gave the driver a banknote. The Vegas Lounge might be the best club in town, I thought, or it might just be the one that tipped taxi drivers the most for bringing punters to their door.

Two big, slope-shouldered men in tight suits stood either side of the entrance, their no-nonsense faces illuminated by a green and pink neon sign over the door. Immediately I was planning how to fight them. One was a gym bunny who spent too much time working on his arms and shoulders – he had the skinny legs of a man forty pounds lighter. Snap the ligaments of his knee with a kick from the side, draw the other one away and watch for a weapon. They looked me over as I approached, no doubt making the same kind of calculation.

I passed between them into an anteroom formed by heavy swags of ruby red curtain hanging from the ceiling. Several more doormen stood in the shadows. A sharp-faced woman wearing a green evening dress and a necklace of jade beads greeted me with a perfunctory smile, then led me over to a table bearing a vase of white lilies with spotted throats.

'Entrance to Vegas Lounge is thirty dollars,' she said.

'That's a fancy price for a garage with a bit of neon stuck on the front,' I said.

She shrugged, causing the skin beneath her necklace to stretch over her ribcage.

I paid her the money and she pulled a section of curtain aside to let me through. There were twenty or thirty low tables, each with a glass-shaded lamp that gave off a corona of dim, pinkish light. Groups of men lounged in sofas and armchairs. A few of them raised their heads, then looked away when they saw that I was ready to meet their eyes. The light gave their faces a peculiar appearance, swollen and a little effeminate. A tired-looking girl dressed in tight white shorts and a sequinned halter-neck bikini top showed me to an empty sofa opposite two men of about fifty. A bottle of brandy was set on a side table between them. Neither of them looked up when I sat down. One was reclining in his chair with his head thrown back, taking long pulls on a thin cigar while the other leaned in and talked.

I ordered whisky. The walls were bare brick painted with thick black paint and decorated with photos of movie starlets from the forties and fifties, all tilted chins and undulating hair. The bar was a long table draped in red baize, manned by two men in black trousers and ridiculous frilled shirts.

The girl brought my drink. As she leaned over to place the glass on the table, the cigar-smoking man behind her ran his fingers up the inside of her thigh, causing her to shy away and slop my drink on the table.

'Be careful! Your new guest does not want whisky in his lap.'

He slapped her on the leg and grinned at me.

'Macedonian girls. They look OK, but they don't know how to behave. They have to be taught. You are English, I think. From London?'

He had an oval of neatly clipped beard around his chin and

upper lip, a narrow nose and sunken eyes. I shook my head and looked away.

'Silent type, huh?'

I felt him staring at me and turned to meet his eye. The expression of lascivious entitlement was so repulsive that I looked at his companion instead, a small man whose demeanour was full of furtive hostility. After a moment, the two of them turned back to each other and continued their conversation.

I took a long swig of my whisky and tried to relax. I'd never set foot inside a brothel before, so what was I expecting? Raucous soldiers and buxom girls, tickles and squeezes and hearts of gold? None of that here. These johns were all rich and middle-aged. Their eyes flicked greedily over the bare limbs on parade, while their desires crouched in the shadows, biding their time.

Get out, I told myself. This place is all wrong.

Yet I too was entranced by the depravity of the Vegas Lounge. My eyes dwelt on creases and clefts. Lust pawed impatiently inside me. Then, serving a table on the far side of the room, I saw the sleepy-eyed girl from the troll's house. At least, I thought it was her – by this time I wasn't focusing so well. Her blonde hair was pinned into a loose knot at the back of her neck and she wore the regulation shorts and bikini top – an altogether different girl from the one who'd allowed her dressing gown to slip open and smiled at me in the doorway of the house on Syrna Street.

It would be better if she didn't know I was here – she no doubt despised the clientele of the Vegas Lounge. I could find her another day, now that I knew where she worked. I lowered my head and watched her discreetly, but in any case she was too busy serving – and fending off – the circle of laughing men at her table to notice me.

Then my befuddled mind caught hold of another thought: she lived in the house of a man who had tried to dent my skull with an iron bar. The troll might even now be waiting in the yard with a troupe of outsized doormen. Cautiously, I scanned the faces around me. The troll wasn't among them. Anyway, how could he have known that I'd end up here? None of the bouncers seemed to be taking a particular interest in me.

After a while, I allowed myself to think that I might not be in danger after all. That's how drunk I was. Before long, the woman with the jade necklace came over, put another whisky down in front of me, and perched her angular bottom on the arm of my sofa.

'You like a nice girl, sir?'

'Sure,' I said casually.

The man opposite watched me with a smirk on his face, then waved his cigar at the woman. 'Show your new guest to room sixteen,' he told her.

'Nice young girl for you,' she said. 'Is that what you like?'

I nodded, thinking that she wasn't making much sense. Why would I want a not-nice old girl?

'Price is two hundred,' she said. 'You come with me.'

She stood up and I followed her to a door at the back of the lounge. Beyond was a waiting area with candles set out on shelves along one wall, their scent doing little to mask the high, salty smell of human bodies. Two hundred dollars was a lot more than I'd been expecting, but she had a card reader to hand.

'For champagne, you see?'

She handed me the receipt, went to a cupboard stacked with linen and took out two white towels, then beckoned me along a narrow corridor with rooms on one side that were little more than plasterboard partitions. I heard a grunt and a slap from one of them as we passed. Even then I could have turned round and walked away, written off the two hundred dollars and saved myself from the corrupting embrace of the Vegas Lounge. We reached the last door. Room 16. She handed me the towels, unlocked the door and ushered me inside.

More candles, flushing the thin walls with a sickly orange cast. A bedside table with an ashtray and a table lamp that gave no light. A low bed with a white sheet stretched over it. The door shut behind me. Where was the girl? I stepped further into the room and heard an intake of breath. My eyes grew accustomed to the darkness and I caught sight of a figure squatting on the far side of the bed, out of reach of the candlelight. I dropped the towels on the bed, sat down with my back to her and turned on the lamp, thinking that she would come to me when she was ready. After a moment, I felt her climb onto the bed and tap me on the shoulder.

I turned and there was a small girl kneeling beside me. I mean, a child. A child dressed in a flimsy nightdress, hands stretching the hem over her bony knees, eyes cast down. She's been sent in to prepare the room, I thought stupidly. The real girl will be here in a moment. No one came and the truth crept over me. This is what I had bought with my two hundred dollars: the right to take my turn with this child, then pass her on to another of the guests of the Vegas Lounge. Shock gave way to fury. The girl looked up at me in alarm. I ran to the door. The woman with the jade necklace was watching from the waiting area, a cellphone held to her ear.

'Come with me,' I said to the girl. 'I'll get you out of here.'

She shrank away. I took her arm and she started to cry. The door opened behind me: the bony woman, pointing above my head. I looked up and saw a camera.

'All on video. You and this little girl. Let go now, you are hurting her.'

I looked into the girl's face and saw it was true. I released my grip on her slim wrist and the woman pulled her away. One of the doormen loomed in the doorway. The gym bunny with the skinny calves. I already knew what to do with him. My kick took him on the side of the knee and the joint buckled. He reached for something to steady himself but there was nothing and he toppled to the floor, hampering the man behind him so that he stumbled as he rushed me. I dropped my forehead into the bridge of his nose and the impact was so violent it almost knocked me out, too. I hurdled his body and sprinted along the corridor, then burst through the door into the bar.

'Get out!' I bellowed. 'Out, now!'

The clientele didn't like that. I picked up a side table and flung it across the room. It crashed into the back of a man who'd stood up from his sofa and was turning for the exit. I saw the cigar-smoking man standing five yards away, so I seized a bottle of champagne and hurled it at his head. He ducked and I ran over and punched him in the mouth, then ploughed on through the lounge.

I came to the makeshift bar, lifted it off the trestles and rammed the tabletop into the frilled shirts behind. A cohort of doormen had gathered behind me, but none of them wanted to be the first to take me on. The room was emptying fast. The curtain round the lobby got torn down and fell like a net over the crush of retreating men. I got in among them, hammering my fists, elbows, head into every face that came within range. There was such a throng around the exit that the doormen couldn't get to me now, even if they'd wanted to. A few moments later, I was out through the door.

* * *

I got less than five hundred yards down the street before an unmarked saloon sped past and pulled up. Two men piled out, aimed handguns at me and shouted. I slowed, looked back: a police van parked across the street behind me, uniformed men fanning out. I thought of making a run for it, but I was drunk and worn out and it didn't seem worth the risk. The Vegas Lounge wasn't the kind of place to press charges and a police cell was as good a place as any to spend the night.

I put my hands above my head and waited for them to approach. Two of the uniforms searched and cuffed me, while the men from the saloon holstered their guns and lit up. They locked me in a cage in the back of the van and we set off for the centre of town. At the police station, formalities were kept to a minimum. They didn't seem interested in me, and I wondered how often they carted troublemakers away from the Vegas Lounge. You can't keep a brothel in a place like Skopje without reaching some kind of an accommodation with the local police. Five minutes later, I was lying on the floor in a windowless cell, which mercifully I had to myself.

Connections circled in my head. The sleepy-eyed girl who lived at 77 Syrna Street, where I'd dropped off a twelve-year-old girl after saving her from exposure in a forest in Kosovo, was employed at the Vegas Lounge, where they sold underage girls for sex. Coincidence? Possibly. But when I'd come back to look for her, the troll in charge had tried to kill me. And what of the priest who'd given me the address? He'd told me there was UNHCR paperwork to show the children he sent there were in official hands. He was lying. Or the papers were forged and he'd been duped. I searched desperately for some mistake in the logic, but there was none.

I rolled around on the cold concrete floor and these specula-tions rolled with me, pointless and unanswerable. My bruised fists remembered the havoc I'd created among the clients of the Vegas Lounge, but the memory brought with it no satisfaction. There was no redemption to be found in the righteous fury I'd unleashed on the assembled sinners, and no hiding from the truth: I'd laid waste to the Vegas Lounge to exorcise a mood of self-loathing and despair that had got me in its clutches ever since I'd killed the boy in the farmhouse loft. Nor could I unburden myself of the image of the girl on the bed in Room 16. Could I have taken her with me, if I hadn't flown into a rage instead? Too late now. I remembered how she'd tapped me on the shoulder and held the nightdress over her little girl's thighs. Another garish memory to add to those I'd accumulated over the last few days, like warts on a once smooth face.

The alcohol took over and I fell into a fitful sleep – to be woken some hours later by the clang of iron bolts being drawn back. The door swung open and there stood Clive Silk, my MI6 liaison. Behind him were three wingmen, cussed old sergeants with fat fists and small, cold eyes.

Silk started reading from a document he had ready. 'You are hereby arrested under Section forty-two of the Armed Forces Act nineteen ninety-six, on suspicion of committing an offence under the Child Abduction Act nineteen eighty-four, namely abduction of a child.'

'Filthy nonce,' said one of the sergeants.

There was a gratified expression on Silk's square, doughy face. We'd never got on. 'Do you want to make this easy for yourself,' he said, 'or shall we do it—'

'The hard way,' I said, taking him by the throat and driving the top of his head into the chin of the sergeant behind him.

Just before they took me out, I thought of something else. The girl I had rescued... I didn't even know her name.

Anna

12

My dearest, darling Katarina, my sweet angel, my beautiful child, how could I have lost you? My head seethes, scrabbles, swoons with the loss of you. I cannot think for the loss of you. My heart beats without point. I do not sleep for fear that hope will desert me while my mind is off guard. I am drained out, blinking at emptiness.

* * *

The past rearranges itself in my mind until it seems as if everything colluded in the events of that horrible day. It began with a call from the secretary to Mikhail Ongoric, vice-principal of the University of Pristina, requiring my attendance at a meeting the following Friday 15 January. There would be no school that day and Katarina implored me to let her stay in our apartment on her own. I was worried about the war between the Kosovo Liberation Army and our Serbian masters, but I agreed. There had been bombs and raids and killings in Pristina, but not in our district. A sensible twelve-year-old girl – even a Kosovar girl of mixed Albanian-Roma parentage – would be perfectly safe. Besides, we had good neighbours who would take care of her if anything bad should happen.

On the Thursday I saw a gang of men dressed in black, with black gloves over their hands and black balaclavas over their faces, marching through the Albi shopping mall and barging people aside as if they did not exist. *Specijalna Antiteroristička Jedinica*, President Slobodan Milošević's pet fighting dogs. I lost heart. I couldn't leave Katya alone with Milosh's bullies about, so I rang my ex-husband Franz's mother in Talinic. There has never been any fighting there because it's a Roma village, and as such regarded with contempt by the KLA and Serbian army alike. I arranged to drop Katya off at one and pick her up by six at the latest. 'Oh,' said Grandmama, 'make an old woman happy, Anna, and leave her with me forever!' Katya was cross with me, though in truth she loves spending time in Talinic. Her Roma cousins treat her with awe because she is so pretty and clever, and they stage boxing matches and dances in her honour.

I drove her to Talinic in my *Fiat Frikshëm*, as we call it, my Fiat Frightful, and arrived in Vice-Principal Ongoric's office at two. The meeting was to discuss his application to the Serbian Ministry for Further and Higher Education for the funds required to institute a new course in international relations. It was pointless. Belgrade were never going to fund the course because they don't know anything about international relations and if they did they would never leave the teaching of it in the hands of a claque of clever-clog Kosovars like us – as Ongoric would have known, had he not been such a gullible clod. Nevertheless, we combed through the proposed curriculum at tedious length, searching for evidence of intellectual imbalance; social, racial, religious, political, gender or cultural bias; and, finally, at just after four-fifteen, deficiencies in relevance to the administrative and/or commercial and/or cultural needs of the greater Serbia.

On our release, my friend and colleague Eleni rolled her eyes at me and we agreed that our fortitude in the presence of V-P Ongoric's weary quest for impeccable balance in the matter of doomed funding applications to Belgrade warranted the very best coffee in all of Kosovo. We went to the Italian Café on Novotny Street and had a good grumble. I lingered over the thick swirl of caramel-coloured foam on top of my espresso, then had a second cup because the first was such a delicious luxury.

At five-twenty, I stood up abruptly and said I must hurry because I'd promised to collect Katarina by six and even though Talinic was only half an hour away by Fiat Frightful, the traffic would be bad. The traffic was bad. My way out of town was blocked by a bus that had got its wheel jammed in a broken drain cover. The policeman who should have been redirecting the traffic stood around flirting with the driver and giving her cigarettes and nudging her until I got out and politely asked him if he might stop the traffic on the other carriageway for long enough for some of us to get by and was told to mind my own business or he'd inspect my vehicle and find some reason to give me a ticket. I got back into the Fiat Frightful and waited.

A team of mechanics arrived and unloaded a large jack from the back of their rescue truck. Everything will be fine, I told myself. Very soon you'll be holding Katya tight in your arms. She'll squirm away because she wants Grandmama to see she's too grown-up to be hugged and kissed like a little girl. Grandmama will make me sample a spoonful of her revoltingly runny sour-cherry jam while she tells me how adorable Katya is. She would never confess it to me, but she feels guilty that her darling boy Franz ran off and left me shortly before Katya's second birthday and never comes round to see us nor sends any money.

I didn't get to Talinic until six-twenty. It was dark. The sky spat rain on the windscreen. My nephew Sammy and friends, who usually congregate by the gas station smoking cigarettes and making obscene gestures at passing cars, weren't there. I parked outside

Grandmama's house. She ran from the doorway and fell to her knees in front of me.

'They took her away, the sons of whores! We didn't know, my darling Anna, we would have stopped them, Piotr would have killed them first, we didn't even know they were here, damn them to hell…'

My husband's younger brother Piotr came out and led her back to her chair by the stove. His son Sammy was seated at the table, hands held out in front of him. His eyes were red from crying, his face white. Piotr dusted off the seat of the chair opposite with his big hands, then looked at me, his face rippling with misery and shame.

'They took her, Anna. They took Katarina.'

'What do you mean? Where is Katya?'

'Go on, Sammy.'

'I made a rude sign at them,' said Sammy. 'I didn't know…'

'What are you talking about?' I said, standing up. 'I must take Katya home now, I hate driving in the rain—'

Piotr banged the table with the flat of his hand. 'Sammy, speak!'

'They were in this fancy pickup so I showed them my arse. They stopped and got out and we ran. They chased us down behind Grigor's and we got to the river, then one of them caught me and hit me.'

He raised his T-shirt. In the centre of his skinny boy's stomach was a patch of bright red, dark at the centre.

'But Katya wasn't with you,' I told him. 'She never hangs out with you boys.'

'She was by the river with Kezia and Silvio. They were making a bonfire. The men said are you from the village and Katya said no and they said why're you here and she said what's it got to do with you.'

He looked at me, wretchedness gaping in his eyes.

'Go on,' said Piotr.

'They said she shouldn't be hanging out with effing Roma scum.'

'Why didn't you protect her, Sammy?' I asked. 'Why didn't you all run away?'

'I don't know, Aunt Anna.'

'Then what happened?'

'Then they took her.'

'No, Sammy,' I whispered. 'Don't say that... Don't.'

'They said where're you from and Silvio said she's from Pristina and they said OK we're taking you home so you don't have to be with these dirty Roma. One of them picked her up and she kicked and kicked so he dropped her and then two of them got her and she kicked some more and scratched one of them in the eye but they took her to their pickup and drove her away.'

'No, not Katya. Please...'

'It was a Toyota.'

'We've got men out looking for them,' said Piotr. 'Grigor's called his cousin in Drenas, in case they go that way.'

'They can't just take her away...' I said, imploring them to save me, to undo everything that was said.

'Maybe she's back in Pristina, Aunt Anna,' said Sammy. 'Waiting for you.'

* * *

Time stalls. I'm stuck forever in Grandmama's kitchen, Sammy crying, Piotr bleak as stone. The past leans back through the life we had together. The future no longer exists.

* * *

Piotr drives me home and all the way I pretend to think, Oh, Sammy's probably right, she'll be waiting when I get there. She's rung Milo and Nina's bell and they've buzzed her in and Nina's made her hot chocolate and Milo's put on a wildlife video. Right now, Katya's sitting neatly at the table and answering their questions about school and what she wants for her birthday and whether she'd like another homemade sweetmeal biscuit. Piotr moves his mouth around the words he would like to speak but cannot. He's a good man, but shy and proud. He will never forgive himself that he could not prevent it. It is unmanly. He would rather be dead. I feel his shame pulsing beside me. I'm concentrating on the moment when Nina pulls open her door and Katya skips up behind her and looks at me with her clear blue eyes and says, *Hi, Mum, can we get a take-away, since you're so late?*

Of course, Katya my love, my dear sweet angel, we'll have a takeaway. We'll have a thousand million takeaways, our flat will be crammed with tinfoil cartons and uneaten portions of shredded cabbage, the aroma of spicy chicken wings will permanently scent the air.

'What is it, Anna, what has happened?' says Nina when she opens the door.

'I don't suppose Katya dropped by, did she?'

'Oh, Anna, no. Has she gone missing? Please God she has not. When did you last see her? You must tell me if there's anything I can do. Milo still has contacts, you know?'

There is no circumstance so dire as to be beyond the influence of Milo's contacts, Nina believes, and their willingness to be called upon is never in doubt. Milo worked in government, though in what capacity is unclear, and he retired ten years ago. Whenever Nina mentions his contacts, Milo looks anxious.

'I'll say a little prayer,' says Nina.

'Thank you, I'm sure she'll turn up soon.'

I'm sure she'll turn up soon. I'll say this many times and no one will contradict me. No one will say, *I'm not so sure, Anna, you might have lost her forever.* The little lie protects me from pity and solicitude.

Already I can do a quick smile with my mouth and cheeks that is completely dissociated from what's inside me.

*   *   *

We live in a three-room apartment near the centre of town, which we are lucky to have. After a day at the university delivering ill-attended lectures, holding less-than-animated seminars and researching the migration of warlike tribes in north-eastern Turkey, I usually go to Katya's school to collect her. My sweet-natured, composed and rather serious twelve-year-old girl stands at the gates, waiting for me. For a treat, we might take her friends Magda and Sofia to the zoo, followed by an ice cream at the Yankee Doodle Dandy Diner – *Where sprinkles come free!*

'What do you want to do?' asks Piotr.

The apartment is cold. Blackness presses against the windows. The fridge buzzes. Her not being here makes everything seem separated out. They picked on her because she looks different from Kezia and Silvio and the others, I realise. Outsiders are vulnerable. The Ottoman rulers understood that, that's why they kept their inner circle close.

'Do you know how to get in touch with Franz?'

'No... I can try.'

I see in Piotr a trace of his-brother-my-husband's default preference for not being responsible, and it makes me feel weak and alone.

'Last I heard he was in Izmir.'

Turkey. That figures. Scamming the pensions off jolly German widows. Fucking them, probably. How I loved that man, that filthy Roma with his big smile and soft eyes, his brown skin that smelled of cedars and sunlight.

'Find him, Piotr. You must. I'll make a list.'

I compose the list in my head, but all it comes to is this:

1. Hug my Katya's little body and feel her try to squirm away and not let her.
2. Buy my little Katya a takeaway and sit next to her on the sofa and watch TV.
3. After she has gone to bed, go in to turn her light out, lean down to kiss her warm cheek, feel the slightness of her arms around my neck.

I inhale deeply and the breath shudders in my throat. A moan I didn't mean to make, a sob I expected to suppress. Piotr takes me in his arms and I drown.

* * *

The list. Focus. How long since they came and took my life away? Just three hours, a little more. Hours such as once stole past unnoticed now divide themselves into minutes and linger on. Even seconds last longer than they should. I make Piotr call everyone he knows. Roma clans are terribly well connected, though only with each other. The calls take a long time because there is always *business* to discuss. Discussing business is important – more so than actually doing it, which is time-consuming and presents the Roma male with too many opportunities for a demeaning failure. At least there is a family to call. Who do I have? A mother who died of breast cancer. A father who went to California to sell real estate to Yugoslav expatriates, married a Guatemalan sweatshop 'entrepreneur', and now lives in San Diego, where he spends his wife's ill-gotten wealth on lavishly upholstered sailing boats. Some aunts and uncles who disapprove of me. A slew of cousins who don't even know I exist.

The list.

Call the police. Visit the police.

'Piotr, get Sammy to write everything down. You know, how many men, what they looked like, the pickup. Anything he can think of.'

'He can't write. Never was much good at school. Lazy.'

'For fuck's sake!' I scream at him. 'Get him to tell someone who can write.'

'OK, OK. I'm sorry, Anna.'

He's never seen me lose my temper. Hardly anyone has. In the faculty at the University of Pristina I am better known for my mildness and passivity than for my work on the early years of the Ottoman Empire.

The list.

Call the police. Visit the police.

Call or write to everyone I know.

Say a little prayer.

13

In the morning, Piotr drives me to the police station on Yevgeny Street.

'What will they do with her, Piotr?'

'Shit, Anna, I don't know. Maybe you'll get a ransom demand.'

'When? When will I get a ransom demand?'

'They might wait until the police've lost interest and the family are desperate. A week. Maybe two.'

'I'm already desperate,' I say. 'The police have already lost interest,' I continue, remembering the cruel labour of my phone call to the duty sergeant the previous night. 'I only got an appointment this morning because I said I was connected with the KVM.'

'KVM?'

'Kosovo Verification Mission. Here to make sure the Serbs do what they're told.'

'Waste of space.'

'How will I pay the ransom? You'll help me, won't you?'

'We'll get the money. Don't worry about that.'

He draws back his shoulders and sits upright in his seat. He's made a promise, and he will keep it. He begins to drive a bit less like the car is towing a trailer precariously loaded with several tons of straw. Piotr is OK. He's going to help me. My eyes fill with tears. It happens so fast that when I look down to find a tissue in my bag, a stream of salty water drops into the compartment where I keep my keys.

We arrive opposite the police station. 'Be strong,' he says. 'Don't let them wriggle out of it. There are still laws in this fucking country.'

'Not for us there aren't. There is only one law: leave while you can.'

He asks me if I want him to come in, but I say no. I want him back home, waiting by the phone for when Katarina rings to say she is fine, really, the men in the pickup dropped her off at the bus station and then she took the wrong bus but by total good luck she ended up near Sofia's house! So she went and stayed the night there and she did try to call me, really and truly she did, but her phone's battery was dead and Sofia's mum has been disconnected for not paying her bill.

* * *

I sit on a bench just inside the entrance to the police station, between a door that does not close properly and a man hunched defensively over his knees. All I can see of his face is a bloodshot eye beneath a swollen eyebrow that resembles a large, hairy cater-pillar. The duty sergeant keeps insisting that there is no chance of Inspector Jankovic being able to see me today.

'I have an appointment. The police here keep their appoint-ments, I'm sure.' My voice is both ice cold and shaky, because fury and despair have not yet worked out which is in charge.

'Lost your daughter, right?'

'Yes.'

'And she is how old?'

'Just twelve.'

He gives me a world-weary look. Why did I say *Just twelve* instead of *Twelve*? It sounded as if I was trying to make a point.

'You've checked with her boyfriend's family?'

'She doesn't have a boyfriend.'

Another look.

After an hour and a half, my neighbour lies down on the tiled floor, ignoring the smears of mud and whatever.

'He's waiting for an ambulance,' says the sergeant.

Eventually, Inspector Jankovic arrives, takes a quick look at me over the counter, says, 'One minute, please,' and disappears. Not one but forty-six minutes pass. He returns and takes me to an interview room painted pale cream and furnished with a single red plastic chair. Through a small oblong window high in the wall opposite I can see a small oblong of perfectly grey sky.

'I'll stand.'

He disappears again, returns carrying a pad of lined yellow paper and dragging a second red plastic chair. The feet of the chair scrape and bump across the floor. I look down and see splashes of some dark substance dried into the concrete.

'Missing person, yeah?'

He is sweating. The skin around his jaw is glabrous and unnaturally thick. I don't want this man to find my daughter, I think suddenly. His fingers are sausagey and stained with tobacco.

'My daughter. Katarina.'

Already there is a hollowness in the sound that means her. It appals me to see him writing it down on his yellow pad, in this room where people come to have their tragedies recorded and filed away. He takes down my contact details. He doesn't trouble to check the number he has written down because he knows he will never use it. As soon as he's rid of me, he'll go upstairs to his office, tear the sheet off, scrunch it up and toss it at a bin marked *Crimes committed by Serbs against Albanians*. The bin is already full of scrunched-up yellow paper. If he should miss, he won't even bother to get out of his chair and pick it up.

'When did you last see her?'

'About eleven-thirty yesterday morning. I took her to her grandmother's for the day.'

I give him the address and he looks up from his writing, a smug expression on his face.

'Talinic – Roma village, yeah?'

'Yes.'

'You left your daughter in a Roma village and now she's gone.' It's all he can do to stop himself grinning.

'I left Katarina with her grandmother – it's OK to leave children with their grandmothers, don't you think?' The shakiness is gaining ascendance over the iciness.

'Depends on the gran.'

'She was playing with her cousins and got abducted by an armed gang in a pickup,' I say, desperately trying to stay calm. 'I don't see what the ethnic make-up of the village has got to do with it.'

'Let me get this straight. Her grandmother is your husband's mother? So where is he, your husband?'

'I don't know. He left me ten years ago.'

A decade it may be, but still I feel the shame creep over me. The stupid bitch married a Roma man and guess what? He ran away!

He clears his throat. 'Might be worth checking with him, yeah?'

'Sir, his brother is getting in touch with Katarina's father right now. In the meantime, there are witnesses who saw her being driven away in a Toyota pickup. You have to go to Talinic and talk to them.'

'Witnesses? The kids she was playing with?'

'And some older boys.'

'All members of your ex-husband's family, yeah?'

He has stopped taking notes. What happened has already been settled: an estranged Roma dad arranged the abduction of his daughter; mum has been sold some ridiculous story about a gang of militia carting her away in a pickup; now she wants us to sort it out. Typical. He's closing the case in his mind. You make a complete dog mess of your private life, he's thinking, then blame the Serbs.

'They're a very tight-knit community, these Roma.'

'Spare me the platitudes,' I say angrily. 'She's a twelve-year-old girl and at least half a dozen witnesses say she was abducted. Doesn't matter what your prejudices tell you, does it, because you still have to investigate. Isn't that one of the benefits of being part of the greater Serbia? The anarchy's not supposed to start until *after* you've left, remember?'

'I wouldn't take that tone in here.'

He looks me up and down, slowly. I've crossed the line – and given him licence to do the same. Even in that stuffy room, I feel the heat off him, the hormones rousing themselves as he examines my breasts and legs. I've made it personal, alluded to matters of politics and ethnicity – so now I'm not just a member of the public reporting her daughter missing, but a Kosovar woman of fuckable age who's making trouble. Why don't I kick and scratch, like Katya did when the men carried her away?

'Kids get handed round Roma families like second-hand cars.'

'Do they? So that's it? I have to find her myself?'

'Start with Gran and go from there.'

'She's twelve years old—'

'I can't file a missing person report until she's been gone for twenty-four hours. Call me at six, if she hasn't turned up.'

'You're not even going to Talinic?'

'Talk to Gran, yeah?'

14

Piotr sleeps in Katya's room. He's like a decent version of his brother-my-husband, sober and steadfast where Franz is flashy and sly. But the decency is lugubrious, oppressive even. It offers nothing, yet demands to be taken seriously. It is horrible to see him emerging from Katya's room – as if my lissom daughter has metamorphosed overnight into a slouching, black-haired giant. He hasn't seen me watching him. He stands in the corridor in a Bosch logo T-shirt and tracksuit bottoms, prodding at something with his big bare foot. After a moment he scratches the back of his head and bends down to pick the something up. It's a biro top. He twirls it in his fingers, then looks up and sees me and drops it. His awkwardness seems like a wholly unnecessary side-effect of Katya's being taken away from me, and again I feel angry with him.

I feed him eggs and toast, then get him to drive me out to Talinic. I dread Grandmama's wails, but I have to speak to Sammy again. And Kezia and Silvio. The older boys are not smoking cigarettes outside the gas station and it seems to me that the village is deserted, silent and frozen with shock. We turn into the street where Grandmama lives and I see a crowd outside the stairwell to one of Talinic's apartment blocks. There's a girl, teetering and voluminous in white chiffon, inside a palisade of strutting, smoking men in black suits.

'Shit,' says Piotr. 'Sasha's wedding party – I forgot.'

It's easily done – the Roma are avid celebrants. Aside from the weddings, christenings, funerals, memorial days, birthdays, confirmations and first holy communions, there are innumerable contests and competitions: fistfighting, cockfighting, dancing, musicianship, horsemanship, and a host of other feats whose importance is in no way compromised by their obscurity. The prize is eagerly sought and always the same: the victor wins the right to trumpet his (always his, the women have better things to do) supremacy in the contested sphere until the next competition is held. Not long after we were married, Franz was *obliged* to absent himself for an entire weekend in order to celebrate an elderly Talinic man's victory in a competition for the best collection of Turkish music on cassette (the judging based on each contestant's ability to inspire foot-tapping, dancing and tears among his audience). Furthermore, the men of Talinic are inclined to declare incidental triumphs in their endlessly recurring feuds with neighbouring villages and families, and to call for these to be properly observed.

My daughter's kidnapping by a gang of Serbian militia is now the lesser priority. I must drive Piotr to his apartment, wait for him to change, then drive him back to the community hall opposite Block 3. It's only two hundred yards each way but he's ashamed of being late. The confection in white is being corralled indoors by a supernumerary constellation of bobbing pink clouds. There is panic inside me, aching for release.

'Wouldn't be fair to spoil her day,' Piotr mutters. 'Do you want to come in?' He looks shiny and, I'm suddenly and painfully aware, quite beautiful in his clean white shirt and burgundy suit.

'What do you think, Piotr?'

He looks down at his hands.

'I'll be at Grandmama's. Send Sammy over as soon as you can. Make him come.'

I drive slowly across the village. I was part of this once, but now I'm an outsider again. The ties that were weakened when Franz ran away have been severed entirely by the abduction of his daughter. I'd assumed Grandmama would be at the party but she isn't. She's sitting by her stove, weeping.

'Oh Anna, you have news for me, Anna? Say you have news for me.'

I shake my head.

'I know in your heart you blame me. You say to yourself it was the fault of that cursed Roma family. And where was Franz? He should have been here to protect his own darling Katya. Where was he, the lazy wretch! There was nothing, nothing I could do, Anna. It was over before I even knew. That sweet girl who we all loved—'

I can't bear it. I step outside into the cold.

'He should have been here! Franz... His own dear daughter!' Grandmama shouts after me.

I start to walk. I'm not necessarily seeing things the way they are just now, but still the village looks ugly. Four apartment buildings in cream-painted breeze block, eight overseers' houses, all built for the cement plant a kilometre to the south. When the plant closed and the workers left, Franz's extended family (over a hundred of them, eventually) moved in. The uncongenial concrete of the unlovely village became overlaid with the richly patinated fabric of their lives, so in the end you could hardly even see it. Or I couldn't, anyway, not the way I can now. Talinic was the scene of my seduction, it was my Verona, my Baghdad, my Kathmandu. A handsome, black-haired man sold me a cast-iron scallop shell basin at a flea market, then offered to carry it home in his strong brown arms. So handsome and black-haired that a week later he is walking me along this pounded-rubble street, flashing his teeth at passers-by. He's put on

a clean white shirt for me, a strong brown arm has taken ownership
of my waist. We turn here, step down behind the yard at the back of
Grandmama's, where he bends and picks up my ankles one by one
so he can take off my shoes.

'They'll get dirty,' he says.

We start across the meadow but the soles of my feet wince at
the thistles and stones and I lean on him and beg him to carry me,
which he willingly does, his broad hand flirting with the small of
my back. He walks to the river, this warm little chit in his arms,
and ducks below the lowest branch of a huge alder tree. There's a
little bower he's made, the cunning bastard, with a bolster of hay
and a bottle of wine cooling on the riverbed. He reaches for me
and I feel the easy power that rolls in his limbs. The cool air and
his warm lips bring goosebumps to my naked shoulders, shudders
to my breast. The demure academic with her dusty passion for the
nomads who once galloped the high plains of eastern Turkey now
yields to a wanderer of her own, feels the rude tickle of crushed
hay beneath her thighs. He could trace his lineage back through
centuries, as if he cared. The feel of my lips parting for his kisses
is all that matters to him now. I wrap my arms around my Roma
prize, while the alder shakes its great boughs and the swallows skip
down to the river to drink.

How the aunts and uncles whispered! Meek, modest Anna
Galica, in the arms of a swarthy Horahane! And before you could
say *How disgraceful*, she was married! And then (*Aha!*), pregnant!
They could say what they liked, I was drunk on it, woozy and rav-
enous as a bey's whore in the foothills of Mount Ararat. I wanted
it all, every drop of it. I lay in his arms and invented our delicious
future: we travel to Paris where, because of his exceptional talent
with horses, Franz has been offered the reins of a prestigious racing stables. I have several more beautiful children and bring them
up in a sunny *maison de maître*. I write books, instead of merely

translating them, novels and essays and memoirs and who knows what. I look up from my desk to watch my husband canter across the field in front of the house, the limbs of his powerful bay flowing beneath him. Later I find him in the stables grooming the mare he has entered for the races at Longchamp. He is whispering something in its ear and I tell him to stop and whisper in mine.

I walk down to the river, to the place where Katya was begotten and then taken away. There's nothing to see or understand here, only a yawning melancholy in the clumps of trodden yellow grass, the shivering alder trees, the passage of brown water between sodden riverbanks. There's a patch of wet ash and charred wood where the children had their bonfire, and a circle of sticks that forms an arena for dancing or other kinds of ceremonial play. Weddings are the most popular, Katya said, followed by christenings. I look for her footprints in the mud, and perhaps I find them, but it's been drizzling and the outlines are smooth. There are bootprints, too. Men have stood here and considered taking my child away. They're in a dangerous mood, their fragile manhood offended by the sight of Sammy's bared arse. The one who's in charge sees Katarina. She's different. She doesn't belong here with these *filthy Roma*, he thinks. She can come with us. That'll teach the gypsy scum. One of them takes hold of her, but she kicks him. *She kicked and kicked*, Sammy said. My heart gulps and I find I am moaning as I circle the damp cinders.

It's evidence. It needs to be preserved. There should be red-and-white-striped tape like they have for car accidents. How can this be less important than a car accident? I'll come back with a camera. Dread heaves inside me. I'm going to show Inspector Jankovic some photos of a muddy field. He'll take them with a smirk and file them in the bin with the notes he wrote on his pad of lined yellow paper. The very few notes he took because he thinks her Roma father took Katarina, abetted by his Roma family in Talinic, all of them habitual liars and practised child abductors. He'll see Grandmama's stricken face and think, *She can't fool me, the old fraud.* Why should he waste his time because some overheated Kosovar bitch can't keep her knickers on when a bit of Roma rough strolls by?

I'm rescued by the sight of Sammy, Silvio and Kezia standing by the fence round Grandmama's backyard. I set off towards them, stumbling like a mad thing in the dank, sticky field.

* * *

'I wrote down everything,' I say to Eleni in the Italian Café next day, handing her a photocopy of my notes. 'Descriptions of the men. How they were dressed, their accents. One of them sounds very distinctive: *He had clothes like a soldier. He was bald with a tattoo of a snake on his neck. When he talked, the snake's mouth moved.*'

'The very model of a Serbian policeman,' says Eleni. 'Bald as in no hair, or shaven-headed?'

'I don't know. Another was fat, wearing blue overalls. Two of them had cowboy hats, one in black leather, one in what I guess was felt. That one was carrying a shotgun – a shotgun, Eleni. To deal with a bunch of mouthy kids.'

'Did you speak to them separately?'

'No. I thought it would help them remember if they were together.'

'So they took it in turns to speak and the others listened and agreed?'

'Yes. Sammy came in to Pristina and we went to the Toyota dealership and identified the pickup. It's a Toyota Invincible fitted with something called—' I check the notes— 'a Road Muscle Body Kit. Surely there can't be many like that. Look at it!'

I show her the printout. The red toner was low and the vehicle looks like a cartoon.

'If they weren't telling the truth, Anna… Well, you made it easy for them.'

'Not telling the truth? What do you mean? Why wouldn't they?'

'Because… Maybe Franz really is behind this.'

'Not you too, Eleni. You can't believe that.'

She sees my furious expression and blushes. 'I'm sorry, Anna. I just don't see how you can rule it out.'

'Er, because he was my husband?'

'I know, and he was a lovely man, I always said that. But not exactly reliable. Men can be possessive of their children, just as much as women.'

Eleni is a social psychologist and we are straying into her area of expertise. She is also one of the least tactful people I have ever met. These are both good reasons for curtailing this conversation, even though there is nothing else I can talk about. I look into her big, anxious face – anxious because she loves me and shares my grief with a sincerity that makes me long to fold myself into her arms and weep (something I do often these days).

'If it was him, we'll soon find out. And at least she'll be safe.'

Safe with Franz; with anyone else, not safe. Eleni sets out the options with her unerring instinct for causing distress without meaning to.

'I'm going to carry on with this line of enquiry, anyway,' I say hurriedly, standing up to leave.

Eleni stands, too. Her big, clumsy body knocks the little table and I have to lunge to prevent two espresso cups and a side plate sliding to the floor.

'I'm sleeping at yours tonight,' she says, bringing the hefty flaps of her dark green boiled-wool coat under control.

'You don't have to. Piotr is still there.'

'All right, tomorrow then. Or as soon as he's gone. I'll read these notes and see if I can think of anything. Go now, Anna, or you'll be late.'

Line of enquiry... Who are you kidding? You're a distraught mother, drifting uncontrollably between immobility and hysteria. You're also hosting a seminar called *Worship on the Road: Religious observance among Turkish nomads, 1450–1530.* Only three people have signed up for it, but I can't back out or the university will dock my pay.

15

When I get back there's a note from Piotr on the table. *Had to go home. Call tomorrow. P.* The apartment is empty of everything except loneliness and loss. This is how our home is now, how it will be. Silent. I step into Katya's room and there's enough of her there to sustain me. I curl up on her bed and cry for a while – not sobbing but whimpering from deep within.

I won't give up, I won't abandon hope for fear of despair. I go and make a cup of coffee. On the fridge door is a photo I took on a picnic in Germia Park last summer. I'll use it for the leaflet I'm going to do. Katya's sitting on a rug with her legs folded beneath her. There's chicken sandwich quarters, a sliced tomato and a stack of potato chips neatly arranged on a yellow plastic plate in her lap, and she's coiled her hair behind one ear so it doesn't get in the way while she eats. Such an orderly girl! She saw my camera and sucked in her cheeks. 'Mum! Why're you always pointing that thing at me?' The protest was not credible. A few weeks later I came across her and Sofia practising to look cute, pouting at the mirror in the hall. 'Ooh, you look gorgeous,' said Sofia with a giggle.

I lay out the text and the words stare back at me from the screen of my laptop. The gulf between what they mean and what they

mean to me is so great that I'm momentarily confused. *Missing...*
Last seen in Talinic... Please contact... Is this all that need be said?
You see leaflets like this in news reports from refugee centres, held
up by weeping mothers or pinned to noticeboards behind rows of
craning heads.

I'll have to scan the photo on the machine in the faculty office.
If I had a key I'd drive over there right now, but instead I go to bed
and all night I'm tapping on turned shoulders and stumbling past
bare-faced doors, whether awake or asleep I cannot tell. At nine the
next morning I'm outside the university building, waiting to be let
in. However, the bulb on the scanner has broken and the replacement has to be posted from Germany.

'I ordered it three months ago,' says V-P Ongoric's secretary.
'There's a print shop on Ceruleska Street we sometimes use. It's
not far.'

It's not far but there's a notice on the door: DUE TO ADVERSE
TRADING CONDITIONS, WE HAVE BEEN FORCED TO CLOSE. By
the time I've found a printer who has survived the adverse trading conditions, it's already three o'clock. The man at the counter
declares he can't do a thing until tomorrow. As a Serb born and
bred he would usually defer jobs from Albanian women for weeks
or even refuse them altogether, his manner implies; but he is prepared to rise nobly above the ethnic divide on behalf of the missing child.

'No, not tomorrow morning, tomorrow afternoon. You're lucky
to get it done at all, given the way things are,' he says accusingly.

The way things are is all over the news. The World Service of
the BBC has been reporting the massacre of forty-five civilians during a raid on the village of Račak, a KLA stronghold not fifty kilometres from Pristina. The attack was co-ordinated by men dressed
in black, with black gloves over their hands and black balaclavas
over their faces. The first body the reporters discovered had been

decapitated. Meanwhile, a peace conference is mooted. Serbian and Kosovar-Albanian leaders must sort out their differences under the stern gaze of representatives of the six Great Powers. If not, NATO has legal authority to bomb Kosovo into oblivion.

* * *

I make a start on the letters. *Dear President Rugova…* Or perhaps, given the personal nature of the letter, I can get away with *Dear Ibrahim.* I was introduced to the president of the widely unrecognised Republic of Kosovo at a reception held by the Writers Union three years ago; he favoured me with a wan smile. Since then, I've translated for him five times – three diplomatic papers and two circuitous legal opinions from a barrister in London who I hope was not paid by the word, as I was. *Dear President Rugova, I hope you will not mind this approach, but…* Why so apologetic? Because it's shameful to lose your twelve-year-old daughter – everyone will think so. She should have been more careful, especially with the way things are. I wasn't careful. While Katya was being abducted, I was licking espresso froth off a wooden spill in the Italian Café.

Dear President Rugova, as a consequence of my careless and naive disregard for the way things are, my daughter has been taken from the town of Talinic by an unknown gang in a Toyota Invincible with Road Muscle Body Kit. They carried shotguns and wore stupid leather hats. Probably Serbs – who else could get away with snatching a child in broad daylight? I am keen to get her back before we are bombed by NATO. Please help.

I delete it all and start again, a sober, respectful letter, and by the end of the day I've written twenty more in the same vein. I'll send them by both email and post, although neither service is reliable in the Kosovo of January 1999 – whether this is a form of oppression or a symptom of general collapse is impossible to say. I tramp along the ice-crusted street to buy stamps, then go back to the police station with the pack of evidence I've prepared for Inspector Jankovic. I've included the picture of the Toyota Invincible with Road Muscle Body Kit Sammy and I got from the dealership, beneath which I have written: *This was the type of pickup driven by the men who took Katarina Corochai away from Talinic on 15 January 1999. Signed by her cousin, Sammy Corochai.* Sammy managed to write out his name in the space below, though the effort made him go bright red and the letters are uneven in size. I've also attached copies of the statements of Sammy, Kezia and Silvio, and the pictures I took of the meadow behind Grandmama's. I lay the pack down on the counter for the duty sergeant to inspect.

He inspects me instead, then turns back to his more important paperwork. 'Leave the stuff with me, I'll make sure Jankovic gets it.'

'No. I want to speak to him in person. Do you have children?'

He doesn't answer.

'Last time I was here, you rolled your eyes when I said my twelve-year-old doesn't have a boyfriend. It sounded as if you had experience of girls of that age. Do you?'

He's a neatly turned-out man with short, greasy hair and a trim brown moustache shaped like the cow-catchers you see on pictures of steam trains in the Wild West. Half policeman, half communist bureaucrat. His eyes are watery and the skin of his cheeks is flaking. I suspect that rustic militiamen make him snuffle with disapproval.

'You see a lot from behind this counter, I can tell you.'

'None of it good, I guess.'

'Oh, I wouldn't say that,' he says, though I'm sure he would have if it hadn't entailed agreeing with me.

'They grow up at different speeds, don't they?' The attempt at chattiness sounds ludicrous in my ears. 'I mean, you see some twelve-year-olds who look sixteen or seventeen and others who are still little girls.'

'And you know who's the last to know when the little girl grows into a big girl and gets herself into trouble? Her mother.'

Along with the tone of worldly admonishment, there's a glint in his oystery eyes – he likes mention of big girls in trouble.

'Last time I was here, the theory was she'd been abducted by her father. Today, she's run off with a boyfriend. What will it be tomorrow, I wonder?'

He gives a frown of warning and picks up his pen. I turn away and walk back to the bench with my evidence pack. I have brought with me a printout of a journal article I ought to read: *Recent Excavations in Eastern Anatolia: Holy Days and Feasts, 830–890 AD.* I open it and immediately want to feel Katya's little body snuggle in my lap, though in truth it's years since she last did so. When was the last time? I hunt for the memory, distraught that I may lose it forever and have nothing to replace it with. The report is dull and excessively cautious, and offers nothing I can usefully incorporate into my research. An hour later, I go back to the counter, hand the folder full of evidence to the sergeant, and leave.

*   *   *

Next day Eleni and I collect the leaflets from the printer, then tour the sombre valleys of southern Kosovo in the Fiat Frightful, looking for a Toyota Invincible with Road Muscle Body Kit driven by a bald or shaven-headed man dressed in army gear with a tattoo of a snake on his neck. Eleni has stuck the ghostly printout to the dashboard with Blu-tack.

'You think we might miss it?'

'We know nothing about cars, Anna. Better safe than sorry.'

The words make me clench my teeth. Safe, sorry – which shall we choose? I know, safe! I glance at the picture but it's impossible to acknowledge that this bestial car could ever have anything to do with Katya. Then I'm imagining her inside it, scratching the snake tattoo that writhes beneath the bald man's jaw and screaming for help. This is my whole life right now. Only the loss of Katya means anything, and it's too terrible to think about.

I've identified nine towns and villages in a twenty-kilometre radius of Talinic – excluding any which are not predominantly Serb or do not have police stations – and marked them on the map Eleni has spread over her lap. She's not good at orienteering and has to keep rotating the map so it's facing the same way as us. The road narrows where chunks of tarmac have broken off and tumbled down a gravel chute. That's good. I can concentrate on driving.

What will we do if we find the snake-man? I take a sidelong look at Eleni's oddly dished profile, her flattish nose, soft, broad cheeks and prominent chin. If I asked her, would she help me kill him? We're close, but I've only known her since she moved up from Tirana eighteen months ago. She's not used to being a passenger and her feet are working the pedals in panicky counterpoint to mine. She turns to direct at me another of her exhaustingly anxious looks. Her pale brown hair has been cut in a girlish fringe and I've wondered several times whether to tell her that a woman of her majestic appearance should never indulge her hairdresser's frivolous side.

'Thanks for coming with me, Eleni. I know you think it's a waste of time.'

'Oh no, not at all.'

This trivial lie brings a look of dejection to her face.

'I need to do this, since the police won't.'

'Do watch the road, please— Anna!'

We swerve round a pothole and the Fiat's outer wheels flirt briefly with a stretch of friable verge.

'Oh!' says Eleni. She covers her terror by making several folds in the map. 'We'll find Katya, one way or another. I just know it.'

I know it by instinct, she's implying, for want of any logical reason. I'm grateful for her loyalty, but it doesn't matter what Eleni thinks. The Fiat Frightful rattles and stinks as it trundles up the side of a not-very-steep valley. We are (or should be) just five minutes or so from the first town on our itinerary. It's good to be out doing something, but we are nervous. Eleni and I are Kosovars, that is to say, Albanian Muslims or Muslim Albanians – it doesn't matter which since we are not very committed on either score. Anyway, we are not going to be welcome.

'We'll just distribute the leaflets,' I say. 'We're not accusing any-one of anything, but someone must know where Katya is.'

'What if we see this hideous car?' Eleni asks.

'Then we'll start knocking on doors. I wonder if I should offer a reward. How much, do you think?'

'Oh, Anna, I don't know. Didn't you say Piotr thinks there'll be a ransom demand? Maybe we should just wait for that.'

We enter a dreary little town and I park the Fiat Frightful out-side a house supported by an assemblage of rickety scaffolding poles. We each take a handful of leaflets and set off in opposite directions. It isn't going to take long. The place looks pale and exhausted, as if it's suffering from an incurable disease. The first letterbox I come to has been screwed shut and I have to fold the leaflet and jam it between the door and the frame. Katya's face looks out at me and I feel like I've done something callous by sticking her there. I wish I'd chosen a different photo. The suggestion of a pout makes her look older than she is, and less innocent. Not everyone understands girls of this age. They experiment with being adults, and are interested in the effect they can have on those around them. I refold the leaflet so her face doesn't show and walk back down the cracked concrete path to the street.

It takes less than twenty minutes to deliver leaflets to my half of the town. I find the police station, but its windows are boarded up. Walking back to the car, I see Eleni arguing with a man wearing a dirty tracksuit with stripes down the arms and legs. He's big and aggressive, but Eleni is standing her ground.

'You're not welcome here,' the man shouts. '*Shiptar* cow.'

'I'm not asking for your welcome,' says Eleni fiercely. 'I'm asking if you've seen this girl.'

'No, but if you find her, bring her round and I'll give her a good seeing to.'

I'm right up close now, and I slap him with all my strength. He's too astonished to duck the blow. He curses, draws back his fist. I'm so consumed by rage that I hit him again. Eleni gets her forearm against his throat and shoves. He staggers backwards and trips over the roots of a dusty old bush that's pushed up at the edge of the road.

We run for the car, climb in and lock the doors. The Fiat Frightful always takes at least three turns on the ignition to start and it isn't going to make an exception this time. In the rear-view mirror, I see the man pull himself upright and lumber towards us, mouth hanging open, face red. By the second turn, he's got both hands on the handle of Eleni's door and the car is rocking from side to side. The third turn is long, and slows into spasms as the battery weakens... Then the engine cranks into life and I ram the gearstick forward and accelerate away down the road. The man trots along beside us for a few yards, then bends to cough as the Fiat Frightful envelops him in a pall of oily smoke.

16

This is how it is. I tell Piotr to find Franz. I write letters. I make phone calls. I lurk outside the police station to harass Inspector Jankovic whenever he enters or leaves the building. Eleni and I haunt the predominantly Serb villages in the vicinity of Talinic – two strange Albanian women in a smelly yellow car. Not just square-headed farm-labouring type Albanians, either, but godless, urban ones from Pristina. KLA sympathisers, probably, scouting the village for their terrorist menfolk. The leaflet with the pretty girl is just a front. Albanians are born liars.

I stand on street corners in Pristina, tugging at the sleeves of passers-by. Have you seen this girl? No. Toyota Invincible with Road Muscle Body Kit? Yes, isn't it distinctive. No, I haven't seen it. Take a leaflet, anyway, take ten or twenty, because the printer has set aside his antipathy towards Albanians in the interests of his business and I can get new stocks run off in just a few hours. People are polite and tuck them into a pocket or a bag, but later I see them spilling from rubbish bins or stuck to the pavement. Katya's face, clean, glossy hair coiled behind one ear, bearing the imprint of a wet boot-sole. It's a hard thing for a mother to see.

Days pass. A week passes. No ransom demand. Nothing from

Istanbul or Ankara or Izmir or anywhere else Franz might have wandered to. Surely someone in his family keeps in touch with him, says Eleni, trying not to sound indignant. Inspector Jankovic finds a secret way to get in and out of his office. One by one the feelers I've put out come trudging back and shake their heads.

* * *

Two weeks... I get a call from an aide to Ibrahim Rugova, president of the devolved (but still Serbian) Republic of Kosovo. My heart leaps into my throat, my mouth dries so fast I can barely confirm my name. But it's not about Katya. He's called to remind me that I've agreed to translate for them if the peace conference ever gets off the ground, which finally it has. The conference will open on 6 February at the Château de Rambouillet, near Paris.

'I apologise for the short notice,' he says excitedly. 'The arrangements have only just been confirmed.'

'Did President Rugova get my letter? About my daughter?'

He doesn't know. I explain why I cannot go and the aide seems puzzled: the abduction of my only child is a matter to be set aside, surely, in the interests of this historic opportunity to settle the future of an independent Kosovo? He stresses the word *independent*, as if this must clinch it.

'My *daughter* has been *abducted*,' I repeat. 'I'm not about to run off to Paris.'

'This is just the sort of criminal type activity we can stamp out once the Serbs are off our backs.'

'This particular instance of criminal type activity can't be stamped out,' I say furiously. 'It's already happened. The answer is no.'

When I report this conversation to Eleni, she takes a different view.

'Go, Anna. You'll be surrounded by the most powerful men in Kosovo. If you can get even one of them to make a fuss about Katarina, that could be the break we need.'

'I'll be surrounded by powerful *Albanians*, Eleni. Katarina was taken by a Serb gang.'

'We don't know that for sure—'

'I've already written to Rugova and what have I got? An invitation to a fucking peace conference.'

My anger crushes poor Eleni into silence. We are sitting in front of the little TV in my sitting room to watch the seven o'clock news. A bouncy young government minister has been dispatched to the PTC TV studio in Belgrade to trumpet Milošević's latest pronouncement on the future of Kosovo. His voice has a tone of bright desperation – as if he personally has been ordered to hold the forces of disintegration at bay. Behind the smooth blue studio backdrop, Serbia is barging and banging its way into a corner. We know well how cornered rats behave. The shadow of Bosnia darkens our lives. Only Milosh cannot see it: his old woman's face and stupid, piggy eyes are a picture of misplaced patriotic defiance. He really does believe that Russia will start World War Three rather than let its old ally be humiliated.

The next item opens with a glamorous lady standing in a clearing surrounded by scorched trees.

I'm here at the scene of one of the worst atrocities yet committed by the terrorists of the so-called Kosovo Liberation Army on the forces of law and order in this troubled region. The small town of Kric lies not far from the border with Macedonia. This is a peaceful place, where people make an honest living from their smallholdings or work in the forestry business. The night before last, it was torn apart by a savage attack. Such is the level of destruction you see here that it is hard to piece together what happened, but it appears that the local captain of police was lured to this place along with a number of his friends. They were set upon and murdered by a KLA gang, and their bodies and vehicles burned. What you see here now is all that remains – the destruction so complete that forensics experts say it will be at least four weeks before we can confirm the identities of everyone who died here in such horrific circumstances two nights ago.

'Kric is east of Pristina,' says Eleni, an unexpected hint of martial pride in her voice. 'New ground for the KLA. No wonder the Serbs are alarmed.'

The item closes with footage of a tow-truck slithering down the track and out onto the road, dragging a burnt-out pickup behind.

'Eleni, look!'

'What?'

I'm standing up, gesticulating at the screen.

'Toyota Invincible, with Road Muscle Body Kit!'

'Are you sure?' says Eleni as the footage ends.

'Those arches over the back wheels. And it was black.'

'It was *burnt*.'

'I've been staring at a photo of that thing for weeks. I think I'd recognise it.'

'We'll watch again at ten.'

I'm a fervent, passionate, desperate believer that this was the vehicle in which my Katya was driven away, but I daren't try to convince Eleni in case she says something tactless. For the next three hours, my heart teeters over a chasm of disappointment. The image of the listing chassis with its charred paintwork and warped roof is stamped in my mind. I can neither connect it with Katya nor think of anything other than its connection with Katya. Eleni calls a friend who does PR work for the Kosovar leadership. The dead men were members of a militia gang called Bura. Tempest.

'They give themselves these names because they have the all-round maturity of fourteen-year-old boys,' she says. 'Anna, you mustn't get your hopes up—'

'Don't, Eleni, I can see what you're thinking. Let's say that was the pickup they were driving when they took Katya. Then she may be somewhere in Kric, right? Waiting for us to come for her. After this attack, they may feel she's too much trouble and let her go. How far is Kric?'

'About fifteen kilometres. But it's at least an hour from Talinic – I don't understand what these Bura were doing there.'

'Why does it matter?' I say crossly.

Eleni lowers her eyes. Her shoulders are quivering. I go over to console her, pressing my cheek to hers.

'I don't know how we'll get through this!' she bursts out. 'If that car isn't... I won't say it, Anna, it only annoys you. I wish I could do more. You're so strong and I'm no kind of a friend.'

'Eleni, you're the best possible friend!' I get up and sit beside her on the sofa, taking her hands in mine. 'You couldn't have done more. You've been my rock, right from the start.'

'More like a pillow, I'm afraid.' She smiles at me and dabs her eyes with a handkerchief.

'That's right, my pillow. Much better than a hard old rock. Though it's true that you are a bit bossy sometimes.'

She laughs and we comfort each other with kind words and tea and snacks until ten o'clock. We sit close to the screen and stare at the tow-truck with its grotesque cargo, but it's no more conclusive this time.

'Anyway,' I say, 'we'll go there tomorrow and find out for ourselves.'

* * *

We drive out of Pristina early next morning and reach the crest of a high ridge. A break in the trees reveals the contours of the valley beyond, the forested slopes torn by machinery tracks, the mangy squares of scraped earth where the trees have been felled, the dirt-flecked mounds of crusted snow left over from the last fall. At the foot of the valley, a small town lies hunched beneath dark swathes of conifers.

'I think that may be Kric,' says Eleni, rotating the map through a hundred and eighty degrees. 'But... Oh dear, I'm not exactly sure where we are.'

The Fiat Frightful backfires as we decelerate down the far side – it dislikes slopes, up and down alike. A little way along the road is a windowless police van, parked at the entrance to a track. A quantity of red-and-white-striped plastic tape (the kind they don't bother to use for crime scenes involving twelve-year-old Kosovar girls) extends from its bumpers into the undergrowth on either side. A uniformed policeman is leaning against the van and watching us.

'The place where the Bura were attacked, do you think?' says Eleni.

I do. We drive slowly past the policeman without daring to look at him, then come to a sign announcing our arrival in the town of Kric. The first big house we see has a pale patch in the shape of a shield above the door, outlined with grime.

'The police station,' I say. 'Hiding itself from the KLA. We'll start there.'

'Let's not accuse anyone of anything just yet, Anna,' Eleni warns.

We park in a square with an Orthodox church and two huge sycamore trees, then walk back to the police station. I am filled with euphoria because Katarina may be inside, waiting for me. We will drive back to Pristina together, chatting about her adventure – for that is what it is, now that it is over. I watch her clear brown eyes and beautiful, earnest face in the rear-view mirror as she answers

Eleni's silly questions. What she really wants is to get me alone and wheedle a new pair of trainers out of me – to replace the ones that got ruined when I put them on the radiator to dry and the leather cracked, which she'd told me would happen because she'd read the instructions that came with them from cover to cover and under the *Care of your new trainers* section it said that you should always let them dry out at room temperature. She wants a hug, too, she wants to be wrapped tight in her mother's arms, but quick because she is twelve now and girls of twelve don't hug for ages and ages. A mother knows things about her child that her child may not wish to know herself. It's knowledge to act upon, while pretending ignorance. Children vacillate constantly between aspiration and regression, every day's a wild ride full of swooping highs and shuddering lows. I'm telling myself this as we hurry down the main street of Kric. Children have to negotiate the gap between who they are and who they would like to be, I lecture myself compulsively. It's exhausting for them, and the least a mother can do is to try and keep up. I'm feeling conspicuous because there's no one else about and Eleni's boiled-wool coat, though practical, is a curiosity. In Salzburg, where she bought it, they are popular. In southern Kosovo, less so.

The house is Balkan vernacular, two storeys, rendered and painted off-white, steep, green-tiled roof. It should have matching green shutters pinned back either side of the windows and an iron-work verandah, then it could call itself a villa. There's no sign of the burnt-out Toyota Invincible.

'Let's check the yard,' I say, setting off for the back of the house. There's a high wall and double gates topped with barbed wire. The gates are open. As I come level, I see it: the wrecked vehicle lolling on the tarmac. The flared wheel arches hang like batwings over the skeletal remains of the rear wheels. I can just make out the word TOYOTA embossed into its tailgate, and then in smaller letters on the right, *Invincible*. I taste the sweet, acrid smell of burnt rubber on my lips and without warning I'm tipping sideways into Eleni's arms as the sky yaws overhead. She holds me by one arm and strokes my shoulders as I throw up on the pale grey tarmac.

'What are you doing here?'

There's a woman at the back door.

'She's not well, as you see,' says Eleni.

'Take her away. I don't want to clean up her mess.'

'So wait until it rains,' says Eleni. There's a hardness in her voice I haven't heard before.

'Fucking Albanians.'

I straighten up and look at the woman. She's about fifty, heavily built, hair tied in a square of black cotton. She holds a broom out to one side of her, like a soldier with a spear.

'Who owns this car?' I ask. 'I have to speak to the person who owns this car.'

'He hasn't got much to say for himself, seeing as he's dead,' says the woman, and raps the railings with her broom.

'What was his name, then? Did he have a snake tattoo on his neck?'

'Burnt to death by ugly squareheads,' says the woman, her eyes narrowing. 'Why're you here? I don't like it.' She looks back over her shoulder and shouts into the house. 'Bojan!'

'I must know whose car this is, this Toyota Invincible. I'm looking for my daughter. I've lost her.' I walk rapidly over to the steps. 'Can I just come in and look around?'

She doesn't answer. A slope-shouldered boy in his late teens appears in the doorway behind her.

'Go tell Jacek there are two Albanian bitches here, asking questions and looking for trouble.'

The boy's small eyes dart around in his slack-featured face. I'm reminded of Inspector Jankovic, the sense of a man assessing the extent of his power over me, trying out scenarios in his mind. I'm

136

half way up the steps when the woman upends her broom and jabs me in the stomach.

'Bojan, go!'

The boy runs back into the house.

'KLA types,' says the woman. 'Come to gloat, have you? I reckon you know something.'

'We're leaving,' says Eleni, taking me by the arm and pulling me back to the foot of the steps. 'And we're not making trouble but looking for my friend's daughter. We think she was taken away in that car. She's twelve, with black hair, pretty. Perhaps you've seen her?'

The woman's face is impassive as a slab of oak.

'Not too pretty, I hope.'

Eleni leads me back across the yard, out through the gates and up into the street behind the house.

'We'll search the town,' I gabble. 'Someone must know where Katya is. There are mothers here, they'll understand. Go home if you like, Eleni. Go and get help. Leave me here.'

Eleni takes me firmly by the shoulders. 'Anna, we've found the car... Maybe we've found the car. Now we need to be careful and work out what to do. Otherwise, you'll be arrested. Or worse.'

'Because I want my daughter back?'

'Because you're an Albanian, in a Serb village that's just been attacked by the KLA. Suppose they search the car and find the map?'

The map... with local police stations marked in biro. And a picture of the exact same make of vehicle as was destroyed in the KLA attack. I can't reply. Eleni is right. I moan and fall into her arms, the boiled wool of her Salzburg coat scratches my cheek. We hear footsteps clumping along the main street below. Booted men, coming to deal with the troublemakers. We flee back to the square and drive the wrong way out of town, and it feels like I've lost Katya all over again. I want to turn round and go back straight away and start knocking on doors. Eleni plays voice of reason, though she

137

hates herself for it. I must talk to Inspector Jankovic again, she says, while she enlists the help of the UNHCR.

'If we keep it official,' she says, 'with everything on the record, then they'll have no excuse.'

'There is no official.' I'm shouting in frustration now. 'They don't need any excuse. There's a war on and we're the enemy.'

'We don't know for sure that was the pickup we're looking for,' says Eleni for the hundredth time. 'And if Katya is there, we mustn't give them a reason to take her somewhere else.'

This thought torments me. The woman with the broom might be talking to the men fetched by Bojan right now. *Get the girl out of here, those women are trouble.*

17

I drive back to Kric next day – alone, taking a camera so I can photograph the wreck of the Toyota. The police-station gates are locked shut. The burnt-out pickup has gone. There's a dog licking tentatively at the oval of dried-up sick. I go round the front and knock at the door, ready to confront the woman with the broom. No one answers.

Back in the square I see a noticeboard by the church doors. It lists the times when services are held: Mass, evensong – and tomorrow at six the priest will hear confessions. This is where the Bura come to be forgiven. I'll catch the priest when he's finished, when the sins are fresh in his mind. I'll look him straight in the eye and beg him to tell me what happened to Katya. I'll fall to my knees and beat my breast. I'll do anything he asks of me, if he will only part with the secrets of the confessional.

It's a plan, something to which I can pin my tattered hopes. I zigzag through the streets of the dreary little town, the cold squeezing at my heart. The River Pec runs alongside the main road, then bends away to follow the line of the valley. It is said that in this river lurk spirits that will snare the souls of passers-by and can only be quelled by the singing of songs sanctified by inclusion in a service of the Orthodox Christian Church. It's not wide, but fast-flowing and powerful, its surface glassy black and full of unspecified menace. In ten minutes I've reached the far end and counted 137 doors. When I've knocked on them all, I will have found Katya. Or not. The prospect of failure makes me shrink inside my skin.

The shut doors of Kric have big locks and curtained fanlights. I step up to the first and there's no bell or knocker so I have to bang with my fist. It doesn't sound right. It sounds feeble, uncertain. No one answers. I try another and a dog barks from within, I can hear its nails scrabbling at the letterbox. I knock, ring, bang along the street, but the locks stay locked and the bolts bolted. I haven't even seen a curtain twitch.

Half way along the next street, an old woman answers from within.

'Wait, I'm coming…'

I listen to her shuffling down the hall and fiddling with the lock.

'Oh dear, I can never…'

Finally it opens. She's tall and bony and bent, with scabbed shins beneath the frayed hem of her dress. I show her my leaflet. 'This is my daughter. I'm looking for her. I think she may be somewhere in Kric.'

The old woman hands it back and shakes her head sorrowfully, then beckons me inside. I follow her into a sitting room. There's a charred log smouldering in the grate and a washing-up bowl by her chair, which she's been using to piss in. She points at a sagging sofa. 'Will you sit down, please? I don't get many visitors.'

'I'm sorry,' I tell her. 'I don't have time. I'm looking for my daughter. If you see her, will you…'

It's pointless. I leave her standing there, stooped and sad. As I pull her front door shut behind me I hear a cry from somewhere up behind the main square, and it jolts me like an electric shock. Katya! I'm sure of it! I heard her cry like that at the hospital when she dislocated her elbow and some clumsy old doctor tried to fit it back together. She cried out in just that way. A lilting wail of protest, ending in an intake of breath. I'd know it anywhere. I run down the street, convinced that in seconds I'll turn a corner and find my Katya leaning from a window or climbing the fence of a backyard. She's a good climber, determined and lithe. I come to the end of the street and look left and right but she's not there. I stand panting and spinning on a patch of broken cobblestones. Call out again, my darling Katya, call again, my sweet child!

Silence.

'Katya!'

My voice has a wild power, like no noise I've ever made before.

'Katya! Katya!'

Her name cannons off the rooftops, flounders in the heavy air.

Silence.

'Katya!'

A car rumbles suddenly up behind me and blasts by so close it whisks at my coat. Hostile faces stare back at me from its rear window. I won't be deterred. I feel in my heart that I've heard Katya cry out for me, but in my head the doubts insinuate themselves like little gobs of poison. The cries of children are not so distinctive… A woman, maybe, or a boy, or a dog… I'll carry on knocking from here, where the cry came from, if it came from anywhere. The houses in this street have yards out back with makeshift shelters for chickens or pigs and workshops with oily tools lying about. I peer through broken fences and see hundreds of places where the abductors of children may hide their prey.

Knock, ring, bang. A woman of my age opens her door, a baby tucked into the crook of her arm.

'Have you seen this girl?'

'No,' she says. 'No!' the baby repeats, brandishing a plastic spoon. The mother turns away and slams the door with the heel of her foot. 'How would you feel if your baby was taken away from you?' I ask the shut door.

I keep seeing chainsaws: hanging from nails, resting on sections of tree trunk – there's even one lying on the rear shelf of a car, where you might expect to see a box of tissues or a teddy bear. And I'm being tailed by a pack of dogs which bark and skitter away when I walk towards them, then slink up closer as I press a bell and listen to a cheery ding-dong that doesn't get answered. After twenty more doors I've provoked nothing but an irritable shout and the sound of a window being clamped shut.

*   *   *

By nightfall I've walked across Kric four times, looking for doors I might have missed, listening for cries I might have misheard. Why are the streets empty? Because it's cold. Because the Serbs feel angry and ill-used. They lock their doors and grumble: they are decent, hard-working people, while the Albanians are lazy and dishonest. Several times I hear a car idling nearby, then see it flash across a junction. It's a dark red Skoda estate. I've written down its registration number. I'm scared. I hurry back to the square. A wind has blown in and the sycamore trees rattle and shed bits of bark and broken twig.

I get into the Fiat Frightful and drive out of town. As I pass the police station, I notice that the Skoda is following me. Its headlights slither around inside the car, illuminating my hair, my neck, my face as I turn back to look. The Fiat slows and slows on the hill and I have to drop down to second gear. When did I last get the oil changed? The Skoda comes up close, right up close so I can hear the bellow of its engine. In the rear-view mirror, I see that it's full of men with watch caps pulled down low over their foreheads. They're going to ram me from behind, shunt me off the road and down into the woods. The accelerator pedal is flat to the floor but still I'm losing speed. They'll climb out of the car and come loping after me, pulling long knives from inside their coats. The radio hisses – you can't turn it off, only down. My headlights yellow and flicker and I think they might give out. Then I see the top of the hill. I focus on the column of pewter sky between the trees and don't see the windows of the Skoda wind down, arms reach out.

Gunshots. I duck down and bang my forehead against the steering wheel. The Fiat slews across the road. I haul the steering wheel down in time to veer away from the ditch, but the car stalls, rolls back. Sharp cracks split the forested darkness. I've stopped breathing. Handbrake! I hear laughter. The driver of the Skoda leans on his horn and the ugly howl scoops every thought from my mind. I'm trembling so hard I can't do anything to save myself. A bony-faced man with deep-set eyes appears at my window. He shakes his head from side to side, then draws his hand across his throat.

He walks back to the Skoda. The car turns round and they head back into Kric. Twice on the way home I have to pull over and curl up across the front seats to get the trembling under control.

* * *

'The pickup that was used to abduct my daughter is in Kric – or it was,' I inform the duty sergeant with the cow-catcher moustache and flaky skin. 'It's the one that was destroyed in the attack there a few nights ago.'

'What do you know about that?' he asks sharply.

'Nothing. I saw it on the news. The boys who were there when my daughter was abducted gave me a description of the pickup they were driving – there's a picture in the pack I gave you. I saw it in Kric the day before yesterday. It's the same one, I'm sure of it.'

'You went nosing around in Kric, after what happened?'

'Yes. I was asking if anyone had seen my daughter and these men attacked me.'

'How?'

'They shot at me. They drove a red Skoda estate – here's the registration number.'

He doesn't touch the scrap of paper I push across the desk. 'Any injuries? Bullet holes in your car?'

'No.'

'So they missed.'

'They were shooting to frighten me, to get me out of town.'

'They didn't in fact attack you.'

'That's not the crime – the crime is that they took my daughter. You have to investigate this. You have to…'

The words catch in my throat. I've steeled myself to be rational and composed so that my demands prove irresistible, but instead I am falling apart. I step away from the counter and arch my hand over my eyes to squeeze the tears away, then take a number of deep breaths.

'I'm going back to Kric,' I inform him when I've pulled myself together again. 'You could advise me not to go, but that would mean admitting that I might be dealing with the people who abducted my daughter.'

'You shouldn't go into any town where you're not known and stir things up with the locals. Especially after they've been attacked by the KLA. You have been warned.'

'Oh, they know who I am.'

* * *

The men of Kric scare me, but they cannot scare me off. I'm not a member of some impertinent rival militia, but a mother searching for her child. The church occupies one side of the square with the sycamore trees. I park and walk round it. It's a puzzling building: pre-Ottoman, I would say, but most of it seems to have been destroyed and rebuilt without the flamboyance that must have characterised the original. Usually in such cases there's a mosque nearby, built to overshadow the temple of the lesser faith in respect of scale, craftsmanship and grace. But Kric does not have a mosque, only this bare church. I push through the doors into the incense-haunted murk of the interior. It is colder in here than outside. My eyes adjust, and I make out a black-robed figure sitting in a large upholstered armchair by an incongruously small and plain beech-wood lectern. His hands extend over the arms of the chair and one of them is flapping impatiently. He is muttering something, and I don't think he has seen me. I walk up the aisle and when I'm ten yards away, he starts and holds out his hand.

'Wait there.'

His voice is sonorous, as if he is taking a service. I sit down on the nearest chair and he resumes the strange hand-flapping. His chair is not an ecclesiastical item, but an easy chair for the home. The church is like a junk shop, every wall a patchwork of pictures, icons, effigies, glass vases and candlesticks, crucifixes and items of tarnished silver. There are shelves stacked with torn brown envelopes, boxes of postcards and laminated service sheets. The priest mutters and nods his head, then makes an elaborate sign of the cross. His expression is hard, but his features have a drunk's querulous laxity, his cheeks flabby and his eyes unable to rest.

Suddenly I realise that the benediction was for me and the priest is waiting for me to approach and make my confession.

'There.'

He points to an embroidered kneeler on the floor in front of him, to the left of which is an icon propped against a stack of books. I kneel.

'Well?'

'I need your help, Father. My daughter…'

The priest's tatty black slip-ons are parked by his chair. His wool-clad feet emit a rancid smell that cuts through the fug of stale incense.

'You are here to confess. Get on with it.'

'My daughter was taken from me and brought to this town. My twelve-year-old daughter. I came to ask if you've heard anything that might help me find her.'

He is silent for a long time. The icon depicts Christ crowned with thorns, his head tipped down, his eyes raised heavenwards. His expression must be intended to portray suffering beatitude, but the artist has made him look like an imbecile. By contrast, much skill and effort has been devoted to painting the thorn-pierced flesh beneath the line of his scalp, the gouts of blood like jewels on his brow and cheeks. I feel unsteady on my kneeler.

'You don't wish to confess,' he says eventually. 'You cannot even be a Christian, or you would not ask me to defile the sacrament of confession.'

'You don't have to tell me anything. Just… If she is here, in this town, you could nod your head or something. Is she?'

He shakes his head. 'Not even a Serb.'

'We're all Serbs, aren't we? That's what this war is about. But that has nothing to do with it. I've lost my child! Was she ever here? You must know.'

'There is nothing for you here.' He edges laboriously forward in the seat of his armchair. 'Get out.' He stands and turns his back on me, starts to shuffle towards the altar.

'You're one of them, aren't you,' I say, getting up from the kneeler. 'You give them absolution and then you share a bottle of raki together. You're disgusting, you're a disgrace to the Church.'

I carry on insulting him as he propels himself slowly towards the sacristy door behind the altar, but I don't follow. When he has gone, I lash out with my foot and send the stack of books and the hideous icon sliding away across the tiled floor. Confession is over. I go outside and hear footsteps running. The Fiat Frightful is slumped. The two front tyres have been let down. I don't have a pump. There are dozens of people in Kric who could help me, but none of them will. It's dark and there's a sharp smell of woodsmoke on the air. I get out my phone but the signal is weak so I set off up the hill behind the church. After a while I come to a children's playground, a square of tarmac with a swing and collection of old tyres arranged as an obstacle course. The signal's better and I call Piotr and explain what's happened.

'You should've let me take you, Anna. You know what these people are—'

'Yes, all right, Piotr. But please, can you come and get me?'

I told him I'd wait in the church. The thought of going back inside fills me with horror, but it's probably safer than sitting in the marooned Fiat. It's quiet in the playground and I think I may as well stay here until it gets too cold. I crouch down beside a huge, rotten tractor tyre and then see that I can climb inside it. I'll be well hidden, and sheltered. I wedge myself in between the sidewalls and settle my back into the curve of the tyre, then my foot presses down on something hard. I pick it up and tilt it towards the ambient light from the square below, but still I can't see what it is. Too heavy and crude for a bracelet. It has four finger holds and some kind of ridged frame… Knuckleduster.

Fear see-saws inside me. A knuckleduster, discarded in a children's playground, like a yo-yo or a toy car. That's the sort of town Kric is. The grip is padded so you can strike as hard as you like without hurting your fingers. I shrink back into the tyre and listen to my heart preparing for flight with a series of thumps so heavy that my whole body shakes.

The cold seeps into me but I dare not move. After I don't know how long I start to shiver. Really shiver, more like shuddering. What if Piotr doesn't make it and I'm forced to spend the night out here? I pull the knuckleduster over my fingers, just in case I have to defend myself, then lever myself stiffly from the tyre and make my way back down the hill. There's no moon tonight and not much streetlight beyond the square. The priest has locked up his church and fled. There's not even a porch to sit in. What if the big woman from the police station finds me crouching in a corner with a knuckleduster clamped in my fist? I wander for another ten minutes, circling the area round the playground, and finally end up back in the tractor tyre. Soon I hear an engine from the direction of the square. It stops and a car door slams. I wait for a few minutes to see if the vehicle drives away again, but it doesn't, so I run back down to the square.

A loud scuffing noise, a boot scraping gravel across tarmac, then a series of thumps and a grunt.

'Who asked you here, monkey face?'

I turn the corner and see Piotr down on one knee beside the Fiat, panting, head bowed beneath his thick hair. Three of them. One is leaning against the bonnet of the Fiat and spitting something on the ground. The other two stand over Piotr. One of them swings his boot into Piotr's ribs, the other draws back his shoulder for a long, clubbing blow at his head. I run towards them, rage lashing and boiling in my blood, fingers clamped over the padded grip of the knuckleduster. Piotr has a footpump in his hand – he lifts it up to shield his face and the man's fist drives clumsily into its steel frame. Then Piotr is up, and he's a big man, brave and dangerous. His assailant steps back – straight into the trajectory of my swinging arm and the dull weight of the knuckleduster at its tip. The brass ridge crunches into his temple. He gives a cry of shock and sways backwards, sprawls. He raises himself on one arm and manages to shuffle a short distance away before collapsing. I turn to see Piotr drive his fist into the solar plexus of the man who kicked him. The air leaves his lungs with a heavy sigh and he doubles over, wheezing for breath. The third man has disappeared.

Piotr crouches down by the Fiat and starts trying to fix the pump hose to the tyre valve.

'Piotr, leave that and let's get out.'

He looks up at me. There's a bloody rip in the skin along his jaw. 'You don't want to take the Fiat?'

'No. Please, Piotr. There could be more…'

He's agonisingly slow about stowing the pump in the back seat of his pickup, starting the engine, reversing out of the parking space. I look at the man whose eye-socket I mashed with the weapon still clamped in my hand. He's lying on the tarmac, a semi-circle of glossy darkness by his ear. I feel sick. Also, euphoric. I hit a man and laid him out. For a moment I want to do it again.

'Are you OK? What's going on, Anna?'

'I'm fine. You're the one who got hurt.'

He adjusts the rear-view mirror and looks.

'It needs stitching,' I tell him.

We take the first turning off the main road out of town and pull over so I can knot a scarf over his head to stop the bleeding, then drive back to Pristina.

* * *

I sit in the hospital waiting room while they stitch up his lacerated jaw. It was a glancing blow, the duty nurse informs me, otherwise it could have cracked his jawbone.

'People don't seem to just hit each other these days. They use all sorts. Brass knuckles, saps, chains.'

'You think it's got more vicious recently?'

'There's a war coming. Some people can't wait to get started.'

And it's true that the hospital waiting area displays the bloody consequences of this skirmishing. There must be twenty men in there, arranged on blood-splotched gurneys, faces puffed up and split like rotten fruit. There's a war coming... I knew this, didn't I?

On the way back to my apartment, I look out at the high buildings on Esstorvec Street and imagine them torn open, lumps of rubble clinging to their iron sinews, concrete floors concertina'd, beds and curtains and china ornaments spilling into the street like the filling from an over-stuffed sandwich. The night air is hounded by sirens, the sound of vengeance, of settled scores. How else was it going to end, this decade of persecution, these years of strutting contempt? But I didn't see it so clearly then. After Bosnia, I told myself, they'll see reason, they'll be prudent, they'll talk and talk and talk, as they're paid to do. Anything's better than war.

'Is the pickup registered in your name, Piotr?'

'Um... No. I mean, the plates are made up.'

'Leave it in the vacant lot behind my building until you can sort out new ones. The only thing is, it may get stolen.'

Piotr shrugs.

'I guess you'd have said if you'd heard from Franz.'

'Lauri went to Istanbul on Friday. She'll track him down.'

'Or if not, she'll have a bit of a holiday.'

The streetlights of Pristina flicker and dim – the electricity supply hasn't been dependable for weeks. Franz is not coming back. I have lost my only child. I'm brawling with Serbian thugs in strange towns and hiding illegal vehicles. Everything is already in ruins.

18

Eleni comes round with supper the next evening. When she has finished chiding me for twice going to Kric without her, we sit down to watch the news and there it is. *KLA in new attack on town in mourning* reads the strapline beneath the newscaster's desk.

> The town of Kric was in a state of shock last night, following a brutal assault in the town square. Three men were on their way to church when they were set upon and beaten by an unknown number of assailants. One of the victims has been detained in hospital in a serious but stable condition. Only five days ago, eight men from the town were ambushed and murdered by KLA terrorists, and the police believe the two incidents are connected. As the hunt for the perpetrators is stepped up, the people of this peaceful, hard-working town have been warned to brace themselves for further attacks, and the atmosphere is tense and fearful.

The rest of the report is read over a picture of a man propped up in bed wearing a sky-blue-check hospital gown. The top left-hand quarter of his head is subsumed by a mass of lumpy tissue, crisscrossed with stitches. There's a tube up his nose and some kind of monitor taped to his other temple. I remember what I used to think when I saw such photos: How could anyone do such a thing? What kind of hate drives you to put someone in that state? Now I know. It wasn't hate but rage, and I don't feel any remorse. No one thought I was the sort of girl who'd marry a Roma man ten years older than her, and no one thought I was the sort of woman who would put a man in hospital, either. I didn't know myself.

Eleni sees I am transfixed by the picture. 'Is that your one, Anna?'

'I suppose. I didn't look at him closely.'

'Well, take a good look now – what a warrior! Behind that modest façade, the fury of the Amazons courses in your blood. That'll teach them to tamper with the Fiat Frightful.'

'It wasn't the car, Eleni, it was Piotr.'

'The dumb brother-in-law doesn't deserve you, Anna. Nor does the dumb brother, come to that. *An unknown number of assailants!* Two to be precise. One of them quite small expert in the early Ottomans.'

The dumb brother-in-law rings half an hour later.

'The police were in Talinic today. They took away Grigor, Zak and a couple of others. I was out or I guess they'd have had me.'

'On what grounds?'

'A round-up, they called it. Grandmama's in a state. Think it's connected to… You know, to last night?'

'When did the police last arrive in Talinic and start rounding you up, as they call it?'

'I can't remember.'

'So yes, it's connected.'

'I got the Fiat back.'

'Piotr, that was a stupid thing to do. You could have just left it.'

'Not me, Mikhail's uncle. He's got a tow-truck, went out first thing in the morning. He fixed the tyres and changed the oil for you. Says it's the least he could do.'

'Please thank him,' I say.

I find that I am crying and have to hang up. Eleni is mopping up something in the kitchen – something I swear she has mopped up a hundred times already. I tell her about the arrests in Talinic.

'I'm dragging them down with me – and for what? For nothing.'

'Don't, Anna. You're not to blame. They need no excuse to persecute the Roma.'

'It's not just that. They're saying, if you come near this, we'll beat you and lock you up, you and all your family. They're warning us off, right?'

'Us?' Eleni shrugs. 'Yes. They are warning us off – us and everyone else who is not a true Serb. And look how well they are doing – the BBC is saying forty thousand people have left already.'

'How can they do this, Eleni?'

'They have power over us, and this is how they choose to use it. Milošević in Belgrade, Jankovic in Pristina, the Bura in Kric – they can all do whatever they like. As for us, we can bow our heads to them, or join the refugees.'

*   *   *

I haunt the town of Kric like a ghost, looking for Katya without expectation of finding her. I'll do this until I get another clue. What else? I walk out along the river to the farmsteads and loggers' huts beyond. I pass and re-pass and pass again by the track that leads up to the clearing where the Bura died, but I dare not go and look. I saw the blackened trees on the news and I'm afraid of what I might find. The men in the Skoda estate car don't bother me now. I'm just a bad smell that is fading, a dirty conscience that the priest has wiped clean. Katarina isn't here any more, if she ever was here, if the wail I heard from the streets above the square was ever anything other than the sound made by a yearning mother's heart.

153

I stop going to Kric and hand out leaflets instead – at the bus terminal, the train station, government offices, hospitals, schools. I write more letters and emails, imploring people to help me, and get pleas of helplessness in reply. *I wish there was something I could do, but with Kosovo falling apart...* Bitterness spills into me.

'You're doing everything you can,' says Eleni. 'No mother could do more.'

'I could have left her at home, or not sat around drinking coffee after meeting with that fucking old fool Ongoric.'

'One day the phone will ring and it'll be the UNHCR in Skopje, saying they've taken her in,' she says soothingly. 'I'm quite sure of it.'

She doesn't look sure and I am not soothed. Eleni's company is becoming unbearable. Whenever we meet now, her anxiety takes my despair by the hand and leads a hysterical dance. If you're shrivelling up, you want to do it alone.

'Have you thought any more about Rambouillet?' she asks, after a period of miserable silence. 'I know you hate the idea of leaving Pristina, but I'll be here for you.'

She's been going on about the powerful men who'll be at Rambouillet ever since the call from Rugova's aide; but my mood swings and instead of being annoyed that she's brought it up again, I feel touched – and ashamed of my harsh thoughts. Eleni may be tactless sometimes, but she is also a devoted friend who won't stay silent just because I'm in a bad temper.

'Yes... I mean, no,' I tell her. 'It's probably too late, anyway.'

'Nonsense. You know they asked that dolt Kreshnik from the history department to go in your place? They'll be happy to get rid of him.'

'I don't know what to do, Eleni.'

'Go. Hashim Thaçi will be there. He'll know how to contact these Bura. Tell him what a hero he'll be when he arranges for Katarina to come home.'

I imagine the fate of my daughter interrupting the deliberations of the conference delegates. KLA leader Hashim Thaçi, whose *nom de guerre* is the Snake, pins the Serbian Minister for the Interior against the cracked porcelain of a Rambouillet *pissoir* and threatens to tear his face off if anything should happen to young Katarina. President Rugova declines to sign the peace agreement until his favourite translator's daughter is set free. She becomes a *cause célèbre*, her fate and the fate of a nation inextricably entwined. *Katarina of Kosovo: how the release of a kidnapped girl unlocked the door to peace in this troubled region...*

Eleni is right, I should move among these people, engineer a shove from on high. The shove is passed on, mutates from favour-asked to polite-request to demand-with-threats, in which form it arrives in Inspector Jankovic's email. *Rise up off your fat arse, Janko, and get this girl back. Or you can kiss the pension goodbye.*

My own detective work has come to this: if Katya was in Kric, she's not there now, not after I blundered in. The men who abducted her are probably dead. In order to persuade Inspector Jankovic to drop the idea that Katya was snatched away by her Roma father, I now have to get him to investigate his dead colleagues in Kric instead – his dead colleagues who have recently been the subject of a news broadcast which elevated them to the status of fully fledged martyrs of the greater Serbia.

I have a little weep in Eleni's arms, and next morning call Rugova's aide to tell him I've changed my mind. I'll go to Paris. The future has to come about somehow.

19

I get to the airport early on the appointed day, all torn up with doubt. Am I right to leave Pristina? Will I be able to persuade the Kosovar leadership to help me find her? I know most of them already, at least to shake hands with – the community of intellectuals in Pristina is not extensive any more than it is well funded.

'Anna, I am happy that you are with us,' says President Ibrahim Rugova, arriving with a small entourage. He takes me by the shoulders and kisses me on both cheeks, then holds me at arm's length and regards me with his soft, mournful eyes. 'Not just the best translator in Kosovo, but the best linguist, too. You will be our secret weapon.'

'Thank you, Mr President. I'll try and look menacing.'

Observing that my smile is unenthusiastic, the President moves on to inform me that there's a delay because Hashim Thaçi has been barred from leaving the country.

'So childish. Of course, we will not fly without him.'

He receives a nudge from his aide, who leans sideways and whispers in his ear.

'Of course, your daughter, Anna – is there any news?'

'No. I mean, I have some leads, but—'

'We'll make time to talk about this, Anna, I promise.'

We wait at the airport for six hours. The departure lounge is hermetically sealed: we inhale exhaled air, scented with stale coffee. Sandwiches salute from brightly lit shelves, but no one feels like eating. A man in a boiler suit slides a scissor-shaped mop down the corridor, then back again. It is not properly called a mop, I decide, madly trying to distract myself from the empty wastes of time howling around me, since it isn't wet. Rugova's aide makes a series of calls. The diplomatic network hums in his ear, propelling him on an unpredictable route around the maze of grey foam chairs. There are children playing amongst the chrome stalks of the stools at the coffee bar and I watch them furtively, feasting off their giggles and shrieks.

'You know, they will try to split us,' says Rugova to his co-delegate and rival Rexhep Qosja.

'Shouldn't be difficult.'

Various self-deprecatory remarks are made on the subject of the Kosovar tendency to disputatiousness. These are quite touching to hear, in such chronically disputatious company.

'This time we must stand together. Else they'll just pick us off.'

Hashim Thaçi arrives and at last we depart for Paris; only to endure a further interval of terminal-time at Orly Airport, waiting for the *motorcade*, as Rugova's aide insists on calling it. All motorcades in the vicinity of Paris are already spoken for, and we have to make do with a fleet of taxis. At the cordon round the Château de Rambouillet a surly French policeman searches my bags and takes away my cellphone.

'I need it. I'm expecting to hear from my daughter. She's gone missing.'

'Protocol,' says the policeman.

'What protocol? Give me back my phone or I'm not going in.'

Rugova's aide steps over. 'Anna,' he says to me while smiling at the policeman, 'no one is allowed to take phones into the conference. It was all in the pack we sent you.'

The aide's manner is unctuous, but in fact he is cross that the arrival of the Kosovar delegation has been undignified by this outburst – and from a translator! Making a fuss, he believes, is a privilege strictly reserved for heads of state.

'And if my daughter calls over the next two weeks?'

'If it's an emergency,' says the aide, 'then I'm sure we can sort something out.'

'It's an emergency,' I tell him, my face reddening. 'Sort something out or I'm going home.'

The threat is empty and everyone knows it.

'Right now, Anna, we need to get into the chateau. I'll deal with this, I promise.'

'You do that,' I tell him, repacking my bag and thinking that if he doesn't, I can always leave in the morning.

We pass through the *cordon sanitaire* and wait in the reception hall to be shown to our rooms. In the ladies, I meet a frisky blonde girl in her early twenties, refreshing various aspects of her deeply textured maquillage. Noticing the official translator's badge pinned to her bosom, I address her first in Albanian, then in English, and finally in Serbian – which draws a heavily scented sigh of relief, a becomingly wide smile and an offer of chewing gum. Her name is Marta.

'And you're here to translate?' I ask.

'Ooh, I hope not,' she says, giving a little flourish of her round bottom. 'I'm helping to look after them, mostly.'

And I'm here to persuade powerful men to help me find my daughter, I think, which makes both of us frauds. The powerful men have already been shown to their quarters, but it is another hour before we underlings are directed to our far-flung rooms. Mine is a wedge-shaped space excavated from an area of attic formerly set aside for roosting bats and now mainly occupied by a wardrobe so weary that it is leaning against the wall beside it. I unpack, then can't sleep for wishing I hadn't come.

20

The Rambouillet Peace Conference is billed as the last chance to end the persecution of Kosovo's majority Albanian population by the Serbian government of Slobodan Milošević, neutralise the Kosovo Liberation Army, and bring peace to the people of the region. Our gracious hosts, the Contact Group of ministers from France, Germany, Italy, Russia, the UK and the USA, have declared their intention to arrive at a political settlement that will offer 'substantial autonomy for Kosovo' while simultaneously respecting 'the territorial integrity and sovereignty of the Federal Republic of Yugoslavia'.

There is barely a single word of this mercifully brief declaration that is not violently disputed by either or both parties to the negotiation.

* * *

Daylight reveals that the Château de Rambouillet consists of two four-storey wings, a pair of slim towers with steep conical roofs, and an ancient turreted citadel of the kind traditionally used for the ill-treatment of downfallen kings. As you descend from the attic, the ceilings become higher, the windows larger, the carpets thicker, the decor more swirly, the portraits more ghoulish, and the light fittings more likely to work. But even on the ground floor, it is a shabby chateau which no one loves. A leaflet available in the entrance hall explains that Marie Antoinette called it a *crapaudière gothique*, a gothic toadhouse, and refused to live there. The ceilings sway with strands of blackened cobweb that may once have threatened the coiffures of the court of Louis XVI. The whole building is not much bigger than a village school.

Breakfasting Serbs and breakfasting Kosovars occupy different rooms, because these are *proximity* talks: the delegates do not actually have to speak to each other. To require these saintly politicians to sit around a table together would place an unbearable strain on their tempers and their self-esteem. Anyone would think we paid them to sort these things out! I chew on a Kosovar-allocated croissant and wait for the moment to collar Rugova's aide. When I do, he is pleased to inform me that I cannot leave Rambouillet. It's in the protocol pack I didn't read: *For reasons of security and to protect the confidentiality of the negotiations, attendees are required to remain within the confines of the Château de Rambouillet for the duration of the conference.*

Panic balloons in my stomach. My eyes film over but I'm too shocked even to blink the tears away.

'I'm doing my best, Anna,' says Rugova's aide. 'Be patient. Work with the team today, then hopefully we'll get you your phone call.'

He hands me a spare copy of the protocols and hurries away. This can't be right – is France no longer a free country? I'm a translator, and already sworn to secrecy. I'll leave when I please! I would say this to the aide, but he's now on the far side of the room, being obsequious to Hashim Thaçi. After spending the last few weeks with Eleni, it's disorienting to be among people for whom the loss of my child is just an unhelpful distraction. Folded into the back of the protocols is a sheet of paper I don't think he meant to leave there, with photographs and contact details for all the Kosovar delegates. What's the point of this, I'd like to know, since our phones have been confiscated?

* * *

We have been assigned the ground-floor ballroom, while the Serbian delegates occupy a salon on the floor above (the symbolic import of this arrangement has been discussed at length). Our chairs are undersized and upholstered in a lobster-coloured velvet which clashes with everything, and our conference table is so elderly and over-polished that it creaks at the merest touch of a Kosovar elbow. A set of French doors gives access to the *Allée de Cyprès chauves de Louisiane*, along which it might be pleasant to stroll for a moment of statesmanlike contemplation. However, the doors are misaligned and can only be opened by a trained servant.

Proceedings commence with a visit from our co-host, the British Foreign Secretary, accompanied by an adviser who is not introduced. The BFS is a curious, pointy little fellow, all clipped ginger bristles and bulgy eyes. He starts by thanking us for coming and asking if we are quite comfortable, before suggesting that we make time to admire Rambouillet's cultural treasures (making particular reference to the splendid Pierre Julien sculpture of Amalthea with Jupiter's Goat to be found in the Dairy), and observing that he himself finds the historic surroundings quite inspiring at this, *ahem*, historic juncture.

'We are here to fight for an independent Kosovo, not wander round looking at old statues and soaking up the atmosphere,' says Hashim Thaçi.

The BFS receives my translation of this pronouncement with a goaty expression on his face. 'Of course,' he says. 'And the dedication and integrity you bring to these proceedings is highly valued by the Contact Group, I do assure you. I have here a preliminary draft, which I invite you to consider. The issues are familiar, of course, but we need to look at them with fresh eyes and open minds.'

Next we are treated to a homily on the limitations of the Rambouillet Conference. There are matters of agreement in principle, and then there are matters of execution. The two are not to be allowed near each other. In fact, all contentious issues are forthwith to be defined as matters of execution, and as such debarred from scaring off the matters of agreement in principle, should any of these shy creatures be spotted during the course of our sojourn at the chateau. The question of the democratic will of the people of Kosovo, for instance, is the *sine qua non* of matters of execution, since it can only be determined by execution of a referendum.

'Not so,' says Rugova mildly. 'The outcome of a properly conducted vote on independence may be safely assumed. If that were not the case, it would already have been held.'

'Well put, Ibrahim,' says Thaçi.

'Let's be realistic, gentlemen,' says the BFS. 'We're not going to sort out everything here. It's too much to expect. But we can set out the ground rules, negotiate in good faith, see where it takes us, yes?'

His affable tone arouses the ire of Hashim Thaçi.

'No, it is not too much to expect,' shouts the Snake, as soon as the words are out of my mouth. 'The democratic will of the people must be respected or the conference is a sham.'

'Our first duty is to negotiate a peace for the people of Kosovo,' the BFS replies. 'If we fail to reach an agreement here at Rambouillet, war may be inevitable.'

I translate, replacing *may be* with *is*, for both semantic and political reasons.

'Better war than slavery,' Thaçi declares. 'Kosovo for the Kosovars!'

The delegation breaks into spontaneous applause. The British

Foreign Secretary hides his bewilderment behind a fixed smile, then pushes back his chair and scuttles from the room.

* * *

We take up our coloured pens (green for yes, red for no, blue for discuss further) and pore over the future of our beloved Kosovo, as defined by the preliminary draft. But first, speeches must be made, stands must be taken, hands must be placed on hearts or thumped on the creaky table. I want to go home.

The speeches end and the delegates make a preliminary stab at drafting their response to the preliminary draft. A few carefully chosen words of Albanian appear on paper. We have begun! Now I must translate them, then translate them again in several different ways so the meaning of each version can be weighed in the balance – and the counter-balance, too. The words must be picked over until exhausted, examined for nuance, interrogated for evidence of hidden agendas, and finally challenged over their constitutional rigour and linguistic immutability. Even definite and indefinite articles are not spared, for who can say that a stray 'a' will not cause a catastrophe?

Hashim Thaçi's attention is drawn to the word *disarm*. He taps it disapprovingly.

'Is there perhaps any ambiguity here?' asks Ibrahim Rugova, the most experienced diplomat among us, and a poet of some repute.

I explain that *disarm* has the subsidiary meaning *overcome objection by means of charm*, but that in the context of a series of clauses about the notoriously charm-averse fighting men of the Kosovo Liberation Army it can safely be taken to indicate that they must hand over their guns. There is a shaking of heads, a drumming of fingers, a hiss from Hashim Thaçi. *It's a peace conference, duh?* I would have said, had I not been instructed to speak only when specifically requested to do so. Out comes the red pen to perform a ceremonial dismissal of the word *disarm*.

It is now observed that the actual phrase is *disarm immediately* and that the word *immediately* could perhaps be substituted with a phrase (*suggestions please, Anna*) such as *in the medium term* or, better still, *when [certain conditions to be confirmed] regarding [insert later] have been met*. There follows a debate about what certain conditions might be later inserted, led by one of our advisers, Colonel V. Adjani, whose career in the Albanian secret police apparently entitles him to claim expertise in the matter of the security of the people. *Expertise in wielding electric batons in the matter of the security of the Communist Party of Albania, you mean*, I would have commented, if specifically requested to do so.

'Never come between an Albanian and his gun,' Hashim Thaçi announces.

Everyone nods. Colonel Adjani lights a thin cigar and places it in the centre of the oval of greasy bristle which surrounds his creased, tar-brown lips. One side of his mouth is lumpy and there's a patch of red under the bristle, as if he's been punched. While the delegates debate the question of security, I run through possible reasons for punching Colonel Adjani. This train of thought occupies me for some time.

Eventually it is agreed to dispense with *disarm immediately* in favour of *lay down their arms on a timetable to be agreed*. The delegates congratulate themselves on appearing to have made a concession while in fact giving nothing away. This tremendous coup has taken three hours to devise and we are weary. Shadows incline like dozing sentries along the unreachable *allée*. I should like to walk along it with Katya. I take her hand, her fingers are warm in my palm. A child's touch is not only gentle, it lacks expectation – and so, clumsiness. She considers herself too old for hand-holding, but the setting lends the gesture a formal air and I have my treat.

How beautiful she looks, pale as a spring flower among the stiff old cypress trees.

*   *   *

The day's work ends but the phone call is not forthcoming. Rugova's aide wears a sympathetic face, but his eyes say the request is an affront which has caused him extra work. It's distasteful and, yes, embarrassing! Did we have to invite this mousy woman along, and why is she not being mousy?

I leave him and go in search of President Rugova, tiptoeing among the huddle and crush of men-who-will-not-talk-directly-to-each-other-even-though-they-should. I find him outside the dining room.

'Mr President, may I talk to you about my daughter, Katarina?'

'Anna,' he says gravely, 'you must remind me of this again when the conference closes.'

'Is there anything you could do right now?'

He sees my red eyes and unarranged hair. It's not enough. He fears I will make a spectacle of myself, and of him. He steps back.

'This is really not the time, Anna. You understand that.'

This really is the time, I want to shout at his dapper little form as he joins an eddy of people near the main entrance. The likelihood of finding a missing person lessens with every passing day.

I repair to the bat-loft and put on lipstick and perfume, a tight skirt and the cream cashmere cardigan Franz stole from the MiniMax department store. You're just fulfilling the Roma stereotype, I told him. That's not why I took it. I took it so I can feel your soft, furry breasts, he replied, feeling my soft, furry breasts. Like little bunny rabbits, he decided, reaching for the hem of my skirt. I was sexy, then. Today, nothing is further from my mind.

I go back downstairs to wander the salons and corridors in

search of Hashim Thaçi, and eventually spy him drinking brandy with Colonel Adjani. I lurk behind the folds of a brocade curtain until the Colonel goes off somewhere, then walk quickly over. Thaçi listens to me with cold curiosity.

'These Bura shits deserved everything they got,' he says.

'Do you know how to contact them?'

'I'll ask around, but they've probably moved her on by now.'

I stand there, too shocked to ask what he means and terrified that, given how I have dolled myself up for him, the KLA leader may demand a sexual favour in return for helping me find Katya. The bunny rabbits pose without enthusiasm or abandon. I am not sexy now. Thaçi gives me a quizzical look, then takes a mouthful of brandy and waves me away.

21

Next morning, Rugova's aide reports that the Serbian delegates have succeeded in inspecting the cover page of the draft agreement. Greatly dismayed, they are demanding that the title be changed from *Interim Agreement for Peace and Self-Government in Kosovo* to *Agreement for Self-Government in Kosmet*. Their intentions could not have been more bluntly put: first, Kosovo is hereinafter to be known by its Serbian appellation Kosmet, in recognition of the fact that it is, always has been and always will be Serbian; second, they are not interested in peace. Unable to continue their deliberations until the offensive cover page has been amended, they spent the rest of the day getting drunk and singing patriotic songs.

The Kosovars debate this outrage until interrupted by delivery of a formal note from the British Foreign Secretary, to the effect that an unnamed Englishman has arrived at Rambouillet for a private interview with Colonel Adjani. This note causes both awe and irritation among the Kosovar delegation – in the hierarchy of Rambouillet, the Colonel is of rather lowly status. But this must be an intelligence matter, a spy-on-spy encounter, they speculate, noting that, immediately prior to the conference, diplomatic pressure was applied to have Colonel Adjani removed from the list of

Kosovar advisers. The man himself listens to the discussion with monumental impassivity and declares himself mystified. He does not look mystified, he looks smug and lights a cheroot. He smokes so many of these things that his nose has narrowed and his eyes have sunk back into his skull.

The interview/meeting/spy-on-spy encounter takes place at eleven sharp. I am to play the role of interpreter. The English spy is a disappointment. The word *prim* is usually reserved for women, but this man, who does not give his name, is prim. He has thin lips and waxy cheeks. We shake hands and his grip is clammy. He has a buff folder under his arm and an eager, pink-faced woman a few years younger than me in his wake.

The anonymous English spy approaches the table. Colonel Adjani is already seated, and gestures for his adversary to sit beside him. The spy takes the chair opposite instead. Ha! The game has begun. I wonder if I should translate: *The English spy declines your courteous gesture, which he judges disingenuous, and asserts his superiority by sitting where he pleases.* Having negotiated this moment of hazard, the English spy nods at his assistant and arranges his folder on the table in front of him.

'Thank you for taking time out from your busy schedule to meet me this morning, Colonel Adjani,' he says. 'I will not keep you long.'

Colonel Adjani looks bored.

'I would not be here if the matter for discussion did not have the potential to impact your negotiations on the future of Kosovo. That is a measure of its seriousness.'

Colonel Adjani leans sideways in his chair so that he can stare at the pink-faced woman's legs.

'Before we begin, I would like your undertaking that you will not give the British government or any of its agencies or employees as the source of whatever you may find out during the course of this meeting.'

'You want to tell me something in secret,' the Colonel observes.

'Quite so,' says the English spy. 'Do you agree to this condition?'

'OK, why not? I do not know you, MI6 man, and we have never met.'

'Good,' says the English spy, though it is obvious from his frown that he does not like being addressed as MI6 man. 'So,' he continues, 'I have indicated the importance of this interview. You should know, Colonel, that there is mounting pressure on the International Police Task Force to investigate your brother Haclan.'

'They'd be better off looking at the price of a taxi instead. Now that's a scandal,' says the Colonel.

The English spy is momentarily startled by the Colonel's levity. 'There is concern at the highest level,' he resumes, 'that your brother's criminal activities in Skopje and elsewhere will bring the Kosovar cause into disrepute.'

'Our cause is noble,' declares Colonel Adjani. 'No wise or just person would deny us the freedom we crave. It is a cause for which all Kosovar-Albanians will take up arms when called upon, all of them, down to the very last man, be he ten years old or a hundred and ten!'

He goes on in this vein for a minute, while the spy fiddles with his ring and his assistant tucks her legs out of view.

'The Colonel says that his cause is noble,' I begin, hoping to cut him short. He holds up his hand to shut me up and carries on. By the time he's finished, I've forgotten how he started, but it hardly matters. I invent some suitably nationalistic bombast and conclude by saying: 'You'd better get on with it, Mr Bond, because he can do this all night.'

The English spy looks at me sharply and the pink-faced woman studies her fingernails in order to stop herself laughing. Colonel Adjani sees them and frowns. 'I told him you're very busy and could he come to the point,' I say in Albanian. 'I hope that's OK.'

The Colonel studies me from his sunken eyes.

'I have no interest in his point.'

'Perhaps you would confine yourself to translation, Ms…' The English spy studies my name-badge. 'Ms Galica.'

'Sure. If only there were something to translate.'

'Ask that girl if she'll let me fuck her in the arse,' says Colonel Adjani.

'The answer's no,' I say. 'She won't.'

'How do you know? English girls aren't such prudes as you Kosovars. Even the Serbs get to fuck their translators.'

'You know why that is? Because they're not translators.'

'Shall we get on?' says the English spy. 'If Haclan is arrested by the IPTF while the conference is in progress, which seems increasingly likely, there may be charges or allegations that will be disastrous for the reputation and credibility of the Kosovar negotiating team. The timing could not be worse for you. It's not just that Haclan is your brother – it has been reported in various media that he is close to the KLA leadership.'

'*It has been reported in various media*,' Colonel Adjani mimics, in revealingly fluent English, before reverting to his native tongue. 'The famous British SIS now gets its intelligence from the gossip columns. Some spy you are.'

'The public perception of an association between your brother and the Kosovar leadership is what matters here.'

'Don't arrest him,' says the Colonel. 'Problem solved.'

'We cannot interfere at the operational level. Surely I don't have to explain such things to a man of your experience.'

'But still you are here, interfering,' says Colonel Adjani. He pauses while I translate, then goes on: 'OK, I'll call my brother. Dear Haclan, you must leave Skopje. Leave now, they want to arrest you. They always want to arrest me, says he. No, this is different, I tell him.' Colonel Adjani pauses to eyeball the English spy. 'How is this different, MI6 man?'

'There is new information about Haclan's operations in Skopje – detailed and very damaging information. That's all I'm prepared to say.'

'The woman who took her lies to the UNHCR won't be helping you any further.' He stares at the English spy, daring him to share some dark look whose meaning I do not understand. 'But perhaps you mean this British man you have detained, this UNHCR officer. *Bryan Harley…*' He says the name slowly and with emphasis. 'The new information is from him, I think.'

'How do you know about Harley?' asks the English spy suspiciously.

'I read it in a gossip column.'

'I don't think so. No details have been released.'

'You are holding this Bryan Harley in secret,' the Colonel says. 'You locked him up in his apartment and interrogated him about my brother, but you have not charged him with any crime. This is illegal, I believe, under your ancient English law of *habeas corpus*. Are you above the law, MI6 man?'

I am so taken aback by the Colonel's sudden concern for Harley's human rights that my translation is wooden, but the English spy is impatient to reply.

'I am not at liberty to discuss this further.'

'Why not? In here, everything is secret, for sure. We can say what we like.'

'You need to call your brother and tell him to shut down his operation in Skopje and leave. I have made arrangements for you to have access to a private telephone.'

'So you can listen? What kind of fool do you take me for?'

'Then find some other way.' The English spy is exasperated. He thinks he is doing the Kosovars a favour, but the interview has been a disagreeable charade. 'These things have a momentum of their own,' he goes on. 'It would be in your interests to act immediately.'

'And yours, or you would not be here,' Colonel Adjani retorts.

'If you fail to persuade your brother to avoid his imminent arrest, you will be doing your people a grave disservice.'

'You care nothing for my people,' says Colonel Adjani, reverting to declamatory mode. 'Milosh has insulted you, and for old times' sake you would like to give the Russians a kick in the balls. Therefore, you will bomb Serbia and Kosovans will die. But that's OK. That does not matter to you.'

'I don't know what you're talking about,' mutters the English spy. 'This meeting is at an end.'

* * *

I get my phone call at lunchtime. Eleni's in a fluster, but there's no news.

'No one's called or emailed, then? And the police haven't got back to you?'

'They shut the police station yesterday. I'm sorry, Anna. It's got ugly here. The Serbs are lashing out while they still have the chance.'

* * *

I accost Hashim Thaçi after dinner and ask him what he meant when he said Katarina had probably been moved on.

'I told you I'd ask around, but don't push it,' he says severely. 'Wait to hear from me.'

He turns his back and I hurry to my room, undress and get into bed. I already know what he meant: the men who took Katya don't have her any more. I realised that when the red Skoda stopped following me round Kric.

Piano music and laughter drift up from a salon full of Serbs below. Another night at the Prison de Rambouillet, wrapped tight in its velvet folds, stitched up with protocols and principles and rules of engagement. Colonel Adjani's words reel through my mind. *Kosovans will die.* The English spy did not disagree. People are running away – tens of thousands of them. It's in the papers every day. *Kosovans will die.* Eleni thought so, too. They'll break us all to bits. They'll burn us and choke us and bury us alive. *Kosovans will die.* No one knows which ones. Katarina is Kosovan. To be exact, she's half Albanian, half Roma, with ancestors from India and Turkey. She works hard at school and is a little shy and earnest. She's pretty, with bright, hopeful eyes. She doesn't deserve to die.

22

Newspapers are not allowed at Rambouillet, but the fat wretches have somehow sneaked through the *cordon sanitaire*, and next morning the assembled dignitaries discover that the world's media have misjudged them. This convocation of grave, diligent politicians, resolutely defending the interests of their people while still finding space in their austere souls for that wise pragmatism which is the hallmark of true statesmanship, is being portrayed as a gaggle of shameless freeloaders, who spend their days lying recumbent on some stretch of goose-down-stuffed upholstery, ravaged by indigestion and incapable of engaging with the diplomatic realm unless by issue of the occasional belch. One (French) newspaper has acquired the catering department's accounts and calculated that already enough alcohol has been consumed to keep the entire chateau in a stupor for the duration of the conference; and further, it reveals, the *plateau de fromages* offered round at every meal is loaded with no fewer than twenty varieties of cheese – several of which are not even in season!

The Kosovars find this depiction hurtful. The Serbs, Marta tells me, regard it as some kind of conspiracy that they are too tired to unravel. The Contact Groupies are livid. The agreements in principle are as elusive as ever, and now they are being jeered at. Their inner amanuenses are hastily excising the chapter of their memoirs in which they credit themselves with the salvation of Kosovo. The morning briefing is peremptory; at lunch, the super-abundant *plateau de fromages* has been replaced by a single Brie of colossal girth. If nothing else will, this shattering privation must surely drive the delegates to make peace.

Some of the Kosovar delegates have received death threats from hardliners back home. Your people lie bleeding in the hills of their beloved homeland, runs the narrative of the KLA campfires, while you eat cheese and grovel. A declaration that allows for any outcome other than independence would be a betrayal of the Račak dead.

I am being forced to take part in a farce, while my daughter is *moved on*. Extra bureaucrats and advisers and specialists have arrived to help break the deadlock, and Rambouillet is full to bursting point. But still the conference is constipated. Not a paragraph is accepted, not a phrase nor a word, no, not a syllable, not even a letter is even in principle agreed.

* * *

A cadre of NATO officials arrives to brief us on – whisper it not – the prohibited matters of execution. Their faces are grim-set and grey. Perhaps they've just come from inspecting the bombs tucked up in their numbered steel cribs. There's execution for you, there's an implementation issue lying in wait for Kosovo. The NATO men are passionate devotees of Kosovan autonomy, apparently. And Serbian integrity, I'd like to know? Rugova smoothes the cravat at his throat, which he wears as a symbol of the throttling of Kosovo by the imperialists of Belgrade.

The NATO men leave to brief the Serbian delegation, who are carousing on the floor above. The Kosovar team is left alone and the mood quickly becomes petulant. They've located the limits of their power and found it extends no further than the right to squabble with each other in a dusty room at the *crapaudière* and hope the Serbs foul up. I listen to them wearily for an hour. You said this. But you said that. Who did? Not I. Categorically so. In writing, or just categorically? Check the minutes, Anna, check the drafts, the revisions, the emendations and the strikings-out. Consult the versions once thought superseded but now significant once more.

'The will of the people is for an independent Kosovo,' Colonel Adjani declares, stroking his bruised mouth with a brandy-addled hand. 'If it takes a NATO assault to kick Milosh out, let's get on with it.'

I pick up three folders of paperwork and slam them down again. 'You stupid fucking shitholes!' I scream, as the densely annotated drafts slide across the gleaming rosewood table. 'You jumped-up, preening *cjaps*! You wave your fucking donkey *kollodoks* about like anyone gives a fuck what you think!'

The Kosovar delegation is silent with astonishment.

'What do you know about the will of the people, you prick? The will of the people is to not be bombed! You know what the Contact Group think of you *zuzar*? They think you're a bunch of fucking criminals and they're embarrassed to be anywhere near you. They only got you along so they can pretend it's a peace conference. Well it's not a peace conference, it's a declaration of fucking war. So sign some bits of paper and go home. Any bits. Here, sign this.' I pick up a folder and fling it at Colonel Adjani. 'Then they can bomb us all to hell in our own fucking names.'

'Get this bitch out of here,' says the Colonel.

* * *

I steal a set of six teaspoons as a gift for Eleni, and leave a note for President Rugova, apologising, and one for Hashim Thaçi, reminding him that he's agreed to help me. I get my phone back and call Eleni but she has nothing new to say.

'Everyone is leaving Pristina,' she tells me. 'Nina and Milo went yesterday.'

Nina and Milo are Serbian Catholics. If they don't feel safe, no one should.

'Can you pick me up at the airport? My flight gets in at nine-twenty.'

'Of course I will. Anna, I think we should go to Skopje for a few days. We'll hand out leaflets and visit the UNHCR.'

'I've written to them four times and called them I don't know how many.'

'They can't brush us aside so easily if we are there in person. It's for the best. We can stay in my uncle's apartment.'

* * *

I was by then so hollowed out I would have done anything she'd proposed. The main roads into Macedonia were choked so Piotr's Uncle Mikhail loaded the Fiat Frightful onto his truck and drove us to Skopje via a maze of mountain tracks. Up there on the bare plains with the jutting peaks standing hard and imperious against the bare sky, I suddenly felt very close to Katarina, and it dawned on me that there were ways of being together that did not require actual presence or contact. Then I felt appalled, because I realised this was how I might think about her if she were dead.

James

23

Clive Silk's three wide men couldn't believe their luck. It was unusual for a member of the officer class to be arrested at all, rare for that officer to be in army intelligence, and unheard of for the slimy Rupert to resist. They set about their work with ill-disguised glee – the hangover I'd earned the night before making their job a whole lot easier than it should have been. They concentrated on my back and thighs – no doubt motivated by the knowledge that for the next four hours I'd be trussed up in a slung canvas seat on a military flight into Brize Norton. The blood pooled in my bruised legs, and by the time we landed I was a jangling rictus of cramp.

They had to drag me by the armpits to the car waiting outside the terminal. We drove for three hours and it was dark when we arrived. They attached a tag to my left ankle with a tamper-proof band, then fed me tinned soup and cold toast and insulted me while I ate. I was escorted upstairs and locked in a small bedroom. I crawled to the bed, tried to get onto it. Failed. Curled up. Slept. A night of ugly, sinuous dreams that clambered over each other like foraging rats.

* * *

'Up! Shower!'

A bruiser I hadn't seen before stepped into the room.

'Fuck me,' he said, 'so that's what a paedo smells like.'

I hobbled along the corridor to the bathroom. As soon as I was in the shower, he opened the door and took my clothes. I soaped my hands and ran them over my bruised, lumpy body. I was a mess, and the physical injuries weren't the half of it. I was furious that I'd been arrested on this vile charge, and longed for the moment when my superiors' embarrassed faces would feel the scorching heat of my outrage.

Yet some part of me welcomed the swellings and contusions as the just desserts for a sinner of such recklessness and violence. I'd failed to deliver the girl I'd carried out of Kosovo to the proper authorities, for no better reason than that I'd been possessed by a feverish desire to return to action and prove myself a worthy member of TJ Farah's SAS unit. I'd been wrong to do what I'd done to the boy in the farmhouse loft and the Bura leader in the woods: too eager to kill, and then too weak to refuse to kill.

Then there were the men who'd pursued me near Syrna Street. Self-defence? Picturing the scene in the back of the van, I wasn't sure that plea would pass muster. Finally, I'd allowed my inebriated lust for a dyed blonde in a dressing gown to dupe me into taking a taxi ride to the Vegas Lounge – a place that any fool would immediately have recognised as a cesspit of depravity. The brawl that followed might have salved my conscience, but I was uncomfortably aware that, for all the righteous grandstanding, I'd left a child behind, in the clutches of her abusers.

I stepped out of the shower and dressed in the tracksuit bottoms and white T-shirt which lay on the stool where my clothes had been, then went to the frosted-glass window and pushed open the fanlight – the only part that wasn't locked. Beyond the house was a scrubby field occupied by a small flock of daggy-bottomed sheep.

The land rose in a shallow slope surmounted by a large stack of straw wrapped in tattered black polythene that rippled and flapped in the gusty wind. I shut the fanlight and knocked to be let out. After a long wait, the bruiser came and unlocked the door. He didn't step aside, so I was forced to push past him.

'Watch yerself, filthy perv.'

He barged a meaty shoulder into my sternum so that my head snapped back against the doorframe. I was going to have to get used to this.

The view from my room wasn't up to much, either: an apron of muddy grass surrounded by a high stone wall, a track leading to an expanse of conifer bisected by a narrow lane. The sky bore down on the horizon like a wall of putty-coloured mud.

Half an hour later, I was delivered to the kitchen for breakfast, supervised by the other two members of the night shift. They weren't in uniform – ex-military, I guessed, employed by whatever private security firm had the contract to run this place. One of them leaned against the frame of the back door and picked his nails, while his mate perched on a stool by the counter, his large haunches engulfing the vinyl seat. I ate off melamine crockery, using plastic utensils: cereal, toast, lukewarm instant coffee which they'd obviously spat in.

'If it was me, I'd feed slimy nonces on dog shit and broken glass.'

'And a cup of cold piss.'

Allowing these bullies to wind me up was the worst thing I could do. My Int Corps superiors wanted to take me off the map for a while, that much was obvious; but why go to the expense of a safe house with its three rotating shifts of three bruisers each and its no doubt inconvenient location? I chewed a corner of burnt toast and looked round the kitchen – an assemblage of laminated chipboard and plastic trim that could have been described as utilitarian if it hadn't been falling apart. The kitchen gave onto a hallway with the front door and staircase, and a short passage with rooms either side.

'I want a phone call,' I said. 'And get me Clive Silk. When you've done that, take this tag off my ankle.'

'Did you say something?' the man on the stool asked his companion.

'Not me, mate. Maybe there's an infestation. You know, roaches or vermin or suchlike.'

'There's a bad smell, that's for sure. Slimy, if you take my meaning.'

'Yeah, sort of noncey.'

They sniffed the air theatrically, then smirked at each other.

* * *

They locked me up again and I examined the tag strapped to my ankle – it was cheaply made, but still impossible to open or detach without sounding the alarm.

I spent the next hour walking round and round the room, examining handles, hinges, brackets, screws – anything that would furnish me with a tool or a weapon. There was a shelving unit incorporating a column of small cupboards and a hanging space from which the pole had been removed. The bed was a flimsy divan that would be useful only if my warders had a pathological fear of upholstered pine. The window tilted open about four inches, at which point it was impeded by steel blocks screwed into the slides. As I pushed at them pointlessly with my thumb, a car pulled up in the lane. Three men got out and walked round the side of the house. A minute later, the three who'd guarded me overnight were driven off.

Less than an hour into the wakeful portion of my captivity, and already I had nothing to do. Have another look at the window. Grip it top and bottom, like so, and you can pop it clear of the slides. My knuckles whitened and I realised I was already twisting the frame.

I felt sick, empty. Do something. I checked the bed again. It was nothing. I could tear it apart in ten seconds flat. Do anything.

Remember how his dying heart pulsed through the knife-grip?

Yes, I remember.

The boy dead in the loft, fear and loneliness draining from his eyes: remember how it felt?

Exercise, I told myself. Get a routine going.

I leaned against the wall and stretched, and the protests from my bruised limbs distracted me. I went at it hard, every rep I knew, demanding that my body find the energy to keep my mind at bay. As I worked, I noticed that a section of floor was uneven and springy. A loose floorboard: the sort of place workmen mislay tools or leave bits and pieces they can't be bothered to take out to the skip. A screwdriver or a chisel, I fantasised. Something to investigate, anyway. Something to plan. I imagined lifting the length of timber to reveal my hoard.

* * *

At midday I was taken downstairs for a microwaved lasagne served with a garnish of sneers. There was a row of dog-eared paperbacks set out on the counter by the kettle.

'Could I have one of those books, please?'

'Slimy Nonce wants a book. What do you think?'

'We couldn't allow it. Some of the characters might be kiddies.'

'He'll get all hot and sweaty. Next thing, he's spunking all over his fucking room.'

'Wouldn't be right.'

I told myself that their choreographed mockery meant nothing to me, but in truth it was hard to take.

'We wuz going to let his royal sliminess have a walk in the garden after his lunch,' one of them went on.

'Can't be allowed. Not when he's looking for an opportunity to have hisself a wank.'

* * *

Back in my room I decided to investigate the loose floorboard. I'd spent the last few hours clinging to the hope that it might hide something miraculous, and now felt a sentimental reluctance to see that hope dashed. Get on with it, I told myself, or you'll never find the girl you fed to the dogs in Skopje.

I moved the bed aside so I could get to the corner nearest the loose board, waited until I was sure the noise hadn't alerted my handlers, then lifted the carpet off the spiked gripper tacked along the skirting and rolled back the underlay. The board was nailed down at one end, but the other had lifted enough that I could get my fingernails into the grain and start easing it up. I could hear a TV from the ground floor, the voices of my handlers conducting a desultory, stop-start conversation, but the noises weren't coming from the room below mine. The one who was supposed to be posted outside my door had sloped off to bed in the room next to the bathroom half an hour ago, and the occasional snort suggested he was asleep.

Once I had my fingers in under the board I could pull harder, but the nails protested and I had to take it slowly, pausing after every little creak. Five minutes later I was lying on the floor, my fingers scrabbling among the dust and wires between the joists.

I set my haul out on the floor: eight pages of the *Sun* newspaper, dated 11 October 1978, and a piece of broken glass that looked like it came from the base of a Coke bottle.

Hallelujah.

It was ridiculous to feel so disappointed. *You weren't seriously expecting a chisel, were you?* I stuffed everything back down between the joists, replaced the floorboard and rolled the carpet into place. I lay down on the bed and tried in vain to sleep. What would happen now to the girl I'd dumped in Syrna Street? I was the only person who knew what desperate trouble she was in, but I was being held in this grim little house somewhere on the other side of Europe. I could not save her. But I must. I would.

24

After breakfast next day, one of the bruisers diverted me down the passage off the hallway. The door to the room below mine was open and I looked in as we passed – a dining room that didn't look used. That was good. I could move around upstairs without attracting attention. The bruiser hustled me into the sitting room on the other side of the passage, and there was Clive Silk. He'd disposed himself across the sofa in a languid manner and was studying the ceiling. *I'm a highly intelligent spy on a highly sensitive mission*, his demeanour announced. I wasn't fooled. The skin of his face was damp and his tie looked as if it were throttling him.

'Captain Palatine – good to see you've recovered. You were in a bit of a sorry state last time we met.'

I didn't answer.

'Funny kind of place, this – looks like it's been parachuted in from Woking or Croydon or somewhere. They treating you OK?'

I sat down opposite him and folded my arms. I thought I could damage Clive Silk quite badly in the five seconds it would take the hired hands to arrive.

'I've come to tell you what happens from here on. Obviously you're in quite a bit of trouble. No point pretending otherwise.'

'You have forty-eight hours from my arrest to get me in front of a court and lay charges,' I said. 'Forty-eight hours is already up, so you're committing a criminal offence by holding me here.'

'Correct. And you smuggled an underage girl over the border from Kosovo. The driver said you had your arm round her in the back of the Land Rover. Then I guess she spent the night in your apartment.'

'She had nowhere else to go,' I said, thinking that, in the right hands, it would be a compellingly sordid piece of evidence. 'Have you spoken to Sergeant Farah?'

'Denies all knowledge of the girl, and so do his unit. They were hurrying to get an injured man back across the border, if you remember.'

The story as agreed. It didn't exactly help my cause.

'Farah's report says you couldn't keep up,' Silk went on, the corners of his thin mouth betraying the momentary twinge of pleasure this detail gave him. 'Three days later, you were filmed in a club called the Vegas Lounge that's under investigation for child prostitution. You must see how bad it all looks. Where is this girl now?'

'I took her to a house at seventy-seven Syrna Street. I was led to believe it was run by the UNHCR. Does that address mean anything to you?'

It wasn't the sort of question people like Clive Silk answer. 'So you left her there,' he said. 'Anything else I should know about?'

'The girl who took her in I saw later at the Vegas Lounge.'

'This gets worse and worse,' said Silk. 'And then?'

'I don't know. Do you have the tape?'

'A copy. The Skopje police have the original. You, on a bed with an underage girl. Unfortunate.'

I ignored the provocation and asked: 'Did the police tell you they'd arrested me?'

'They didn't need to. We'd had the Vegas Lounge under informal

189

surveillance for several days before you dropped in. You didn't exactly go incognito.'

'You're watching it? Why haven't you closed it down?'

'Don't be naive, Palatine. None of this is in our jurisdiction – UK intelligence is an interested party here, that's all.'

'There are girls being abused at the Vegas Lounge every night. If you don't do something about it, you're complicit.'

This argument cut no ice with Silk. He didn't feel complicit at all. 'We'll pass on any relevant intel, of course,' he said.

'Did it occur to you to *talk* to me,' I said bitterly, 'rather than fabricating this arrest?'

'The Skopje police are in possession of a video showing a British army officer— Well, you know what it shows. How would it look if we'd got you released, then just let you wander off? We have to be able to demonstrate that you've been properly investigated.'

'Now that's been done,' I said, 'you can let me go.'

'I'm afraid not. There are wider issues in play, which I'm not able to explain to you at this time.'

'So this isn't just about me,' I said. 'You're not even that bothered by a bit of child prostitution. Why is MI6 handling this rather than the Int Corps?'

'Because the wider issues are outside the Int Corps remit.'

'And these issues are?'

Silk didn't reply. I looked into his eyes. They were a faded blue colour, slightly filmed-over, but the pupils had an anxious, startled energy. Silk was essentially a weak man for whom the corporate structure of MI6, allied to his sense of his own cleverness, provided the extra ballast he needed. It was galling to have him lording it over me, but he wasn't enjoying it as much as he should have been.

'The night I was at the Vegas Lounge,' I said, 'pretty much everyone was army, NATO or UN.'

'Did you recognise someone in particular?' asked Silk. 'Or was there just a general twitching of the Palatine halo?'

'I've been to embassy cocktail parties. The guests at the Vegas Lounge looked much the same.'

'Why were you at the Vegas Lounge? You haven't said.'

'I don't feel the need to explain myself to you,' I said, 'now I know my arrest is part of some charade dreamed up by you and your team in the MI6 playpen.'

'But once inside, you thought you'd hire an underage girl, then start a drunken brawl.'

'I lost my temper when I found out what was going on in the bedrooms,' I said coldly.

'Not because you didn't get your *champagne*?'

A pulse rocked in my neck, so heavy it made me nod. The urge to spring forward and kill Clive Silk was strong. I didn't know if I could contain it. Silk had seen it. He made as if to stand up, thought better of it, shouted:

'Ackford!'

One of the old bullies trotted in.

'You're going to regret that remark, Clive Silk,' I said.

'Oi. Cut it,' said Ackford.

'Captain Palatine can go back to his room,' Silk ordered.

'Right you are, Sir.'

'You know how sensitive this sort of thing is, Palatine,' said Silk, an expression of the unjustly accused playing over his rubbery features.

I stood and stared down at him. 'So sensitive that I had to be locked up in a safe house with this knuckle-dragger for company?'

Ackford hissed and stepped in, then realised he couldn't hit me with Silk there and stood with his head thrust forward, inches from my ear.

'You'll be held here for another two weeks. That's all I can tell you at this point.'

191

* * *

MI6 won't do anything about the Vegas Lounge, I thought, when they'd locked me in my room. Whatever network of corruption was allowing the place to operate, they weren't going to unravel it. Silk and his colleagues and masters regarded such tawdry affairs as beneath their dignity. Geopolitics was their game, and they played it among themselves as far as possible. The lives of ordinary people were a complication easily set aside, an inconvenience easily forgotten. No, they'd leave the messy hands-on stuff to others – it didn't much matter who. In the meantime, it would suit MI6 to survey the goings-on at the Vegas Lounge from a position of interested detachment: such places were prime sources of intel, especially the precious kind that enables you to add new names to the list of influential people you can blackmail.

Besides, what Silk had said about Skopje being outside their jurisdiction was true. And the knowledge that an incriminating videotape of a British army officer was stored in the evidence room at Skopje police station would hardly encourage MI6 to press for a formal investigation into the Vegas Lounge. What else? I was missing something. Why exactly did they need me off the map for the next two weeks? I thought back over our conversation but couldn't work it out.

Brooding wasn't going to get me any answers. I sat on the floor with my left leg stretched out so the ankle tag was next to the corner of the bed, then raised the bedframe and smashed it down onto the plastic case. The thick plastic band that secured it ripped into my shin, but I hammered it again, and then again, until the case split down its seam. I prised the tag apart and tore out its innards, expecting the alarm to sound immediately. It didn't. I counted the seconds: five, six, seven, eight— The monitoring unit downstairs whooped into life. Seconds later, I heard swearing outside, a key scratching in the lock. I shoved the bits under the mattress, then sat with my back against the door and managed to hold them off for long enough to clip the plastic case shut. I rolled aside and the door flew open.

'You cunt.'

'I don't want this box attached to my ankle.'

They pulled me up, got me by the throat, slammed me against the wall. One of them kneed me in the groin. I lay on the floor and retched for a while. When I'd recovered enough to speak, I said: 'You can tag someone when they've been convicted of an offence. Otherwise, it's illegal.'

'You pull that one again, I'll tag your fucking cock,' said the one who had kneed me.

He knelt on my neck while the other two went downstairs. I thought of allowing myself the pleasure of snapping this one's spine and making a run for it. Twist his foot to get him off balance, drop knee-first into the small of his back... But there were two more to get past, and two further shifts of three men each, probably located less than five miles away with an off-site monitoring unit to alert them to any goings-on at the house. They'd already be out looking for me. An abortive escape was the worst possible move I could make.

A moment later, the alarm stopped shrieking and the two who had gone downstairs returned. One of them cut the broken tag from my ankle and handed it to his mate while he fastened a new one in its place. Seeing the empty plastic case clutched in the bully's knobbly fist made me feel better than I had for days.

'We can tag the nonce,' he grunted in my ear, 'or we can tie him up like a mad dog instead, if that's how he likes it. Not a problem.'

* * *

I lay on the bed and examined the innards of the tag. There wasn't much to it: a master unit listens out from somewhere in the house, like a mother duck keeping tabs on her chicks; at regular intervals, the RF chip in the ankle tag emits a cheep of the required frequency. If the tag fails to cheep as expected, the mother unit sounds the alarm.

The chip didn't seem to be damaged. It was connected to a battery to extend its range, but although the wiring was intact, the tamper-proof circuit fitted to the case had broken when I'd prised it open. Because the alarm hadn't gone off immediately, I knew this circuit worked passively – by disabling the chip so it couldn't send its cheeps to the mother unit. On a more intelligent device, of the kind used to tag offenders on parole, the alarm would have been triggered the moment the circuit was cut. I felt a moment of glee that the place had been equipped with such a crude system.

I went and had another look at the mechanism that stopped the window opening. It had started to rain. Drops clung to the pane, quivering in the wind, then burst and slipped down the glass. The two steel blocks squatted inside the guide-rails, screwed down snug and tight. I pushed the window open as far as it would go and stared down through the narrow gap. My eyes settled immediately on a green plastic box against the wall directly below. It was like a small version of the grit hoppers you see by the roadside in winter, with a sloping lid and a metal latch you could use to secure it with a padlock. The lid was down, but it wasn't locked.

I could lower myself onto that box when I escaped – it looked solid enough. I twisted my head sideways and pressed my cheek against the window to get a better view. What was inside it? I pulled the window shut and went back to the bed, pushed the mattress aside and picked at a corner of the ticking that covered the base. I used the broken glass to cut out a large oblong of material, then sliced it into strips, knotted them together and made a noose at one end.

There was plenty of daylight left, and they wouldn't come for me until after dark. I opened the window and lowered my makeshift fishing line. The strips of nylon jinked in every gust, so I hauled up the line and weighted it with the broken glass. It didn't make much difference. Forehead jammed up against the lower edge of the window frame, I watched the knots in the nylon strips zigzag across my narrow field of view, but however much I twitched and tugged, the thing was impossible to control.

I carried on, excitement giving way to frustration. It was like a fairground fishing game that nobody ever wins. Then the wind dropped and the spattering drizzle turned into a downpour. That did it. The nylon strips got wet, making them heavier and easier to manoeuvre. The noose flopped over the latch. I tugged gently and it tightened. But as it took the weight of the lid, it slipped off. I pulled the line up. This wasn't going to work.

I smelled fishfingers frying below. I should stop, be satisfied with the progress I had made, try again tomorrow. But I was too agitated to resist having one last go. I remade the noose so that the weight of the glass would help to tighten it and lowered away. It took three attempts to lasso the latch. I jiggled the line until I thought it would hold, then slowly, surely, lifted the lid on the green plastic hopper far enough to look inside.

A pair of wellington boots. Some shapes I couldn't make out in the failing light. I pulled a little harder to get the lid up to vertical. The noose slipped off. The lid banged down.

I hid the line, then banged my fist against the cupboard door. It didn't sound much like a plastic lid slamming shut, but it would do. I counted to five, then did it again. They unlocked the door and charged in, just in time to see my fist strike the cupboard door for a third time. I reeled back and gazed stupidly across the room.

'Now, now, Slimey, that'll do.'

'Missing his mumsie, is he?' said the other.

'Bet she's not missing him. Wishes she'd never had him, filthy paedo.'

They kept this up while I ate burnt fishfingers and sliced white bread. This time I really didn't care.

25

I remade my fishing line several times that evening, and eventually hit on a way of using a second line to draw the noose tight when it was hooked over the latch. However, my warders were active in the morning and I wouldn't be able to try it out until the following afternoon. I went to sleep wondering whether I'd done anything to make them suspicious. Fortunately, they were the kind of geezers who have a superstitious awe of technology and believe that an electronic tag cannot possibly be bypassed – as my futile antics of the previous day had already confirmed. They didn't think I could escape and it made them lazy. They spent too much time snoozing and watching TV and didn't check on me as often as they should.

I acted very chastened and cooperative when they took me to shower and fed me the following day, and perhaps they noticed a change in my demeanour, for the men became morose, as if any mood other than utter dejection was an insult to their custodial skills.

The business of reconnecting the tamper-proof circuit on the broken tag very nearly defeated me. I set the battery aside, then experimented all morning, making tools with splinters of wood from the loose floorboard, and ties with nylon thread. Several times

I nearly flung the bits and pieces out of the window. I cracked it only after working out that I could wedge the components into a gap at the edge of one of the cupboard shelves, which allowed me to work with both hands. I set it up so that I could reattach the battery in one simple step, then fetched my fishing rig from beneath the loose floorboard and set to work.

The lid of the green plastic box came up neatly enough, and I managed to get it to swing back and rest against the wall. I'd been right about the wellington boots. There was also a pair of baggy socks and a few lengths of twine. It didn't look promising but I worked on, moving one of the socks aside and eventually exposing the handle of what looked like a pair of garden secateurs.

I got the twine up first and there was enough to replace most of the cumbersome strips of ticking. Even so, it was almost dark before I had the secateurs in my hand. They were a good tool, old but with a strong blade and a long enough handle to give leverage on the slides of the window frame. A little rhyme occurred to me as I hid my escape kit and straightened up the bed:

> When Ackford appears,
> I'll snip off his ears
> With my secateurs.

By the time I heard a key tap at the lock, I was as close to a picture of sleepy innocence as it is possible to appear in the eyes of a man who thinks you're a paedophile.

* * *

Back in my room after supper, I worked on the window with the secateurs and had the blocks free within twenty minutes. I pushed the window wide open and plotted a route: lower yourself onto the box, put on the boots – they'd taken my shoes away on arrival – across the grass to the garden wall, over and away down the lane.

The last step was to get ready to disable the tag at my ankle as soon as I'd connected up its replacement. If the mother unit clucked for a response and got two cheeps in reply, rather than the one it was expecting, the alarm would certainly go off. How long would I have? It had taken eight seconds for the alarm to sound when I'd broken open the case the previous day, so the interval between clucks was at least that long. But I'd have no way of knowing what point in that interval had been reached when I reconnected the battery. I might have eight seconds or more; I might have none.

This was assuming the replacement tag worked at all. Another unknown.

I picked up the glass and began to cut through the band that secured the tag to my ankle. If I broke the tamper-proof wire embedded in the plastic, that would be that. But I needed to be able to rip the tag from my ankle fast when the moment came. I worked round the tie, sawing gingerly towards the centre until I dared go no further. There was a fair thickness of plastic left, but a hard tug on the case and the band would snap, disabling the tag. Then the mother unit would never know the cheeps that said all's well had come from a chip and a battery laboriously wedged in place by a cupboard shelf.

The TV went off at ten-thirty and by eleven-thirty the house echoed with whistles and grunts from the bruisers disported on their couches and beds. I pushed open the window. It was cold, with a steady, chafing wind humming in the trees. The puddles in the track beyond the wall gleamed like pools of oil. I put the secateurs in my pocket and knelt over the chip and the battery. I ran through the movements my hands would make, from the delicate work on the chip to the violent wrenching of the tag from my ankle. If the alarm went off, so be it. I had no better ideas.

I checked that the chip was securely wedged in place, took several deep breaths to compose myself, then pressed the wires home with a splinter of wood and reached for the tag. The tie cut into the skin of my ankle, snapped. I counted the seconds. Got to eight. Nothing. Ten. Twelve. Silence, blooming softly through the house. Fifteen, twenty. A fox barked from the fields and I've never heard a lovelier sound come coursing through empty air. Thirty seconds. I stared at the chip and the battery, not wanting to breathe in case I disturbed it.

After a minute, I knew it was safe to leave. I stepped softly to the window, swung over the ledge and lowered myself down, then dangled from one arm and reached up with the other to shut the window as far as I could – I didn't want anyone to notice a cold draft under my door. The plastic box was a yard beneath my feet, but suddenly I didn't trust it. I swung sideways and jumped clear. Grabbed the boots from the box, sprinted to the wall and threw them over. Climbed. Picked up the boots and ran, refusing to let my feet flinch from the flintstones embedded in the icy mud.

Two hundred yards from the house, I stopped and pulled on the boots. Too small. I cut slits in the toes with the secateurs, then ran on to the end of the track. From here the lane cut straight through the trees. I had no idea where I was going, but it was sweet relief to feel the rubber boots slapping on the wet road, the night air numbing my hands and cheeks.

After half an hour or so, I emerged from the wood and came to a village – a few streets with a solitary streetlamp by the bus stop. I checked the timetable: Shakers Wood. Two buses a day, running between Great Yarmouth and Sandringham. Judging by the schedule, it was a fair few miles to either. Just along from the bus stop was a cul-de-sac of bungalows with cars parked out front. I would have liked to have stolen one, but the army hadn't yet taught me how to hot-wire a car.

I walked up the cul-de-sac until I came to a ramshackle place with an ancient Triumph Herald parked in front of the garage. As I got closer I saw that the garage doors were ajar. I slipped inside, pulled the doors shut and felt round for a light switch.

The striplight flickered on and revealed a large pile of dilapidated furniture, partly hidden under dust sheets. I was just about to switch the light off and leave when I noticed a bicycle wheel poking out from behind the arm of a sofa. I had to move a stack of broken chairs to get at it, but that done I had in my hands a handsome black racing bike with a leather saddle and the words Jack Taylor emblazoned on the downtube. It was half a size too small for me, there was a cheap braided wire lock round the rear wheel and both tyres were flat. But there was a pump slung under the crossbar... It was worth a try.

The secateurs did for the lock and when I pumped up the tyres, they held air. I lifted the rear wheel and pressed the cranks and the hub spun silently. I hadn't expected to complete my escape on a bicycle, but why not? I replaced the dust sheets, turned off the light, wheeled the Jack Taylor out into the cul-de-sac and climbed aboard.

I'd done some competitive cycling at university; this bike was heavier than I was used to, the rear brake was useless and the gears didn't like changing; but once you got up to speed, it loped along as smooth as a cantering greyhound.

I headed west, because I was going to need TJ Farah's help now, and he lived near the SAS HQ in Hereford. The landscape was flat and I followed dead-straight drover's roads across low-lying fields. A quarter moon appeared from behind a fringe of wind-torn cloud and the marshland glistened as if criss-crossed with silver thread. I had a following wind at my back. Weeting flew by, Hockwold cum Wilton, Prickwillow, Haddenham... Ten, fifteen, twenty miles, the signposts said. I'd taken the bike around two a.m. A person who is reasonably fit can maintain a speed of seventeen or eighteen miles an hour. I was more than reasonably fit and reckoned I could do twenty once I got a rhythm going. By the time they unlocked my empty room at seven-fifteen, I should be a hundred miles away. I didn't think the owner of the bike would notice it was missing, and there'd be no reports of stolen vehicles in the vicinity. So they'd assume I'd gone on foot – implying a search with a radius of forty miles at most. A huge area, but I'd be far outside it.

My mind unclenched, and for a while there was nothing but the sensation of carving through time and space, light as a whistle on the air. I kept to back lanes and B roads, taking the westerly option at every junction, stopping to drink at water butts and farm-yard hoses. Fenstanton, Hail Weston, Thurleigh… The landscape started to roll: big, desolate fields ploughed into jumbled slabs of gleaming earth. The wind backed round to the north and drove the clouds away, and the new air was so cold it was hard to breathe. The wellington boots slapped at my calves. Weariness entered my legs, and every little hill had me panting. The flying Jack Taylor became an old steel bike again.

I had to re-fuel, eat. But it was still an hour before dawn and I had no money. The wind moaned in my face, bearing a smell of wet coal. *This is where you earn it,* I told myself. *You won't get back to Skopje on a tide of euphoria.*

Dawn crept into the sky at my back and that buoyed me for a while, but then the cold was gnawing at my bones and I knew I couldn't go on. I passed a sign to Wellingborough, then came to a halt alongside a Dutch barn stacked with bales. I wheeled the Jack Taylor round to the sheltered side and buried it under a pile of loose straw, then made a burrow for myself and crawled in.

26

Hunger woke me a few hours later. I stood up unsteadily and a rat which had crept close to my body for warmth scurried off across the concrete floor of the barn, shedding bits of straw from its greasy back. I tidied myself and tried to work out what time it was. Nine at least, probably nearer ten. I was officially on the run.

I cycled into Wellingborough and found the railway station. Reasoning that I looked like a beggar, I started to beg. It wasn't the most sensible way to start my life as a fugitive, but by now my hunger was such that no other consideration counted for anything at all. People inspected askance my mutilated boots, dank tracksuit bottoms and grubby T-shirt and most of them diverted accordingly. I thought how quickly I had crossed the border between relative contentment and absolute catastrophe – and perhaps some passers-by saw it, too, because I soon had enough money for a No. 3 Breakfast at the ambitiously named Royal Café, which occupied a noisy berth under the arches just to the south of the station.

After mopping up the last smear of egg, I found an Internet café and paid for half an hour's usage, then got into my server using a tricksy little backdoor I'd installed because people like me are not just paranoid, we are prescient, too. I accessed my cellphone backup and noted down TJ's number, then cycled round in search of a call box. Wellingborough seemed to be phasing them out, and the one I finally found in a semi-industrial quarter of town didn't smell well used – at least not for making phone calls. I fed my last forty pence into the slot and dialled, praying that TJ was back from Kosovo and hadn't already been dispatched on another op.

He took about twenty rings to answer. I heard a child yelling excitedly, *My turn, Dad, it's my turn, isn't it? Dad!*

'Hi, how are you today?' I asked brightly. 'I wonder if you'd have a moment to talk about some financial offers we have exclusively for customers in the Hereford region.'

He gave a deep sigh, read out a number and hung up. It would be a pre-paid phone – all of us in this miserable business assumed that our regular phones were tapped. I called him back, gave him the number of the call box, and finally we could talk.

'It must be fucking hard being you, Jimmy Palatine.'

'You heard what happened?'

'Some. When did they let you out?'

'They didn't.'

'Shit. Any bodies?'

'No. I have to get back to Skop, TJ. I need help.'

'You need more than help, you need a fucking miracle. You need Dr Who and his fucking Tardis.'

'It's not about me. That girl, I made a bad, bad mistake. I handed her over to a gang of pimps. I have to get her out.'

'You do not have to get her out. What you have to do is stay away from Kosovo. They're going to shit all over it anyway.'

'I can ID some of them, including the one who tried to kill me. I know where they're based. At least—'

'I don't want to hear about every half-arsed thing that's happened in your life, Jimmy, so shut the fuck up. I'll help you one time, no more, because you helped my man Azza, who'd not've even needed help if I'd been doing my job. So there it is. Where are you?'

'Wellingborough.'

'Station car park, eighteen hundred tomorrow. Send a pic of your gobsmacked face.' He read out an email address. 'Call me at nine to confirm.'

'Thanks, TJ, I really—'

You said it was my turn, Dad! I heard, then the line went dead. For a moment I felt like that child, needy and persistent, though quite without the charm.

* * *

I went back to the café and sent TJ a passport photo I had on file, then cycled out of Wellingborough. Time is cruel. I had not one single minute to spare, and it had dumped in my path an immovable interlude of thirty hours. Space will not compromise. The distance between a country lane outside Wellingborough and Syrna Street, Skopje, could not be contracted or sidestepped or cajoled into setting its topographical exigencies aside. I was not Dr Who. I had no Tardis. I couldn't risk an airport, so would have to get to the continent by boat, then south by road and rail. Timetables, connections, night trains clanking into sidings for interludes interminable and unexplained. I pedalled slowly.

A sign told me I was thirteen miles from Northampton and I remembered that was where Father Daniel's order was based. Since I had time on my hands, I decided to pay the place a visit. I was still suspicious about the priest, unsure what, if anything, he knew about Syrna Street; but I could go incognito. I stood on the cranks and the Jack Taylor sprang forward. Forty minutes later I rolled up to a pair of iron gates under a stone arch with a brass plate set in the left-hand pillar: *Order of St Hugh*, it read, and beneath it, *Visitors please use the entrance on Huddleston Road.* Beyond the gates, a gainly old Elizabethan manor house had spread its red-brick skirts in an acre of grounds. Towering chimney stacks decorated with elaborate zigzags and crenellations held themselves aloft against the low grey sky. To one side was a small chapel and a graveyard; to the other a short gravel drive led to a low-built annexe.

I cycled past an ornamental garden of geometrical lawns and box hedges and turned into Huddleston Road, then left the Jack Taylor in a hedge on the other side of the road and strolled up the drive. The annexe had half-glazed double doors and I peered inside at a row of wooden chairs and a table set against the wall beneath a reproduction of da Vinci's *The Last Supper*. I tried the door and it opened.

The table was set out with leaflets and photocopied sheets: service timetables, information about something called St Hugh's Tuesday Club, and a history of the order with, on the inside cover, a photograph of a large man with showily arranged white hair and a red face. *Father Wulfstan Murray-Bligh*, read the caption, *Rector General*. I skimmed through the introduction. St Hugh's 'is a mendicant order with active participation in apostolic endeavours, dependent on the alms generously donated by its patrons and supporters,' it explained. On the third page was a photograph of the refuge, taken from far enough away that you couldn't see how run-down it was. 'Opened in May 1996, our refuge in southern Kosovo takes in orphaned children from across this troubled region, and with the grace of God helps them to start new lives. Funds are urgently needed to allow us to continue this important work.'

I heard a key in the lock of the door to the main building. It was opened by a man in priestly garb with close-cropped red hair. His pale face was heavily lined around the mouth and nostrils, as if his expression had set hard after decades of inactivity, though he couldn't have been more than thirty.

'Can I help you?' he asked, his demeanour making it clear that he would rather not.

'I wonder if I could have a glass of water?'

The priest studied me with his small green eyes. 'Wait here, please.'

He went back into the house, shutting the door behind him. A few minutes later, the Rector General himself bustled in.

'What can I do for you, young man? My name is Father Wulfstan.' He held out a beefy hand.

I shook it. 'I just dropped in to see if I could get a drink.'

Father Wulfstan's face was even redder than in the photo, purple almost, and thick-skinned around the jaw. But what the image did not show was how strong and well-proportioned his features were – broad, sloping brow, shapely nose and generous, big-lipped mouth.

'Water you wanted, yes,' he said. 'Father Neil is getting some now. He doesn't trust you, thinks you're a pikey! Good heavens, those boots... I must say, you do look absolutely destitute. Come in for a moment.'

He ushered me into a panelled dining hall lined with portraits of saints and other dignitaries, whose faces, replete with either suffering or disapproval, stared out across a large mahogany table. Father Neil returned, the cheap grey carpet slippers he wore slapping the tiled floor. He handed me a glass of water, then hovered nearby.

The warm atmosphere was releasing from my clothes a smell of old sweat and dirty straw, which seemed especially offensive in this dignified room. Evidently the same odour and the same opinion of it had also occurred to Father Wulfstan. 'May I offer you a change of clothes?' he enquired. 'By good fortune, one of our order is about your size – in fact, looking at you now, I'd say you and he could almost be brothers.'

'Thank you,' I said. 'Much appreciated.'

'Father Neil,' said the Rector General, 'go to Father Daniel's room and find clothes for our visitor. A complete set, shoes included. He can change in the downstairs cloakroom. Then bring him to my study.'

Father Neil did as he'd been ordered without comment – and without altering the rigidly disagreeable expression on his face. Five minutes later, dressed in black trousers, white shirt and pale grey V-neck pullover, and shod in a pair of rubber-soled black shoes, I was shown to the Rector General's study.

It was a grand and opulently furnished room with a leaded bay window occupying most of one wall, a capacious fireplace with a carved stone mantel, and a pair of glass-fronted cabinets containing a display of silverware – crosses, chalices, platters, bowls, thuribles and incense boats all jostling for space on their broad shelves. The Rector General was rummaging at his desk, which was covered completely with hundreds of items of paperwork. These had formed themselves into a kind of miniature dune, with peaks and drifts spreading out onto side tables positioned at strategic points round the desk to catch the overflow. He looked up as I entered.

'A significant improvement, though the jacket is a little tight for you. Please sit.'

He directed me to a red armchair, made a gesture of impatience at the mess on his desk, then came round and dropped his considerable bulk into a sofa opposite. 'A glass of sherry?'

He already had one in his hand, nearly empty. He refilled from a bottle on the coffee table, then poured one for me. I took a mouthful: it had a musky perfume and was unpleasantly sweet. There was a stack of boxes beside his desk, each bearing the same logo as appeared on the bottle in front of us. On the carpet next to the boxes was a neat pile of broken glass.

'Father Neil is making you a sandwich. I am curious about

you, I confess. We don't get many visitors, especially fine young men like you.'

'I'm down on my luck, that's all,' I said, feigning irritation in hope of averting further questions.

'You don't have to tell me if you don't want to,' said Father Wulfstan amiably. 'When you are young, you may fall unexpectedly. Perhaps it is not your fault, but you fall. And you do not know where the fall will end.'

This diagnosis seemed at once kindly and faintly sinister. I decided to wait for the food, eat it and leave.

'You must always believe that our Dear Lord will provide for you,' the Rector General went on. 'And indeed, He will do so very shortly, in the form of Father Neil's sandwich.'

He finished his sherry and poured himself another.

'I read in your leaflet that you have a refuge in Kosovo,' I said.

'Yes indeed, run by Father Daniel, the dear man whose clothes you are wearing.'

'What made you decide to set up there?'

'No doubt you think it odd that a Catholic order should carry on its good works in a region where most of the population are Muslim and the Christians themselves are Orthodox. But I promise you, we are very ecumenical in all we do, most especially when children are involved. Daniel's mother was Albanian, you know, and he speaks the language. I thought it a good opportunity for him to bring succour to his kinsfolk in that war-torn region.'

'So Father Daniel is at the refuge now?'

'Oh yes, he would not leave his poor charges for anything. A man of simple faith and unquestioning obedience to the Order of St Hugh – and to God. I often give thanks that I was able to save him.'

'Save him? What did you save him from?'

'Great unhappiness. Or perhaps despair is the better word. His father was a brute, you see, obsessed with money and free with his fists. When he was fourteen, his mother ran off and took him with her. She left him with us and fled abroad. We've had him ever since. The father was found dead. Well, to be truthful, he was murdered. Suspicion fell on the mother, of course.'

'So he hasn't seen her since?' I said. My own mother had died in a cycling accident when I was a teenager, and I felt drawn to the story of Daniel's loss.

Father Wulfstan abruptly stood up from the sofa – he was surprisingly athletic for such a big man. He picked a small silver bell off a shelf by the door and rang it hard. 'Father Neil!' he shouted, when the summons was not immediately answered. 'Father Neil!'

The young priest appeared, and stood with his hands clasped neatly behind his back.

'Cut two slices of bread and put a piece of cheese between them,' Father Wulfstan said harshly. 'How long can that take? Go on, the poor man is half starved.'

The Rector General returned to his sofa. He took his mane of white hair in both hands and smoothed it luxuriously back over his forehead, drawing the skin of his face so tight that patches of white appeared in his rubicund cheeks.

'Daniel does still cause me concern,' said Father Wulfstan. 'Rather, I suppose, as you would, were you in my charge. May I offer to hear your confession? Of all the sacraments it is the most consoling. You may protest that you are not a Catholic, but God will not turn his back on any heathen who has the grace to reach out to Him.'

I was a Catholic – by upbringing, at least – and hearing these words I was struck by the realisation that everything about the headquarters of the Order of St Hugh reminded me of the boarding school where I had spent my adolescence: the frowning saints and waxed floors, the comfortless warmth and disinfected smell, and even – no, *especially* – this big, genial, sherry-soaked man sat solidly on the sofa opposite me.

Father Wulfstan went prattling on and only hunger kept me in my chair. Just then I heard a scrunching of gravel from somewhere outside.

'Are you expecting a visitor?' I asked.

'No indeed,' said Wulfstan quickly.

Too quickly. I stepped over to the window and saw the bonnet of a police car. I ran back to the dining hall. Voices from beyond the door to the annexe. I crouched behind it and a burly policeman stepped through. I came up fast beside him and drove my fist into his midriff, heard the breath rush from his lungs. I shoved him sideways and stuck out a leg. He tripped and the side of his head crashed against the mahogany table.

I swung the door open. A lanky young constable stood in front of me, his face frozen in a moment of fearful indecision. Our eyes met and I wanted not to hurt him, but there wasn't time. I feinted a punch with my right, and as his hands came up to protect his jaw, stepped in and drove my elbow into his temple. I caught him as he fell and lowered him on top of his colleague, who was leaning against a chair and fumbling for his radio.

'Run if you like,' boomed the Rector General from the far end of the dining hall, 'but your soul will not escape judgement.'

Both policemen's radios were now hissing and yammering away, but their owners weren't in any state to answer. I took the handsets and backed out into the annexe, then stepped over to a side window and checked the gravel drive. One squad car, empty…

I ran outside. A split-second later I was doubled up over my knees and staring at the grey carpet slippers of Father Neil. I squinted up at him. His expression had finally found a reason to change: narrow lips widened to reveal a row of uneven teeth, eyes shining with excitement. The golf club he'd swung into my ribcage was poised for a second blow.

'Don't move,' he said.

I came out of my crouch and my knuckles were dislodging teeth long before the head of the club whipped harmlessly round behind my back. I ripped the shaft from his hands and swung the bulb of wood into his thigh. He gave a yelp and started to whimper and crab away, dragging his dead leg after him. I dropped the club and ran round the back of the house.

As soon as I was out of sight of the driveway, I sprinted to the perimeter and carried on round, keeping below the height of the wall. One of the handsets I dropped in a flower bed; the other chattered away at me: Romeo Oscar Three Two was on its way, then Bravo Lima Two Zero. I reached a place where I had a view of the driveway and looked over in time to see a police BMW hurtle through the gates. The Jack Taylor was about half way between us and there was no cover. The doors flew open and three policemen jumped out. Two of them ran for the door, the third got on his radio. If he turned round, he'd see me. I thumbed the handset and spoke through gritted teeth:

'Suspect went towards the chapel. Repeat, towards the chapel. Shit… Get me an ambulance.'

The one with the radio must have heard me and fallen for the ruse. He called the other two and pointed towards the chapel. As the three of them hurried off on their wild goose chase, I vaulted the wall and sprinted across the road.

ETA one minute. You OK, Mikey?

I pulled the Jack Taylor from the hedge and ran to a side road. Siddington Lane. The corner was overhung by a bulging privet hedge. Once behind it, I'd be safely hidden, at least for a moment or two. A siren was howling from somewhere towards the centre of town. In the periphery of my vision I saw a uniform running across the ornamental garden.

Suspect on foot, male, six four or five, well built, black trousers, grey sweater. Appears unarmed, but violent. Approach with caution.

I got into the lee of the hedge. The siren stopped and I heard a vehicle idling somewhere nearby. The driver gunned the engine and seconds later a Range Rover surged past the neck of Siddington Lane. I hitched the radio to the waistband of my trousers, climbed on the bike and stood on the pedals till the old steel frame got up to speed.

Suspect on foot... Well, no. I listened to them fanning out, dispersing methodically over the streets and side roads and footpaths. This was their patch and no suspect-on-foot was going to give them the slip. *Bravo Lima Two Zero check Siddington Lane, confirm.* Suspect now a mile away and flying. *On Siddington Lane, no sign of him yet.* I reached a crossroads that told me I'd left Northampton four miles behind.

Mikey's radio's missing. Has anyone got Mikey's radio? Repeat, has anyone got PC Wakefield's radio?

I tossed it into a hedge and carried on west.

27

After twenty miles of hard cycling, I began to think I'd got away with it. They'd scour the streets and the countryside around St Hugh's for an hour or two, then assume I'd gone to ground and start on sheds, garages, overgrown shrubberies, patches of wasteland. It could be four or five hours before they admitted to themselves that I'd slipped the net.

Wulfstan must have had an email or fax from one of Clive Silk's lot, telling him to ring immediately if a man answering my description turned up. He'd made the call while I was changing into Father Daniel's clothes. Silk had been very quick off the mark, but I couldn't work out how he knew about the Order of St Hugh. He must have found out that the girl had been at their refuge in Kosovo, though I hadn't told him – he hadn't even asked. There were refugees on the move all over the region and she could have come from anywhere. I'd told Silk I'd left her at 77 Syrna Street, though, and he knew about the Vegas Lounge. Maybe he'd already found a connection between these places and the refuge. In that case, all my worst fears were confirmed.

I'd escaped recapture and had a clean set of clothes to show for my visit to the Order of St Hugh – that was something. On the downside, I also had a couple of damaged ribs, courtesy of Father Neil's golf club. The bones clicked and creaked like cracked knuckles. It's not easy to cycle without moving your torso, but I tried.

* * *

On the run in hostile territory: I'd been trained for this, though not with rural Northamptonshire in mind. They knew roughly where I was now and I would have to go cautiously, but I felt confident they wouldn't find me again. I wasn't going to give myself away by using a cash card because I didn't have one, and they still didn't know about the bike. Keep moving. Avoid human contact. Don't attract attention.

That became difficult when a blowy, spattering kind of rain began to fall. People do cycle in the wet, but not usually dressed in a fertiliser bag they've picked off a barbed-wire fence. After another hour in the saddle, I started to flag and the cold got to me. My shoulders stiffened up, my legs felt like logs of sodden wood, my ribcage ached.

Then I came across a stack of bagged potatoes and onions by a farmyard gate with an honesty box nailed to the post. I robbed it of five pounds and 46 pence and cycled on to the next village. I bought a flimsy plastic pac-a-mac for one pound fifty and spent the rest on food, keeping forty pence back for the phone call to TJ.

I sat behind a hedge in a muddy field, cramming my mouth with pork pie and wondering what to do for the next twenty-four hours. Somewhere warm to sit would be a good start. I'd seen signs for Leicester and although it was twenty miles away, I had plenty of time to kill and there'd be a library that might stay open late. I could hole up there until closing time, then replenish my larder from the rear of a supermarket before finding somewhere to spend the night.

* * *

I sat in the overheated Edwardian grandeur of Leicester Central Library and read newspaper reports of the goings-on at the peace conference in Rambouillet. It was early days, but things didn't look promising. The term 'Chateau fatigue' had been coined to describe the state of the antagonists, who it seemed had not yet summoned the energy actually to speak to each other. MOBILE PHONE LEAKS PLAGUE KOSOVO TALKS ran one headline. Delegates had been rousing themselves from their torpor sufficiently to make off-the-record calls to the media on illicit phones, to the great irritation of the grandees in charge. Reading between the lines, it was clear that the Serbs were calling NATO's bluff: there was no legal basis for demanding peace under threat of war, they'd persuaded themselves; and anyway, the West is timid, its people lazy and fat. They should have looked more closely into Tony Blair's eyes, I thought.

I returned the newspaper to its rack and picked up a book from the returns shelf: *The Murder of Roger Ackroyd* by Agatha Christie. A strange story – a perfectly executed formal dance which ends, not in justice, but with Poirot, studiously genteel to the last, coercing the murderer into suicide. It kept me occupied until six, and I was casting around for another to take me through to closing time at nine when I spotted an area of shelves given over to a newspaper archive of large bound volumes and tins of microfiche.

Father Daniel was in his mid-thirties. He'd been left with the Order of St Hugh when he was fourteen, about twenty years ago – 1978 or '79. I found the 1978 tin and loaded the first reel onto the reader. They had only national newspapers, but still, an unsolved murder, a fugitive wife... The reel clattered in its guides and the pages streamed by. It took me two hours to find it, a story from the *Lowestoft Journal* syndicated in the *Daily Telegraph*:

Trawlerman found dead at Oulton Broad home

The body of John Cady, age 53, has been found at his home on Dell Road, near Oulton Broad South Station. Police were called when fellow trawlerman Phillip Nash reported that Cady's boat, the *Suffolk Rose*, had been left unattended since his return to port on Sunday. 'I've never known John leave the *Rose* for so long,' said Nash. 'He loved that boat more than anything.'

On searching his Dell Road house, police found the body of a man, presumed to be Cady. Early reports indicate that he had been repeatedly stabbed, and police have opened a murder enquiry. His wife Irene and their 14-year-old son Daniel are missing, and police have appealed for information about their whereabouts. Irene Cady, who is of Albanian descent, came to Lowestoft in 1965 and found employment as a chambermaid at the Royal Hotel, where she is thought to have met her future husband. Their Dell Road neighbours say the Cadys kept themselves to themselves. 'Irene always had a smile for you, and she kept her house very neat,' said Elsie Gardiner, 72, 'but they never had visitors.'

Daniel Cady had recently started work on his father's boat. 'John was old school,' said Nash. 'He had a bit of a reputation among the local hands. But we were shocked when he took his son to sea. The deck of a working trawler is no place for a boy.'

The article was dated 16 October 1979. I looked in vain for a follow-up – Irene Cady had escaped arrest, it seemed, and the police never looked for anyone else. She must have left her boy with the Order of St Hugh in Northampton, then fled the country somehow. I wondered why she had chosen that place. It wasn't convenient; nor was the Order well known. At any rate, Father Wulfstan had evidently not handed poor Daniel over to the police – a considerate if risky decision.

I left the newspaper section and went in search of the library's solitary Internet terminal. I had to wait my turn, but when I ran a search for the Cady family, I got lucky: a librarian and amateur genealogist from Maine had lovingly traced his family history and set it out in a website entitled *All Things Cady: Our Family Story*.

It turned out that John Cady was the only son of a man who, in the decades following the Second World War, had owned half the Lowestoft fishing fleet. Most of the boats had been laid up or sold off during the sixties, but it was a fair guess that, far from being a modest solo trawler captain, John Cady had been a wealthy man. If that was the case, then his fortune would very likely have passed to Father Daniel.

* * *

I spent a cheerless night in an empty lock-up, then cycled on to a village a few miles south of town and called TJ.

'Change of RV. Car park of the Peeping Tom in Burton Mawsley. Six miles north-west of Wellingborough. Look for the water tower. Same time and don't be late.'

'Why, what happened?'

'You tell me. No, wait. Don't tell me, Jimmy, for I do not want to know.'

He hung up. The cracked perspex window of the call box looked out over a rainswept road, a clump of cottages with tiny windows and tiny painted doors, an empty bus shelter, a shop sign shuddering in the squally wind. Why was there no one else I could turn to? A grim, reproachful kind of loneliness flooded through me. I thought of the girls I'd been out with: Corinna, for instance, who looked into my eyes and asked me what I was thinking, first with curiosity and affection, then with mournful resignation, finally, terminally, with exasperation. What was it about me that she had liked and wanted? And what had she seen that made her step away? Or not seen… Making love to me was like opening the door to someone and finding they weren't actually there, another girl had said. I was empty, then, a void, the human embodiment of my definitively soulless career.

I chewed on a stale croissant I'd fished out of a bin at the back of a Tesco store the night before – as poor a consolation as I no doubt deserved, but it made me feel better. Back on the Jack Taylor, I meandered south-east, navigating by the drone of traffic on the A6, brooding and cursing this limbo into which I'd been pitched. At four in the afternoon, I saw the water tower, a white-ribbed cylinder like a giant chef's hat, and pedalled into Burton Mawsley, past the Peeping Tom, then on to a copse just outside the village. I hunched under my pac-a-mac and watched the crows tumble around the treetops like scraps of charred paper, until darkness fell and they settled to their roosts, swayed this way and that by the bitter February air.

* * *

TJ Farah isn't as mean as I've depicted him. It's just that in the space of ten days I'd idolised him as the very model of the supremely effective combat soldier, then resented and mistrusted him, then feared him as the embodiment of a world of casual savagery that had sucked me almost unawares into its dark heart. Now, confounding that panoply of ill-assorted feelings, I depended on him.

In the pub car park was an immaculate sapphire blue Jaguar, parked up with its nose facing the exit, two men inside. I got closer and saw Peanut in the passenger seat. Neither of them looked round as I climbed into the back. The interior was like the late-night bar of an executive hotel, all cream leather upholstery and ambient blue lighting. They were watching a mixed martial arts film on a portable DVD player.

'Have a look at the neck on that, Jimmy. Like a fucking hippo.'

'S'why the fat fuck can't get out the way,' said Peanut. 'One more chop to the teeth, he'll be eating from a liquidiser.'

'Peanut here is thinking of going in for this MMA stuff when he retires,' TJ remarked. 'I've told him after about five seconds with one of these steroid queens he's going to get pissed off and go in for the kill. What d'you reckon, Jimmy?'

'I should imagine that's against the rules.'

'There you are, what did I say?'

'What the fuck does Jimmy P know about it?'

'Peanut, it's play-fighting,' said TJ. 'Not fucking murder.'

He handed me an envelope containing a passport – my new name was Anthony Skinner – and two hundred pounds in cash.

'What's the matter,' he said, 'you expecting a good-luck card signed by all the lads?'

'I can't get the girl we found out of my head, that's all. Thanks for this, TJ.'

'There's a hundred other girls like her dying a fucking horrible death right now, Jimmy. Bombs, bullets, fires, fists, whatever. You can't save them.'

'I saved this one. Then I handed her over to a gang of pimps.'

TJ was regarding me thoughtfully. 'You look like you're sitting on a thistle.'

'Cracked rib.'

'Breathing OK?'

I nodded.

'It'll pass. I got called in by some little pimp called Silk. Know him?'

'My MI6 liaison,' I said.

'Practised his whole fucking playbook on me – promises of this, threats of that, hints of the other. Then he tells me there's matters of significant national interest at stake and it's my patriotic duty to turn you in.'

'Did he say why?'

'Take a wild guess. Do your own frigging patriotic duty, I wanted to tell him, if you even know what it is.'

'Came for me, too,' said Peanut. 'Puddle of wank.'

'They arrested me on a charge of child abduction,' I said nervously.

'Bollocks. You know something, or Her Majesty's Secret Slimeballs think you do.'

'I wish I did.'

'Might help to work out what it is.'

No one spoke for a minute. Play-fighting grunts filled the interior of the car.

'What happened out there, TJ?'

'Plenty.'

'That night in the woods.'

'The Bura boys? They thought they were the most evil mother-fuckers in southern Kosovo. Turned out we were.'

'That's it? Like gangs on a council estate? I thought we were soldiers.'

'What the fuck do you think soldiers are? Gangs, tribes, races, nations – they all need to do some killing every so often.'

'And when they do,' said Peanut, 'it's murderous bastards like us get the work.'

'So I am *one of us*, then,' I said uneasily. 'I thought you weren't convinced.'

'I like you, Jimmy,' said TJ. 'You're the silliest fucking Rupert I've come across in a good many years, but OK, Ollie was right, you're one of us. Most people can't kill – most soldiers can't kill. You train them to do it, but if they ever do, they hate themselves for it. They fall apart – you've seen it, we all have. But you can kill, Jimmy Palatine. I've got a photo of you doing that lame fuck with the corpse tattoo. You press your blade against his bare skin and you lean in. You're not bothered by his pleading eyes or his orphaned baby daughter or whether you'll go to hell for it. No, you're working out the best way to get the tip of your knife into his gristle. So you *lean in*. Like you're pushing a mate's car or something.'

I remembered the scene. It had set up camp in my mind, every detail saturated with its own slippery but indelible meaning. A cold, cold memory that made me shiver in my plush leather seat. Could you not kill just because you had to? How did TJ know I wasn't falling apart? My head felt swollen with unwanted feelings. TJ fired the ignition and the instrument cluster winked, illuminating the smooth underside of his jaw. The world might be handed over to murderous bastards and their paymasters, but the oil pressure was good, the airbags were present, the brakes were functioning correctly. I'd never felt such a gulf between the things around me and the things within. I heard TJ sigh, and when I looked over, I saw how hard his face was set, even in repose.

'Not many like us, Jimmy,' he said. 'There's Silks fucking everywhere, but Farahs and Palatines? Not so many.'

'What about Peanuts?' asked Peanut.

'Only one, thank fuck – or three, if you count your nan's haemorrhoids.'

Peanut aimed a jab at his ribs, which TJ was laughing too much to parry.

'Out you get,' he said to me when he'd recovered. 'I've got another life to live, one that doesn't involve sitting in a pub car park with your miserable face for company.'

'What happens to that photo you took?'

'This one?'

TJ pulled a print from his shirt pocket and passed it to me. I didn't like what I saw. It was all much too clear.

'Goes in the vault, Captain,' he said.

'The vault?'

'Insurance policy – keeps you Ruperts honest. No one needs to see it.'

'S'long as you behave y'self,' said Peanut.

'So you guys have a whole stash of—'

'Out. No point telling you not to do anything stupid because you can't help yourself. But keep it simple, right?'

28

I retrieved the Jack Taylor from the copse, ate the rest of my food, and rode east. The moon was weak again, and dogged by cloud. I studied the contours of the road ahead and was careful to avoid any rut or ridge that might throw me off or buckle a wheel – or if not that, cause bits of rib to grind against each other. My mission had begun, and I was not to be delayed by such things. I must find the girl and restore her to a place of safety. I must do whatever it took. I'd be *one of us*. I'd be a murderous bastard. When it was over, there'd come a time for searching through the unshriven byways of my soul. Until then: *keep it simple*.

The pac-a-mac was not much more than a few shreds of plastic now, so I cycled into Huntingdon and spent some of the money TJ had given me on a black rain jacket and a JCB-logo baseball cap. A fine rain hung in the air, so the hedgerows and trees and fields and the shapes of church towers and country manors looked soft and grainy, like pictures on an old television set. I ate in the saddle, stuffing down bread and cheese and lumps of sodden cake that fell apart in my fingers.

The food kept me going for thirty miles or so, then I started slowing down and had to snatch a few hours' sleep in a stable somewhere south of Newmarket. I got to Harwich just before eleven a.m. There was a golf club to the south of the international port. I cycled up the short tarmac driveway and locked the Jack Taylor in a rack behind the clubhouse, sheltered by a corrugated plastic awning. That bike deserved a safe berth after all the favours it had done me. Then I set off round the perimeter of the course until I reached a small network of streets alongside the docks.

I soon found what I was looking for: a café that served lorry drivers waiting for the ferry over to the Hook of Holland. I ordered spaghetti Bolognese and sat down opposite an old trucker. His forearms bore tattoos which had softened and spread into the wrinkled, tawny skin. He was small for a trucker, and looked dead beat. For sixty pounds he agreed to let me hide out in the sleeping compartment of his cab. He said his name was Luke, that he was from Leytonstone, and that he knew David Beckham's uncle. Then he clammed up.

His lorry was parked in a holding area outside the terminal gates, along with thirty or so others. It wasn't fenced, but there were cameras everywhere, mounted on high posts, snouts cocked at the apron of tarmac below.

'Thirty-six-wheeler Daf, blue trailer.' He pointed it out.

'I'll join you in half an hour,' I said. 'Shake hands, so it looks like we're parting company.'

I walked back the way we had come, looking for a way to get to the door of the Daf without being caught on CCTV. There was a children's playground at the end of a residential street at right angles to the lorry park, and I saw that from there I could cross the road and get in amongst the vehicles under cover of a row of empty containers. The rain was good: no one was out unless they had to be, and those that had to be had their heads down. Once I was out of sight of the cameras, I walked around for twenty minutes, then circled back to the playground and took off my jacket and baseball cap. I sloped past the containers to Luke's truck. Maybe the cameras hadn't seen me, but Luke had: the passenger door swung open and I pulled myself up into the cab. He had the curtains drawn.

'You can give me the sixty now.'

I handed over three twenties and he pointed to a steel ladder that led to a narrow hatchway in the roof of the cab. The sleeping compartment had about six inches of headroom and smelled of dirty feet and engine oil. I lay down on a vinyl-covered mattress in the semi-darkness and went to sleep, only to be woken an indeterminate amount of time later by a series of thumps from below.

'We're going through. You snore like that, they'll think I've got meself hitched up to a pig.'

The brakes spat air and the lorry pulled forward. We rolled through the gates and into the terminal, on for a few hundred yards, then bounced to a standstill. After a ten-minute wait I heard the cab door open.

'All right, Lucky? You get those tickets you were after?'

'Nah. Fucking tout. Daylight robbery, the price he wanted.'

'Always next year.'

Bangs from the rear of the trailer, then the lorry rumbled down the gangway onto the ferry. Tyres squeaked on the rubbed steel of the car deck, shouts echoed off the walls, chains clanked. Lucky poked his head up through the hatch.

'I'm going to the bar. Sleep tight.'

* * *

Lucky was well known on the Dutch side, too, and no one wanted to poke around in his private sleeping quarters. Anyway, they weren't looking for renegade intelligence officers, but for illegal immigrants clinging to the chassis or suffocating inside the container. I found out he was going to Mannheim, and for an extra tenner he took me there – dropping me at a service station where I could get a lift south. By dusk I was in Frankfurt; an overnight ride in the company of a voluble Slovenian took me to Klagenfurt; I made Zagreb by lunchtime.

The direct route to Skopje was via Belgrade, but I could imagine the Serbian authorities taking great pleasure in disrupting the itinerary of a lone Englishman with a passport that might not withstand close scrutiny. I changed my remaining cash at the bus station and got a ticket for Dubrovnik. The coach ground laboriously south, exiting the main road every half an hour to lumber into some sleepy town. At the newly established border with Montenegro, we stopped altogether. The crossing was closed – no one knew why. It would reopen at six-thirty a.m.

A man of my size could occupy the seat in only one position – which happened to cause my cracked rib to flex with every intake of breath and again with every exhalation of breath. At seven-forty-five an official in a uniform of comic grandiosity checked our documents and handed out forms. At eight-thirty he collected the forms. At ten-fifteen we lumbered into Montenegro. An hour later, we lumbered out.

The Dubrovnik–Tirana leg was no better. There was an overnight bus to Tetovo, a few hours west of Skopje, but our driver was determined we wouldn't make it and we didn't. I lay on a bench inside the bus station and tried to sleep while maintaining a sufficiently ferocious expression to deter the beggars and robbers who haunted the place. It seemed to work. The damaged ribs did some knitting overnight, and when I woke I was able to stretch a bit without gasping for mercy.

The bus left at dawn and was rammed full. I stood swaying in the aisle while a boy of about seven ransacked the pockets of my trousers. When I frowned at him, he froze; when I looked away, he started again. Eventually, I simply grinned and pulled out the pockets to confirm that, as he surely knew after half an hour of indiscreet rummaging, they were empty. He grinned back. I gave him a half-packet of biscuits from my carrier bag and he ate them immediately, then handed back the wrapper. Elbasan, Librazhde, across the border into Macedonia, then north along the lake to Struga and Ohrid, where a number of elderly holidaymakers disembarked with a cargo of tightly clamped bags. Kichevo, Gostivar, Tetovo. After the long, disjointed journey, the proximity of Skopje now seemed miraculous.

My final bus ride started an hour later. I watched through the window as the sky swung down and darkness drew in, softening the contours of fields and woods. We bustled through the still, sombre landscape, a little box on wheels, splaying the road ahead with a waxy yellow light and leaving a brief outburst of engine noise in its wake.

29

I hadn't even got off the bus in Skopje before I saw someone I knew: an American NATO official who several weeks earlier had subjected me to an inept attempt to pry out some intel on Serbian military supply lines into Kosovo, because he suspected (correctly) the British knew more than we were sharing. I pulled the baseball cap low over my face and joined a crowd of people jostling their way out of the terminal to fight for a place in the bus queues on Nikola Karev Street.

My plan was to walk to Maria's. Her restaurant was directly below my apartment, which was quite likely under surveillance, but the kitchen gave onto an enclosed backyard accessible via a derelict theatre on the parallel street. It would be pleasant to sit in Maria's apartment, eat the daily special and drink a carafe of her especially oily wine while she scolded me for whatever it was I deserved scolding for and her children hunted for an opportunity to amuse themselves at my expense. Tomorrow morning, I could start to set the world to rights.

A few yards outside the terminal I stopped. Staring up at me from the pavement was a picture of a girl. Even in the gloomy light from the streetlamps overhead, I recognised her.

The girl I'd left at Syrna Street.

I picked it up – a leaflet, torn and smeared by the feet of passers-by. It did not show the miserable, frightened bundle I had carried out of Kosovo – just an ordinary girl having a picnic on a sunny summer's day. But there was no mistaking the pretty oval face and lustrous eyes; she'd even tucked her black hair behind one ear, exactly as she had when I'd given her a plate of pasta in my apartment. I turned the leaflet over. *Have you seen this girl?*

I looked quickly around me, heart thumping in my chest. Whoever was handing these out might not be far away. I searched the thronged concourse, then started to walk round the terminal. On the second corner stood a slight woman in her mid-thirties, wearing a dark blue parka with a fur-trimmed collar. Her face was pale as milk, her hair dishevelled. I watched her accost a tall, smartly dressed man – I had the impression he would usually brush such people off, but there was something about her that compelled his attention. Even from forty or fifty yards away, I could see her dark eyes glittering, the graceful arc of her neck as she looked up at him, the gravity of her demeanour. I too was transfixed. The man took the leaflet and listened politely, before moving off with an apologetic shrug. Her head dropped, then she braced herself for another attempt on another shoulder-shrugging passer-by.

I hurried over to her. The bleakness in her face was frightening.

'I have seen this girl.'

'You've… Katarina…' Her eyes searched mine with such clarity that I felt stripped bare.

'Is there somewhere we could talk?' I asked.

'Yes. Is Katarina all right? Is she…?'

'She was when I saw her. That was about two weeks ago.'

'Where is she now?'

'I'm not sure. There's a refuge in Kosovo, not far from the border—'

'Come back to my apartment.' She took me suddenly by the wrist, as if frightened I might try to escape. 'My car's not far away. This refuge, is she there now, do you know?'

'I… Perhaps. I'm not sure. I've only just got here,' I said lamely.

'You will help me find her?'

I nodded. She led me to her car, a decrepit yellow Fiat parked in a side street five minutes' walk from the bus terminal, and we climbed in.

'What is your name?' she asked.

'James Palatine.'

'I am Anna Galica, Katarina's mother. I want to ask you many questions, James Palatine, but now I am so agitated… I don't think I can drive and listen to you at the same time. I am not familiar with Skopje.'

She turned the key and the starter motor pulsed hectically for a few seconds, started to die, stopped, turned over again. I felt huge inside her car, a vast, sweaty thing, reeking of desperation, scalp skewed against the roof, legs crammed into the footwell. A series of grumpy coughs from the exhaust and the engine whined into life. She eased the gearstick forward until it clunked into first, and pulled out sharply into the street.

30

As we careered across Skopje, I took a surreptitious look around the interior of the car: it was strewn with books, files and papers, the remains of meals eaten on the go – sandwich packs, apple-juice cartons, and perhaps a dozen limp ice-cream tubs from a place called the Yankee Doodle Dandy Diner. *Where sprinkles come free!* it said in multi-coloured letters on the lids. A blue vinyl overnight bag lay on the back seat, half covered by a damp raincoat. The radio was making a tuneless whistling noise and an empty wine bottle clanked against a seatbelt buckle at every bump in the road.

We drew up at a set of traffic lights and she said: 'I can't wait. At least tell me what were you doing in Kosovo when you saw Katarina?'

She looked over at me and I felt a current of empathy pass between us – made all the more powerful by the expression in her large, unblinking eyes. The reserve with which people usually guard themselves from strangers was entirely absent. She was sad and angry, she was weary, she was struggling to keep her spirits up. She was determined. Her eyes showed all this and did not care who saw it.

'I'm in the British Army,' I said. 'Or at least, I was. I'm not so sure right now.'

'You ran away?'

'Yes. I've been accused of something I didn't do and—'

'It doesn't matter. How well do you know Skopje? Right now, I am lost.' She brought the car to a standstill outside a shuttered mini-market and indicated the glovebox. 'There's a map. The address of the apartment is written on the front.'

I extracted the map and looked for an interior light to read it by. She pushed open her door and the light came on. 'Nothing in this horrible car works properly. And I see it doesn't fit you very well.'

'I have to say it'd be more comfortable without the seat.'

She gave me a dutiful smile, from which I saw that she was glad I had made the joke, even if she wasn't disposed to laugh at it.

'I don't really know Skopje. I lived here for a few weeks, that's all. Do you have a rough idea where we are?'

'The apartment is in Čair, off Kemal Sejfula, at the north end. We can't be far away.'

I squinted at the tiny lettering.

'They teach you to read maps in soldier school, I expect.'

I found it eventually and we pulled back into the traffic, then quickly got lost again. I had to keep opening the door to turn the reading light on.

'Turn the map upside down,' she advised, 'if it helps.'

Čair was in the old town, a tangle of run-down, cobbled streets sandwiched between the Gazi Baba Park and the Ilinden army barracks – where weeks that seemed like years ago I'd been to a reception for the officers of foreign army units stationed in Skopje. Our Macedonian hosts had drunk too much, and there'd been a lot of strutting and bristling, punctuated with bursts of gaudy laughter.

Eventually we parked outside a six-storey concrete block with a peeling ochre balcony on each floor. I refolded the map and tried to cram it back into the glovebox, but it snagged on a sheet of printed A4. Anna was already standing on the pavement, waiting to lock the car. The paper had a badly photocopied image of a Toyota Invincible exactly like the one I had driven up into the forest with the Bura in pursuit – fat wheel arches, polished chrome, brutish snout. I tucked it under the map, shut the flap and got out. Why would Anna Galica have a picture of such a thing? The fantasy wheels of a man in her life, perhaps. Anyway, I surely didn't know her well enough to enquire about the contents of her glovebox. We entered the building and climbed the stairs to the fourth floor.

'My friend Eleni will think the worst when she sees you,' she said. 'This is her uncle's apartment – his wife died a few years ago. He's in California, waiting for things to settle down.'

Before she could unlock the door, it was opened by a large woman dressed in a burgundy woollen skirt and an elaborately embroidered cream cardigan. She had a broad, kindly face with lightly pockmarked cheeks. Her inquisitive brown eyes surveyed me suspiciously, then Anna reproachfully.

'This is James,' said Anna. 'He's going to help us.'

She stepped past her friend, drawing her by the arm towards a room on the far side of a tiny hallway. I shut the door behind me and stood there listening to them arguing in Albanian. Eleni spoke in a sensible tone undermined by a trailing edge of hysteria. Anna was matter-of-fact. After several minutes, she beckoned me in.

'Come, James. We're making some tea.'

The kitchen had a small blue-painted cupboard, numerous wooden shelves lined with strips of floral wallpaper, a narrow stainless-steel sink and an ancient enamelled stove.

'Sit down, please,' said Anna. 'You make everything look so small.'

I took a chair at a wooden table set against one wall. In front of me was a stack of leaflets. Eleni was filling a kettle and declining to meet my eye. Everything was in abeyance, and I sensed that, as much as she longed to hear news of her daughter, Anna feared what I might tell her. For now, she could hope and believe that the arrival of this stranger was the first step on the road to a happy reunion with her daughter; once I'd said what I knew, that consolation might be exposed as a cruel fiction.

'We'll be more comfortable next door,' she said suddenly, and hurried out of the kitchen. Eleni gestured for me to follow, an expression of deep foreboding on her matronly face.

The little sitting room was like a shrine to the embroidery skills of Eleni's deceased aunt, and to the artistic skills of Eleni's uncle who, it seemed, spent his retirement painting watercolours of Macedonian ruins – there was a work in progress on an easel by the door to the balcony. I spent a lot of time looking round vaguely at the embroidered rugs, cushions and antimacassars, and the pallid pictures of once-glorious things because I didn't want to meet Anna's eyes. I'd been over my story a thousand times, but never in a form tailored for the girl's mother. I should have told her everything, of course. Instead, I kept stalling... Though I barely faltered over the reasons for my brief tour of southern Kosovo, which, for political and military reasons, I had most reason to conceal.

'You were planning to bomb Kosovo – before Rambouillet even started?' Eleni said. 'How could you dare!'

'Not planning, preparing,' I said feebly.

Eleni pulled her cardigan tight and flexed the muscles of her heavy shoulders. I told them how I'd found Anna's daughter shivering in a ditch not far from Father Daniel's refuge – I didn't say how close she was to death – and taken her to my apartment, where I'd fed her spaghetti with tomato sauce, and in the morning borrowed clean clothes for her to wear. Anna drank in my words and the tears streamed down her cheeks. What a fraud I felt, then, seeing in eyes swollen with emotion how she took me for a saviour, a guardian angel, a knight in shining armour. How could I disabuse her of those comforting delusions? How could I tell her that I'd left her daughter in the hands of a pimp and gone back to Kosovo to play the murderous bastard in a night of slaughter in a forest outside the town of Kric? And then, how my clumsy attempts to undo my terrible mistakes had led me to the squalid backrooms of the Vegas Lounge? Better for her, I told myself all too readily, to believe that I was the hero she needed me to be.

Eleni consoled her friend with interjections in Albanian and hugs and squeezes which Anna pushed away in her eagerness to draw my story out. When I got to the point where the sleepy-eyed blonde took Katarina into the house on Syrna Street, I stopped again.

'That's as much as I can tell you. Your daughter was OK when I saw her last. I'm sorry, but I don't know what's happened since.'

'But you saved her life,' said Anna. 'You saved Katya's life. I…' She wiped her eyes. 'It's a miracle that you found her. And now I've found you. I'd almost given up hope. Thank you, James, thank you. So now, she's back at the refuge, do you think?'

'We must hope so.'

The stilted quality of this reply did not escape Eleni's notice.

'What do you mean, *hope so*?' she said sharply. 'I am sure you checked.'

'I couldn't get hold of Father Daniel. Then I had to go back on tour for a few days…'

'To *prepare* the destruction of Kosovo.'

'Eleni, let James finish. It's not his fault.'

'And after your tour?' said Eleni haughtily.

'That was when I got into trouble. They'd seen me crossing the border into Macedonia with a girl— With your daughter. They thought I was… Well, I don't exactly know what they thought, but I was arrested.'

'That's ridiculous,' said Anna. 'You explained, of course?'

I could see from Eleni's face that she thought it ridiculous, too, though not for the same reasons. She saw the loose ends of my story flapping pathetically, and she feared that the whole edifice of half-truths was about to unravel.

'I tried, but they took me back to England and locked me up. I escaped – I'd only just arrived in Skopje when I saw the leaflet and found you.'

'Why did you escape?' asked Eleni. 'Since you have not done anything wrong.'

'Anna's daughter is the only person who can prove that. I came back here to find her.'

'I must call Father Daniel now,' said Anna. 'Do you have the number?'

I didn't. And I dreaded the call being made.

'I will look for it,' said Eleni. 'Father Daniel is a member of the Order of St Hugh, you said. And what was the village called?'

'I don't know, we passed through very quickly.'

I hadn't told them about the scene in the farmhouse, either. Eleni produced a map and I showed her the place. The farmstead wasn't named, but the church opposite the refuge was: the Orthodox Church of the Holy Saviour and Saint Panteleimon. She went to a small wrought-iron chair by the window, picked a telephone off the floor and dialled a number with a determined air.

'You can check with Maria at the café – she didn't see Katarina, but she lent me the clothes. I know this must be a lot to take in…'

Anna stood up and walked rapidly out into the hallway, then rapidly back again. 'James, I already believe you. Eleni doesn't want me to get my hopes up, that's all.' Eleni confirmed this by glowering at me from her iron chair. 'I've waited so long for something good to happen, and now suddenly you arrive and it feels as if I lost her only moments ago and I want to hold her in my arms again so much I can't bear it.'

Directory enquiries took a long time to answer. Anna paced the room and kept stopping to look at me, as if she doubted that I really existed. She made more tea, then told me I must be hungry and brought some dry crackers and a tube of fishpaste. I went to the bathroom to clean myself up and on the way back cannoned into a side table and sent a small collection of china horses sliding to the floor.

'What happened to your daughter?' I asked, once the horses had been tidied up.

'Katarina,' she said. 'You must call her Katarina.' She told me how a gang of Serbian militia had snatched Katarina from a Roma village where she'd been staying with her grandmama, how she'd managed to trace the vehicle they'd been driving, a Toyota Invincible with Road Muscle Body Kit, how they'd seen its charred remains being towed from the forest near Kric after a KLA attack.

Things slid into place, then, assumptions and deductions realigning themselves like a puzzle of sliding panels in a gothic chamber. It was the Bura crew who had taken Katarina; and it wasn't the KLA who had attacked them but I and my SAS comrades on a rogue mission of revenge. I remembered the chief's office, the crucifix and girly pics, the seatless chair and box full of knuckledusters. A sick feeling crawled in my stomach.

'Katarina's uncle rescued me from Kric one night. We got into a fight. When was it you found her?'

'The twenty-eighth.'

She went to the kitchen and returned with a newspaper cutting. 'That was the night before the attack.'

I know, I killed one of them myself, I thought. But what good would it do Anna to know this?

'And then on the twenty-ninth you took her to this place on Syrna Street. So Katya can't have been in Kric when I was looking for her there – I didn't go until the thirty-first. I was so afraid I'd alerted them and they'd taken her somewhere else.'

'Hush,' said Eleni. 'I can't find a number for the refuge, but I'm calling the Order of St Hugh in England.'

'I was sure I heard her cry out,' Anna said mournfully.

She stood up. We waited in silence, listening to the faint *burr burr* of the phone. I imagined the Rector General's study in the stately old Elizabethan manor, its handsome window and ranks of polished silver. The phone rang out and I felt an ignominious sense of relief.

'It's late,' said Eleni gently. 'We can try in the morning. They will help us. Certainly they will help us.'

'Katarina's at the refuge right now,' said Anna, with a bravado that shamed me to the core. 'I am so sure of it. If we can't get Father Daniel on the phone, we'll just go and pick her up tomorrow.'

'We should visit the house in Syrna Street first,' said Eleni.

'I'm going to see Katarina soon,' Anna said, looking at each of us in turn. 'I feel in my heart I will.'

31

I slept deeply, without dreams or interludes of wakefulness, but in the morning I found that my feet had snapped the armrest off the end of the sofa. I was searching in the upholstery for some bolt or bracket by which I might reattach it when Eleni came in, dressed for the day in another of her sensible skirts and armoured cardigans. She stopped to observe me kneeling by the stricken sofa, then stepped out onto the balcony to smoke a cigarette.

'You don't know your own strength, I see,' she said, coming back inside but leaving the door open behind her so that the room quickly filled with cold air.

'I'll replace it, as soon as I can.'

'It must be repaired. It is an ugly thing, but to Uncle Semyon it is the place where his wife sat. The caretaker can do it. What will Father Daniel say when I speak to him?'

'I don't know,' I replied, but the lie was a poor thing.

'Katarina is not at the refuge.'

'I don't know that.'

'Why do you suspect it?'

'I didn't like the look of the house where I left her. It felt wrong.'

'But anyway, you left her there.'

'I had to get back on duty. And there were queues at the UNHCR building.'

'Queues?'

She hid her annoyance by returning to the balcony for another cigarette. I joined her. The bleached-orange rooftops of Skopje lay before us like a dirty old quilt tented by ranks of bony knees.

'I think you are a straw, Captain Palatine, which Anna is clutching at,' she said. 'I have the saying correct?'

I nodded.

'This makes me sad. I will call the priest now, before she wakes up.'

She found a notepad and biro and set it open on the wrought-iron chair, then went to the bathroom, came back, smoked another cigarette, and finally managed to sit down and pick up the phone. Her call was answered straight away. By Father Neil, I guessed. She spoke insistently and had to repeat her demand several times.

'This is a serious matter,' she said eventually. 'The Order of St Hugh may not obstruct our search for a missing child.'

There was a short delay, then Eleni took down a number and read it back. I recognised it as the refuge landline. She thanked Father Neil and put down the receiver, lifted it again and dialled. Someone answered and they spoke in Albanian. The look on Eleni's face confirmed what I already knew.

'Katarina is not there.'

Eleni hung up and her handsome face crumpled. She looked forlornly about her. 'The refuge is closed. They have not seen her. A horrible man. He did not listen. He said the children have gone and he could not help us. Then he put the phone down.'

'Did he say where they'd gone?'

She couldn't answer but simply shook her head.

When she had recovered a little, she tut-tutted at my travel-worn clothes and produced a sweatshirt and pullover of her Uncle

Semyon's from a chest in the hallway. He was a big man, evidently. She made coffee and we ate sweet rolls with cherry jam in unhappy silence, interrupted by Eleni observing several times that at least Anna was enjoying a really good night's sleep. That was a luxury she hadn't enjoyed since... She spilled jam on her cardigan and scraped it off with a buttery knife. I went to the bathroom, came back and straightened the sofa. She smoked another two cigarettes. After the second, she rushed straight across the sitting room and into the hallway.

'Anna, Anna!'

I sat on the sofa, gripped by an urge to blunder from the claustrophobic apartment and lie alone with my sins somewhere beneath the yawning sky. The cries from the bedroom across the hallway wrapped themselves round my head like a skein of softest, stifling silk, tamping down my senses until a wailing darkness was all that remained. And the sound commingled in my mind with the keening noise that had filled the air outside the farmhouse and drawn us down to the scene of slaughter below. The sound of a mother's anguish, bright and pure as the blood from a new-made wound.

'If you want to go, you should. Go now.'

Eleni, standing over me, gripping her shoulders. I looked up and saw determination in the set of her mouth, anxiety fluttering in her eyes.

'If you stay, you may not sit with your head hanging down like a cow at milking.'

I met Anna's eye when she emerged from the bedroom. 'I'm sorry about this,' I mumbled. 'I wish—'

She waved me aside. 'I can't talk about this now, James. I still believe you will help us – that's all. Go to this house on Syrna Street and... I don't know. Do whatever it is you do. Then come back and tell me, will you? Please?'

I promised her I would.

'Eleni, do you have a spare key for James?'

Eleni fetched one from the sitting room and handed it over with a reproachful look.

'Do you need money?' asked Anna.

I admitted that I did. She reached for her handbag and found a couple of creased notes. I took them, thanked her, and quickly left.

32

I walked south, keeping to the backstreets parallel with Kemal Sejfula, then entered the Gazi Baba Park. It was another cold day, with skies the colour of a wet cotton sheet. There was no one about.

Eleni was right: I must stop moping and focus on finding Katarina. It was two weeks since I had left her in Syrna Street, but the trail would not have gone completely cold. I tried to sort out what I now knew about her abduction. The Bura gang had taken her in mid-January, Anna had said – an act of vengeance on a Roma village, because Katarina's cousin had bared his arse at them. A petty insult, but bigoted thugs like that need no better excuse. They probably despised the Roma even more than they despised the Kosovars. Nor would they necessarily have known what they were going to do with her. They were Serbs with guns, and in the Kosovo of January 1999, Serbs with guns were inviolable. But then they had taken Katarina to the refuge and dumped her there. Why go to the trouble? If they didn't want her any more, why not simply throw her out?

My thoughts were interrupted by a harsh smell of woodsmoke drifting through the trees, and voices – a low shout, a child crying. Ahead was a stretch of open grassland and there were people there, hundreds of them, encamped in little groups around makeshift tents and smouldering fires. Everyone was lying down, as if they'd been put under a spell, except for twenty or thirty who had formed a queue that didn't seem to lead anywhere. On the far side of the field were three police vans surrounded by helmeted men with their backs turned. With their white vehicles and shiny black uniforms, they looked like a parade of aliens lined up between the patchwork of refugees in front of them and the drab woods beyond.

As I skirted the camp, some of the policemen climbed into one of the vans, which then swayed off across the muddy grass. Four or five people joined the pointless queue. An aeroplane toiled overhead, the disembodied moan of its engines dwindling in the shapeless sky.

I reached the eastern perimeter of the park and turned south again, using the regular thump of trains shunting in and out of Skopje to guide me to the railway track and the ribbon of scrub alongside it. When I came to the place where I had lain down beneath the brambles after killing the two men by the van, I hurried past like a man avoiding a posse of brawling drunks.

I took a side street that entered Syrna Street thirty yards from the house, walked to the corner, and bent as if to tie a shoelace. Everything was just as I remembered it: the fallen porch and broken-down wall, rustling plastic sheeting on the roof, satellite dish sprouting from the ruined pickup out back. A brutal, comfortless place. How could I have left Katarina here? I scanned the street for watchers. Nothing. I gave it ten minutes, before working my way round to a dirt track that ran along the back of Syrna Street. At the far end, three boys were throwing stones at the rusted carcass of a car. There was wooden fencing round the back of number 77, but it was an easy climb onto the corrugated-iron roof of one of the shacks that lined the yard.

The first thing I saw was the brindled dog, circling disconsolately at the entrance on Syrna Street. It heard me, started away, then emitted a ragged bark. I jumped off the roof into the yard and ran for the cover of the satellite dish. The dog skittered off round the corner and into the street, tail tucked between its legs. A window scraped open in one of the upstairs rooms. I squinted through the mesh of the satellite dish and saw a man looking down into the yard. His gaze fell on the dish and for a long moment he stared down at my scanty hiding place. I stayed stock still. A rough voice called from behind him and he turned back into the room.

In the back of the pickup was a plastic milk carton that had been cut in half and filled with nuts, bolts and washers. I stripped to the waist and filled my T-shirt with a handful of the oily steel lumps. Twenty seconds later, the back door opened and I heard footsteps coming towards me across the yard. I tucked in behind the tailgate of the pickup and braced myself, holding the sap so there was a foot of slack to swing and working out the steps I would take when the moment came to strike. He was alongside the cab now, but he'd stopped. Check beneath the pickup and he'd have a view of my shins. Three paces on and he'd see the rest of me. *Forget everything*, I ordered myself. *Don't hold back.* His feet scrunched in the dirt. One pace, two. Three.

I swung backhanded and the steel-knuckled wrecking ball whipped through the air. If I'd let go, it would have flown fifty yards down Syrna Street. I didn't. It slammed into his cheekbone. He gave a whisper of shock and dropped like a bag of sand off the back of a truck. I stooped to break his fall and dragged him under the pickup. I didn't have time to do more. He'd been told to go down and check the yard, and the man who'd given the order would be waiting for his return.

I slipped through the back door and into a kitchen that was rancid with the smell of stale milk and old meat-grease. Across the room was a door to the hallway, where a narrow staircase led to the first floor. A TV was on up there, a smoothly garrulous voice, eruptions of insincere laughter. I hadn't even reached the turn half way up the stairs when the TV snapped off.

The tread creaked beneath my foot. Footsteps in one of the rooms. I sprinted up the next flight, reached the landing, stopped. There was a man pointing a gun at me from the far end of the corridor.

I was expecting the boiler-suited troll who'd swung a length of iron at the back of my neck, but this one was smaller, about fifty, bald, with sharp little eyes and an expression of entrenched biliousness that suggested he'd have no qualms about shooting me.

'I'm looking for a girl,' I said, remembering that the troll had initially taken me for a misguided john.

'You stop!' He raised the gun, and said something I didn't understand, indicating my right hand with a toss of his head.

A misguided john who happened to be bare-chested and carrying something heavy in an oil-stained T-shirt… This wasn't going to work. How good was he with that gun? A small-calibre semi-automatic, a hurter rather than a stopper. I was level with a door to my left. It was open a crack. I dived.

No shots, just a bang as the door swung back against the wall. I rolled to my feet and sprang to the doorway. Silence, then the high-pitched blips of a cellphone keypad. Summoning help.

I stepped out and hurled the sap at his head. It was going to miss him by a foot, but he shied anyway. The phone clattered to the floor. I ran at him low, like a sprinter from the blocks. His forefinger torqued over the trigger. Still three yards away from the black O at the end of the barrel. I swerved, braced for the bullet.

A black shape lurched into the gunman from behind. He staggered. The muzzle flashed. The bullet whacked the plasterwork to my right and I had him, fingers clamped on his wrist, thrusting his gun-hand aside. I bounced him down and his head cannoned into the knees of the man behind him, who toppled against the wall and slid awkwardly to the floor.

The gunman struggled briefly, but the tip of my shoulder had crunched into his jaw and there wasn't much fight left in him. I unpicked his fingers from the gun, stood, and drove the heel of my shoe into his groin. He curled like a salted slug and retched. I looked over at the black-clad figure propped against the doorframe, hands and feet bound with cable ties. Father Daniel Cady.

* * *

A film of sweat covered his face, which was deathly pale except for patches of puffy red around the cheekbones, where he'd been slapped.

'More of them... On the way.' He was in so much pain he could barely get the words out.

I picked up the gunman's cellphone. The number was up on screen but he hadn't had time to press call. I ran down to the kitchen and returned with a knife to cut Father Daniel free. As I helped him to his feet, his jacket and shirt rode up at the back and I saw a pair of dark bruises ripening over his kidneys. Heavy blows, well aimed. I left him leaning against the wall while I dealt with the gunman, who was still coiled over his groin. I searched his pockets and found more cable ties, which saved me the trouble of knocking him out.

I hitched Father Daniel's arm round my neck and hauled him along the corridor. One of the rooms we passed had mattresses laid out round the walls, blankets and a few bedraggled items of clothing. Small, female things... A dormitory – but it looked abandoned. In fact, the whole house looked abandoned. We hobbled down the stairs and out through the kitchen door. The priest sat on the doorstep to steel himself for the next leg while I retrieved the clothes I'd left beneath the pickup. The gun felt cumbersome and incriminating, and I wasn't sure I wanted it. A Czech-made CZ 83, chambered for fifteen rounds – but when I pulled the clip I found only two. I wiped it down and dropped it in the back of the pickup.

Father Daniel was in no state to clamber over the roof of the shack, so we slunk out of the yard and across the road, back towards the railway track. Every time he put his left foot down, he gasped. I didn't want to hustle him along in case he was bleeding internally; but neither did I want the *more of them* he'd warned me about to turn up while we were still dawdling along the pavement opposite the house.

I'd done plenty of damage to this gang, and they weren't the sort to take it with a philosophical shrug. The troll had a brutish authority about him and, more than that, he was no fool: he knew I'd bested him in the fight out front when I'd broken his elbow, and he'd walked away, judging correctly that I would not pursue him. He had plenty of armed men at his beck and call, and I did not like the way they went about their work. There'd been something theatrical about the savagery of the Bura, something self-regarding and a touch neurotic. These men had no such flaws. For them, violence was a job – probably not even all that well paid. A Bura would never have carried a weapon loaded with only three bullets; but to the man I had taken out in Syrna Street, it was no more significant than having to do a day on a building site with a broken shovel.

I got the priest into the cover of a line of scraggy thornbushes alongside the railway track and lay him on his side to rest. He moaned softly for a while, then his breathing eased and he started muttering. I leaned in a little so I could hear what he was saying. 'Our Father, Who art in Heaven, hallowed be Thy name. Thy Kingdom come, Thy will be done…' It brought to mind the puerile variation we'd chanted in the chapel at school: *Our Father, Who art in Heaven, Harold be thy name.* A bubble of laughter escaped my lips, and he turned his head and gave me a mournful look.

'Sorry,' I said. 'You able to talk?'

'Sure. I think so.'

'Did Katarina ever come back?'

He shook his head. 'I haven't been at the refuge for a while, I… I had to come here to Skopje.'

'Syrna Street has nothing to do with the UNHCR,' I said. 'But I suppose you didn't know.'

'No, I've never seen the place before. They would have killed me. I thank God you came.'

'What were you doing there?'

'I was looking for something, I don't know what. To help me find out what happened to Katarina. It was a stupid idea.'

'Is that why you left the refuge? The person who answered the phone said it was closed.'

'It can't be closed. There are still so many children there.'

'Who did you leave in charge?'

His expression was blank and I couldn't tell if he'd heard.

'I tried so hard to help them,' he said.

'Did you see any sign that anyone still lives at Syrna Street? When I took Katarina, there was a girl of twenty or so, blonde hair?'

'Just those two men. I think they saw me arrive.'

There was an ominous, empty, rolling sensation in my chest. Suppose they were preparing to leave Skopje and set up somewhere else, taking Katarina with them?

'You better or worse than half an hour ago?' I asked.

He sat up stiffly. 'Better.'

'Let's go. I'll be as gentle as I can.'

33

It took two hours to get him to Eleni's apartment. On the way, I explained where we were going and said that since we weren't absolutely sure what was going on at the house on Syrna Street, it might be better not to say too much about it to Katarina's mother. He was too ill to protest.

I couldn't fathom him out. He was clearly very naive – he hadn't even changed out of his dog collar for his perilous visit to Syrna Street – and of fragile character; but above all, it seemed to me, Father Daniel Cady was self-absorbed and inclined to self-pity. The look I had noticed when we'd talked outside the refuge, inviting you to feel sorry for him without knowing why, was now even more pronounced. Why had he deserted the children he was supposed to be looking after and come to Skopje on a quest which he must surely have known was beyond him? He'd denied that the refuge was closed – but hadn't asked me what I knew.

Then again, he had just been beaten up. And given everything he'd been through – traumatised by his father, abandoned by his mother after a night of bloodshed in Lowestoft, and betrothed ever since to an eccentric little order of the Catholic Church – given all that, why shouldn't he feel sorry for himself?

I stopped for a kebab and called Eleni on Father Daniel's phone. She and Anna were at the UNHCR, being herded around like refugees, she said indignantly. I told her what had happened and she was there at the door of her uncle's apartment when we arrived. She'd made up a sickbay in the bedroom, complete with Ibuprofen, a thermometer, bottled water, two clean towels and a plastic bucket. She seemed in awe of the injured priest, but by this time he'd taken another turn for the worse and couldn't do anything but lie on the bed and pray. His devotion seemed touchingly familial, like a child reaching for a special toy or asking for a kiss.

* * *

Once we had him settled, Eleni went back to the UNHCR and I took a taxi to the Vegas Lounge. I wanted to find the sleepy-eyed girl again, see if I could get her alone. I was sure that, as long as she felt safe, she would tell me where I could find Katarina.

It wasn't a brothel posing as a nightclub any more, it was a crime scene. The apron of tarmac out front had been cordoned off with red-and-white tape, bowing and clattering in the cold wind that had got up as darkness stole over Skopje town. The perimeter was guarded by half a dozen uniformed police, and the two unmarked cars next to their van suggested the detectives were out in force, too. The sign above the door had that grubby, disenchanted look unlit neon always has, and the two pointy trees by the front entrance now lay on their sides, displaying their dry brown underskirts.

A small crowd had gathered and I joined them. Two men came out of the fire exit at the side of the flank wall, one of them talking and tapping a leather folio while the other nodded. The latter took off the polythene bootees he had on over his shoes and dropped them to the ground. The man with the folio went back inside, while the other marched over to one of the cars and was driven away.

I scanned the crowd for someone who might speak English and spotted a man in his sixties, smartly dressed. I moved next to him.

'Do you know what happened here?'

He turned to look at me, his face grave. 'They came to close it down. But anyway it was closed. There were two girls inside, dead.'

He saw the shock on my face.

'It is what to expect. This is a bad place.'

'Do you know who they were? How old they were?'

'How old? No.'

He moved away. The younger girls would be their prized assets, I told myself quickly. Why harm them? But Katarina was trouble, a liability – an English soldier had come looking for her and already he'd killed two of their number and injured two more. If the troll and his men were cutting their losses, cleaning up...

I could not leave here without knowing, could not face Anna without knowing. I circled the building, looking for a way in. I passed a rubbish bin and delved around inside, came up with a newspaper and a few bits of crumpled A4 paper. I smoothed them out, laid them over the newspaper and walked on.

The area behind the building was just a few square yards of unlit dirt bordered by a ten-foot-high wall, with a small block of flats beyond. I jogged round to the flats and down a side-alley to a backyard with a caretaker's hut and a row of rubbish bins. I pushed one of them against the wall and climbed up. No one was guarding the rear of the building and the uniforms at the front had their backs to me. I swung over the wall and sauntered to the corner by the open fire exit. I straightened my clothes – my black rain jacket was just what the detectives had been wearing – and watched until I was sure no one was about to enter the building, then walked along the side wall, inspecting my scraps of paper and ticking off imaginary items with one finger. Reaching the fire exit, I put on the polythene bootees the detective had discarded and stepped through the door.

A man was walking towards me. A puzzled look came over his face. I reached down to adjust a bootee, then turned sideways to let him pass, readying myself to run. But he didn't challenge me and I watched him turn out of sight beyond the fire exit.

I was in the narrow corridor along which I had followed the bony-chested woman twelve days ago. A plane of bright, blue-white light lay over the wall ahead. Voices. They were in the waiting area with the scented candles and towel cupboard. The voices got louder. I stepped into a room to my right. It was dark, but I made out the shape of the bed and the bedside table and the tin tray of condoms gleaming in the light from the corridor. I hid behind the door until the voices had passed. There was a camera above my head and I noticed that the cabling turned down and followed the corner before passing through a rough hole a few inches above the floor.

I stepped back into the corridor and found a low door with no handle, a few inches ajar. I pushed it open and ducked into a tiny room, barely four feet across, with a pair of monitors and a keyboard set on a table. I tapped the keyboard and the screens lit up. One of them showed a desktop strewn with icons representing the security cameras in the Vegas Lounge; the other, an empty room. The image shivered eerily in its frame. I went through the icons one by one – a parade of squalid grey rooms. I had five cameras still to check… I clicked the next and the screen filled with brilliant white light and swooping shadows, figures moving across the cold gaze of an arc lamp set on a tripod by the door. Behind them, glimpses of the bodies on the bed. Pudgy, white, awkwardly arranged, like a pair of discarded dolls.

I tapped at the zoom control and the camera jerked towards the nearest corpse. I saw hips, pubic hair, breasts – I had held Katarina against me and I knew this was not her. I panned over to the other. She was smaller, plump, with her knees drawn up so I couldn't easily make her out… Then I saw her hair – a halo of pale yellow against the stark white of the sheet. Katarina was dark. It was not Katarina. I did not have to squint at her face to be sure, because I knew who it was: the sleepy-eyed girl from Syrna Street.

I killed the screen. I was aching with rage. A grinding, bone-shuddering kind of rage that made the walls of the tiny room vibrate. I kicked open the door and stepped into the corridor. The lights flickered as if they were about to fail. Beyond the fire exit, the world appeared as a painted screen patrolled by painted shapes from a dimension I did not inhabit but only saw from afar and pitied for the frail illusions of goodness and reason that sustained it. Animated uniforms, trees upset, dead neon. The little crowd of starers watched me, their faces wary and sad. I ducked under the tape and walked away. No one tried to stop me.

I took a bus back into the centre of town. The dark streets filed past – hopeless places, leading nowhere. The house on Syrna Street had been abandoned, the Vegas Lounge shut down. How long did we have? If you mean to kill to cover your traces, it's the last thing you do before you go. Not days, hours. And my only two leads cold as lumps of clay in a winter field.

34

I got back to Eleni's apartment just after eight and found them talking in the sitting room. Father Daniel was perched on the edge of the chair by the telephone, leaning stiffly away from his bruised innards. They were drinking brandy and soda. Eleni offered me a glass but I felt too agitated to drink. They switched to English. The priest was talking about Katarina. The woman who'd brought her in wouldn't say where she'd found her, he told us, and refused to give her own name. It wasn't uncommon for children to turn up like this.

'Kosovo is falling apart,' said Eleni. 'Any day, you can be thrown out of your home by men who are drunk with how power-ful they are. It makes them sick, so sick they think it is OK to kill people. And always it's the children who suffer most, the innocent ones.' She looked sorrowfully at Anna – and then immediately seemed to regret it and forced a smile of encouragement onto her face instead.

'But that's not what happened to Katya,' Anna said. 'She must have told you I was still alive?'

'It's the first thing they say when they arrive, always,' said Father Daniel. 'Their mothers and fathers are waiting for them and can they please go home? It breaks your heart to hear it, truly it does. But I was never able to track down any of their families. Not one.'

'But I am sure you believed Katarina,' said Eleni. 'She is old enough, and a very sensible girl.'

'So I did,' he said. 'I asked if I could telephone you, but she didn't know your number – it was on her cellphone, which she had lost. You do not have a landline at your apartment, I think?'

'We just used cellphones,' said Anna unhappily.

'She told me you worked at the university,' said Father Daniel. 'I called them and asked for a Mrs Corochai, but there was no one by that name.'

'At the university, she uses her maiden name,' said Eleni, her voice barely more than a whisper. 'Galica. But Katya must have known—'

'We never talked about it,' said Anna. 'I wanted her to be proud of being half Roma. I couldn't keep the name myself, I was too angry with Franz. Anyway, I'd published a few articles under my maiden name. But I didn't want Katya to wonder why she had a different name from me, so I just… I never…' She covered her face with her hands.

'I'm afraid I just assumed your name was Mrs Corochai,' said Father Daniel. 'I didn't ask Katarina, and I didn't like to tell her I couldn't get hold of you. I promised I would write to you at the university, and that was a comfort to her. I notified the police in Pristina, but I heard nothing. That was to be expected – you have to leave a message and they never call back. They used to send an acknowledgement if you wrote to them, but they don't even do that now. There must be so many lost children… Of course, I wrote to your home address, which Katarina gave me. But there was no answer. I suppose it never arrived?'

'The post does not work any more,' said Eleni. 'Not for us Kosovars. It can take weeks for letters to get through. Anna has been in Paris, then she came straight here – as I suggested.'

'Oh, dear Lord, I am sorry. It was a pattern I had become so familiar with, you see – the requests for help or information, the long wait, then disappointment, always disappointment. It was very hard on the poor things. It seemed cruel to allow hopes to linger.'

He shifted gingerly in his chair. Anna had not taken her hands from her face and the conversation was too painful to continue.

Eventually, Eleni turned to me and said: 'You found nothing at Syrna Street? Nothing at all?'

I glanced at Father Daniel, hoping he might answer, but he wouldn't meet my eye.

'We didn't have much time. I'll go back and search it properly.'

'I thought you would do that this afternoon?'

'No. I... I just walked around a bit. To clear my head.'

'To clear your head. How pleasant for you.'

I fumbled for a way of changing the subject and came up with the question I'd been meaning to ask Father Daniel: 'You say you had UNHCR paperwork for children being transferred to Skopje. Did you have a set of documents for Katarina?'

'He can't have done,' Eleni interrupted. 'We were there today and they have no record of her, none at all.'

'But I did,' said Father Daniel. 'The UNHCR provided transit papers for the children before they left. There was one for Katarina – she was due to go to Skopje anyway, a few days after she ran away, along with five other girls. Everything was stamped and signed in the usual way. I had no way of knowing—'

'Who signed them?'

'The same person as always – a case officer called Bryan Harley.'

Anna pulled her hands away from her face. 'Harley? That was the man I told you about, Eleni. An English spy came to Rambouillet to talk to Colonel Adjani. They'd detained a UNHCR officer and had him locked up at his apartment – his name was Bryan Harley, I'm sure of it.'

'Bryan Harley has been locked up?' said Father Daniel, his face aghast. 'It can't be true... He dealt with all the children we sent to Skopje.'

'The papers he gave to Father Daniel were false!' said Eleni.

'We don't know that,' I said quickly, though in truth I think we did. 'Did they say why Harley was arrested?'

Anna shook her head.

'Anna, I'm so terribly sorry,' said Father Daniel, his head bowed and his voice no more than a whisper.

Anna turned away and we lapsed into silence again. Eleni poured out more brandy and this time I asked for a glass. A UNHCR case officer was providing fake documentation for children being trafficked – the word could not any longer be dodged – from Father Daniel's refuge in Kosovo to 77 Syrna Street. I thought of the semi-circles of pink, greedy faces in the dim light of the Vegas Lounge and wondered if Bryan Harley had been one of them.

'Why was Colonel Adjani being told about this?' I asked, breaking the long silence.

'He has a brother called Haclan,' said Anna tonelessly, 'a gangster who is also close to the KLA. The English spy told Colonel Adjani that the International Police Task Force were about to arrest Haclan. He said Haclan was discrediting the Kosovar cause and must shut down his operation and get out of Skopje.'

Haclan Adjani. The troll from Syrna Street had a name.

'This English spy warned Haclan off?' I asked. 'So he could escape arrest? He actually did that?'

'Yes,' said Anna. 'I also heard that they tried to ban Colonel Adjani from attending the conference.'

She looked round at each of us in turn and the expression of shocked nobility on her face was deeply affecting. 'This is what happened to Katya, isn't it? They're a gang of child traffickers. She was... I sat beside Colonel Adjani day after day at Rambouillet. I sat beside him and I didn't know... All along his brother had my Katya. I sat beside him and... There was no way to connect them. It seemed like a different world. But it was the same world, just different ends of it.'

There was nothing more to say. The whole tragic and capricious narrative had now been set out (aside from some elements I still felt too ashamed to supply). Why dwell on the pitiless details? None of this would bring us closer to finding Katarina.

Eleni went off to cook supper – she had managed to find lake trout in the market, a great treat, she said, without any trace of conviction. Father Daniel asked if he might go to the bedroom to lie down.

'Nothing's really changed, Anna,' I said, when we were alone. 'We mustn't give up.'

She rounded on me. 'Give up? Why would I give up? You give up. You say you need to find Katarina to prove your innocence, but I don't believe you. What are you even doing here? Eleni says you are a liar, and she's right.'

I was ready for this – I'd been ready ever since I'd met her at the bus station – but still it was difficult to take. She stared at me and in her gaze I read the particular character of her suffering. She'd lost everything. She blamed herself. She felt useless, bewildered. Hope was draining away, and every revelation I dredged up took her closer to the point when hope would run out. And beyond hope? The unimaginable, the inescapable betrayal: reset the clock and start life without Katarina.

'There are some things I can't tell you. Things that make no difference.'

She looked at me, proud and bleak, and the anger left her eyes as quickly as it had possessed them.

'Do you think I will judge you, James? Do you think I have any choice about whether to trust you?'

'You can trust me, Anna. I swear you can.'

She sighed and leaned back in the sofa.

Eleni passed through and smoked a cigarette on the balcony. 'Five minutes, then we can eat,' she said on her way back. 'I'll tell Father Daniel.'

'We have two clues we didn't have before,' I said to Anna. 'I'll find Bryan Harley first, then Haclan.'

'Will you, James? I don't think so. You are just one man.'

I asked her to describe the English agent who had come to Rambouillet to interview Colonel Adjani, and when she did so, I had a pretty good idea who he was.

'Did he fiddle with a signet ring on his left hand?'

'Yes. Do you know him?'

'His name is Clive Silk – he's an officer in British intelligence.'

'Will he help us?'

'I don't think so. He's the one who had me arrested.'

Clive Silk had seen the evidence against Bryan Harley, I realised, and probably interrogated him, too. That was how he'd made the connection between the refuge and Syrna Street. When I'd escaped from the safe house in Norfolk, it was no more than a simple precaution to alert the Order of St Hugh.

'Come and eat the fish,' said Eleni at the door.

Father Daniel was already seated at the little table in the kitchen, but when Eleni put a plate in front of him, the whole lake trout laid neatly across the centre and small piles of buttered carrots and potatoes either side, he stood up without speaking and walked slowly to the bathroom. A few seconds later, we heard him being sick.

'The poor man is unwell,' said Eleni, trying in vain not to look offended.

Anna went to see if he was OK and came back a few minutes later, having helped him return to bed. I was reminded of the poem I'd found at the front of his Book of Prayer. *Torn scales, pink slime, a thousand drowning eyes.* We ate in a silence broken only by nervous conversational gambits from Eleni that flapped into desultory inconsequence like bits of old newspaper blown along a pavement. The weather was unusually wet. Skopje was a much more interesting city than it might first appear, did I not think? The fish tasted more of mud than fish.

After clearing away, we went back to the sitting room and Anna turned on the TV. The ten o'clock news came on and fate lashed out again. An English UNHCR official by the name of Bryan Harley had been found hanged in his Skopje apartment.

35

I lay on the floor in the bedroom, with Father Daniel's groans wallowing round the walls. It did not seem sensible to move him, so Anna and Eleni had decamped to the sitting room. When it became obvious that neither of us were asleep, I said: 'You took a turn for the worse earlier – was it the fish?'

Peering at him through the gloom, I could just make out his mouth moving as if in speech. But he said nothing.

'I thought maybe you were allergic?'

'I don't… no, not allergic. I just…'

'Your father was a trawlerman in Lowestoft, right?'

'How did you know that?' he said, suddenly strident.

'I looked it up in a newspaper archive.'

'It's a shock to find you've been prying into my private life. I don't know by what right—'

'I was trying to find out about Katarina, that's all. I didn't have much to go on.'

He sat up slowly and set his knee to jiggling up and down on the floor. The tension hummed off him like an electric charge.

'Then you know about my father.'

'Yes. It must have been traumatic for you.'

'And for Ma. But my father was a brutal man. He tore us apart.'

'The papers said neither of you were found. How did you end up with the Order of St Hugh?'

'She left me there before she fled the country. The Order was based in Lowestoft at the time.'

'So Father Wulfstan looked after you from the age of fourteen?'

'How do you know that name?'

'I dropped by their house in Northampton while I was on the run. Father Wulfstan gave me some of your clothes to wear, then called the police.'

'Did he, then. What else did he tell you?'

'Nothing much – I wasn't there long.'

'I'm sorry, I don't mean to be bad-tempered,' he said, reverting to his usual, modest tone of voice. 'I can hardly think straight. I keep remembering all the girls I sent down to Skopje – they were mostly girls. I'd wave at them as they drove off in our Mitsubishi camper van, and they'd wave back and grin with excitement. Oh, my dear God, how many did we send there… I can't even count them in my head.'

'You weren't to know.'

'And then after Syrna Street, what happened to them, do you know?'

I told him about the Vegas Lounge. I didn't feel like sparing him the detail. There was something about his reaction to the discovery that the children in his care had been prostituted by a gang of traffickers in Skopje that was… I won't say false, but constrained or repressed. It was as if his own self-pity left not much room for pitying anyone else.

'God consigned them to my care,' he said when I had finished. 'And I did care for them. I did. To get some of them off to safety in Skopje… It seemed… The UNHCR… Dear Lord Jesus Christ, forgive me. I prayed for guidance before coming to Kosovo, you know.

I beseeched Our Lord to tell me if it was right. I had no experience of looking after children. And my own childhood was… was…'

'Troubled?'

'Oh well, I'm not the first to suffer a little, and I won't be the last. My mother was a good and lovely woman, that I am sure of.'

But she killed your father and left you with Wulfstan, I thought.

'She came and found you when you opened the refuge?'

'Yes – that was nearly three years ago. She'd settled in northern Albania. I was so happy to see her again. She couldn't come to England because… Well, she couldn't. And Wulfstan said that if I went to her, the police would follow and I would lead them to her door.'

This seemed improbable, but Father Daniel was not a worldly man.

'Do you know where your mother is now?'

He did not reply for a moment; when he did, his voice was soft and bitter as ash: 'She was the woman you found in the farmhouse.'

Priest, priest, she'd cried, pointing at her phone. *Priest…* Not calling for a priest, but for her son. And I'd sent him down there to find his own mother eviscerated in her chair.

'I wish I'd known. I'm sorry.'

He didn't answer, but lay down again and drew the bedclothes up to his chin. I was relieved that the conversation had ended, for now I felt guilty that I'd judged him so harshly. A little while later, I heard his breathing slow and he started to snore. I could hear Anna and Eleni whispering in the sitting room; but even when they fell silent half an hour later, I couldn't sleep.

I was beginning to understand what had been going on in the background between MI6 and their political masters. The Vegas Lounge was a scandal-in-waiting – and bore uncomfortable similarities to the child-trafficking scandals that had disgraced the UN's intervention in Bosnia a few years previously. Worse, the place was run by a brother of one of the Kosovar delegates at Rambouillet and a known associate of the KLA. If the scandal blew while the peace conference was in full swing, it would hand a massive PR victory to the Serbs and their Russian sponsors and upset the delicately balanced diplomatic rationale for military intervention in Kosovo. The threatened NATO bombing campaign was supposed to be a humanitarian intervention, which made it both legal and politically acceptable; but the ethical facade would look pretty threadbare if some of the people you were siding with ran an underage brothel in Skopje.

They'd decided to keep a lid on it. The relevant security agencies would have received a subtle diktat to the effect that now was not the time to move on Haclan Adjani. I'd found out what was going on and they'd locked me away in Norfolk without a second thought. But the UNHCR was also involved, because of Bryan Harley, and that was a thornier problem. They'd tried to prevent Colonel Adjani attending the peace conference, but evidently failed. A few days later, Clive Silk had met him at Rambouillet and, in effect, tried to help a child trafficker slip the net. If that got out, he'd be crucified.

Everything I'd seen since coming back to Skopje confirmed that Haclan had got the message and was shutting up shop. I went through what Anna had told me about Silk's visit to Rambouillet and an idea came to me. I turned the idea over and over, examining it from every possible angle. It didn't look that good from any of them, but it was the best I could come up with and we were running out of time.

36

I got up an hour later, dressed in the narrow hallway, then left the building. It was two-thirty a.m., the darkest time of night. I set off at a jog and in twenty minutes arrived at the far end of the street where my apartment was located.

Looming above me was a boarded-up theatre with an elaborate fire escape clinging to its back – the sections of rickety ironwork were a feature of the view from my bathroom window. The theatre was a haunt of homeless people – many times I'd observed them squeezing through a section of boarding. I found the place, prised open the gap, and entered a narrow strip of yard that was choked with rubbish lobbed in from the street. At the top of three wide steps were the main doors, their glass knocked out and replaced by oblongs of plywood, which had in turn been kicked in. The night was bitter and I guessed the people who took refuge here had retreated inside.

I made my way round the back and found the foot of the fire escape. It was a Manhattan-style affair, with cantilevered sections designed to be lowered from above, but someone had left a length of tatty cord attached to the bottom ladder. I pulled it down and the whole structure shuddered, then showered me with flakes of rust. This didn't seem like such a good idea now, but I needed a gun and there were two in my apartment. I started up and made it to the first landing. I felt with my fingers for the bolts which fastened the platform to the wall and found that half of them had rusted away. Six more flights to the top... I don't know what was worse about that ascent – the sonorous groans emitted by the fire escape as due notice of its imminent collapse, or the sound of unidentified lumps of decaying ironwork thudding onto the tarmac below. Eventually I made it to a small dome with a balustraded walkway, which gave me a good view of the street below.

They hadn't made much effort to conceal themselves: a white Mercedes saloon was parked twenty yards down from Maria's, its windows fugged up and a styrofoam takeaway box in the gutter below the passenger door. These were not professional intelligence operatives, not even freelance ones. There was an outside chance they were local police, but I guessed my former colleagues would find it hard to convince Skopje's finest to devote their precious time to the capture of a junior British intelligence officer, whatever lies they told about me. No, they had to be Haclan Adjani's crew. How had they found out I was back in Skopje?

Seeing them there outside Maria's, brazenly watching my apartment, made me angry. I worked my way quickly round the parapet until I came to the side that bordered an alley separating the theatre from the block next door. A jump of no more than five feet, with an easy landing on a flat tarred roof a few feet lower down. In one movement I stepped up onto the balustrade and launched myself out over the black gulf between the two buildings.

It was further than I'd thought and my trailing leg caught the edge of the roof, but I toppled forward and rolled to safety. There were no more alleys to leap now, just various reassuringly solid walls and tiled roof-slopes. In less than a minute I was dropping down onto the back extension directly above my bathroom, which was out of sight of the watchers in the street. I clambered in through the metal window – which was too warped to be shut properly, but had the merit of being securely embedded in the wall.

The bathroom stank of old urine. The WC hadn't been flushed last time I was here, with Katarina, because the cistern leaked and I'd tied the ballcock up with a rubber band. I took off the lid and saw it was stuffed with sheets of balled-up paper. I opened one out and straightaway recognised the tidily flamboyant handwriting: these were the missing pages from the back of Father Daniel's Book of Prayer. Katarina must have got up in the night, torn them out and hidden them here.

I shut the door to stop any light filtering through to the front window, then flipped the switch and slowly extracted all the scrumpled paper from the cistern. Blood pounded in my throat as I smoothed the sheets out one by one on the bathroom floor. I put them all the same way up. I arranged them in three straight lines. I fussed over the creases. Why had Katarina hidden them here? Because she'd wanted me to find them? I looked for page numbers so I could put them in the right order. Anything to postpone the moment when I actually had to read them.

The first bore a poem, set out so it occupied the exact centre of the page. Most of the writing was in Albanian, but like the poem I had found in the front of the book when I'd been waiting in the BFPO to send it back to Northampton, this one was in English.

> Say a little prayer
> To cleanse your mouth of wickedness,
> Say a little prayer
> To save your lips from sin.
> Say a little prayer
> And give yourself to godliness,
> Say a little prayer
> And let your Master in.

I skipped uneasily over the next few pages, until I came to a passage of Albanian. I'd picked up enough of the language to be able to work my way through a newspaper article, with the help of the dictionary I'd bought at the airport on first arriving in Skopje. I fetched it from the sitting room, knelt on the lumpy grey lino of the bathroom floor and started to translate.

Heat belted off the radiator, cold blew in through the window, the cistern dripped. My mind carried unknown words from the pages of the book to the columns of the dictionary. *Adult... Obedience...* I hunted for meanings and dreaded what I would find at the place in the column where my finger came to rest. *Punishment...* It was a dark moment in my life. To be panicked by the knowledge that you belong to the same world and the same species as the author of some sheets of handwritten paper torn from a book – that is to be panicked by something you can never escape.

Bedtime Story, it was called.

Once upon a time there was a girl who felt sorry for herself. She was in the care of a kind man of God, she had a roof over her head and food to eat, and she was taught to read and write, but still she grumbled and complained. The kind man who looked after her asked her to help with some grown-up things he could not do by himself. He was lonely, you see, with only children for company; and because he was a man of God, who spent his whole life doing good things for others, he would never have a family of his own. So it was only fair that she should help him in these grown-up ways, to show she was grateful to him for looking after her so well and making sure she was warm and had food to eat. She knew she should have done these things gladly and with a willing heart, as God asked, but still she was stubborn and difficult. In the end, the good man asked God what to do. You must punish the girl, God told the good man, until she shows obedience. But I don't want to punish her, said the good man. You must, God told him, for that is how I wish it to be. So he did punish her and she didn't like that because it hurt. But she knew that it was right that if she refused to do what God and the good man wanted, she should be punished. And although the punishments made her cry, she understood that they were good for her and would make her better.

Now, go to sleep, children, and God bless you all, in the name of the Father etc. Think about what I have said to you, and in the morning you must try to do what God wants you to do without being difficult or complaining.

And then there was a page entitled *Cleanliness*.

Do you know what it says in the Bible? Cleanliness is next to godliness. Our outsides get dirty and we can clean them with water and soap, which God has given us for this purpose. But not many people know that we can clean our insides, too. We brush our teeth by reaching into our mouths, don't we? And we clean our ears, and we even push our fingers up into our noses to find the dirt. So why should we also not reach into other parts of ourselves and clean them, too? You have been brought up in ignorance of these things, but I can help you make yourselves clean so that God will love and welcome you into his Church and not cast you out because of the dirty smells that come out of you and the dirty things you harbour inside yourselves which you are too lazy to clean. I will show you how to make yourselves clean enough so that God will love you, and there are two parts to it: first, there is the inspection, so that we can find the dirt; and then there is the cleaning itself, which can hurt quite a lot when you are not used to it…

I turned the page without reading any further, hoping to find that this was as bad as it got, that there were other items Katarina had torn out which would make the regime at the refuge seem less appalling. I checked my watch: it had taken me forty minutes to get this far. I worked feverishly through another page.

Do you know what gibber means?

No, Father.

Well, I want you to imagine the very worst pain you can, even worse than being whipped for a long, long time, or having your fingernails pulled out, or bits of skin cut off. I think you can believe that you would scream and scream and scream when you were having this pain. But if this pain goes on and on forever and never stops, well, you can't scream at the top of your voice forever, can you?

No, Father.

No, after a while, maybe an hour or a day or even a few days, you get tired and you can't scream any more. Now, the noise you make when the pain is still terrible but you are too tired to scream is called a gibber. And do you know where you hear this noise the whole time?

No, Father.

You hear it in hell! You hear it a long way from hell. As soon as you get close to hell, the gibbering fills your ears. When you come closer still, you see why they gibber in hell. You see the Devil's bony black pigs, which are always hungry. You see their sharp teeth tearing the skin from people's legs and gnawing at their bones. Would you like that to happen to you?

No, Father.

No. And the reason I am telling you about gibbering is because I don't want you to go to hell. You know that when you are bad and don't do what I tell you to do, God is watching. And if there's one thing in the world our Dear Lord in Heaven loves more than anything else it is His Church, which is like His home on Earth, and the people like me who work in His Church are like His family, you see? So if you children are disobedient or disrespectful towards me, God hates that so much that anyone who does it, well, can you guess what He does?

No, Father.

He sends them to hell and the black pigs gnaw the skin from their legs and crack open their kneecaps with their big jaws. And then they gibber, oh, how those poor children gibber! So just remember that if you ever say anything or do anything to harm the Church or God's family, which is people like me, well, God will find out and and He knows what to do.

Father Daniel's Book of Prayer was a record not of his spiritual development, as it claimed on the front cover, but of his depravity. I should have been expecting this, for wasn't it he who told me to take Katarina to the house on Syrna Street in the first place? But ever since I'd found him there, bleeding inside from the fists of Haclan's men, I'd felt ashamed of my suspicions.

How gullible I was! He'd come to Skopje not to find Katarina, but to find the Book of Prayer. These pages, in which he had assiduously recorded his abuse of the children in his care, would incriminate him. Katarina understood that. Perhaps she had seen him poring over them, absorbed in lascivious contemplation of the procedures by which he gratified his desires. Katarina had seen how important the book was, and had had the courage to steal it.

But why had she torn out the pages that described the horror inflicted by Father Daniel? A primitive urge to dispel the evil they contained? Why not give the book to me? Because Father Daniel's threats had worked their foul enchantment, I guessed. She hadn't been long at the refuge, so might not yet have heard Father Daniel reading out the passage I had just translated. But some time during the night she'd spent in my apartment, she'd woken up, taken the Book of Prayer into the bathroom to read and found it for herself. Then she'd cast around in panic for some way to undo her defiance of the priest and his vengeful God. She hadn't wanted me to find these pages – quite the reverse. She'd torn them out and hidden them, to save herself from the black pigs of hell.

This was all speculation, of course. But thinking of the terror she must have suffered that night, I felt engulfed by sadness and a renewed sense of guilt that I had done so little to help her.

I didn't translate any more passages of text, but I spent another hour deciphering some of the pages of notes he kept for each of the children in his care: what made them frightened or sad, whether they were suspicious or trusting, straightforward or secretive, stoical or easily reduced to tears. By this means he was able to tailor the suffering he inflicted. He was a skilled, patient groomer, who presented his victims with a simple choice: be pious and obedient, or face eternal damnation. Piety and obedience were exacted by Father Daniel in numerous ways, all of them either physically or psychologically sadistic. The prospect of eternal damnation was conjured up at every opportunity, and especially last thing at night. The inspiration was biblical, but the delivery matter-of-fact and educational in tone. *And by the way*, Father Daniel added to the end of another of his 'bedtime stories', *I've seen some of the Devil's pigs in the woods, just a short way from here. Their lips are too skinny to cover their long teeth and the spit drips from their jaws because they are always hungry.*

For the pious and obedient, there were little rewards – the right to sit in this or that chair, or go to bed late, or listen to music on the priest's MP3 player. For the rest, there were punishments and the promise of hell. And presiding over this was God – Father Daniel's God, whose Church was His home and whose priests were His family. God never forgave anyone who said anything bad about His

Church or His priests – especially not children who knew better, as they did – but sent them gibbering to hell. Even if they did not know what they were saying *was* bad, He sent them to hell. For this reason, it was safer to say nothing at all.

On the final page, Father Daniel had written out the *Salve Regina*, the prayer recited for the final bead of the rosary:

> Hail, holy Queen, Mother of Mercy,
> Hail our life, our sweetness and our hope.
> To thee do we cry,
> Poor banished children of Eve;
> To thee do we send forth our sighs,
> Mourning and weeping in this vale of tears.
> Turn then, most gracious advocate,
> Thine eyes of mercy towards us;
> And after this our exile,
> Show unto us the blessed fruit of thy womb, Jesus.

As a boy of nine or ten I had been required to recite this prayer daily. Kneeling on a waxed wooden pew in the school chapel with the gritty reek of incense smoke in my mouth, I chanted the fulsome words and felt their stifling melancholy. I lived in a *vale of tears*. The *mourning and weeping* was mine. I would weep and weep until the moment when the *blessed fruit* was shown unto me. Did I have to look? Would I be ready? I asked one of the monks what it meant.

'Stupid boy,' he replied scornfully. 'It means you are dead.'

Reading it here, written out in Father Daniel's book of corruption, the prayer seemed like an excuse. We're all in exile, we're all filling the heavens with our sighs and cries. In a sinful world, sin is inevitable. The headquarters of the Order of St Hugh in Northampton came back to me in a swirl of polished parquet and sweetly perfumed sherry. I pushed the papers away across the floor, overwhelmed by a taint both vile and familiar, like a mouthful of vomit.

After a few minutes, I realised I must leave. I stuffed the torn-out pages into an envelope and retrieved what I had come for from the steel box in the wardrobe – my Sig Sauer P228 and a couple of spare clips. I was more used to the Browning but the Sauer was easier to conceal. If only I'd kept the gun I'd taken off the man in Syrna Street, I could have spared myself this. Was anything Father Daniel had told us true? He'd tricked me into delivering Katarina to Syrna Street. He'd sat opposite Anna and feigned shock when told that Bryan Harley was implicated in child trafficking. He'd wrung his hands over the fate of the children in his care. He was nerveless and cold as a snake.

I left by the back stairs, which had a fire exit into the alley behind Maria's restaurant. I was in no fit state to leap from buildings or swing on fire escapes. How did their operation work? Groomed at the refuge, given a foretaste of their new lives by a sadistic priest. He runs a few background checks in case they've accidentally acquired a child with connections, a child who is not utterly helpless and alone. Bryan Harley prepares the paperwork. They're taken across the border and handed on to Haclan Adjani. A bony-breasted woman locks them in cubicles at the rear of the Vegas Lounge. They crouch by their assigned beds, the sickly stink of scented wax in their nostrils.

I ran back to Eleni's apartment. When I arrived, I would kill Father Daniel. No. First, I would make him get down on his knees before Anna and confess what he had done. Then I would kill him. In Eleni's apartment? Take him somewhere else. On foot – or in Anna's car. Suppose she objected? Father Daniel must surely know something that would help us find Katarina.

My pace slowed. I felt like a child deprived of a treat. The sense of disgust returned, sour and all-pervasive: disgust with the priest, and with myself. I arrived at Eleni's building and leaned against the wall by the door. Dawn was reaching along the tops of the houses, coaxing a little colour from clay-tiled roofs, from painted sills and curtains drawn over bedrooms where ordinary people slept. What could I tell Anna now? *I handed Katarina back to her abuser, but it's OK because I'm going to take him away in your car and kill him.* Should I even tell her what he had done?

I let myself into the apartment, knowing that I would succumb to whatever compulsion came over me when I saw Father Daniel asleep on Anna's bed. But when I opened the door to the bedroom, Father Daniel had gone.

I sat in the kitchen for an hour and considered my plan. In the end I decided that nothing had really changed. I opened the door to the sitting room and leaned against the doorway. The soft, warm smell of the sleeping women made me doubt myself, and for a moment I wanted very much not to wake them and explain what I had in mind. I stood a while longer, watching a strip of sunlight meander over the parquet floor beneath the curtains over the door to the balcony. The events of the night had left me in shreds. I shouldn't have been deciding anything.

But Haclan wasn't going to wait sportingly on the sidelines while I sorted myself out. I went back to the kitchen, made tea and brought it to them. They sat up, Eleni bleary and indignant, Anna immediately alert, as if sleep were merely wakefulness with your eyes shut.

'What is it?' said Anna. 'James, what's happened?'

'Do you know where Father Daniel went?'

'He's gone?'

'Never mind. We're going to get Katarina back.'

37

I went out and paid a taxi driver to take the pages torn from Father Daniel's book to Maria, along with a letter explaining what they were and asking her to deliver a copy to the UNHCR. I said I was sorry I hadn't been to see her, but if she looked out of her window and saw two bored men sitting in a small pile of takeaway remains, she would understand why. Then I bought a roll of gaffer tape, two pre-pay mobile phones, a spare battery, a micro screwdriver set and a soldering iron, went back to the apartment and settled down at the kitchen table to build the tracking device I had in mind. The tiny articulations needed to locate the flimsy wires and deposit the microscopic blobs of solder were unfamiliar employment for hands that had spent the last two weeks engaged in various acts of violence, and I found the job unexpectedly calming.

Eleni had spoken to a colleague in the Social Sciences Department whose speciality was the history of gangs in the south Balkans.

'The Adjanis are like Mafia,' she told me, jabbing the table with her elbow so that I made an inadvertent weld. 'Catholics, from the Mirditë region originally – they often have a cross tattooed on their chests so they get a Christian burial. They are widely feared for their brutality. This branch has three brothers. Vasilis, who was at Rambouillet. And Haclan – there is plenty to know about him, none of it good. They say he has operations in Skopje, Athens and Istanbul, and they traffic girls from all over. These are the people to whom you delivered Katarina. But I see in your face that you already know this. I hope you will be good enough to tell us everything soon, Captain Palatine.'

'What about the third brother?' I asked, to distract her from demanding that I do so immediately.

'Peter. My friend did not know about him. There may have been a family feud. Anyway, Peter does not seem to be associated with the family now. Perhaps he is just an ordinary man.'

Suppose they'd already taken Katarina to Athens or Istanbul? I saw now why they'd gone to the trouble of procuring the forged UNHCR documents from Bryan Harley. The border with Macedonia was barely even marked, but other crossings would not be so easy to make without official paperwork.

I couldn't worry about that now. Eleni went out to hire a van – Anna's Fiat was too distinctive for what I had in mind. Anna was searching through her conference papers for the sheet of paper she'd got hold of at Rambouillet which had contact details for each of the Kosovar delegates. She was sure she still had it… Sighs of frustration issued from the sitting room; and then she decided it must still be in the car and went out. Twenty minutes later she returned, brandishing a folded sheet of paper.

'You found it, in your car?' I said. 'It's a miracle.'

'Tidy people like you see only mess, James, but I promise you my Fiat Frightful is very highly organised. Even the ice-cream tubs have a purpose.'

'Which is?'

'They are a calendar. I know I had ice cream on this day, therefore that paper which I was reading when I ate it must be nearby. There. Such a thing would never even occur to you, admit it.'

I didn't admit it because I was looking at the document she'd located in the Fiat. There were photos of each of the delegates. Colonel Vasilis Adjani was the cigar-smoking man I'd punched in the Vegas Lounge. Clive Silk's watchers would have seen him go in, and MI6 would have worked on the assumption that I'd seen him there – and knew who he was, or might find out. Another reason for keeping me holed up in Norfolk while the peace talks took place: I had actually sat opposite a member of the Kosovar delegation to Rambouillet in a brothel that hired out underage girls.

'What is it, James?' Anna came and looked over my shoulder. 'That's him, near the bottom. The second number is his personal cellphone.'

'I hope he goes for it,' I said.

'He's clever. No, he's cunning. You must be careful not to say too much.'

She took a map of Skopje into the sitting room, while I downloaded the software I needed to her laptop and set about the configuration, working my way through a long list of pointless parameters which the hacker who had coded the GPS controller must have hoped would one day prove how far-sighted he had been.

'Why has Father Daniel run off?' Anna said, rushing into the kitchen. I could feel her stark eyes fixed on my forehead. 'There was something odd about him. I don't think it was just bruised kidneys he was suffering from. Surely he could have tried harder to contact me when Katya was at the refuge?'

I'd asked myself the same question. Well, I knew the answer now. 'I guess we got all we could from him, anyway,' I said, pretending to focus intently on a screen full of function calls. 'Maybe he's gone off to try something of his own.'

'I hope so, because I don't think our plan will work,' she said, her voice dipping into despair. 'It's too complicated. So many things can go wrong.'

'If it fails, we'll try something else.'

'He's not answering his mobile. Eleni rang them in Northampton again. They said they hadn't heard from him for months.'

Eleni came back then, and saved me from further participation in the pretence that Father Daniel was just an oddball priest with a heart of gold. I worked on, and a few hours later had a pair of matched GPS devices: send a blank text to one, and the other would wake up, return the coordinates for its current location, then go back to sleep. My main concern was power: GPS is hungry and I wasn't sure how long the tracker would hold out. But with the extra battery, I thought it would last for three or four days. I left the tracker on the balcony and went out into the street to test it. The master unit refused to send a blank text – some operating system wrinkle designed to make the phone more user-friendly.

I found the line of code that called the function and remarked it out, checked that it all worked correctly, then left the batteries to charge while I downloaded a geographical information database I'd used when preparing for the operation in Kosovo. It covered most of the Balkans and, among other things, enabled you to show long-lat coordinates on a map. It didn't take kindly to Anna's laptop, so I uninstalled as much as I could and eventually got it up and running. The display was maddeningly slow to refresh, but I thought it would do the job.

* * *

I left the apartment and followed Eleni's directions to the nearest call box. On the way, I practised Clive Silk's voice: a flat, slightly pinched delivery, on the verge of a whine. Don't push it, I told myself, it's not the voice but the details only Silk could know that will make this credible. I loaded the coins and dialled Colonel Adjani's cellphone. He was still at Rambouillet, but from what I'd read in the papers in Leicester Central Library, the cellphone ban was being ignored.

'*Tjeta*,' said a gruff voice.

'We spoke at Rambouillet about the activities of your brother Haclan,' I said.

'Who is this?'

'You haven't acted on my advice. Perhaps you weren't listening properly.'

'Perhaps I no speaking English,' said Colonel Adjani.

'The interpreter wasn't needed at Rambouillet and she isn't needed now. Haclan is still active. More than active. This cannot continue.'

'Haclan, Haclan. Forget about Haclan. He is not your concern, MI6 man.'

'The priest from the refuge in Kosovo is preparing to speak to the International Police Task Force in Skopje. If this happens, we cannot stop them arresting your brother.'

'So, make it not to happen.'

'He's meeting them at six this evening, at their offices above the Kisela Voda police station. Warn Haclan. Do it now.'

'You people, you flap and you squawk like old hens.'

'A colourful metaphor for a non-English speaker,' I couldn't resist saying. 'There will be no further warnings.'

I hung up. I shouldn't have goaded him, but I thought I'd got away with it. Anyway, the message had been delivered and I was sure Colonel Adjani would pass it on to his brother. Haclan would have his doubts about the story, but I didn't think he'd have any reliable means of checking it out: informants in the regular police would be part and parcel of his trade, but he surely couldn't have penetrated the IPTF. He might reason that the priest would not report what he knew for fear of incriminating himself – but the priest was a strange man, and who could say he had not been stricken with a bout of bad conscience and decided to come clean? Why take that risk, when all they need do was watch the police station in case he showed up?

More than anything, I was counting on the fact that Father Daniel had been Haclan's prisoner the previous day. They'd turned on him for some reason, beaten him, then allowed him to escape. Here was an opportunity to get him back.

* * *

I hurried back to the apartment and snatched a few hours' sleep. When I woke, the hairs on the nape of my neck were bristling. I joined Anna and Eleni in the sitting room.

'Let's look at the route.'

'You don't have to do this,' Anna said. 'You can change your mind.'

I said nothing. I did have to do it. We laid the map out on the table. I decided it would be safe enough to wander a little when, disguised as Father Daniel, I reached the streets around the Kisela Voda police station. It was vital that they spotted me, preferably not too close to my purported destination, either, whose proximity might unnerve them. But they didn't know which direction their quarry would be coming from, so they too would be circling Kisela Voda. It was a district of wide boulevards and official buildings. There were several good escape routes and the streets would not be thronged with pedestrians. That was perfect for them.

Anna had the more difficult job: she had to follow in the hired van, which would mean stopping frequently along the way to allow me to catch up. We chose a route without one-way streets and with plenty of places where it would be easy to pull over.

'Won't they drive away very fast after they have attacked you?' asked Eleni.

'Then we will drive fast, too,' said Anna.

'Why don't I go in Anna's Fiat – so we have two cars to chase them?'

'You'd need to be able to communicate with each other,' I said. 'Even then, it's a difficult thing to do. Better you watch where their vehicle goes so Anna can concentrate on driving.'

'If they do capture you, James, they'll discover you are not Father Daniel. Then they will hurt you, won't they? Or even kill you?'

'Please, Eleni!'

'Well, won't they?'

'I'll just have to make sure they don't.'

Anna cut my hair short at the sides and made it flop forward over my forehead like Father Daniel's. Her hands were gentle and deft against my scalp, but when she stood back to study the effect of her work, they began to tremble. I changed into the plain black suit, grey shirt and dog collar Eleni had bought while out hiring the van.

'We should all bring our passports. And I ought to have a hat.'

My JCB logo baseball cap was not the kind of headgear Father Daniel would wear, so Eleni went through the chest in the hall and came up with a wonky affair in black felt with a broad brim. If I tilted my head forward, the hat hid most of my face. I inspected myself in the mirror. It was good that we were doing this after dark because to me the disguise looked superficial to the point of absurdity.

'I could not tell you two apart,' said Eleni. 'It makes me feel quite odd, as if I am looking at a ghost.'

Anna gave her a look of vexation, then caught sight of the Sauer I had tucked into my waistband.

'I don't want you to get killed on our account. It won't help at all.'

'I promise not to. Please bring these spare clips for the gun.'

'You can't promise anything,' said Anna, putting the ammunition in her bag. 'Just don't think you have to be heroic – it will only distract you.'

'They're expecting a frightened priest and they'll get me. It's nearly five o'clock – we have to get started.'

38

We drove down Kemal Sejfula and they dropped me just south of Nikola Karev, about fifteen minutes from the river.

I walked fast, the brim of the hat pulled down over my face. I kept to the right-hand pavement, walking in the same direction as the stream of traffic beside me, so that Anna and Eleni would be facing the same way as the gang's vehicle when, once they'd finished with me, they took off. I couldn't turn and check every car that came idling up behind me, and I felt horribly exposed.

It won't happen here, I told myself. *Too soon.*

I practised listening to engine noises, discounting big diesels and anything that sounded too decrepit to make a good escape vehicle. It didn't rule much out. We entered the old town, where the streets were narrow and thronged with people. I slackened my pace and turned onto Boulevard Philip II, which led directly down to the river. I guessed they'd have spotters on the bridges, with their vehicle or vehicles parked close to the police station, in case I arrived by cab.

I walked across the bridge, holding onto my hat to stop it being picked off by the rough gusts blowing off the river. Half way across, I stopped and gazed thoughtfully down into the black waters of the

Vardar River. Anna and Eleni passed slowly behind me. When the tail lights of the van pulled up on the far side, I followed.

A few restaurants lined the south bank, but the pavements were deserted. I followed the road down between a looming chain hotel and a municipal car park. I was ten minutes' walk from the police station now. The street was wide and although well lit, the lamps were high and gave a cold, fluorescent sheen to the concrete and glass walls of the hotel. The perfect place for a killing. So where were the killers?

The traffic was lighter here, vehicles coming up fast, so at least I had a chance of sensing if one of them decelerated. Anna and Eleni had pulled over just beyond a bus stop, and I walked quickly to get past them. Now there was a small park to my right. I stilled my breathing and shook out my arms to let the tension go, and all the time my eyes flickered over the slabs of gleaming steel and glass sliding along the road beside me. Three minutes since I'd crossed the bridge. Time enough, if I'd been spotted.

I had.

A BMW, cruising towards me on the opposite carriageway. A face staring at me from the rear window, lips twitching in speech, finger pointing. Anna was ten yards behind me. The BMW slowed and drew in towards the kerb, making space for a U-turn. I reached to adjust my dog collar, lest they be in any doubt that I was Father Daniel.

I watched for their move. The park was unfenced, but there wasn't much cover for the first twenty yards, just a statue of a group of soldiers leaning towards the sky.

A long blast on a horn. I turned. The BMW was heeling across the traffic, windows gaping. In the passenger seat I saw the big, impassive face and dark eyes of the man who had tried to crack open my skull in Syrna Street. Haclan Adjani.

I sprinted for the statue, got its broad plinth between me and the BMW. Doors slamming, the car surging away from the kerb.

I ran straight into the park and watched the BMW's lights swing right at the corner and follow the road round. Footsteps behind me, right and left. The BMW drew up on the far side of the park, three or four hundred yards away. I ran through lines of low hedging and skirted a bandstand that stood in a blaze of light in the centre of the park, its white colonnades so clean and new they looked like plastic.

I headed into a brake of ornamental trees, though their slender trunks would give scant cover. Two men were running in from the place where the BMW was parked. I saw a dart of orange, heard the vicious snap, the bullet whining as it split the cold air ten yards to my left. A second shot from the men behind me crunched into the bark of a tree to my right.

I hit the side road along the rear of the hotel. They were still over a hundred yards away, and it takes luck to down a running man with a handgun at that range. I was tempted to use the Sauer to keep them honest, but then they'd know for sure I wasn't Father Daniel and the longer they harboured doubts on that score the better. I dashed across the street without bothering to zigzag. The head-lights of the BMW shone from the corner. Which way now?

Cast-iron railings separated the sidewalk from a strip of con-crete paving along the wall of the hotel. I looked left and right for a way into the building... There! A delivery bay with a down ramp barred by a pair of high gates. I raced towards it. Locked – and too high to climb quickly enough. Haclan got out of the BMW and stood watching me, one arm in a sling across his stomach.

I was stranded on a narrowing stretch of pavement, my pur-suers fanning out along the edge of the park behind me. One of them crouched and raised the snout of his weapon. His bullet whanged off the crossbar of the railings and a chip of cast iron struck my cheek. A second bullet snapped into the wall, just about head height. A jolt of adrenalin booted at my heart. I ran – towards the BMW, because I was facing that way, and because Haclan wasn't firing. He'd stepped out of the car merely to enjoy the spectacle. They loosed off round after round, like shooting at a pellet-scarred tin soldier rattling along a rail at a fairground booth. Time ticked down, my legs slowed, my arms took turns to reach ahead of me. My mind rehearsed the moment of impact, the heavy slug tearing flesh, parting nerves, splintering bone.

Then I saw something. A skylight. One of a row set in the paved area on the other side of the railings, but this one wasn't like the rest. Brown, tatty at the edges. Twenty paces away. I slowed to a jog. It was broken, repaired with a square of chipboard and a bit of plastic sheeting. Bullets whirring and snickering... I took it all in: the height of the railings, the blunt shapes of the spikes. Ten paces. The opening, just wide enough, the chipboard brittle. Three paces. The possibility that I'd misjudged. Two paces. The fact that I had no choice.

I seized the third spike back from the broken skylight with my right hand and vaulted, putting all the power I could through my arm to turn forward momentum into height. I felt my weakened ribs crunch as I torqued through the air, but I got one foot on top of a spike, released my grip, and caught my balance for long enough to take aim at the skylight. It didn't look so big now but I was on my way, battering feet first through the square of chipboard, splinters tearing at my arms, the frame flying past, plunging down and praying for a safe passage and a soft landing.

I got neither.

My left shoulder crashed against the frame of the skylight and a jag of chipboard gouged a furrow in my neck, then snagged the tip of my ear and ripped through the cartilage. I landed off balance on a concrete floor, and the square of plastic sheeting slipped out from beneath my feet. I slammed down on hip and elbow, lay there with my bones throbbing, blood dripping over the dog collar and pooling on the floor.

I rolled onto my side and pulled myself upright, groggy and stiff but more or less intact. I reached for the Sauer, but it wasn't there. Dislodged in the fall. There was a dim glow from the street, but not enough to see much. I'd make an easy target if I turned on the light so I searched the floor with my hands, but couldn't find the gun.

I tried the door. Locked. It was strong and close-fitting, the kind a hotel chain fits on a room where hazardous materials are stored. Shadows lunged across the room. I looked up to see the wan streetlight blocked out by the figure of a man peering over the railings.

The room was lined with racks of steel shelving, holding mops, brushes and boxes of cleaning products. I found a bottle of bleach, and another of bathroom cleaner with a nozzle and trigger top. Two men were now climbing the railings above the skylight. I emptied the bottle with the trigger top and filled it with bleach, adjusted the nozzle to give a jet, then climbed the shelves to one side of the skylight until I was hunched against the ceiling. I held my breath and stayed very still.

Voices, feet scuffing concrete, the rasp and click of a clip being loaded. I could sense their reluctance to lower themselves into this dark basement, even though there was probably nothing down there but a priest unconscious on the floor. After a moment, the silhouette of a head appeared in the opening. A gun inched uncertainly forward.

I reached up and aimed the nozzle at the face behind it, squeezed. There was a roar and the gun-hand shot backwards. A second gun appeared and fired twice into the floor. I dropped the bleach and stretched up for the shooter's wrist, got it in one hand, grabbed it with the other, then swung down off the shelves. He didn't have time to brace himself. His head and shoulders scraped down through the skylight and my bodyweight did the rest. His head cracked into the floor, and his body flopped after it like a puppet with the strings cut.

An engine running in the street, a shout. Haclan, regrouping. I flipped on the light and saw the butt of my Sauer beneath the shelving rack. The lock was a good one and it took three carefully aimed shots before I could barge the door open.

* * *

I stepped out into a dimly lit passage and saw a uniformed man retreat smartly from the corner ahead of me. If he'd been sent to investigate, then someone else would already have called the police, and they didn't have far to come. I ran along the low, narrow passages around the basement until I found the service lift. It was jammed open by a wheeled hopper full of bags used by guests to send their clothes for cleaning. I shoved the hopper into the lift and hit the button for the top floor. While the lift trundled upwards, I searched through the laundry bags and found a couple of T-shirts to mop the blood from my arms and neck, then sorted out a black polo-neck sweater that would cover the dog collar, and a fawn overcoat. My trousers were ripped but I couldn't find a replacement and the overcoat would cover the worst of the damage.

On the top floor I encountered a party of well-dressed diners making their way along the corridor from the passenger lifts, following signs for the Skyway Restaurant. I hurried past them, T-shirt clamped to my neck. I took a flight of stairs that led to the roof, ran to the parapet above the back wall of the building.

The BMW had driven off. I worked my way around the roof and noticed that on one side of the building there was a walkway which gave access at third-floor level to the shopping mall next door. I moved on to the front of the hotel and looked down at a short arc of brightly lit asphalt that curved in beneath the canopy over the entrance. A group of porters had gathered, one of them giving orders and pointing. A man and a woman came out and were bundled hastily into a waiting taxi. No sign of the BMW, nor of Anna and Eleni's van. As I changed into my new clothes, the darkness was cut by the keening of a siren, then a series of jabbering pulses as the approaching police vehicle cleared the traffic from a junction. Time to move on.

I ran back down and rode the service lift to the third floor, reasoning that the police would expect a fugitive to use the stairs and would shortly have them covered. I found the entrance to the walkway and stepped between rows of glass-fronted cabinets with sensually posed perfume flasks, wristwatches reclining on Alpine swards, crystal swans necking beneath cones of halogen. This surreal scene gave way to a galleried shopping arena, with a few groups of people browsing the brightly lit shopfronts. I thought I might bleed to death before I found the lavatories, which were hidden by an artful *trompe l'oeil* of a curved wall.

Once inside, I stripped to the waist and sluiced cold water over my ear and neck. My shoulder was livid and swollen where it had banged against the frame of the skylight, but nothing was broken. The ugly, ragged scrape in my neck pulsed as blood pumped in the carotid artery – a splinter of chipboard had missed it by millimetres. My arms were cut up, too, but the only really troublesome injury was the inch-long nick in my already-damaged ear, which bled with joyful copiousness whenever I pulled the T-shirt away. I rinsed the cloth, tore it into strips and bandaged my head, then redressed. The overcoat was a fancy cashmere, and from the collar down I could pass for a wealthy Skopje businessman; from the collar up I looked like a desperado who's run head first through a barbed-wire fence and been patched up by a passing drunk. I could have done with the shabby hat, but it was probably sitting in a labelled evidence bag in the back of a police car by now. It couldn't be helped. I'd been here too long already.

I went back into the mall and left by the main entrance, then turned towards the river. I went cautiously, head down, dawdling at corners to check for followers. On the embankment road, a bus came past and I ran for the stop. The driver waited, though when he saw my ripped-up neck and soggy bandage he looked as if he wished he hadn't. I rode the bus for several stops, then got out, crossed the river and walked back towards the old town.

39

I bought a black watch cap to hide the bandage and holed up in a cluttered little café just off the souk. I had nothing to do now but wait for Anna's call. The proprietor juggled a huge spit of chicken meat onto his grill and tended it lovingly while talking football at me in broken English. It was clear from the collection of greasy posters and flags pinned to the wall behind the counter that his first love was FK Vardar Skopje and his second Aston Villa. Having nothing to contribute to a conversation about either, I nodded or shook my head on cue, and was rewarded with the first serving from the spit, served in a hot flatbread with sliced tomato and a powerful-smelling garlic sauce.

'No bottle, no!' he ferociously declared, smearing it onto the bread with the back of a spoon. 'I make myself. Julian Joachim, best striker in England football, yes?'

'For sure.'

'Left foot, right foot, head. Always in the net!'

The hot, spicy food and loquacious company were soothing as the touch of a mother's hand in fever. I found myself think-ing of all the cafés I'd visited over the last few weeks – Maria's, the Royal outside Wellingborough Station, the lorry drivers' haunt by Harwich docks, and now this place that already felt so familiar – and they strung themselves together in my memory like knots in a cord, markers of moments when the chaotic trajectory of my life intersected briefly with normality. Moments of respite... Yet also reminders of how far adrift I was, how hurled about and swept along and consumed by the dark and insatiable appetites of my enemies. I'd aligned myself with the power of a mother's love, of her anguish. But still, I'd left another body on the floor of the hotel store room. Dead? I hadn't even checked. Either way, I was a killer. And I felt gloomy, then, because I did not know where being a killer would take me next.

The proprietor came over with a glass of red wine.

'For you. We drink now. To Vardar! To Aston Villa! Hurrah!'

'Hurrah,' I said.

'You sad man,' he observed. 'Maybe Birmingham fan!'

I laughed with him and slugged the velvety wine that smelled of blackberries and warm earth. He refilled my glass and we drank again. Wasn't this how life should be? An exchange of camaraderie over chicken and red wine. The trivial circumstance of human kinship. I looked up at my host's generous, piratical features and grinned at him. It doesn't take so much to be a happy man, I thought. Aston Villa, cheap wine, a willingness to make your own garlic sauce. The phone buzzed in my pocket.

'James, we thought you must be dead.'

'Very much alive, thank you, Eleni.'

'We lost them. It was my fault. We followed the car, but then—'

'Where did you see them last? Are you there now?'

'Yes. They had another car near the station. We followed that one. The BMW was too fast. It was a Volkswagen...' I heard her consulting Anna. 'A Volkswagen Passat. Grey. I got it mixed up with another car.'

'Give me the address, I'll come and find you.'

I ran into the street and found a taxi. Thirty-five minutes later, I was crouched in the back of the little van, Anna's haunted face turned towards me, Eleni clutching a map in both hands. It was upside down, I noticed. 'We heard the shooting,' she said. 'Dear James, what happened to your neck? And your ear?'

'It's fine. Tell me what happened.'

'The BMW waited by the park until we heard sirens, then it left and we followed it to a place near the railway station. Most of them got into the grey car that was waiting and the BMW drove off.'

'Did you see who drove it? The man with his arm in a sling?'

'No, he got into the grey car.'

'The BMW was probably stolen. Show me where they went.'

'They crossed the river on Belasitsa, then took the main road east, Alexander Makedonski, here,' said Eleni, her large white finger fluttering uncertainly over the map. 'They came off at Andonov-Chenko and we followed them for about two kilometres. Left onto Alija Avdovikj, then left again, Durmitorska Road. But when the car stopped, a family got out.' She looked anxiously at Anna. 'The streets are so dark. All I could see was the red lights on the back of the cars.'

'You did your best,' said Anna. 'Did we really think we could follow these men to their front door? We're university lecturers, not policemen or spies. It didn't work, that's all.'

'Eleni, show me where you think you started following the wrong car.'

'The junction of Andonov-Chenko and Alija Avdovikj. There was so much traffic, I couldn't—'

'Look at the route,' I interrupted. 'They followed Alexander Makedonski out of town, then took a smaller main road, then perhaps Alija Avdovikj. There are plenty of other exits off Alexander Makedonski but they chose this one. Which tells us they were heading for this area.' I circled it on the map. 'I'd say they're holed up somewhere less than five minutes' drive from here.'

'Maybe thirty streets,' said Anna, starting the engine. 'How long will it take, do you think, James? Half an hour?'

'Eleni should go back and get the Fiat,' I said. 'They might have seen the van.'

'Anna, do you want me to stay?'

'No. Call me when you get to the apartment.'

'Good luck, my darling Anna,' she said, and bundled herself out into the street.

I climbed into the passenger seat and worked out a route that zigzagged back and forth across our search area. It would take two hours at least. All the stiffness and soreness in the various damaged bits of my body was gone. I dared not tell Anna, but I really did feel that Haclan was close.

*　　*　　*

It was a district of light industrial units, most of which were locked up and looked disused. High walls topped with broken glass, fenced-off yards with warehouses, sheds, office huts, lock-up garages, unlit corners, barriers formed by stacks of timber or piles of sand or skips full of rubbish… Every turning seemed to have a dozen places you could hide a car. We crawled along the broken roads, the van's wipers thumping from side to side, laying drifts of gritty slush against the edges of the windscreen, further obscuring our view of these obscure places.

'We may have to try again on foot,' said Anna, when we'd covered every street at least once. 'Or maybe cover a bigger area. What do you think?'

'We should do the whole route again in reverse, so we approach every street from a new perspective. We'll see things we missed first time.'

Different things that were more of the same. Hiding places.

Hidden places. Locked-up places. Dogs too hungry to wait out the sleet, sniffing at drains and gullies choked with sodden debris. A boy on a bicycle that was too large for him, lifting his feet up as he freewheeled through a puddle of melted slush. The search area was too precise, too optimistic. There were many reasons why you might avoid this or that junction and take a less obvious route – for instance, to stop for petrol or food. Or because you'd seen that small white van and the two women inside it enough times to make you suspicious.

'I don't think we will find the car on the street,' said Anna decisively. I could sense her dismay, picking away at the kernel of hope which all the accumulation of facts and inferences had so far failed to crack apart.

'Let's finish our route, then decide what to do next.'

We finished. We drove back to our starting point in silence, then started again. I was staring through the side window, feeling drained out by the pitch and yaw of the long, grim day, when I saw a shape that was somehow familiar. A certain curve. Polished chrome shining from the gloom, blunt rubber cap. There was something about that curve of chrome which demanded to be recognised.

'Stop.'

'What is it, James? What did you see?'

'I don't know. Back up a bit.'

Polished chrome. An inch or two. Above the line of glass chunks embedded in the wall.

'Wait here, Anna. It's probably nothing.'

I crossed the road and walked along the wall to a pair of wooden gates. There was a gap between the gatepost and the wall and I peered through into a big yard with a pair of prefab huts and a couple of vehicles hunched in the gloom. The gap was narrow and I couldn't see much to either side. I pressed my cheek against the brickwork and got the angle I needed to see why that unexceptional shape had set off such a strident alert in my head.

I ran back to Anna. 'There was a vehicle at Father Daniel's refuge, a Mitsubishi camper van with a ladder on the back. It's in that yard. The top of the ladder is poking above the wall.'

'How do you…? Are you sure, James?'

'Not a hundred per cent. I've never seen another vehicle like that one. It's too much of a coincidence.'

'Katarina may be inside it. We must call the police, they can surround the place so they can't get away.'

'I don't think we should – not yet.'

'Those monsters have got my daughter!'

'What can we say? That we've seen a Mitsubishi camper van parked in a yard? They're not going to stage a full-on assault just because we tell them to.'

'The police can't just pretend it isn't happening.' I could see in her face that she knew they could do just that. 'Suppose they drive away?'

I wasn't going to say so to Anna, but I knew that an operation like Haclan's would have a line into the Skopje police. If she called them, Anna might inadvertently be reporting our presence to Haclan. *There's a small white van, parked right outside your den… Deal with it!*

'I'm frightened for Katya. I'm so frightened for her. What can we do if the police won't help us?'

'If they try to take the children anywhere else, they'll use the Mitsubishi. Let me get my tracker in place. Whatever happens, we'll know where they are.'

'Children?'

'We have to assume it isn't just Katya.'

'Yes. OK. Do that, James. Go. Quickly.'

'I need to scout the place. Don't wait here – we can meet…' I pulled out the map and we found a parallel street. 'Give me twenty minutes. If you think they've seen you, drive away and call me when you're clear.'

I felt uneasy leaving her. If I didn't do something, *anything*, right now, I felt I might start to tick like the timer on an unexploded bomb. Anna, meanwhile, was going to sit alone in a dark street and wait. While she waited, she would have to endure the knowledge that her daughter might be less than a hundred yards away, in the hands of child traffickers. I reached out and touched her arm, and when she turned her eyes on me it was like being picked out by a searchlight.

'Don't fail me, James. Or Katya. Don't.'

I gave her arm what was intended to be a reassuring squeeze, but there was so much adrenalin sluicing through me that the hold I took on her was not far short of an act of violence. My clumsiness broke the tension, and she gave a smile full of fortitude and grace.

'Ow. I can't drive if you break my wrist.'

'Sorry. Call Eleni, tell her what's happened.'

I got out and walked back along the street, heard the van pulling away smoothly behind me. I have never felt so much respect for someone as I did for Anna then. I would not fail her. Or Katya.

The sleet had eased and the street hissed and plinked as the meltwater sluiced away down the gutters. I took off the fancy overcoat and hid it under an overturned dustbin – the neighbourhood was sporadically lit at best, and with the black polo neck and the watch cap pulled down tight over my ears, I could hide in any patch of darkness. I started at the gates I'd peered through earlier, kneeling on the pavement and scanning the derelict yard again. I could climb over in a matter of seconds, but that would land me directly between the two prefabs to the right and the vehicles to the left. The wall was a couple of feet higher than the gates and I'd have to negotiate the broken glass; but at least I could pick my spot. There were lights on in both huts and the windows of one were steamed up – from cooking, I guessed. I couldn't see anyone outside, but the light faded rapidly twenty yards in, and Haclan was well organised

– it would be second nature to post a couple of guards while he sat down to his dinner.

I carried on round the block. Haclan's yard was sandwiched between brick-built warehouses, four storeys high, with their windows boarded up and the front gates close-fitting and secured with padlocked chains – it wasn't what you would call a salubrious neighbourhood. In the parallel street, I found the entrance to a narrow archway that had been blocked off with two sheets of corrugated iron nailed to a timber frame. The nail heads were rusty, and when I tugged at one corner of the barrier the whole construction creaked. I checked the street, then wrapped my watch cap over the bottom edge of one of the sheets and worked my hands underneath it. The sheet bent reluctantly upwards, creasing at the lowest nail. It took me four or five minutes to work the corrugated iron back and forth and lever out the nails at one edge until I had an opening wide enough to climb through.

It was pitch dark at first. I edged along the damp brick wall for ten yards, then emerged from the back of the building, where a little ambient light filtered down from the sky and was sucked in by a stale fog that hung over the ground. To my left, the brick wall continued for another twenty yards, then ended in a section of fence the same width as the alley. On the other side of the alley was a wire fence, beyond which were seven or eight teetering stacks of empty pallets.

I pulled the watch cap down low and crept forward. The icy mud slid and crunched beneath my feet. A few paces from the end, I stopped and found myself looking directly into the back of Haclan's yard – I could see the lights from the huts about thirty yards away. The Mitsubishi should be straight ahead, but my view was blocked by a low breeze-block shed. There was a gate in the section of fence at the end, secured by a padlocked sliding bar. The fence was high and too flimsy to climb – and given that the Mitsubishi was over on the far side of the yard, there didn't seem to be any advantage in breaking in from here. I watched the yard for a while longer, mapping its layout in my head.

The door to one of the prefabs swung open and a man stepped out, flicked on a torch and started across the yard. I lay down along the angle of the wall, and the wetness seeped into my sweater. Without warning – I hadn't even noticed the cold until now – I started to shiver. The oval of torchlight zigzagged along the ground towards me and I got ready to run in case it fell on some part of my shivering body. Another torch beam swung out from just behind the wall I was lying against, not more than three yards away. The man holding it stood up and walked over to the front of the shed. Now both men were hidden from view and I was able to retreat to a less exposed position in the alley.

They had a brief argument, their grumbling voices muffled by the damp air, then one of the torch beams set off for the prefab and the other flicked off. I guessed they were taking it in turns to go for their dinner. I stole back to the street and folded the corrugated iron back over the gap, then continued round the block.

There was a vacant lot on the last section, but too far away to offer a third access point to Haclan's yard. Barbed wire had been wrapped roughly round the top of the wooden palings that fenced it off from the street. I unpicked a length and took it back to the alley. Lying prone in the mud, I wrapped the barbed wire round the post and the leading edge of the gate. My fingers were stiff with cold, but I got the wire looped three times round and then twisted the ends together and tucked them into the final loop.

I watched the yard for a few minutes more, but all I discovered was that the man on guard duty had a racking cough. I slunk back to the street and went round the front, retrieved my coat and moved the dustbin against the front wall – roughly adjacent to where the Mitsubishi was parked. Then I went back to Anna – ten minutes later than agreed. She looked strung out beyond endurance, fraying under the strain of keeping both hope and hopelessness in check.

'We need a diversion in the alley at the back,' I said. 'It's dangerous, though. I've wired the gate shut, but it won't hold them for more than a minute or two.'

'What do I do?'

'I'm going to tie the Sauer to the fence, then run a line back to the archway so you can operate the trigger from there, where it's dark. I need to find a length of wire or string, or something—'

'Don't be stupid, James. That will take forever. I'll just go down to the end and fire.'

'It's too dangerous.'

'Everything is too dangerous. Mostly it is too dangerous for Katya. Did you see her there? Was there any sign or...'

I shook my head. 'It's very dark – impossible to know. I'm sorry.'

'That's all right. Shall we go now?'

I didn't persist with my idea. It probably wouldn't have worked. I showed her how to use the gun, told her to fire once by the gate, retreat down the alley and fire again, then get out.

'Don't run,' I told her. 'It's slippery.'

'How should I walk, do you think? Maybe putting one foot in front of the other?'

'Just be careful,' I insisted. 'And don't wait longer than three seconds before the second shot.'

A single, unexpected gunshot is difficult to locate in an environment like that: the report would bounce around the walls of the warehouses or rattle into the gaps between stacks of pallets, leaving just a confused echo in the ears. I needed the second shot to get Haclan's men homing in on the alley at the rear, well away from the Mitsubishi. But was I expecting too much of Anna? As far as I knew, she'd never even held a gun before, let alone fired one in a fog-choked alley.

'It'll kick hard so hold it in both hands. And keep your elbow bent. If it jams, just get out of there, OK? If anything at all goes wrong, in fact—'

'You sound like Eleni. Maybe you should fire the gun and I'll go over the wall.'

'I'm trying to anticipate, that's all. Don't try and go through the gate, will you?'

'I'll do anything to get Katya back. That doesn't make me completely crazy.'

'Sorry. If I thought we could handle them, then… But we can't.'

I unpicked the components of the tracker and rearranged them so the little package would fit in one of the uprights of the ladder, then taped it together again. Anna watched me impatiently.

'Can you call Eleni and see how she's getting on? I could do with one of her uncle's coats.'

Anna spoke to her friend, who had just arrived at the apartment, then we drove in a wide circle to the archway on the far side of Haclan's yard. I showed her the gap in the corrugated-iron barrier and gave her the gun.

'Hold me for a moment, James.'

'Better put that down first.'

She dropped the Sauer into the pocket of her parka, then reached across and clung to me and I felt her heart beating. I remembered holding Katarina against my thudding chest during our flight from Kosovo, and I had that same feeling that fate had brought us together so we could save each other from the different kinds of darkness that had fallen over our lives. Then she released me and I got out of the van and ran round to the wall of Haclan's yard. I took off my overcoat, looked up at the wall I was going to climb, and waited for the gunshots.

The first – shockingly loud in the dank air. I climbed onto the dustbin, keeping my head below the wall, started counting.

One... I threw the coat over the palisade of broken glass, positioned my hands at either edge.

Two... Levered myself up until the ridge of the wall was level with my chest.

Three...

No shot.

Two men running from the prefab. Still no second shot. Jammed. Dropped. Or they'd worked out where the first shot had come from and caught her in the alley. A third man jogged over towards the back gate. The second shot came and he stumbled, doubled over and cried out in shock. I swung over the wall, pulled the overcoat down and out of sight, and ran the few paces to the Mitsubishi. Gunshots hammered out from the breeze-block shed and I feared for Anna fleeing down the dank alley.

I climbed the first rung of the ladder fixed to the rear and pulled the rubber cap off the top of the upright. Over the roof of the Mitsubishi I could see someone unlocking the front gates. A car ignition fired. The tracker was too fat for the chrome tubing. I squeezed and massaged the layers of gaffer tape, eased it back into the tube, but it jammed in the bend and I had to prise it out and try again. I wanted to feel movement inside the camper, but there was no sign that anyone was inside.

They weren't firing any more, but I couldn't see what was going on. I heard Haclan giving orders in his flat, cold voice, and for a split second the urge to kill him ripped through me. Take him, there and then, no matter what. Perhaps I would have done so if the tracker hadn't just then slid obligingly into place. I put the rubber cap back on and climbed down and crouched behind the Mitsubishi. The grey Passat saloon was idling at the gates, its only occupant sitting in the passenger seat, checking his gun. The driver's door was open, a scrap of red from the car's interior lights cast on the dirt below.

Two men were kneeling by the injured man, two more staring towards the alley from the cover of the breeze-block shed. Haclan stood outside the prefab with the steamed-up windows, facing my way, giving orders to a tall, hunched man loading a pump-action shotgun. If I climbed back over the wall now, Haclan would see me. Better to run for the open gates. Fifteen or twenty yards to cover, then I'd be out on the street. The dark, empty, locked-up street, with a carload of armed men on my tail. They could be looking for Anna, too.

I moved to the front wing of the Mitsubishi. Where would the first bullet come from? The man in the Passat, most likely. A scream from the wounded man – they were carrying him to the prefab. I got to the wall in three paces, ran low towards the Passat's lights. Through the side windows of the vehicle, I saw the tall, hunched man turn and walk away from Haclan. I was ten yards from the car. Haclan walked up the steps to the door of the prefab, his head rising above the roof of the Passat. He swung round and our eyes met.

I sprinted for the open door and dived. The gun swung towards me but he was too slow and I thrust his hand aside. The shot cracked out, filling the interior with pulsing noise and the choking reek of the charge. I drove the heel of my hand up into the gunman's nose and his head thumped back against the headrest. I felt the cartilage give, and shoved again until the ridge of his nose collapsed into his face. A snap on the rear window and a thousand cubes of glass pattered onto the back seat. I swung my legs into the footwell and hit the throttle and the clutch at the same time.

The car shuddered on its springs, exhaust jetting smoke. A bullet smacked into the fascia six inches from my hand. Someone yanked open the door behind my seat. I jammed the gearstick forward and released the clutch. The Passat surged forward, grit peppering its undercarriage. The driver's door walloped the gate-pillar and slammed shut. The man behind me was half inside the car. No time to get the rest of him in. No time to bail out, either. The steel skin of the door screeched against the brickwork, and the vehicle shunted sideways. His ribcage probably took the brunt of it. The door came clear of the pillar, and in the rear-view mirror I saw him totter sideways as the Passat slewed out into the street.

40

I drove for a kilometre in a fast, straight line, then took a corner and pulled up. My passenger was still holding the gun, but he was shuddering and his eyes said he thought he was dying. I took the gun and checked the clip: nearly full. I hauled him onto the pavement and sat him up against a wall, then drove on for another five minutes and pulled up outside a Chinese takeaway.

I called Anna, and heard myself sigh with relief when she answered. I gave her the address. There was nowhere to hide the car, so I carried on for a few minutes until I found a quiet cul-de-sac. I dropped the keys down a drain and let down the front tyres, then walked back to the takeaway.

I took the opportunity to order a dish of noodles and sat on the bench beneath the window to wait. A woman came in with two girls in their early teens who squabbled over the menu, then tore it in half and were hustled outside and ticked off at length. One of the takeaway's brown paper bags flopped along the pavement like a species of urban tumbleweed.

I didn't see the van pull up. Anna rushed through the door. Her face was white as chalk and her eyes glittered with barely restrained ferocity.

'Did you do it? Did you get the tracker on?'

'It's there.'

'They tried to come after me but they couldn't get the gate open, so they just shot at me instead. I didn't realise until a bullet hit the bit of corrugated iron I was holding and it stung my hands.'

'You shot one of them.'

'Did I? Yes…'

She stood up, stumbled out into the street and was sick on the pavement. I went out and helped her back to the van. We drove to the other side of Alexander Makedonski and parked in a street of small, well-kept villas. A rapacious-looking power boat called *Sofia* sat on a trailer in front of the garage of the house beside us. The temperature had finally dropped below zero and the tarpaulin stretched over its cockpit was lightly furred with ice.

Anna called Eleni to tell her where we were. I turned on the phone linked to the tracker and waited for it to boot. Now that our assault on Haclan's yard was over, the endorphins coursing through my veins had run dry and various bits of my body felt sore. I touched my split ear and found it had formed a large clot.

Anna finished her call. 'Eleni's on her way – she's bringing you a coat.' She handed me the Sauer. 'I'm OK now. I didn't mean to shoot at him. I was so angry.'

'It was one hell of a diversion, anyway.'

'I did call the police. The woman who answered wanted to know if I'd been drinking. Has there been an actual crime, she kept asking? Hundreds, I told her. Child prostitution, abduction, murder. She gave me a crime reference number to shut me up. We'll send someone round as soon as possible, she said. You were right, it was completely pointless.'

'Got you!'

'What?'

'It works. Look.' I showed her the row of numbers. 'The long-lats

309

for the Mitsubishi. Wherever it goes now, we can find it. How long till Eleni gets here?'

'Twenty minutes or so.'

I powered up Anna's laptop and found the coordinates on the GIS. The Mitsubishi hadn't moved – but I thought it would, very soon. People like Haclan have a fine instinct for absenting themselves when a messy end is in the offing. It was conceivable that he'd abandon Katarina and any other children in his charge, but what I feared most was that they'd take them in another vehicle, one we couldn't track. Still, there was something about that big, frowsty camper van that made it ideal for transporting stolen children. You could imagine it being driven by a social worker or a teacher, but a child trafficker?

'What do we do now?'

'Wait. As soon as they move, we follow. They'll think they're safe and their guard will drop. They'll pass through public places, town centres and suchlike, where they won't want to show their guns. There'll be an opportunity – we just have to be ready.'

'I am ready. Right now.'

'I'd like to be there when they realise all that mayhem was created by a female expert in the early years of the Ottoman Empire. Every crime boss in the Balkans will be working on a joke about it.'

'They were men just like Haclan – marauders, exploiting the decline of the old order to build their own power bases. One empire wanes, another waxes. He would have loved it.'

'Haclan's is waning.'

'Child trafficking was rife, too,' said Anna absently. 'They even made it official. Christian boys seized and trained up as state enforcers, underage girls pressed into the harem.'

'Do you think they knew it was wrong?'

'They didn't think like that – they believed they were one step from divinity. It was right to acknowledge their supremacy, wrong to defy them. I wonder if the children's mothers tried to get them back.'

'I guess there were women just like you, rattling the cages of men like Haclan.'

'I want Katya back. My God, I want her back. Where is Eleni?'

We sat for a few minutes, and then she said: 'Will you hold me again please, James?'

Without saying much more about it, we went and lay down together in the back of the van. Snowflakes fell past the rear window and the silence deepened. The ribbed floor was cold and we sought each other's arms and lay our cheeks against each other's without kissing or wanting to kiss but only for the comfort of it. Her smell was faint, like a rose that has been too long without water. The cramped steel box cocooned us from the outside world and made us oblivious to it, and it seemed as if we had spun off into another dimension – a place for once devoid of choices and meaning, a place where past and future could not make their implacable demands. We were in abeyance, suspended, paused.

She unwrapped her arms from my neck.

'Check the tracker, James.'

I rolled away from her and dialled. The numbers flicked onto the screen. Different numbers. I dialled again. Different again.

'Anna, we're on.'

'We have to wait for Eleni. What can she be doing?'

'It doesn't matter if they get a head start. We shouldn't follow too close, anyway.' I checked the coordinates on the laptop. 'Leaving town, going south. The signal's good. Will you draw their route on the map?'

The more frequently I called for the tracker to report, the quicker the battery would die. But in the intervals between sending requests for the latest coordinates, time slowed to such a degree that I thought my heart might stop in sympathy. The Mitsubishi passed the junction with the A2, which went west to the Bulgarian border, and carried on south.

'Where does it go?'

'Greece – Thessaloniki.'

A border. A port. We had our passports, but if they transferred to a boat in Thessaloniki... The van had a towbar, and for a moment I considered hitching up the speedboat *Sofia* parked in the driveway next to us. And then? Pursue them across the eastern Mediterranean, to Istanbul, Izmir, Cairo...

'How far to the border?'

'Maybe three hours.'

* * *

Eleni arrived at last. I put on the navy blue fleece-lined coat she'd brought me and we piled into the Fiat. Anna drove – I knew the car to be somewhat characterful, and I didn't trust myself not to hammer it to death. Besides, driving would give her something to focus on. As soon as we were on the move, I reached for the radio, which was hissing away as usual, and pushed my fingers into the cassette slot to get a good grip.

'Do you mind?' I asked.

'Please go ahead,' said Anna. 'I've been listening to that station for years and I've never found it interesting at all.'

I levered the radio out of its cradle and disconnected the wiring.

'Blissful silence,' said Eleni. 'What should I do with this?'

I turned to find her pointing my Sig Sauer pistol at the roof – I'd dropped it into the holdall in the rear of the Fiat when we'd swapped cars. The gun sat very easily in Eleni's hand, I noticed.

'Can you find somewhere to hide it?'

She swept a pile of papers aside, then picked one off the floor.

'Dr Galica, you are weeks— No, you are months behind with your marking. Vice-Principal Ongoric will be displeased.'

'B minus, do you think?'

Eleni produced a pen and wrote on the paper, then put it on the floor with the others. 'Done. The Sauer can go here.'

She indicated a tear in the upholstery from which protruded a tongue of stained foam rubber.

'There's no manual safety, but you can decock it,' I said. 'Here—'

'Very useful,' said Eleni, flipping the lever and stowing the weapon in the torn seat, along with the spare clips.

'You've handled a semi-automatic before?' I asked.

'Certainly. I spent two years in the Albanian Army and I was women's multi-disciplinary shooting champion in both of them. Pistols were my best weapon, followed by rifles. Machine guns are noisy and not accurate – a man's weapon, do you think, James?'

'Eleni, you never told me that,' said Anna.

'Well, it is not a thing to talk about in the senior common room.'

'I've never even seen you in the senior common room. To make it up to me, you must do all the marking in the car. B minus for everyone!'

Anna had already proved her mettle; and the discovery that I had a latter-day Amazon marking history essays in the seat behind now made me think that our little retinue might be more formidable than it appeared. We had a pair of guns between us, too – I still had the one I'd taken from the man I had driven out of Haclan's yard: a lousy old Excam Tanfoglio GT 380, but a gun which I knew worked because it had been fired at me.

The atmosphere in the car became almost buoyant as we rattled south along the A1. The city thinned out and the traffic eased. Lorries loomed behind their headlights, then blasted by in a rolling tumult of air. After twenty-five kilometres, the long-lats showed that we were gaining on the Mitsubishi – not very fast, but the sense of optimism was palpable. The snow stopped and a swollen ridge of cloud rolled back, leaving a bright moon in a sky as clean as wet slate.

We left the plains south-east of Skopje and started to climb into sparsely forested hills with patches of exposed rock like scrape-marks left by giant hands. The darkness was studded with lights from distant farmsteads and villages that seemed to pulse like embers exposed to a fitful wind. A hand's-width of fresh snow lay on the road, tramlined by the wheels of vehicles ahead. One set of tracks was broad and carried the imprint of tyres with deep treads.

'The Mitsubishi has off-road tyres,' I said to Anna. 'Those could be its tracks.'

'Can we really be so close?'

'All the farm vehicles round here will have wheels like that,' said Eleni.

'Quite right,' said Anna. 'We mustn't get our hopes up.'

Our own tyres were narrow and almost bald – though the snow was still soft, and with three people on board the Fiat had just enough grip to proceed uphill. We stopped gaining. The gap was about twenty kilometres when we entered a long tunnel and lost GPS contact. Anna pressed the accelerator to the floor and leaned forward over the steering wheel. The fluorescent strips mounted high in the concrete walls sent shadows sliding over her arms as we raced across the wet tarmac, and I experienced again that sense of otherworldliness which had overwhelmed me when I'd lain beside her in the back of the van.

The Fiat came out of the tunnel much too fast and for seconds we were pirouetting towards the crash barrier, a gleaming slab of mountainside and the hollow, blue-black sky panning by turns across the windscreen. The back end of the Fiat thumped into some obstruction beneath the snow and sent us skidding back the other way, but the momentum was gone and we slithered to a halt, the engine clattering feebly in protest.

'I think James might drive now,' said Eleni.

Anna and I swapped places and we ground on. Anna was trying to get the cellphone to call for a location.

'Fast-dial one.'

'It's not working.'

I cajoled her into turning off the phone and starting again. At last the tracker reported in. Still about the same distance ahead. We crossed a pass where a current of funnelled wind rattled the Fiat's windows, then followed a long curve round the peak.

'Is that them?'

Two sets of headlights, shovelling the darkness aside as they set out across the plain below.

'Eleni, are we permitted to think that might be them?'

'Permission granted.'

The descent was nerve-racking. The Fiat felt both heavy and unpredictable, responding to the wheel either not at all or with a ponderous ploughing motion that had us leaning away from the turns like amateur sailors in a heeling scow. The engine was too small to check our speed effectively, but the brakes locked up at the faintest dab. We dropped below the snowline, but the temperature had fallen again and the road was dappled with patches of ice that glistened menacingly in the yellowish haze of our headlights.

By the time we reached the plain, we were nearly thirty kilometres behind. I coaxed the Fiat up to a hundred kph, then a hundred and twenty... But that caused such a frantic howl from the transmission that I settled for a hundred and ten and we drove for an hour, the road taking a series of broad sweeps past Veles, Gradsko, Negotino, before entering another tunnel at the start of the passage through the mountains just north of the border with Greece.

We were less than five kilometres behind when Anna announced that they'd turned off the main road and were heading east.

'There's another crossing into Greece,' she said. 'Just south of Dojran Lake. It looks like a tiny place – I can't even see a proper road on the Greek side.'

Tiny... and probably comatose. I'd been hoping we could challenge them at the border, where there'd be armed police, officials, bright lights, barriers, queues... In fact, I'd allowed myself to believe that within the hour we might reunite Katarina with her mother. At least I hadn't got as far as proposing this plan to Anna.

'Or I suppose they could carry on east, to the border with Bulgaria.'

I picked up speed, trying to suppress the feeling that the rescue of Katarina had always been a hopelessly quixotic endeavour and would now come unstuck. Haclan's men drove east for twenty kilometres, then south again.

'Greece it is.'

I wanted to get close enough to see them at the border, at least, and drove fast along the flanks of a series of hills. We watched the headlights of Haclan's vehicles below us, creeping towards the border. A lake came into view, a sheet of blackness fringed with lights from the houses set round its shores. We skirted the dark water, passed through a pair of melancholy resort towns, then rounded a bend at the southern end of the lake. They were parked up in a layby less than three hundred yards ahead.

* * *

I took the first turning I could, a rough track shielded by a screen of trees, killed the lights, turned the car round and switched off the engine. Anna wound down her window and we could just make out the low thrum of idling engines.

Anna spoke in a whisper. 'Now's the time, James. Isn't it?'

'Let me go and check what they're up to.'

I loped along behind the trees, veering away from the road to avoid gaps in the cover. There was an abandoned tractor on a square of dirt almost opposite their vehicles. I got in behind it. The Mitsubishi and the white Mercedes saloon I'd seen outside my apartment in Skopje were thirty yards away. A little further on, the road was spanned by an awning of corrugated iron; a plastic hut and striped barrier marked the Macedonian side of the border. An illuminated sign above the hut said *Border Closed* in several languages.

Five men were standing round the Mercedes, faces glowing in turn as they took drags on cigarettes. No sign of Haclan. Relaxed, chatting, stretching. This was their habitual route into Greece, I realised: a sleepy little place with underpaid officials pleased to make a bit extra by raising the barrier to a couple of vehicles passing through at dead of night. Switch off the surveillance cameras, take the cash, go back to sleep. Fine for them – but for us, a dead end.

My mind ticked frantically through the options. Buy our way through? Corrupt officials are wary, they like well-established arrangements with people they can trust not to blab – criminals with plenty to hide, for instance. If the bribe was refused, the man might warn Haclan's gang that they were being followed, and we'd lose the advantage of surprise. Take him out, then. Tie him up and lock him in a storeroom. That wouldn't be difficult, but there might be others. And there was still the Greek end of the crossing to negotiate – all I could see of that was a halo of arc light several hundred yards away, at the far end of a corridor of road fenced off with winking lines of razor wire.

One of the men went to the side door of the camper van, slid it open and said something. Two girls came to the door and climbed out. The man directed them to the front, where they stood awkwardly in the glare of the headlights, watched by the semi-circle of smokers. The man gestured at the ground and one of the girls shook her head and started back to the open door. The man caught her by the wrist and slapped her across the cheek. He yelled something and raised his hand. The two girls cowered, then the one who hadn't tried to get away pulled her trousers down and quickly squatted in the dirt. The other girl hesitated, saw the man stepping towards her, then did the same. One of the smokers said something and the others jeered, then spat at the crouching girls. It was horrible to watch.

You can take these five – they'll be two down before they even know they've been attacked.

Shoot it out, with a carload of children in the line of fire?

Have to do it somewhere...

Eleni thought so, too. She was lying twenty yards away at the foot of a tree and her first shot had the outermost of the group of men staggering for cover with one hand clamped over his hip. I pulled the Excam and got the next shot in, and it caught the tail light of the Mercedes. Eleni hit its rear side window and a glittering cascade of glass dropped from the door frame.

Two of the men grabbed the girls and hauled them to the door of the camper van. The Mitsubishi's lights went out, then the Mercedes' too, and we were staring into darkness. A moment later there was a honk and a flash from the road between the border posts. The barrier by the hut cranked upwards. The Mercedes heeled out onto the road and the Mitsubishi lurched after it.

A dark figure rushed into the road near Eleni's position. Anna. She sprinted past me as the two vehicles swept through the open barrier and accelerated towards the grainy light at the Greek end of the border crossing. Anna's voice lashed out, screaming, scraping at the air between herself and the receding back end of the camper van. The vehicle's rear lights came on and revealed the silhouette of a uniformed man jogging towards us between the lines of razor-wire.

Eleni caught up with Anna, wrapped her arms around her waist and managed to wrestle her to a standstill by the barrier. The uniformed man came up, flapping his arms at them and shouting. I could see Eleni's shoulders quaking as Anna hung in her arms – or perhaps it was just the flickering of a failing tube in the fluorescent lights overhead. She faced the man and delivered an imperious rebuke. He turned his back on them with a toss of the head, and the two women walked back down the road towards me.

41

Anna wanted to be left alone, so we helped her into the back seat of the car, then stood by the bonnet while Eleni drew powerfully on a cigarette.

'We could fight our way through,' I said, 'you and I.'

'Too much risk. I should have shot out their tyres.'

'You could not fire on a carload of children in darkness.'

'In darkness, yes. Darkness too deep to reach into. You saw those men… Poor Katya.' She held out the Sauer. 'You want this back?'

'Keep it,' I said. 'I'm yet to win a prize for shooting straight.'

We buried the two pistols deep in the torn upholstery and drove back to the main road, then turned south to the main border crossing. The tracker on the Mitsubishi reported in and Eleni plotted their course. The gap between us had become tangible for those shocking moments at the Lake Dojran border post – across it, faces could be seen, screams could be heard, bullets could be fired. Now it was just a set of points on a map again, a diagram of our impending failure to rescue Katarina from her captors.

They didn't like the look of us at the border: an Englishman with hollowed-out eyes and his ear clotted with blood who had no obvious reason for being there and a curiously grand and very bossy Kosovar woman with her catatonic companion – all packed into a cheap old car of the kind driven by people who are of no account. We were pulled into a separate queue and I thought the game was up – they were certain to find the two handguns. Failing that, my passport would not pass muster – I couldn't even remember my fake name and had to check: Anthony Skinner. Eleni, however, was perfectly composed. She asked me to check where the convoy of Haclan's men had got to.

'They've stopped, a little way from the coast, maybe twenty-five kilometres east of Thessaloniki.'

'I think they will be meeting a boat,' Eleni announced. 'Then we won't be able to follow.'

'We don't know that,' I said quickly. 'They could just be resting.'

'Suppose the boat's already arrived?' said Anna. 'They may be taking Katya down to the coast on foot.'

No one spoke. Eleni pursed her lips and debouched from the Fiat to smoke another cigarette, leaving behind her a large void full of pessimistic speculations.

A young border official marched over, inspected our passports and started to circle the Fiat. Eleni regaled him with a stream of voluble Greek, her voice so full of indignation and admonishment that I thought she might start wagging her finger at him. Whether it was her lecture or the disarray inside the car, he seemed to lose heart and, after rifling through a sheaf of essays and inspecting the fetid interior of a Yankee Doodle Diner ice-cream tub, he waved us through.

'What did you say to him?' I asked.

'I spoke to him like his mother. Men generally do what their mothers tell them, especially Greek men.'

It was five-fifteen when we got over the border into Greece and headed east along the coast road. The pre-dawn darkness had a hollow, ominous weight that suggested daybreak had been postponed. The tracker was stationary, or dead. The Fiat developed a bony clunk from its rear suspension and I felt obliged to steer round every pothole in the heavily potholed road. Anna and Eleni jolted and swayed in their seats. We reached a coastline of shattered rock; beyond it, a leaden sea hemmed at shore-break by a fringe of dirty froth.

'Look for boats moored out there,' I said.

There were a few lights nodding from the horizon, but nothing closer in. Less than fifteen kilometres to go.

'When we get there,' said Anna, 'I'm going to stay with Katarina. Whatever else, that's what I'll do. You mustn't try and stop me. You don't have to come with me, but if you do, don't try and stop me.'

'There's no need to decide that now,' said Eleni. 'No need at all.'

'Once we see how things lie, we'll act quickly,' I said.

'I would so like to feel optimistic about it,' said Anna. 'But I can't.'

Six kilometres. The road ducked inland over a stubby promontory that formed one cocked arm of the bay beyond. We crested the ridge. Everything happened quickly, then. We didn't have to decide how to act. The ship was there: an unlit cargo vessel anchored in the bay, a smut of black on the dull water. Anna cried, Eleni wrapped her arms around her friend's shoulders. I killed the lights and the engine and we coasted fast down a shallow, ramp-like road to the shore.

'They're still here,' said Anna. 'Look!'

The Mercedes had pulled off the road alongside a stretch of rough pebble beach. I stopped the Fiat behind it, threw open the door and was out and running, driving through the clutter of stones, handgun out.

* * *

They'd driven the Mitsubishi along the beach – its rear end was canted over at an odd angle two hundred yards away. People at the shoreline. Two rigid inflatables in the water, heaving around a few yards from the shore. Children being herded towards them.

They'd seen us... They couldn't beach the RIBs with the outboards still running and now there wasn't time to bring them ashore. Haclan's men started shoving the girls into the water, forcing them to wade out to the boats through the hard, slapping waves. The RIBs bounced and snapped at their painters, the men at their helms bellowing to those on shore. One of the boats kept yawing round, the man at its helm unable to get it to lie up. They were loading the children into the other, but none of them would step willingly into the stinging cold sea.

A girl of Katarina's age stumbled and went under. The man next to her had to reach in and fish her out while the others waited. I could see their handlers' impatience harden into fury. Four of them occupied, which left just one to keep us off. He'd got behind the Mitsubishi, and from his gun came a fat capsule of orange flame. The round clattered in the rocks to my right. We kept on, Anna panting at my side. Another bullet spat off a boulder ahead of us and whined away into the murky sky.

Sixty yards to go. Eleni tracked up the beach and lay prone. I drew us down to the shoreline to give her a clear shot. She fired four times at precise intervals. The driver of the empty RIB went down on the third. His boat drifted away from the shore. All but two of the children were in the other RIB now.

The gunman from behind the Mitsubishi was hobbling down the beach towards the boat, firing at me as he went. I stopped, aimed, felt a gust of cool wind blow the hair from my forehead. I shot him in the chest and he staggered under the weight of the slug, then bowed his head and knelt. The men by the boat turned away.

We couldn't shoot at the bucking RIB, not with six children on board, and they knew it. Anna ran on past me, screaming in despair as the last man swung up onto the bow. Then she caught her foot in something and went down hard. I got to the boat, had the painter just for a split second before the sodden rope snaked from my grasp and the rear end of the RIB spun inshore. The man at the helm straightened up the outboard, opened the throttle. I felt the water churn at my knees and stepped backwards to escape the whirring prop. A flat roar from the engine and the overloaded RIB sank back on its haunches, surged out to sea between the rolling furrows of its wake.

I turned to look for the other RIB. It had drifted fifty or sixty yards out. I stripped off and swam after it. The waves weren't big, but steep and jumbled so it was hard to get any rhythm, and the water that slopped into my nose stank of oil and rotting seaweed. The RIB leapt up the slope of a wave, then dropped into the trough, then bobbed into view again. Every time it reappeared, the distance I still had to swim seemed to have lengthened, but at last I was hauling myself aboard. The driver was lolling over the outboard. He didn't seem to notice when I tipped him into the sea. I throttled up and headed inshore, where Anna was standing waist-deep in the sea. She'd got the Sauer from Eleni and had both handguns, spare clips and my clothes held above her head. I helped her into the RIB.

'Did you see Katarina?'

'I saw her. Just for a moment, until I fell. Quickly, James.'

* * *

I spun the RIB round, got her up onto a plane, and we scudded out across the bay. Anna took the tiller while I grappled into my wet clothes. It was just about dawn, though the only evidence of the new day was a brown tinge to the relentless slate-grey of the sea and the arrival of a flock of gulls to squabble over a patch of refuse discarded from the stern of the cargo ship. She was an old-fashioned vessel, low-slung deck fitted with a small crane between a high prow and a superstructure of bridge and cabins at the stern. The other RIB disappeared round the far side of her hull. How long would it take to get everyone off? The sea got steadily heavier and less predictable as we headed out, the rubber bows bouncing off the faces of the waves and the outboard racing as the propeller lifted clear of the water. Anna asked me to take over and I dropped speed. We had another problem: the gauge on the fuel tank read less than a quarter full.

We got to within a couple of hundred yards and I saw three men with automatic rifles lined up along the rail beneath the bridge. *Santa Cristina*, she was called, out of Piraeus. We weren't an easy target, even from a stable deck, but all they had to do was keep us at a distance while they got under way. One of the men raised his rifle. I didn't see where the bullets went, but three cracks came veering through the air. Then one of them got lucky – a round slapped off the cylinder of rubber that formed the port side of the RIB and it was a miracle it didn't burst. I'd seen enough. I turned away and accelerated past the cargo ship.

'What are you doing?' Anna shouted. 'We have to go on board.'

'We can't.'

'Then what?'

Then what? I didn't know. A scrap of black smoke guffed from the cargo ship's funnel and the sea bulged into a pattern of glassy pools at her stern. The big, ugly vessel with its consignment of kidnapped girls got under way, and was soon ploughing through the turn that would bring her on course to sail straight out of the bay.

Stay with it, I told myself. Think of something.

We passed through the neck of the bay and although the waves grew higher again, they were smoother and less tightly packed and I was able to settle the RIB on a fast, even trajectory that quickly drew us further ahead of the larger vessel. The needle on the fuel gauge edged towards zero. As we raced out into open sea, I noticed a couple of fishing boats near the horizon. I headed for the nearer of the two, trying to work out what to do next. The *Santa Cristina* must not leave Greek waters. And we needed noise, something that the sleepiest coastguard could not miss. The boat carrying Haclan's prized assets was slow and had no place to hide, I told myself. And it was likely that her crew were hired hands who, if it came to a choice between fighting alongside Haclan's men or saving their own skins, would certainly opt for the latter. In such ways, I allowed myself to conclude that there was no better arena in which to take them on. I raised my fist and gave Anna a thumbs-up, accompanied by what I thought was a smile, though it may have been more like a snarl. Anna got the message, and I saw in her face that she was grateful for the show of optimism.

For seven or eight minutes we rode the battering waves, a canopy of numbing spray rattling over the gunwales and bubbling on the duckboards beneath our feet. The sky paled and the horizon came clear, slanting away to the west. We arrived within hailing distance of the fishing boat. A man of my age on deck, oilskins up to his armpits; probably his father up in the wheelhouse. Neither of them pleased to see us. The boat was lying up while they worked on the gear, rocking sharply in the chop. Two swathes of net like huge hornets' nests hung from a low gantry across her stern. I took the RIB round to the seaward side in hope that the *Santa Cristina* would not see what we were doing.

'Tell them we're nearly out of gas. Ask if we can come aboard.'

Anna spoke to them in Greek. They scowled at her. The man on deck grabbed a boathook and held it like a spear. She spoke again and the two men conducted a terse conversation. In the end, the father gave the order. I brought the RIB alongside and caught the line his son flung down at me.

'What did you say to them?'

'That they could have the boat.'

I helped the son winch their prize on board, then followed Anna up to the wheelhouse. She was imploring the captain to help us, but he kept raising his arm and barking at her. I didn't want to hurt the old guy, but we didn't have time for a complicated negotiation, either, so I waited for his son to lumber out of sight with the outboard from the RIB in his arms and then came up behind the father and slugged him with the butt of the Sauer. I left Anna at the wheel and ran down to deal with the son, who was climbing back up a gangway. I pointed the Sauer at his teeth and motioned him to the hatch in the centre of the deck. He was too stupefied to resist. Once I had him in the hold, I hauled up the ladder and secured the hatch-cover, then went back up to the wheelhouse with a length of cord to tie up the captain.

The captain came to and attempted to spit at me. I lashed him to a handrail by the door and stood to watch Anna manoeuvre the boat. She'd already swung round so we were heading back towards the *Santa Cristina*, which was slowly approaching the horns of the bay. The fishing boat was handy enough, responding to the helm and holding her course when set. The waves were coming at us on the bow-quarter, and she was easing the wheel over to compensate.

'You've done this before?'

'My father loves boats. He showed me a bit.'

I put the Excam in the drawer of a cabinet where she could reach it easily, then explained what I had in mind.

'It's dangerous, Anna, but I can't think of any other way.'

'We must try. Let's see how much speed we have.'

Once we came to close quarters, a miscalculation could result in several different kinds of catastrophe; but at least Anna would be well protected up here – the glass in front of her was a good inch thick and built to withstand a hammering at sea. She rolled the throttle lever forward and the engine emitted an indignant bellow that set a biro clattering on a formica-topped chart table beside the wheel. There was plenty of power on tap, but like most elderly diesels, this one had long since settled on a comfortable rate of knots and didn't take kindly to being poked.

'How quickly does she stop?'

Anna cut the engine to idle and the boat pitched forward and started to slew sideways. Once we'd lost a bit of way, she hit reverse. The transmission gave a heavy jolt, then the bows drifted to starboard as the propeller dragged the stern off true.

'The prop won't drive straight in reverse, the curves in the blades give it a bias—'

'James, do I look like I need a lecture on marine engineering?'

'Sorry. The boat may handle differently when we're alongside.'

'Thank goodness it has a rudder.' She looked up at me to check I knew she was only kidding. 'Now, make yourself useful, huh? Go scrub the deck.'

Anna, Anna… How did you find the courage to fill this lull before everything was decided with a little light mockery? I was the powerful one, with my broad shoulders and my gun and my murderous eye, but it was you who had the strength to make light of the obstacles in our path, even as the *Santa Cristina* sailed south with your daughter on board.

I put my arm around her slim shoulders and smiled… No, I grinned. Nothing like a snarl this time.

Make yourself useful, huh? It was cold on deck after the fug of the wheelhouse, and I had to keep reaching for handholds because my legs weren't used to the corkscrew motion of the boat as she rode the lumpy waves. I moved among the cables, cords, hawsers, shackles, blocks and winches that festooned the business area of the deck, trying to understand how it all worked. You swung the nets away from the stern on two rusty outriggers, mounted on the gantry and operated by steel cables forward of the rig; after release, the lines that held the nets were controlled by a pair of stout, long-handled winches. I'd get both nets down if I could. Knife… There, in a plastic holster screwed to the inside of the port rail – the blade long and dull but wafer sharp. Flares. In the emergency locker bolted to the bulwark by the gangway, three battered cylinders that looked several decades past their use-by date.

Anna was now steering the boat in a broad U to bring us onto a course parallel with the *Santa Cristina*, but about five hundred yards ahead and two hundred to port. How long now – four, five minutes? Salt-scented air barrelled in from the east, the diesel jabbered. I loaded the Sauer with a fresh clip and zipped it into the pocket of Eleni's uncle's coat, then ran my hands over the winches and cleats once more. If I swung the nets out too early it might slow us down, so I just looked up at the wheelhouse and nodded to show I was ready.

* * *

Anna spun the wheel and the fishing boat angled neatly in towards the course of the ship behind. Men were assembling along the rails on her upper deck. We'd been rumbled now, so I fired the three flares one after the other, and every damn one of them worked – until the first incinerated its own parachute and tumbled down to the sea. Haclan's men were pointing me out, then one of them waved. I didn't wave back. He pointed his rifle and mimed a shot – what fun to be safely out at sea with this particular fool to aim at! We drew in closer, seventy or eighty yards off her starboard bow and maybe three times that distance ahead. Close enough to fire a few rounds, thought the shooters – two of them took aim and I heard the puny crack of their rifles carry past us on the air.

I cranked the outrigger out over the water, hinges screeching like banshees. The weight of the net dangling to port caused the little boat to list in towards the *Santa Cristina*. Anna had cut it too fine… Distinct from the clatter of our diesel, I could hear the dull throb of the *Santa Cristina*'s engines, the churr of her bow wave. All this time, the gunmen were taking desultory potshots at us; but the closer we tucked in under the *Santa Cristina*'s hull, the less of our deck area was exposed to their fire.

I got the starboard net out, then felt the fishing boat lose way. We were being sucked into the *Santa Cristina*'s sea-space, the displaced water sheering off the bigger vessel's hull heaving beneath our keel. Seconds later, we were just where we didn't want to be: a boat's length behind the long ridge of the *Santa Cristina*'s prow and rolling violently in the glistening hump of her bow wave. If I hadn't got immediately down on all fours and found a handhold, I'd've been tossed overboard. Anna gunned the engine and our prop churned the water. We edged thirty yards ahead of the *Santa Cristina*, while Anna fought to keep us from slipping under her bows.

I pulled the knife and looked up at the wheelhouse. She was braced over the helm, struggling to control the bucking wheel. She shouted something, I don't know what, and I crawled over and cut the line that kept the port net furled. Maybe Haclan's men had worked out what we were doing, because bullets now whisked and hummed through the rigging like a swarm of furious insects. I yanked the release lever on the winch and watched the net flop into the sea, then hauled myself across the deck and released the starboard net. The winches clattered as the net-lines raced out through the blocks, and the row of weights at the leading edge of the nets drew them quickly down towards deep water.

There were barely twenty yards between the two vessels when Anna swung the wheel to take us across *Santa Cristina*'s bows. But the fishing boat wasn't responding to the helm any more, only to the powerful turbulence around the cargo ship's hull. We skated chaotically towards the poised axehead of her prow, the deck shuddering beneath me. Now we'd be pulverised, sucked down into the churning brown water with the splintered remains of the fishing boat somersaulting around us.

It didn't happen quite like that. The boat took a sudden lurch and her wheelhouse ducked beneath the looming bows. The two net-lines snaked back over the starboard rail, then slapped against the base of the wheelhouse and jammed fast. Seawater spattered from the heavy cables as their fibres torqued under the tremendous strain. The boat pitched sharply and I was slung like a rag doll into one of the stanchions that supported the gantry. We slammed against the *Santa Cristina*'s hull. The fishing boat shivered along her keel, then gave a long-drawn-out groan and her deck cracked open from wheelhouse to bows. The arm of the starboard outrigger popped the glass from a row of portholes as we scraped along the cargo ship's hull. The seaward rail tipped up through forty-five degrees and a foot of water sluiced across the deck. I slid with it, dazed... But not so dazed that I couldn't see how I was going to be crushed between the two boats.

Then came the sound I'd been waiting for. A clunk, muffled but immense – the *Santa Cristina*'s propeller fouled by the half-acre of densely knotted fishing net we'd dragged beneath her keel. Her engines died with an ugly cough. She pitched slowly into her bows and started to drift. Our engine was silent, too, and all I could hear in the vacated air was the intermittent screeching of the outrigger and the silky, slurping sound of a ton of water sliding back along the *Santa Cristina*'s flanks.

Even drifting, the ship could drag us under, but the implacable force of her progress had slackened and the fishing boat didn't seem to be sinking. The gantry had been torn half off the deck, but the outrigger was still clanging against the last of the line of portholes. It was no more than a couple of yards above my head, and it was open.

If I was quick, I could get aboard the *Santa Cristina*. I looked up for Anna, couldn't see her. But even if she was hurt, she'd want me to find Katarina first, protect her and the other girls until help arrived.

I kicked open the hatch-bolt so the man I'd locked in the hold could escape, then stepped over to the gantry. I climbed fast, the ironwork cold and sharp in my hands. The outrigger flailed back and forth across the *Santa Cristina*'s hull – if any part of me got trapped between the two... Well, it wouldn't be part of me for long. Shouts from above, gunshots behind me. Anna? I grabbed the frame of the porthole as the outrigger swung past, then hauled myself inside before it could swing back and take my legs off at the shins.

* * *

I rolled upright in a cramped cabin, drew the Sauer and ran for the door. A low passage outside. I made it to the forward end and started up a set of steel steps. Shouts behind me, then the crack of a handgun and my hand was stung by a bullet striking the rail. I doubled back along the passage on the deck above, kicking open doors. Half way along I heard boots on the steps. I knelt in a door-way, turned and saw the head and shoulders of a man emerging through the hatch. I fired. The bullet took him in the shoulder and he gave a cry of distress as he slumped back and slid down the steps.

I ran on to the end of the passage and arrived at a gangway that led up to a storeroom with rows of lockers and oilskins hanging from the walls. I was in the base of the superstructure at the ship's stern, with further cabins and the bridge above me. Through a glass panel in the door at the rear, I saw a steep staircase that gave access to the upper decks, but the door itself was locked.

In the opposite wall was a pair of heavy steel doors, one of which was ajar. Beyond was an area of open deck, three men looking down over the port rail at the fishing boat lashed by her net-lines to the

Santa Cristina's hull. Unarmed – probably crew. Another two were grappling with the anchor in her bows. I ran out on deck and round to the far side of the bridge. Someone saw me, shouted.

I heard three rounds snap out and felt a hot jangle of torn flesh along my upper thigh. I stumbled, managed to keep my feet. Another steel door to my left. I flattened myself alongside it and looked back: two men, tucked in behind the loading crane, one of them raising a rifle to his shoulder. I shot at him twice, then tried the door, but whether it was locked or just stiff, I couldn't open it without moving right out into the line of fire. I ran on, hugging the wall and trying not to let the wound in my thigh disrupt my steps. I reached the corner and took cover behind the superstructure of the bridge. I'd arrived at the rounded stern of the ship, looking out at a small area of deck ahead of me.

Dead end. No steps, no gangway. Nothing to hide behind when they came for me except a fat coil of mooring rope next to a bollard. A hatch clamped shut in the middle of the deck, but that would access a storage area, most likely separated from the main hold by a steel bulwark running right across the hull. Even fewer options than I had up here, which was saying something… Already there'd be men either side of the superstructure I was sheltering behind, taking their own sweet time to work their way up to the corners to my left and right. If I made my stand behind the rope and the bollard, I'd be picked off by a rifle fired from the bridge.

The wound in my thigh wasn't disabling – yet. But already blood was slopping from my shoe. I crossed to the other side of the bridge, got low and looked round. Just one of them, hunched at the far end. The crewmen at the rail had gone. Haclan's man hadn't seen me, so I pulled back and took a few deep breaths. I'd deal with him first, then find a better place to take on the rest…

I came out fast and for a second he was startled. I fired, but the bullet clanged harmlessly off a bulkhead light by his ear. My second shot coincided with his first. I saw him drop the gun, clutch at his throat, tip forward. Nerves screeched in my ribcage and my vision went dim. The deck came up and crunched against my jaw. I humped it away and my head fell forward. Sticky hands. Redness at my feet. I'd lost more blood than I'd realised. So much red down there. Sickened, swaying. Well, you would be, out at sea. Get up. Stand.

Swaying, pitching. Me? Or the ship?

Hold onto the rail. Hold it tight. Find Anna. The fishing boat is somewhere below. Lean over the rail, focus. The freighter's hull is a white plane, rising sheer from the shapeless sea. Lean further.

Cold not air. Dark not day.

Anna

42

The policeman reaches out to take you in his arms. He's going to carry you down the wet steel ladder and into the police launch. I watch you recoil and my heart fills with misgivings. Is this the reaction of a traumatised girl to being reached for by a pair of hairy forearms? Or of a stroppy teenager who wants to show she can descend a ladder by herself? Would you have it in you to be stroppy, after all you've been through? What have you been through?

The Katya I left at Grandmama's would not have drawn back. She was trusting and eager for life. But children change so quickly at that age. I want to know if you've been damaged, and it's a mother's thought, freighted with every possible emotion: anguish, solicitude, fright, fury, vengefulness. Selfishness. I want my treasure to be just as she was when I lost her, an untarnished tribute to my disapproved-of adventure as wife and mother. Can she be?

I mean to call out your name, because I don't think you even know your mother is sitting in the back of the police launch, heart so swollen she can hardly breathe. But when I see you, my voice isn't there. *She's not mine any more*, is what I think. She was never *yours*! She is Katarina Corochai. Katarina Corochai, who survived kidnapping by child traffickers. You are her mother, who rescued her. We are neither of us the same. These events which destroyed our lives we did not experience together, but apart. The apartness cannot be undone.

I expel these stupid, pointless thoughts from my wretched, restless head and lunge across the open deck to the foot of the ladder. Men lean on ropes at bow and stern, haunches braced against the tugging waves. Fenders squeak between the bouncing hulls. Seagulls sway on their thick wings and cock a greedy eye at the goings-on below. A gust of reeking sea air presses the hood of your hoodie over your face and you cannot move it aside because the descent is perilous and you have wrapped your arms around the policeman's neck. I've not seen that hoodie before, where did you get it? A man on deck holds out his arm to stop me getting too close to the edge, and I surprise him by seizing it and clinging on. He wants to pull it away again, but doesn't know how.

You've lost weight, Katya. Or maybe not. Pale – well, it's daybreak at sea after a long journey at night. Last proper meal? Last successful campaign for a takeaway supper? Last evening of American sitcoms with Magda and Sofia? Last night between clean sheets with her mother to kiss her goodnight?

Your saviour's boots clump dependably down the thickly painted rungs, your little bottom sticks out over his big arm. *Don't even think of looking at her like that, anyone, or I'll tear your fucking eyes out.* And then… Oh Katya, Katya, you are in my arms, and the contours of your body do still fold into the angle of my hip, your cheek finds the scoop of my neck, your hair tickles my nose. I croon consolations into your ear and my heart goes haywire, my mind flails at speculations too vile to enumerate. *Beaten or spared?* The body does not lie and you feel fragile, my darling Katya, you feel spent. *Humiliated, shamed, defiled?* Your small frame has the brittle lightness of a discarded shell. Where is the supple, rubber-jointed strength I felt in you before?

It doesn't matter. We'll start again, starting now. I'll never let you go, not until you're thirty or forty at least. It's good to start again. Nothing ever stays the same anyway, no matter how much you want it to. Children grow apart from their mothers one way or another and for now it's enough that I'm holding you in my arms again.

I look up and there are five other girls of around your age perched along the benches bolted to the iron walls of the cabin. The launch wallows, the air stinks of diesel, old varnish and salt. How ill they look. Not one of them is crying. Behind their worried faces, the windows run with salty smears. Time has started again. The future pours out its soul.

43

Here is what happened.

From my station in the wheelhouse, I saw bits of rope flip up, rigging twitch, a red-handled tool sent scudding across the deck. It wasn't until I saw the grim set of James's face as he stepped over to release the nets that I realised I was watching bullets. I screamed at him not to. *Go back!* I shouted, over and over. Then the nets were down and I heaved on the wheel and opened the throttle lever to full.

The boat started shuddering and skimming weirdly over the water. It made no difference what I did with the wheel so I just clung on and waited for it to be over. We spun under the *Santa Cristina*'s bows, so close that for a moment all I could see was a huge sheet of painted iron sliding by. Then it was as if we'd been sucked into a whirlpool. We banged against the side of the *Santa Cristina*. There was a violent noise of croaking metal, like sheets of corrugated iron being ripped apart, then the wheelhouse tilted on its side and all the glass from the windows smashed on the floor. I fell against a steel cupboard and bits and pieces from the wheelhouse crashed into me, mugs and biros and chart books and a radio handset that hit me in the stomach and winded me.

The *Santa Cristina*'s propeller got caught in our nets and she stopped. That was when I started to hope again. Real hope, not just pretending.

Our little boat was half capsized and the deck had burst open, leaving a crack wide enough to fit your hand. But we weren't sinking because somehow we'd become lashed to the cargo ship by various ropes and cables and were stuck there. The poor old man whose boat we had stolen was staring at the wrecked wheelhouse with his mouth open. I crawled over and untied him, but he was too groggy to move.

James was climbing the bit of machinery that controlled the nets, swinging wildly from side to side so I was sure he must fall into the sea and be crushed between the boats. Haclan's men were running around on the *Santa Cristina*'s deck, working out the best place to fire at him. I felt such hatred for those men. I took the Excam from the drawer where James had left it and fired until it ran out of bullets. James dived in through the open porthole. They turned their fire on me instead, so I hid below the window frame. I stayed there for many minutes, listening to the grinding, snapping sounds made by the stricken fishing boat. There were more shots, from different parts of the cargo ship. I looked out again but couldn't see what was going on. I was terribly afraid that they would threaten to hurt Katya and the other children, and James would lay down his gun and they would kill him in some dark corner.

About this time I heard a siren out at sea. I raised my head into the opening where the side window had been and saw a police launch entering the bay, going very fast. The fisherman James had locked in the hold was sitting on a hatch-cover with his head in his hands, so I shouted at him to come up and help his father. Then suddenly I felt so frightened that I tipped forwards onto my knees and started to shiver. I'd had everything clamped up and shut down while I looked for Katya. I'd never allowed myself either to believe or to despair. So when it really did seem that I might soon be holding her in my arms again, my body could not cope. My hands went white, my limbs like dough, my heart forgot to beat. My knees had been cut to shreds by the broken glass, but I couldn't do anything except stare at the blood trickling across the floor.

* * *

Eleni had driven the Mitsubishi camper van into Thessaloniki and alerted the police. At first, she said, they accused her of talking nonsense and agreed only to send a patrol car when they could spare one. Then they heard on their radio that distress flares had been fired in the bay to the east of town. That settled it. The police boat was launched and they drove out to the bay in a state of excitement, shouting at their control for backup and discussing with each other how they intended to deal with this gang of child traffickers who had made the once-in-a-lifetime error of allowing their filthy trade to spill over into the area controlled by the Thessaloniki Police Department (without paying their dues, one might have added in a moment of cynicism).

The police launch circled the *Santa Cristina* in a not wholly convincing display of maritime authority, its commander balancing on the foredeck and booming orders through a megaphone. *Santa Cristina, lay down your weapons, lay down your weapons! We are coming aboard!* A second launch arrived, and that freed them to rescue me and the old man and his son from the fishing boat. There followed a farcical scene in the course of which they tried to arrest me while I screamed at them to take me to the *Santa Cristina* so I could see my kidnapped daughter, also to search for James, also not to dare push me around or tie my hands or even touch me.

They took us aboard and we rocked around beneath the open doors of the *Santa Cristina*'s loading bay. More high-decibel loud-hailings, then three of them boarded the cargo ship, while the crew of the second police launch aimed rifles and a water cannon at her upper decks. But Haclan's men had hidden somewhere, and the *Santa Cristina*'s crew had climbed into a lifeboat and were already half way to the shore. Their story in court was that they knew next to nothing about the assignment. Yes, they surmised that smuggling was involved, but child trafficking? No! As soon as they discovered what Adjani's men were about, they protested that they wanted nothing more to do with it, but the evil band of paedophiles held them at gunpoint. They risked their lives to escape – a project they insisted had been initiated well before they heard sirens out in the bay. The police had noticed, surely, how they had left the starboard loading bay open and the gear deployed? In this fashion, they made themselves victims rather than accomplices and all were acquitted.

Later, the officer in command informed me that a ship with captives aboard is the most challenging and hazardous hostage situation in the manual, and success is far from guaranteed. Boarding the *Santa Cristina* without receiving any indication that the gang had surrendered was a serious breach of standard operating procedure, and he'd be grateful if I would plead confusion on this point if questioned in court.

'You were in such a state, Mrs Galica,' he concluded, looking himself rather confused as to whether his actions had been primarily unprofessional or primarily gallant. 'I simply had to do what you said, even though it was so dangerous.'

Haclan's men, demoralised by the disastrous outcome of their operation and the remarkable rate of attrition they had suffered at our hands, were soon flushed out of their hiding places and arrested. By this time, we'd disembarked at the harbour in Thessaloniki and been driven by minibus to the police station, where they fed us a breakfast of rice pudding, sweet pastries and coffee. I watched the careless, unenthusiastic way Katya ate and my heart was heavy. When she had finished, I took her in my arms again, hoping that as long as I could control the sobs, she wouldn't see how close I was to collapse.

They put us in the back office, the interview room being thought 'unsuitable'. The other girls sat in office chairs, studying us solemnly. Orphans, of course – that is what made them good subjects for trafficking. At least they looked as if they had started, tentatively, to believe they might be safe.

'Where is James?' I asked the officer in charge. 'Is he OK?'

The officer looked doubtful.

'He got on board the *Santa Cristina*. You must have found him by now.'

There followed an exchange of crackles and hisses by walkie-talkie.

'They've made a thorough search. Are you sure he was on board, Mrs Galica?'

* * *

All is not well with my poor Katya, but James, I would like you to know that I forgive you. I still do not understand everything that happened, but I could not have got her back without you, and the past cannot be undone.

Anyway, you took the blame on yourself – almost too eagerly, you might say. At the time it felt as if I were using you, your strength and intelligence, your ferocious determination. You were driven by some force that would crush anything which stood in your way. Guilt, rage, madness? Whatever, I wanted it on my side. I was close to despair when you found me outside the bus station in Skopje. I don't say I would have given up, but my efforts to find Katya were beginning to lack conviction.

You could not have given up, even if you'd wanted to. It would never have been enough for you to blame those really responsible. You are a man of rare conscience and nobility, if a little serious (even your sense of humour is grave). Not to mention being easy on the eye, as Eleni observed, the first time she saw you – even though she disapproved of you most entirely at the time! I wish we could have met before Katarina was taken away from me. I will always remember you holding me in your arms in the back of the hired van – the silence, the snow tumbling past the window – and wonder how different things might have been.

James

44

Water. Cold as iron. Lungs pressed shut like meat in a can. Locked up, won't budge. Not for water, nor even for air. Brown brine rank in the sinus.

Save me.

It means you are dead, stupid boy.

Water clasps water tugs. Its limbs are too cold its limbs are too heavy. Save me.

Send forth your sighs.

Mouth tilts clear for half a breath. Wave-slop wallows, slaps, sea swamps in. Cold fingers plug my throat. Too weak to cough. Roll over and rest. Easier like this. Below the darkness teems with half-dead things.

A thousand drowning eyes.

No! My face flies up, salt-grit streams from my eyes, sky light gleams and I'm blasting sea from my throat, sucking air. How many times did that happen? Retching. Water rattles and coos in the chambers of my chest. The ship… I swivel in my barrel of sea. Three-quarters round, the *Santa Cristina*, far away across the shrugging waves.

I'm strong enough to keep my mouth clear of the salt-slop.

Strong enough for now. Drift east. The far side of the bay is only...
Only so far away. Say a little prayer.

*　*　*

Something tugged at my arm. I opened my eyes. Sprawled across
a jumble of rocks, with a girl of about twelve holding my hand in
the air.

'It's OK,' I said. 'You're going to be OK.'

She released my hand and ran off, returned some time later
with an old man in tow. He had a concave face, baggy eyes and a
goitre under his jaw. He knelt over me and started to tear open my
shirt. I smelled raki on his breath.

'Doctor,' he said crossly.

He found the wound in my ribcage, prodded it with his fingers,
then mopped it with the edge of my shirt. He soaked a cotton pad
in something and slapped it over the swollen flesh, bound it up with
a single length of bandage. Then he performed the same impatient
ritual on a furrow left by the bullet that had torn through the outside of my thigh.

'You OK. Go. Go now.' He made a shooing motion with his
hands.

'Give me a lift into town,' I said faintly. 'I'll pay...'

He was already stomping off along the dusty path that led away
from the shore. The girl put a white plastic bag beside me.

'Thank you.'

She twisted her hands together, smiled, and ran after the doctor. In the bag was a bottle of tap water, three dried figs and a half-
loaf of bread with honey drizzled into the crumb.

*　*　*

Had Anna and Katarina been reunited? I longed to know, but for now I was too weak to do anything but lie back and rest my head against a ledge of bare earth beside the path. Out at sea, the *Santa Cristina* was riding at anchor beneath the fuzzy blotch of the sun, a police launch moored to her stern. It must have been sirens I'd heard before I'd fallen overboard. They'd staked out a section of the beach where the RIBs had come ashore, but there weren't any vehicles to be seen, other than the Fiat Frightful stranded a few hundred yards away.

It was confusing to find that the maelstrom of the hour after dawn when we'd fought to keep the *Santa Cristina* from carrying Katarina out to sea had given way to this gloomy and inanimate scene. I realised I must have been out for a long time before the girl found me, maybe five or six hours. I felt very sick, but as one of the army training instructors I'd toiled under was fond of saying, *You can't say, ooh, ooh, I don't feel well, I need to lie down, when there's half a dozen Taliban sniffing your next shit.*

I stood and waved my arms at the vessels out in the bay, but they were a long way off and I couldn't put on much of a show because the movement made the wound in my ribs weep and the gauze pad kept slipping out from beneath the single loop of bandage. At least I was too cold to bleed much. I sat down again and ate the food the girl had brought me. I chewed the crust and tasted the sweetness of the fruit and honey on my tongue – and I vowed to come back some day and thank her for saving me, because until that time, although I'd known I was not dying, still I'd felt close to death.

But now I decided I was strong enough to make my way to Thessaloniki. I'd drifted to the eastern shore of the bay, but the coast road wasn't far. After that, what, fifteen kilometres to town? Four hours in my state. Six maybe. I could hitch a lift, but I hadn't seen or heard a single car since coming to consciousness the best part of an hour ago.

I started gingerly along the path, setting myself targets as I walked: a bend in the path, a wizened old bush, a corner where the grey sea lapped up to the edge of the road. I reached the place where we'd abandoned the Fiat, hobbled over and sat in the driver's seat. The key was in the ignition but I couldn't get the engine to fire. On the fifth turn, the battery died.

I got out and looked for a way across the western promontory of the bay at sea level. There wasn't one, so I had to limp up the road and over the top. I could see Thessaloniki from here, sprawled against the low hills to the north. On the way down, I felt a throbbing, burning sensation beneath my armpit. Later, a thin, trickly sweat broke out on my face and chest. I became conscious of my head bobbing around like a helium balloon, my feet dragging like clods of meat. Several times I lay down at the side of the road and rested. Cars came past, but by the time I'd raised my arm to hail them, they'd gone.

At some point I lay down and stopped seeing or hearing anything at all.

45

The wound in my ribs was infected, my blood poisoned. Days passed, uncountable days filled with uncountable hours of shouting, sweating, hallucinations in which I fought to keep a cavalcade of toothed creatures from gnawing the flesh off my shins. Even when I came to for a moment and saw that the polystyrene ceiling tiles above my head had not been punched open by scabby jaws, I knew I'd be going back to face them again soon. The wound swelled and suppurated. I smelled raki. I smelled vomit. The girl twisted her fingers and begged me to save her. The white plastic bag she brought had a rat inside it. I thought Anna was watching me, but it might just have been striplight sheen playing over the white tiles. At last I slept, and woke to a heavy prod from below. Someone was underneath my bed. An arm reached up and deposited two oranges on the bedside cabinet. An apple followed, accompanied by a sigh of exasperation. Finally, a head appeared.

'Eleni?'

She smiled – a thing of great warmth and beauty. Her eyes brimmed with tears and she kissed me repeatedly, laying her cheek against mine and pressing with such fervour that her gift of fruit rolled off the cabinet again and plonked to the floor.

'Oh, James, thank you, thank you! It is good to see you awake again, really it is lovely… Such a terrible time you've had… Wait, I must call Anna.'

I listened to her gabble into her cellphone, then heard her say *Katya*… I could tell from Eleni's tone of voice that the girl had been reunited with her mother, but the joy I felt was quickly smothered by apprehension. It is one thing to feel guilty, to act like a guilty man, to strive to undo the wrong you have done – but soon I would come face to face with Katarina and see the damage my callow negligence had inflicted on her. I would see it in her manner, in how she held herself, in her eyes.

'They will be here in twenty minutes. Your face is so white, James. You must tell me if you feel ill again.'

I looked around for other patients but there were none, only beds without sheets, curtains tucked into tie-backs, humming striplights.

'How long have I been out for?'

'Three days. They found you lying by the side of the road. You had a bit of bandage which had come undone and flapped in the wind. Otherwise, no one would have found you. Oh dear.' She covered her face with her hands.

'Eleni, you can mourn when I really am dead. In the meantime, tell me what happened.'

'Oh, Anna begged them to look for you, but first she had to take care of Katya, you understand?'

'Of course. I didn't mean that—'

'If we knew you had fallen into the sea, we would have told them to search for you. But Anna thought you were still on the ship.'

'It doesn't matter. How is Katarina?'

'She has been through a terrible experience, more terrible than we can imagine. But we cannot tell how she is in herself, you know?

She doesn't want to talk – this is to be expected. It will take time. What she needs now is the comfort of her mother, plenty of sleep, good food.'

'What about Adjani's men?'

'All locked up. If they face a firing squad – this is possible in Greece – I will volunteer.'

'They're not worth it,' I said, pulling myself into a sitting position while Eleni fussed over the cushions at my back. 'Hired hands. If Haclan hadn't found them, they'd be street thieves and drunks.' I felt weak and sore, but with that sweet languor the body experiences when it is over a crisis.

'You must not be sentimental, James. Gang bosses cannot operate without such people to do their killing.'

'What about the clients of the Vegas Lounge?' I said. 'Who will lock them up? What about the men who knew what was going on but didn't put a stop to it?' And what about Father Daniel, I might have added, had I not remembered in time that I hadn't mentioned the Book of Prayer to anyone except Maria.

'The Vegas Lounge? I have not heard of this place.'

Another thing I hadn't yet mentioned...

'If only there were not criminal gangs,' Eleni went on, without waiting for me to explain. 'If only powerful men did not always want war. If only the world was like heaven and full of angels.'

She looked at her watch, then frowned at me: Anna and Katarina were due soon, said the frown, and now was not the time to discuss the world's more intransigent ills. We chatted about nothing for a while, then I saw her walking across the empty ward with her mother at her side. I drew in my breath, but the surge of guilt did not come. What I mostly felt was relief – that she was alive, that she was safe, that she looked so ordinary in her pale blue hoodie and black jeans so clean you could see the stiffness in the creases. Beautiful, yes, with her pale olive skin and jet-black hair, and graceful, despite the awkwardness of the moment. But really just a girl with her mother, visiting an acquaintance in hospital – a girl who would probably rather be back home watching TV.

Anna was smarter than I had ever seen her: green and red patterned skirt, cream jersey, hair tied back to set off the spare, elegant contours of her face. No one could have guessed what these two had endured. You'd have said it was teenage shyness that made the girl so reluctant to meet my eye; that the shadows in the mother's face were probably caused by having to work late.

Anna kissed me and whispered in my ear: 'She's feeling a bit overwhelmed. Don't think badly of her if she doesn't say anything.'

She pulled an envelope from her handbag and handed it to her daughter. Katarina took it, but I could see that the maternal prompting made her cross, and I was reminded of the impatient way she had hopped out of my arms while we'd been waiting for the ride into Skopje. She proffered the envelope, eyes downcast.

'I can't believe I didn't notice you'd been shot, James,' Anna was saying. 'It seems so ungrateful. When I think of you in that cold water – you must have thought we'd abandoned you, as if you meant nothing to us. I'm sorry.'

No, this is all wrong, I wanted to say. *I could never think badly of you, Anna! And you mustn't apologise to me, if I hadn't been so vain and selfish and irresponsible...*

'Do take it, James,' said Eleni.

'Sorry.'

I smiled at Katarina but still she would not look at me. The card had a picture of two skinny songbirds trilling in a tree. Inside it said, *Dear James, get well soon, Katarina.*

'Did you draw these birds?' I asked feebly. 'They're beautiful.'

Her mother translated and there was silence. I could see Anna and Eleni hoping Katarina would speak, but she only nodded.

'I'm sorry, Katarina,' I said quickly. 'If I hadn't left you at that house, none of this would have happened. I should have taken you to the UNHCR, it was my fault…'

Anna did not translate this time. 'Don't ask her to forgive you, James,' she said gently. 'Not yet. It's not that you don't deserve it, but there's so much for her to deal with just now.'

She was right, of course. Why shouldn't Katarina feel just plain angry for a while? She didn't even want to be here, visiting this oaf in a hospital bed who craved her absolution. I'd spent barely twelve hours in her company, and most of those had been taken up with sleeping and wondering how to get rid of her. The feelings that had stalked me since that terrible night – the guilt, the fury and outrage, the discovery that I might be *one of us* – none of this had anything whatsoever to do with the girl standing by my bed.

'You found Katya in the forest and took her to safety,' Eleni said. 'She would not have survived the night otherwise. Katya will always know that. James, we will never forget how you helped us.'

We all looked at Katarina, but she wouldn't meet anyone's eye.

Anna broke the silence. 'Will you please come to us when you get out? We're driving up to Skopje tomorrow. We'll stay at Eleni's apartment for a while.'

'When will you go back to Pristina?'

'Pristina? Maybe we will never go back. Maybe there will be nothing left.'

'What do you mean?'

'NATO are bombing Kosovo. They got the agreement they needed in Paris three days ago. They couldn't wait to get started.'

46

I slept again, my dreams no longer feverish but simply bleak. I woke and they changed my dressing. The skin hung in a puckered fold over the curve of rib. I was served with a portion of macaroni pie, which I finished in three mouthfuls. They brought me two more. Each came with a small glass of red wine. I don't remember finishing the last. I woke to hear a voice I didn't recognise.

'We can't sit here all day. Perhaps one of the nurses might give him a playful squeeze.'

I opened my eyes and saw Clive Silk of MI6, along with my CO, Colonel Andy Hillson, and another man with a pink, muscular face and a head of sleek black hair, neatly groomed around the temples.

'Good to have you back with us,' he said.

It was morning. The empty ward was bisected by a triangle of sunlit dust.

'I'm not with you,' I said, eyeing Clive Silk. The sight of his smug, I-know-the-bigger-picture face was stoking such a blaze of hatred in my temples that already I felt wide awake. 'Whoever you are.'

The men looked irritable. Their plastic chairs creaked.

'Iain Strang, MI6. The Balkans fall under my remit, lucky fellow that I am.'

'Silk's boss?' I stretched my arm and felt that the sticky stiffness in my ribs had gone. 'What an unwelcome honour.'

'Christ, Palatine, get off the damn high horse for once, will you,' said Colonel Hillson. 'This is important.'

Hillson was the sort of man you set to spy on your closest allies because you can be sure he won't need to know why. Some of this amenability was supposed to have rubbed off on me, I guess.

'Oh, let him sit up there for a while,' said Strang easily. 'The horse'll throw him off soon enough.'

Hillson pursed his lips. 'There are things you don't and can't know about, Palatine,' he said, 'unacceptable though that may seem.'

'Sticking to the things I do know about,' I said, 'you arrested an English UNHCR officer called Bryan Harley and found out he'd been involved in trafficking girls from a refuge in Kosovo. Some of the girls ended up at the Vegas Lounge in Skopje.'

'We make it our business to root out kiddy fiddlers wherever we find them,' said Strang. 'Old fashioned of us, I know.'

'You didn't root it out, though, did you? You hushed it up. Bryan Harley helped you out by hanging himself. You thought I'd seen Vasilis Adjani at the Vegas Lounge, so you locked me up in Norfolk. I didn't even know who he was, but you weren't going to risk me blowing the scandal open just before the Rambouillet peace conference.'

'You'd already embarked on a violent personal crusade,' said Strang drily, 'no doubt driven by the memory of handing over a twelve-year-old girl to a gang of child traffickers.'

'We might have handled it differently,' said Hillson, 'but you went and got yourself videoed at the Vegas Lounge, for pity's sake.'

I had no answer to this, and had to endure a moment of silent admonishment from the three men around my bed.

Hillson sighed. 'One day, Palatine, you might have responsibility for issues of national security yourself. You'll find it isn't as straightforward as you seem to think.'

I stared at Silk. 'And what were the issues of national security that sent you to Rambouillet to inform Colonel Adjani that his brother was in danger of arrest and should shut up shop and leave?'

Strang and Silk wanted more than anything to ask how I knew – but it would be impossible to do so without acknowledging the truth of my accusation. Neither of them spoke. Hillson, meanwhile, looked down at his knees and tapped them busily, in a game attempt to hide his confusion.

'Such melodrama,' said Strang eventually, smoothing back the already smooth hair over his temples. 'Yes, there was a tactical decision to be made over when to move on Haclan, and Rambouillet came into the equation. And your point is?'

'You warned Haclan off,' I said hotly. 'You let a child trafficker— No, you encouraged a child trafficker to pack up and leave Skopje in his own sweet time and with all his precious assets intact, including a consignment of underage girls who ended up on a ship heading out into the Med for God knows where.'

'You put a stop to that and we're all quite moist with gratitude,' said Strang. 'Unfortunately, your Incredible Hulk days seem to be over. Haclan Adjani's gang has been broken up and we managed to prevent the international peace effort being disrupted by a scandal.'

'Peace effort? You mean the NATO bombing campaign? Of course, that's what this is really about, isn't it? Your political masters are so keen to bomb the Serbs that before Rambouillet even started they had us skulking round Kosovo looking for Serbian AA guns. But the Kosovars had to play their part, too. They had to be the heroic underdogs. How would it have looked if the media was suddenly full of stories about brothels full of twelve-year-old girls? It was a risk too far, so you sat on it. Children were raped, Haclan and his club full of clients have all gone free, but that's OK because at least the bombing could go ahead.'

'I'm not going to justify myself to you, Palatine,' said Strang. 'This business is over. It's finished. Digest that thought and then take a moment to consider what you've done. You smuggled a child out of Kosovo and into the hands of men who ran an especially depraved Skopje brothel, which you also happened to visit – something you've never explained. There are two unsolved murders in Skopje which I think have your pawmarks all over them. This is not to mention the shooting of two more men on a beach near Thessaloniki.'

Strang was not a tall man, but thickset and powerful. He leaned forward in his chair and the dark grey cloth of his suit stretched tight over his big, rounded shoulders and heavy thighs. He fixed me with eyes as bright and hard as polished marbles.

'I say it again, Palatine. This is over. Keep your fucking mouth shut. Take a long sabbatical. Weep, wank, pray, whatever you like, but if you and your fucking halo ever cross me again, I'll have you kicked to bits in a pub car park. The old boys you made fools of in Norfolk would relish the job. I might even join them.'

He held my eyes for a long, cold moment. I could feel the triumph coming off him like a tomcat's stink, the groin-thrusting gratification of power exercised by the strong over the weak. But I wasn't having it. I had a strength he hadn't entered into the calculation: I really didn't care what happened to me.

'Arrest Haclan Adjani,' I said. 'Charge him. Do it yourself or make it happen some other way. You have fourteen days. After that, I'm giving what I know to the media.'

'You've got a bloody nerve,' said Hillson.

'I'm calling your bluff, Strang. Put me in court if you like, but I can prove you and your poodle here tipped off a child trafficker.'

I'd been watching his face, at first immobilised by rage, then

361

darkening to the colour of an overripe plum. But for all their devotion to the dark arts by which power is exercised, men like Strang are pragmatists, too, and nothing quells them so quickly as the prospect of their own downfall.

His face rearranged itself painfully into a semblance of good humour, and he said: 'We've caught you at a bad time, yes? You blame yourself for what happened to the girl. It's understandable. But Haclan was always going down – you know that. I'll make it happen, but on my terms, not yours. Deal?'

'Fourteen days. Be careful, Strang. I don't like you.'

Now it was my turn to give him the eye. He stood, thrusting his knees against the seat of his chair so it clattered across the floor, and barrelled out through the swing doors, with Silk trotting along behind him.

'What was all that about Silk going to Rambouillet?' said Hillson, momentarily forgetting that he was my CO and I was due a dressing down.

'You don't want to know.'

'Probably not. We should call it quits, anyway.'

I looked up. His expression was mortified – a man who had witnessed something shameful.

'Make an appointment to see me as soon as you get out of here. I take a share of the blame for this – expected too much of you. We'll find something that'll keep you out of the spotlight for a while, yes?'

47

It wasn't over. How could it be? I wasn't so sure that Strang would respond to my threat and deal with Haclan Adjani. This was a case of child trafficking as foul as anything that had happened in Bosnia, and everyone would feel tainted by it. So much easier to turn away, quoting higher powers, strategic interests, the greater good... Strang wouldn't recognise the greater good if it descended from heaven and sat in his lap. However, he knew how to lift the edge of the carpet and summon Clive Silk with a broom.

Father Daniel was still at large. And what really happened at the farmhouse? I still didn't know. It wasn't that I thirsted for every last gruelling detail – no, only one detail, and it was this: who was the boy I had killed? I did not think he was a Bura – I didn't even believe it was them we'd disturbed at the farmhouse that day. The Bura were fast-cars-and-shotguns types, not the sort to arrive on foot and scurry away up a hillside when disturbed. So who were they? And who was the boy?

* * *

I left hospital two days later, took the train back to Skopje and went to Maria's to pick up the spare key to my apartment.

'No.'

'Come on, Maria. Why not?'

'You are sick. Look at you. Stay in Tomasz's room. When you are OK, I give you the key.'

'I don't want to stay in Tomasz's room. Tomasz doesn't want me to, either.'

'Anyway, I have lost the key. I don't know where. I'll find it – in a few days, maybe.'

The prospect of returning to my dismal apartment was unenticing enough, so I didn't argue any further. I asked her about the pages from Father Daniel's Book of Prayer. 'Did you take them to the UNHCR? What do you think I should do?'

'We. What should *we* do. You cannot deal with this by your own, James. Already you are trying too much. It is not your fault. You did not hurt anyone.'

'Well, in actual fact—'

'Not innocent people.'

'Should I tell Anna now?'

'Tell her what?'

'Oh, I was thinking maybe the truth?'

'Ha. I know what you want. You want her to forgive you for trusting this priest.'

'I wasn't thinking of myself, believe it or not,' I said, offended – but at the same time wondering if the accusation might be justified. 'We all trusted him.'

'It will be better if the girl tells her mother, when she is ready. Anyway, there is nothing definite here.'

'What do you mean?'

'He does not write down exactly what he did.'

'It's obvious what he did, Maria.'

'Perhaps. We will visit the UNHCR and see what they say. Then we can decide.'

I told her how I'd blackmailed Iain Strang.

'This is good,' she said. 'I approve. Adjani and Father Daniel must be dealt with in an official way and I will help you. You are not to go running off and killing them yourself. Do you promise, James?'

'No, Maria, I don't.'

'No dinner for you, then. Look after the restaurant now, while I check on my children. This thing has made me sick with worry.'

* * *

The next evening, I was invited to Eleni's apartment for a celebratory meal of traditional Balkan dishes prepared by our hostess. A big man with shaggy hair was perched on the wrought-iron chair by the telephone – Anna introduced him as her brother-in-law Piotr, who had made the journey down from Pristina to be with us. Our chef was being positive – hysterically positive, you might say. The little apartment echoed to a sequence of bangs, crashes, curses and sighs, and she hurried from kitchen to balcony and back again, trailing tobacco-scented panic in her wake. Away from the field of action, which had brought out her courage and sangfroid, Eleni's neuroticism had quickly reasserted itself.

Anna made polite conversation. Were my wounds healing OK? What was I doing with myself in Skopje? Would I go back to London? Her heart wasn't in it. Mine wasn't, either. I gave airy answers, attempting to make light of it all.

We ate burek with spinach and feta, smoked pork stew, a pear and fig strudel, then vanilla biscuits served with Mursalski tea infused with honey. All of it delicious, but the extravagance of the feast could not disperse the air of awkwardness and gloom that hung over the little room. The eating and the small talk were diversions performed because the question we all wanted answered could not even be asked. *What happened to you, Katarina?*

She sat in silence, crushed by the weight of that unasked question, miserable and still as no child should be. We fussed and tip-toed around her, our voices loud with falsehood. *Do you want more bread, darling one? Just say if you need a rest. We'll get a DVD out later – would you like that?* She picked at her food and communicated only with a nod or a shake of the head.

I found her staring at me once – staring up from the bottom of a dark pit from which she didn't expect to escape. She turned away, back to that lonely place, and I understood then why Maria had said I should not speak about Father Daniel. It was not for me to force the matter into the open. It was Katarina's knowledge, not mine. I had rescued her from Haclan Adjani, yes, but I should not indulge myself with the notion that it was in my power to do more. There was not going to be a rosy ending – not for any of us. I felt like I had when I'd first met them here – a big, clumsy stranger who would not tell them the truth. Whatever Katarina needed to help her tackle the long climb back to normal life, it wasn't me. As soon as the meal was over, I made an excuse and stood up.

'Let me give you a lift somewhere,' said Anna.

'Thanks, but I'd like to walk.'

Piotr stood up and looked as if he would like to go too, but Eleni directed him back to his chair and switched on the TV. We left him with Katarina in the sitting room and stood in the cramped hallway where I had dressed up as Father Daniel Cady. The mood then had been nervous, but also determined and full of brave optimism.

'She is doing very well, James, don't you think?' Eleni asked. 'Just as well as can be expected?'

'Yes,' I said. 'She seems to be coping.'

'She isn't,' said Anna. Her face was riven with despair – all the despair she'd suppressed while Katarina was missing. 'She hasn't spoken to me at all, James. Not a single word.'

'She needs time,' I said. 'We all do.'

'I so wanted it to be all right – and it isn't. It isn't at all.'

She cried and I wrapped her in my arms. It was awkward because I'm nearly eighteen inches taller than her.

'We do this better lying down,' I said, remembering how we had comforted each other on that snowy night when we'd found Adjani's den on the outskirts of town. 'In the back of a freezing cold van.'

She gave a snuffly laugh and pulled away from me. I thought I saw regret in her eyes, but maybe that was just wishful thinking.

'Goodbye, James. Don't… You know, don't be too hard on yourself.'

* * *

My role in Katarina's story had ended. I stood in the street outside and literally did not know what to do.

I went to a bar and couldn't get drunk. I went to the river and found no solace in the oil-black water that slid between the pillars of the Stone Bridge. When I got back, the restaurant was shut up and Maria had to get out of bed to let me in, which gave her a good excuse to scold me. Did I say that Maria is beautiful? Most people see a woman of forty, fat and forbidding, her square face counter-pointed by a pair of mannish spectacles unevenly perched on an aristocratic nose. Actually, what you see is not fat but strength, and the wonky glasses distract from eyes plumbed with kindness and intelligence.

She managed to keep me for three days, and the combination of copious meals and her forthright views on my poor behaviour over the previous month were as soothing as clean cotton sheets to weary limbs. Meanwhile, her children ensured that I had not a single moment to myself. The two girls liked to play weddings and quickly cajoled me into taking the role of priest – displacing an old and very dirty teddy bear and so adding immeasurably to the authenticity of the ritual. I must have said the words *I now pronounce you man and wife* (in English, which didn't seem to matter) twenty or thirty times during my brief stay. Tomasz and his two brothers, meanwhile, having failed to find any weapons amongst my meagre belongings, engaged me on sight in bouts of hand-to-hand combat. More than once I found myself having to interrupt a solemn intonation of the nuptial rites in order to detach a small boy who had taken a mortal grip on my epiglottis.

My physical wounds healed quickly, if not very neatly, once the infection had gone, and I slowly regained the sense that there was a normal world, and even that I might shortly re-enter it. I met with Colonel Andy Hillson, who attempted to debrief me. He was unenthusiastic about the task, and – having no doubt been himself debriefed by Iain Strang – merely confirmed what I already knew.

'I don't have a project for you right now because, frankly, we haven't decided what kind of work you can be trusted with. But I don't want you sitting around feeling sorry for yourself,' he concluded.

'I'm still in the Int Corps, apparently?'

'Not my decision,' he said pointedly, and brought the meeting to an end.

I moved back into my apartment, upon which Maria continued her campaign to keep me busy by declaring that I must pay for my three days' board and lodging by watching the restaurant for her at times when business was slow and my linguistic shortcomings would not be too badly exposed. I was standing obediently behind the counter in mid-afternoon a day or so later when two Coincasa shop girls came in for coffee – the same two who had giggled at me when I'd eaten here the day after our attack on the Bura. They took a table by the window. One of them drew faces on the steamed-up glass while the other flicked through a magazine. After a moment, the one with the magazine beckoned me over.

'You is American, yes?'

'No, English.'

'Ah, yes. We want speak English. You – um – here?'

She patted the bench next to her. She was pretty, with a full mouth and sharp, quizzical eyes beneath not very kempt brown hair. I did as she asked.

'My name is Karela. You name?'

'James.'

The conversation pottered along. Karela slid along the bench until I could feel her warmth as she brushed against me. Her skin had the soft, salty smell of freshly popped popcorn. I answered her questions and smiled at her, and she lowered her eyelids and ever-so-slightly wriggled her hips. Her friend looked annoyed, and I fancy Karela got a kick under the table, though she did a good job of hiding it.

I was just agreeing a time and place to meet her for a drink when Maria returned.

'Soldiers,' she said, affecting a censorious glare, though there was approval in her eyes. It was Maria's firm belief that there were few afflictions a man could suffer that would not be much ameliorated, if not cured altogether, by a bout of good-hearted lovemaking.

'See you, James,' sang Karela as I left the restaurant to go back to my apartment. I wasn't at all sure I should be playing around like this, when what I truly longed for was the company of Anna. But how could I court her now? And what could be more comforting than a fling with Karela? I'd been back in my apartment for less than twenty-four hours and already I'd discovered that, left to itself, my mind circled stealthily back to the lurid scene in the farmhouse loft. Or if not that, then to the poisoned pages of Father Daniel's Book of Prayer. Even when I slept – and I'd been sleeping a lot – I woke up feeling dazed and wary. A fling with Karela was Maria's prescription, and when had she ever been wrong about anything?

48

I pursued my career as junior assistant manager at Maria's restaurant, and every day or so met with Eleni to hear that not much had changed. Anna couldn't join us because she was spending all her time with Katarina.

'They have a long list of things to do,' Eleni told me. 'Anna has bought her smart new clothes and they go to museums or the cinema. Katya doesn't refuse, but whenever they are at the apartment, she goes to the bedroom to be on her own.'

'Has she said anything yet?'

'No. It's very hard on poor Anna.'

It soon became clear that if the only purpose of these meetings was to discuss the progress of Katarina's recovery, they were pointless. Our conversation digressed: politics; the war; our respective families; my *spying job*, as she called it. I discovered that Eleni was an aficionado of Westerns, her favourite being *Destry Rides Again*, starring Jimmy Stewart – a fine exploration of how a society responds to moral leadership, she explained. I think she knew that I was half in love with Anna; and she sympathised, for she was half in love with Anna herself. At our third meeting, she produced a newspaper folded to display a pixelated photograph of a heavy-shouldered man standing outside a courthouse with a lawyer at his side. It was an old photograph, but I recognised the face.

'Look what happened, James. Haclan Adjani is dead.'

She translated the article for me. A rival family, observing how the Adjani clan had been weakened by the collapse of its interests in Skopje, had taken the opportunity to raid their stronghold in northern Albania and pretty much wipe them out. Haclan and three of his men had been knifed and their bodies dumped in a stone drinking trough in the village square. The tree which shaded their bodies had been daubed with an upside-down cross.

'Such violent people. The cross is I think supposed to be an insult – the Adjanis are Catholics, as I told you. But of course their killers are too ignorant to know that St Paul was crucified upside down, and the symbol is seen as respectful. Anyway, now your friend Mr Strang does not have to arrest him.'

'Convenient, that.'

'Do you think he arranged it?'

The newspaper report was curiously lacking in detail – the rival family was not even named. It occurred to me that if MI6 wanted rid of a man whose testimony might be awkward for them, I knew just the sort of murderous bastards they'd dispatch to northern Albania to get the job done.

'Probably not,' I said, feeling in no state to judge whether this paranoid turn of thought was justified. 'It doesn't seem right that he should die in some blood feud, though, after what he's done.'

'Justice is good, but anyway I am glad he is dead,' said Eleni. 'Also, I am glad it was not you who killed him.'

On the way back to Maria's I bought a pre-pay cellphone and went through the rigmarole of calling Sergeant TJ Farah.

'You're like a nasty stain,' he told me. 'What is it this time?'

'I just wanted to ask you something, TJ, there's no need to get the hump.'

'Oh, it's me getting the hump now, is it, not some fucked-up Rupert disturbing my Sunday nap every time he wants his arse wiped.'

'Is it Sunday?'

'No it fucking well isn't.'

'Did you know that St Paul was crucified upside down?'

'Christ on a bike, you really have lost the plot.'

'Just a thought. You won't want to answer this, TJ, but I swear it won't get back to you. And if you don't trust me, you have a photo in your vault of me killing someone in the woods, so—'

'Yeah, all right, Jimmy, ask some more fucking stupid questions and I'll try not to answer them.'

'Were you in the Balkans last week? Specifically, northern Albania?'

'You still in Skop?'

I admitted that I was.

'You want my advice, here it is: leave the Balkans now. Go home. Chain y'self to the settee, throw the key out of the window and drink a bottle of Scotch.'

'I can't, TJ, I have unfinished business here.'

'What the fuck's the matter with you?' Indignation was sending the familiar sing-song cadence of his voice into a chaotic tailspin. 'Serbia's getting bombed to shit. They've already taken out a refugee column. Yesterday it was the Chinese fucking embassy. There's half a million people on the move. Nobody gives a monkey's wank about your unfinished business.'

'I know. Except me.'

His voice softened. 'Take the result, Jimmy. It wasn't the one you wanted, but it's the one you got. Go home. Watch your back. And stop making enemies.'

* * *

Easy for TJ to say – he knew nothing about Father Daniel. When not working for Maria or making good-hearted love with Karela, I sat in a rhombus of spring sunshine at the back of the yard behind the restaurant and read English newspaper accounts of the NATO bombing campaign.

They were written in excitable journalese by flak-jacketed war correspondents and carried photographs that were shocking but beautifully composed, as if to ensure that any compassion they might inspire would be neatly contained. The articles ended with a recital of the soberly smug platitudes that are pasted together to create Ministry of Defence press releases. *Limiting collateral damage through intelligence-directed targeting*, they claimed. Some of that intelligence provided by myself, I reflected bitterly. They were deploying *the latest high-accuracy guidance systems,* naturally, because the campaign was all about the MoD's favourite contradiction in terms, *precision bombing*.

There is no such thing. A bomb is never precise, especially not when tossed into the skies from 30,000 feet. A single BL 755 cluster bomb (of which around 300,000 would be dropped during the NATO campaign) contains 147 bomblets. On impact, each is forcibly inverted by an explosive charge and transformed into a molten slug capable of penetrating the armour plating on a tank. Simultaneously, the bomblet's coiled casing shatters into 2,000 pre-shaped anti-personnel fragments which spray out over a circle nearly a hundred metres in diameter. On average, fifteen to twenty bomblets per cluster bomb fail to detonate, and unexploded bomblets would be found a kilometre and more away from the target coordinates of NATO strikes. These erroneously named 'duds' or 'blanks' are temperamental things: a breath of wind or even a change in atmospheric pressure can trigger them. Precision? I don't think so.

They were using A-10 Tankbusters, too. The A-10 fires 30 mm depleted uranium shells – an effective way of wrecking an armoured vehicle. And, by the by, of turning it into a radioactive playhouse for the use of local children when hostilities end. *Decisive action to avert a humanitarian catastrophe*, the politicians trumpeted, intoxicated with the image of steadfast statesmanship their advisers had prepared for them. *We cannot stand by while the Balkans descend into chaos.* No, I thought, you simply have to join in.

*　*　*

After a series of phone calls in which her obduracy outlasted the ignorance and/or indifference of various administrative staff, Maria got an appointment with the UNHCR. But she didn't tell me about it until after she'd been.

'You are too angry, James, you would frighten them. Then they say nothing.'

'So what did you do,' I said crossly, 'bribe them with a chicken shashlick?'

'There, just like I said. Angry.'

'Sorry. You're right. What did you find out?'

'Eleven children from the refuge arrived at Blace two days ago and were taken in by the UNHCR team. It was Father Daniel who handed them over.'

'Father Daniel? I hope they checked everything properly. Where are the children now?'

'They were transferred to Stankovic Two. A horrible place, but they are safe.'

'What did they say about the pages from the Book of Prayer you sent them?'

'The discipline Father Daniel used was not appropriate, and he should not have been frightening them. But this was all they could know for sure.'

'What about the *internal examinations*?' I asked.

'Ah, yes, they think maybe these were spiritual examinations. There is a phrase Catholics say: *examine your conscience*. It means—'

'I know what it means,' I said, exasperated. 'So this regime of beatings and "internal examinations" is merely *inappropriate*?'

'They will make further investigations. You must be patient, James.'

'I don't understand why Father Daniel took the children to the border.'

'You want him to be one hundred per cent evil. Perhaps he is not.'

'I wish we could be sure the children are OK.'

'You can go to Stankovic Two and see for yourself, but still you won't be satisfied.'

'No, I won't, because who's to say there won't be more? Father Daniel's refuge was the source of Adjani's child-trafficking business, but it was never a business for him, was it? You've seen those pages, Maria. It's an obsession. It's his life's work. You think he'll stop just because Haclan's dead? I don't.'

49

It was still dark when the taxi dropped me at our regular crossing place into Kosovo. I had several pockets full of food, a pair of compact binoculars, a hunting knife and my Browning Hi-Power. I jogged up towards the hills.

It felt good to be running unencumbered through the cold air, while dawn stirred the pools of mist that lingered over the smooth face of the plain. It felt good to be away from the confused, uncertain city and all the hurt it held, to be seeking a resolution that was in my own hands and on my own account. I skirted a succession of wooded hillsides, heading east towards Blace and hoping to find the track that led to the refuge. I didn't see or hear a single patrol: Serbian artillery units had reportedly set up nearby, but most of their infantry were engaged in firing and looting villages further north; and with refugees arriving at Blace in their thousands every day, the Macedonian authorities had better things to do than dispatch their soldiers to sections of the frontier that could only be reached on foot.

I arrived on the flank of the hill above Blace and looked down on the river valley which carried the road to the border and then on south to Skopje. There had been 30,000 refugees, they said, in that no-man's-land between Kosovo and Macedonia; now, the camp was empty. I looked through the binoculars and saw trails of sodden clothing, smeared plastic sheets hung over branches, pushchairs pointing their snapped struts at the sky. A few dozen stragglers were picking at the open mouths of discarded plastic bags. Even though the camp had become notorious, it was impossible to see it abandoned without feeling that some tragedy had taken place.

It wasn't until I swung the binoculars north that I saw the tide of new arrivals awaiting their turn in the hell of the just-vacated holding camp. They were squeezed into a side-track so that the main road could be kept clear, and every square foot of it held a human form. Those who hadn't made it onto the track were waiting in the woods above, and as my eyes became accustomed to the shapes they made amongst the trees, I saw that the entire hillside was teeming with people. The precise, intrusive glare of the binocular lens picked out rope-bound bags over bowed shoulders, the bodies of children slumped in their parents' arms, faces bruised with misery and exhaustion. I swept back and took in the border post itself, the place to which they were fleeing. The steel and tarmac sprawl, set out beneath its dome of bluish, arc-lit air, looked cold and empty as death.

I lowered the binoculars and moved on. After twenty minutes, I came across a thirty-foot crater surrounded by trees snapped off at head height. I looked for evidence that this might be a NATO cluster bomb rather than a Serbian artillery round. There seemed little reason why anyone should pound this patch of deserted hillside. Serbian, I decided.

A couple of minutes later, I heard a series of hard, hollow bangs from the far side of the valley, then the faint whistling of shells... A muffled whump and a plume of earth erupted lazily from the forest on the far side of the valley, closely followed by half a dozen more. I studied the pattern of artillery rounds being lobbed into the sky for signs that the long gun barrels might be swinging my way; but it was a patchy kind of bombardment and I guessed its main purpose was to drive the fleeing Kosovars down to the roads, where they could be more easily herded to the border.

Soon afterwards I came across a group of families sat round the remains of a fire in a damp clearing, the adults talking urgently among themselves while their infants lay huddled in the gaps between them. To one side, a woman crooned over a child in her lap – a child too big to be comfortably held, and whose long, pale shins stuck out like the limbs of a mannequin. Over the next forty minutes, I must have seen several hundred refugees hiding up in those woods.

I knew that if I kept on this bearing I would find the lower of the two tracks that led up to the refuge, but when I did, planted square across it was a Serbian armoured vehicle. Six soldiers were leaning against its plated flanks – evidently very confident in the accuracy of their colleagues' gunnery, since the track ran along the foot of the hill on which the shells had been landing.

I should have backed away at least three hundred yards before circling round them, but I was distracted by thoughts of what lay ahead. Cocky, too – a characteristic of foolish young Ruperts, TJ would have informed me. I smelled the man about the same time as he saw me. Crouched in a hollow of trodden bracken with his trousers round his ankles. He stood abruptly, hands tugging at his waistband. I drew my knife and went for him. Not fast enough to stop the shout in his throat. He saw the blade and ducked sideways, caught his foot in a thicket of stalks, fell. I pounced, swept the curved wafer of steel down towards the sinews of his throat. The bloody hunger, they call it, that smooth, impatient feeling, that palpable surge of blood in the veins, that flash of clarity, cold and undeniable…

But I denied it. I stayed my hand an inch from the stubble of his jaw. Better to go hungry than do this wrong.

He was slight, with a pale, ratty face. His eyes dilated, lips trembled after speech. I put a finger to my lips, then drew a hand across my neck. He raised his head enough to nod, let it fall back, and stared at me groggily. Seeing his white face and the lick of hair stuck to his forehead where his helmet had tipped back, I was glad I hadn't cut him. He looked too much like the boy in the farmhouse loft.

Shouts from the men by the armoured vehicle. Orders. I hammered the pommel of the knife against his temple. He sighed and his eyelids twitched. I plunged twenty yards through the undergrowth, slid down a short bank into a stream, followed its course down the slope for five minutes, then hauled myself up by the roots of an old ash tree and ran on until I pitched head first into a mound of bracken.

I lay on my back, panting as quietly as I could, cocooned between the soft, musty earth and the dull orange of the bracken fronds. Far above my head, the fretwork of twigs at the fringes of the canopy shuddered against the flat blue sky.

The shouts stopped. They'd found him. I listened out for a while, but they didn't come looking for me. Until he came round and told them otherwise, they'd assume I was a refugee who'd been startled by the sight of their defecating comrade and given him a thump on the ear. They wouldn't want to go tramping through the forest in pursuit of such a worthless foe. I stayed there for half an hour while the ground exhaled its sharp rooty smells and the dried fern stalks crackled in time with my breaths. Eventually I heard the grumpy cough of a big engine firing up and the Serbian vehicle rattled off down the track.

I made my way back to the track and jogged uphill, looking for the overgrown path down which we'd plunged in rain-lashed darkness all those weeks ago. TJ would have found it as surely as a fox finds a gap in chicken wire, but I didn't. It wasn't much of a path anyway. I crossed the ditch and clambered up through the woods, and after an hour emerged onto the higher track, with the refuge just twenty minutes away.

50

I stepped back into the woods a hundred yards from the refuge and listened to the birds singing and the whispering trees. The place looked deserted, just as I should have expected. But I hadn't, and felt obscurely disappointed. I worked my way closer and found a hiding place wedged between two stacks of rotting timber. There was the ugly building with its boarded windows and rickety steps up to the glazed front door. Still no sign of occupation.

I looked at the place where the Mitsubishi camper van had been parked and we'd stopped with Azza on his stretcher, staring at the sky through morphine-glazed eyes. I looked down the track to the farmhouse and memories paraded in my mind, as bright and clear as if they'd been polished every day.

You don't have time for this.

I left the shelter of the timber stack, crossed the track and ran up the steps to the front door. Listened to the silence again, then tried the handle and pushed it open. I made a quick search, found no one, then wandered back through the empty rooms. A kitchen with a big catering stove and open shelves with white plates and glasses sitting upside down on squares of kitchen roll, a trestle table and ranks of plastic chairs. A crucifix on the wall, Christ's face turned aside in sorrow and suffering, the clouts in his hands and feet expressively crude and thick. *My God, my God, why hast thou forsaken me?* Well, why? What next, girly pics and a cardboard box of knuckledusters?

No. Dormitories with flimsy little wooden beds, pale brown blankets tucked in tight, a pair of cream wardrobes with doors that wouldn't close. On the wall of the corridor that joined them, a colour print of the Virgin Mary pulling her robe aside to display her sacred heart, decorously rendered in ruby and silver. A large bathroom with three tubs, the enamel scoured grey and lines of black mould around the tiles. And then a room that was different from the rest: a Turkish rug on the floor, an oak desk and chair facing a window that looked out over the valley, electric heater, and a large, high divan bed. Was this where it happened? I sat at the desk and pulled open a drawer full of hanging files. There was a green folder for each of the children – I found Katarina's and opened it.

An admission sheet dated 16 January 1999 – the day after she'd been snatched from the Roma village.

> Katarina Corochai, twelve-year-old girl brought to us by a woman who would not give her name or address. She said she had found the girl wandering lost outside her village. She said she asked around to see if anyone recognised her, but no one did. The woman demanded the usual fee for her expenses, which I paid her, and she left. K is quite hollowed out with fear. She said she was from Pristina and gave me her address.

I looked through the rest of the papers. I was surprised to find copies of the letters Father Daniel had told us about – sent to Anna's apartment, the university and the Pristina police. I'd assumed he'd lied about them. However, there were no replies on file. Perhaps the letters had never actually been sent – of course, it was all just for show. Yet the tone of the notes he'd kept was solicitous. *K still in shock, not eating much and keeping away from the other children.*

There was nothing about Katarina running away. I looked through several files at random and found more of the same. In another drawer of the cabinet I found the document that would have been used to get Katarina across the border into Macedonia – and anywhere else they chose to take her. *United Nations High Commission for Refugees*, it said across the top. A passport photograph was stapled to the corner. The document stated that the subject had been received into the care of the UNHCR in Skopje on 29 January 1999 – ironically enough, that was the day I had left her at Syrna Street. Bryan Harley had signed in blue ink, and there was a countersignature and stamp from the Macedonian authorities recognising Katarina's status as a refugee. You could see how anyone invited to inspect such a document would be impressed by its formality. *The child's papers were in order, sir, I had no reason to suspect…*

The will to carry on looking through the files deserted me. In fact, the will to do anything at all deserted me. Search the rest of the desk, I ordered myself. Something was nagging me, something I'd missed or got wrong.

I found a ledger in which Father Daniel had set out what he'd spent in the running of the refuge. Amounts for food, electricity, stationery, toiletries – and every so often an entry that ran: *Expenses fee ref…* Then the name of one of the children and, in the numbers column, *US$600 cash*. Always the same amount. Father Daniel had paid an *expenses fee* to the woman who had brought Katarina to the refuge. Six hundred dollars was a lot of money for something that should have been an act of kindness.

My heart slumped. Take a stray child to the Catholic refuge near the Orthodox Church of the Holy Saviour and Saint Panteleimon and you can sell her for a tidy wad of US dollars, no questions asked. The Bura would have known that – it was almost certainly why they'd abducted Katarina in the first place. Suddenly I longed for Anna to be here with me, to hear her speak, to see how she would deal with this neatly filed paper trail that bore witness to so much suffering.

* * *

I hauled myself out of the chair and left, feeling as if to stay a second longer would be to risk inhaling a lungful of poison. To the front door and out under the open sky, breathing clean air. The crackle of rifle fire from the hills to the east reminded me where I was – a war zone. I thought I should go back to the files, take some evidence with me, but the idea of returning to that stifling little room filled me with revulsion. The church stood fifty yards away – I'd take refuge there while I decided what to do. I walked up to the arched oak doors between the squat towers and found them already open.

'You'll go to hell, you filthy man. Hell, you hear? You're a murderer, the most mortal of all the sins.'

The words were violent, but the voice that delivered them was soft and mesmeric as the hiss of a snake.

'A murderer, Daniel, who disembowelled his own father. And you accuse me of killing your poor ma? How dare you, when you know full well I was with you when she died.'

All I could see in the gloom of the church were rows of pews and an altar, above which hung a figure of Christ in priestly robes at the centre of a starburst of gilded plaster rays so chipped and dirty it looked as if, rather than radiating light, he was the target of a mortal attack.

'You'll learn obedience or you'll die unshriven and the devil will teach it to you. He'll spoon your soul out through your arse and have it for his dinner.'

The voice came from a wooden confessional box over to the left of the nave, by the sacristy door. I walked silently towards it.

'There'll be no rest for the boy who murdered his own father. What did the autopsy say? You sliced him open, then stabbed him five times. Stab, stab, stab…' He repeated the word over and over in his wheedling voice, as if he were there at the scene, orchestrating the blows.

'You know why I did it,' whispered Father Daniel's voice from the confessor's side of the box. 'To save Ma.'

'I saw the state your mother was in when she brought you to me, it was a sight to wrench tears from an angel. It was a sight to make Satan snap his teeth. You say you were saving her, you stupid man, but all you did was condemn her—'

I came level with the curtain over the father confessor's cubicle and tore it aside.

'Get out.'

I aimed the Browning at his shadowed face, framed in its splendidly leonine mane of hair. Father Wulfstan Murray-Bligh, Rector General of the Order of St Hugh. He didn't move. I should have killed him there and then, but I was too shocked to think straight and I hesitated. I forgot what a big man he was. He turned towards me and gave an affable smile, bracing his hands against the sides of the confessional box as if preparing to stand, then kicked out with vicious speed. I took the heel of his shoe on my knee, staggered back. He charged from the cubicle, head down, thick arms hugging my waist. I couldn't stop him slamming the base of my spine into the carved oak panel at the end of a pew. If the bench hadn't collapsed under our weight, he'd have broken me in half. The gun flew from my hand as I tried to break my fall.

I tried to roll him off as we came down, but he was brutishly strong, with the bulk of a tree trunk. I felt despair. Numbness in my hips, his torso crushing my ribcage, his red, snarling face rearing above me. I seized a hank of his white hair and pushed my arm straight, then went for his eyes with my free hand. My fingers searched for the sockets. He pulled his face sharply aside, and my hooked index finger found the pulp of his nostril. I tore it open, then hammered his temple with the side of my fist.

He bellowed in fury and gripped my throat with one huge hand, creasing my windpipe with his thumb. I started to choke. His hair slipped from my grasp and he got his other hand on my neck. He was panting, open mouth a cavern of wet, purple tissue, tongue thick as a cow's, long yellow teeth. I got one forearm in under his throat and reached for the knife at my belt. Jammed fast by a piece of broken timber wedged against my hip. It was all wrong, all wrong… I'd let myself be drawn into a trial of strength with a man stronger than me. His big eyes were watching me, glittering with pleasure as my room to struggle free diminished, inch by inch. I pummelled at his temple but I might as well have been hitting him with a cotton bud. I tried to shout for Father Daniel to help me, but couldn't even croak his name.

Then some piece of the wreckage of the pew gave way and we dropped a few inches, and in that moment I got my knee up into his groin and levered him up, just enough to give myself respite from his crushing weight. Not from the thumbs compressing my throat, but it gave me hope… And I remembered. He was a drinker. Sherry at lunch. A crate of bottles by his desk. Broken glass on the carpet. I felt around the barrel of his midriff until I found the upper right quadrant of his abdomen. I squeezed and probed with my fingers and felt him flinch. There. A big liver, bloated with toxins and fat.

I summoned all the strength I had left and swung my clenched knuckle into his side. Once, twice, three times… He gasped and tried to twist away. His thumbs drove deeper into the tissue of my throat. I hit him again and again and again, seeking out his weakness with the hard bones of my hand.

I was close to blacking out, but the gasps as my fist struck home told me he was in trouble, and I pounded his gut with ever more brutal calculation, adjusting the angle of my blows to land where they drew the deepest moans. In the end, he had to protect himself. His hands unwrapped from my throat. He groaned and rolled away.

I whooped air through my bruised windpipe, got to my knees, found my legs were working, stood. Wulfstan was down on one knee. I swung my boot into the exact same place where my fist had struck. He screamed and twisted away. I kicked him again and he lowered himself onto his side, drew up his knees, one arm held stiffly over his liver. I kicked him three times more. Long, deliberate blows. He lay there, blood from his ripped nose plastered over his showy white hair. And I stood over him, wondering whether I had the strength or the will or the desire or even the need to finish him off.

'Don't.'

Father Daniel was sitting on the floor, leaning against the confessional. His face was blotched with patches of translucent white. The Browning was in his hand.

'Better I do it,' I whispered.

'You must not sin.'

'And you?'

'Beyond salvation.'

He put down the Browning and crawled rapidly over to Wulfstan's side. I collected the gun and watched. Father Daniel reached for Wulfstan's shoulder. The prostrate man stretched up his arm to bat the hand aside, then suddenly froze. A heavy spasm passed through his massive frame. Cady took hold of the cuff of Wulfstan's jacket and worked the sleeve off his arm. Wulfstan made a low crooning sound in his throat.

'Let me be, Daniel. Hell… I warned you. Dear Daniel… I tried to save you. You and your poor ma. That's all. To care for you…'

Father Daniel reached behind Wulfstan's head and fumbled with the stud of his collar. Again, the big man tried to stop him, but every movement now made him shudder. Father Daniel got the stud undone. The dog collar was stitched at the front to a sleeveless tunic that covered Wulfstan's chest. Father Daniel took two hand-fuls of the black cotton and ripped the tunic off. He threw the collar and tunic aside and looked up at me, his face full of horror.

'There now, see what I've done. Defrocked him. To kill a priest, you see...'

He got to his feet and stumbled over to the place where he'd left the Browning.

'Daniel, look at him,' I said hoarsely. 'He's dying.'

Wulfstan's face was the colour of cod belly, and he was shiver-ing uncontrollably. You lose blood fast from a ruptured liver, and it won't stop bleeding by itself.

'Come with me,' I said, and led Father Daniel from the church.

51

We walked down to the farmhouse, drawn there by some need that did not have to be named. We went slowly because my back was in spasm, and in silence because my throat was so swollen that it hurt to speak.

Instead, I thought about what had happened, and the first thing that came to me was that the handwriting I'd seen in Daniel Cady's notebooks in the bedroom at the refuge was small, scratchy and uneven – nothing at all like the flamboyant script in the Book of Prayer Katarina had stolen.

'I thought it was yours,' I wheezed. 'I almost killed you.'

He looked at me, puzzled.

'The Book of Prayer.'

'It was Wulfstan's.'

The teller of bedtime stories, the giver of treats and punishments, the creator of that monstrous chimera called hell – not Daniel Cady but Wulfstan Murray-Bligh. And when I'd rung the refuge the day after rescuing Katarina... Perhaps it wasn't Daniel I had spoken to, but Wulfstan. The moment this thought occurred to me, I knew it was true. He'd worked out who I was, questioned me to find out whether Katarina had taken his book, then directed me to Syrna Street – Daniel didn't even know it existed. In fact, I now remembered, it was I who had told him the address.

'Wulfstan was obsessed with his Book of Prayer,' Father Daniel said. 'I'd never seen him so angry as when he found it was missing. Usually, he is very controlled.'

We walked on down the track and the farmhouse came into view through a break in the trees. I swallowed and found that the constriction in my kinked windpipe had eased.

'Is it true you killed your father?'

'Ma wanted everyone to believe it was her,' Father Daniel said quietly. 'She had cause enough, God knows. My father had started taking me out to work on his boat, the *Suffolk Rose*—'

'I read your poem – it was folded into Wulfstan's book.' I remembered the note at the end as well, written in what I now knew to be Wulfstan's hand: *Weakness. A terror that will not relax its grip.* 'Some of the lines have haunted me. No wonder you don't like fish.'

He gave me a doleful look, and I saw that he wished I hadn't found his poem.

'Sorry.'

He inclined his head by way of acknowledgement and carried on.

'Every time we came off the boat, my father would beat Ma with a knout because he said the house was dirty. He soaked the knout in seawater the night before, to make it heavier. The house was always clean, it could not have been cleaner. Now that I was one of his crew, he made me watch. He made me part of it, James. Ma looked at me with an awful sadness in her eyes. She thought I'd become like him. I couldn't bear that. I couldn't leave it so. After the third trip on the *Rose*, when we got back and he set about her, I took the knife from my pack and I gutted him, the way he'd taught me. It was just like Wulfstan said. But I had to do it or he'd have killed her.'

Daniel Cady stopped walking and looked down at his feet. His shoulders were shaking and I realised he was crying.

When he'd recovered a little, I asked: 'How did Wulfstan find out?'

'I confessed to him.' Now, along with the grief, there was anger in Daniel's voice. 'I told him everything. When I was done, he said he had to pray for guidance and I was to wait for him. I sat in the confessional box for two hours. It was cold and I was hungry and frightened. I was fourteen and in the space of a week I'd killed my father and lost my mother, perhaps forever. Father Wulfstan was all I had. He came back and made me confess again, sparing no detail. I begged him to absolve me but he refused. He refused to forgive my sin in God's name, as he had the authority to do. Then he told me that over a matter of such seriousness, it was his solemn duty to protect the Order, and so he had taped my confession.

'He played it back to me again and again over the weeks and months and years that followed. He tortured me with it. He said I must atone for my sin by throwing myself on the mercy of God's Church. The first step was to turn over all Dad's money to the Order. My father was a rich man, you see?'

I nodded, remembering what I'd found out in Leicester Central Library: that John Cady, Daniel's father, had inherited a fortune made in Lowestoft's fisheries.

'I had to buy my absolution, though to this day he's never granted it to me. He called himself my mentor and talked in my ear about hell. He's a great expert on hell, is Father Wulfstan.'

* * *

We arrived at the farmhouse. The kitchen had been hosed down and the loft-ladder lay broken on the floor. We found a pair of rickety wooden chairs and sat at the table like two old men. We should have gone up into the woods for safety, but I was too impatient to hear the rest of Father Daniel's story.

'What happened here that afternoon?'

'What happened? It's hard to describe, James. I think something evil took a mortal blow. It died slowly and lashed out with great violence as it went. Does that make sense?'

'Yes, but I meant—'

'You know who struck the mortal blow? Katarina. Yes, it was Katarina. Wulfstan was here when she was brought in. I'd just got back from a trip to Pristina. I welcomed her and took down her details. I tried to comfort the poor child and make her feel safe, then I took her to the kitchen to join the others. Wulfstan was there. He couldn't take his eyes off her. He kept asking her questions, finding reasons to follow her about. She had such a simple grace about her – she didn't know how to deal with this man.

'I tried to keep her away from him. By then I half suspected he'd been abusing the children. He used to come to the refuge every few months and insist that Ma and I go off somewhere for a break. When I got back – well, the children wouldn't speak about it, but they were scared and miserable. Then Wulfstan would leave and I'd tell myself it was nonsense: he wasn't a child abuser. It was what I wanted to believe. But Wulfstan was so mesmerised by Katarina. It was horrible to see him pawing this modest girl with his greedy eyes. And she was so beautiful.'

'*Is* so beautiful.'

I told him what had happened since I'd seen him last. I told him about the Vegas Lounge, how we'd pursued Haclan's gang down to the bay near Thessaloniki and rescued Katarina and the other girls from the *Santa Cristina*. And I told him that Haclan was dead. He listened with head bowed.

When I'd finished, and I didn't spin the story out, he said: 'Katarina's alive, they all are. Thank God.' He looked straight at me for a moment. 'I know nothing about you, James. Nothing at all. Will you tell me how you got caught up in this? I mean, you're a soldier, I know. But if you can?'

'I can. But finish your story first.'

'Yes... Wulfstan, Wulfstan... He could have torn our lives apart, mine and my mother's. He could have had me sent to prison for murder. He could have consigned me to hell – he'd always made me believe that, ever since he'd taken my confession. He and he alone could perform the absolution that would save me. He forbade me to go to another priest and I was too frightened to disobey. I was a prisoner in that place, and hardly noticed the years go by. I did everything he ordered, everything. But when I saw him staring at Katarina, I told myself I'd rather die unshriven than stand by while he preyed on her.'

'So what did you do?'

'I called Ma and she came and helped me with supper. Wulfstan sat at the end of the table and said prayers. The children bowed their heads so low their hair hung in their plates. When they'd gone to bed, I told Wulfstan that next time he came I would stay at the refuge and show him how we looked after them. *Our Saviour provides all the guidance I could possibly hope for, and more, in His wisdom*, he replied. *I will follow wheresoever He takes me.* The words came out easily, but I saw in his eyes that he realised something had changed.

'Ma came back from helping the children to wash. A child tucked into bed and kissed goodnight by someone who cares for her, she used to say, will sleep soundly and wake with hope in her heart. Wulfstan's shadow hung over us, but when he wasn't there... Well, life was hard for us, but we'd found a kind of happiness and I didn't want it to end.

'That night Wulfstan made a sort of confession. He poured us glasses of his precious sherry and admitted that he didn't always meet the high standards of behaviour he set for himself. He sermonised on the challenges and agonies of celibacy. Then he insisted on going to the dormitory, switching the lights on and telling the children a funny story, to show what a lovable man he was. They laughed with desperate mirth and it was awful to see how fear had taught them to dissemble. But still in my weakness I convinced myself that my mentor would now redeem himself. This confession was the first step. Whatever he'd been doing to the children would cease, and soon I would receive the absolution I craved.

'I was woken at two by a shout. I got up and ran to my room, which was where Wulfstan slept when he stayed. He wasn't there. I checked the dormitory and saw that Katarina was missing. I searched the rest of the building, then ran outside and shouted her name. There was no answer. It was very cold and I knew they must have taken shelter somewhere. I went up the track, calling out for her again and again, until I came to the place where we parked the Mitsubishi camper van and saw that it was gone.

'Ma had an old car, so I ran down to the farmhouse. She met me outside – she'd heard me shouting for Katarina. We drove off to find them.

'It wasn't long before we saw yellow lights glowing from a hill-top five minutes' drive from the refuge. We were sure it was him because there was never any traffic around at night. He'd driven up a track which was too muddy for the car, so we parked on the road and made the last few hundred yards on foot. The Mitsubishi's interior lights were on, and he'd spun the rear seats round so they faced each other. It was like a little courtroom in there – Wulfstan sitting in a captain's seat and Katarina kneeling in front of him. As we approached, I saw that he had his Book of Prayer open in his lap, and he was writing in it.

'My mother got to the vehicle first. She pulled back the sliding door and unleashed such a blast of rage and contempt that for a moment I thought she might attack him. He was at first too astonished to speak. Then, when her fury abated, he found his voice. *Be careful, Irene, for your own sake, and the sake of your murderer son.* She shouted back at him that he could do his worst for neither of us cared any more.

'I lifted the tailgate and beckoned to Katarina. Even in this moment of terror, she was so composed and spirited, and saw immediately that this was her chance. Wulfstan reached for her but she was too quick, and in a moment she was running towards the lights of the Volkswagen. I pulled my mother away from the door. She was still screaming at Wulfstan. I'd seen him in this mood before. Nearly always it would end with him drawing back his fist.

'We left him there with his Book of Prayer still open in his lap and ran back to the car. We quickly caught up with Katarina, who had no shoes. I offered to carry her the rest of the way but she refused. We heard the Mitsubishi's engine revving behind us, labouring in the mud as Wulfstan tried to wrestle it round and come after us. But whatever he intended, we made it to the car and drove back to the refuge.

'Katarina slept the rest of the night in the farmhouse with Ma. Later, I heard Wulfstan return, and the next morning at breakfast he behaved as if nothing had happened, though I noticed he was limping. I was too much of a coward to confront him. It was always like that between us. After he had eaten, he packed his bags and left. He had a man who would come and collect him in an expensive car. I often wondered how he got in and out of Kosovo so easily, but I never asked.'

'Did you talk to Katarina afterwards?'

'No, but Ma did. He'd gagged her and carried her from the dormitory. When they got to where the Mitsubishi was parked, she managed to dash the ignition key from his hand. As he crouched to find it, she searched in the dirt for a weapon and by chance came up with a wrench the man who changes the oil must have left there, and when he stood up again, she hit him on the knee. That was the shout I'd heard. He'd gagged her, but he hadn't gagged himself, and so he gave himself away when she hit him. It was a brave thing to do.'

'So after that Wulfstan went back to England?'

'I think so, yes. Anyway, Ma and I agreed that we must never leave the children alone with him again, and Ma reported him to the police in Pristina. Unless we had evidence, they said, there was nothing they could do. Ma decided to contact some of the children who had been taken to Skopje, in hope that they would feel safe enough to speak out. So she called Bryan Harley at the UNHCR.'

'Yes, I saw details of the call in the log on her phone.'

'She couldn't get hold of Harley, so she spoke to someone else. Ma gave this man the names and he said he would check the database and get back to her. The next day a different person called and asked for details from the UNHCR papers, numbers and dates – but he didn't say why. We never heard any more.'

'That must be how they found out about Harley,' I said, 'because those children weren't on the database. When your mother said they'd been sent to Skopje using UNHCR paperwork with his name on it, they'd have been onto him like a shot.'

'I wish they'd called back and told us, then,' said Father Daniel. 'Ma was so angry she couldn't let it rest. A few days later, she came running up to the refuge. She was crying. *Keep away from Haclan Adjani,* she kept saying. *You must keep the children away from him. Don't trust him. Don't cross him. Haclan Adjani will kill you.* I'd never heard the name before – who was he? She told me that Haclan Adjani was a dangerous man, a gangster. And she told me that he was Father Wulfstan's brother.'

'But Wulfstan is English,' I said, astonished.

'No, Albanian. His real name is Peter Adjani. Ma said there'd been a family feud and he fled to England and changed his name, then entered a seminary in Norwich before joining the Order of

St Hugh. Ma's father was a cousin of theirs. That was why she left me with the Order before fleeing the country. I suppose she believed Wulfstan would protect me.'

Wulfstan was the third brother Eleni had told me about, the one who'd disappeared. That was how Haclan had found out I was back in Skopje. Remembering the long form I'd filled out at the BFPO office, I realised that my name and address would have been on the parcel containing his Book of Prayer. Peter Adjani, Wulfstan, had reported all this to Haclan. Whatever the feud had been about, it was over and the three brothers had been in touch throughout.

'Did you know about Vasilis Adjani?' I asked.

'No, but when Anna mentioned his name, I wondered…'

'He's a former member of the Albanian government and yes, he was at Rambouillet. That conversation Anna told us about, when the MI6 officer came to warn him that his brother's criminal activities might jeopardise the Kosovar cause – she said later that Colonel Adjani mentioned a woman who wouldn't be able to help any more. I think that woman was your mother.'

'People knew what was going on, James. People in authority. But still they left Haclan free to kill my mother? If they had arrested him straight away, she might still be alive.'

'They didn't want to arrest him while his brother was representing the Kosovars at Rambouillet. It was shameful and I'm not defending it, but that's the way they think.'

There was a long silence. Father Daniel sat with his head hanging over his knees and I stared out of the door at the buckled concrete yard with its ring of crumbling sheds.

Father Daniel looked up suddenly and said: 'Thank you, James. I haven't said that yet, have I? Without you, Katarina wouldn't have survived and the other children would still be in Adjani's hands.'

'I'm not sure you'd say that if you knew the whole story.'

He gave me a look of kindly concern. I was touched – and surprised. In the short time I had known him, his features had always seemed impassive and melancholy, like an empty shop with a lightbulb glowing dimly through whitewashed windows. I had not thought him capable of registering sympathy.

'Tell me what happened after she warned you about Haclan.' I said. I was nervous now, for we were reaching the point in the story which I had been dreading but still felt compelled to hear.

'Wulfstan came back ten days later, much sooner than expected. As usual, he said I should take time off while he was there. I refused. Then come for a walk with me, so we can discuss your spiritual state, he said. I think you may soon be ready to receive my absolution. We walked for an hour, then I told him I was going back to the refuge. He tried to delay me, but anyway, we got back and the first thing we noticed was that Katarina had gone. Then two men I didn't know came running into the refuge. One of them stared at me, such a dark, dirty look. There were gunshots from the farmhouse and they seemed nervous. Ten or fifteen minutes later, you arrived.'

'If I'd known she was your mother, I would have—'

'It doesn't matter now. They killed her the way I killed my father, then daubed anti-KLA slogans on the wall to make people think it was Serbian militia.'

'I'm sorry,' I said gently. 'What happened after you found her?'

'I ran. My head was full of the horror. I could not go back to the refuge. May God forgive me for abandoning the children.'

'Those men would have killed you too, Daniel. It was better that you survived.'

'I was mad with grief. I couldn't hold my thoughts together for more than a second at a time. I was near the Macedonian border when you called. I listened to your message and told myself Katarina would be all right, because that's what I believed at the time. I was blinded by my own misfortunes. I wandered round with groups of refugees for days and days, doing what I could to help them. Eventually I decided to go to Skopje to look for her.' He paused, then said: 'Ma must have been alive when you found her.'

A picture of the scene of butchery reared in my mind. What could I possibly say to ease his grief?

'I comforted her as best I could. There were three of them, though, not two – the third was hiding in the attic and shot one of our unit. By the time we'd—'

'By the time you'd killed my brother,' said Father Daniel, 'my mother was also dead. Is that what you mean to say?'

I rocked back as if I'd been bludgeoned in the chest. The room reeled before me. The pale throat my fist had crushed was the throat of a boy hiding in terror while his mother was slaughtered below. I'd always known that, hadn't I? It accounted for the feverish aftermath, the feeling of being on the run not just from my actions, but from myself. It accounted for the need to prove myself *one of us*, for only *one of us* could be cold enough to live with such a thing.

'My half-brother, I should say.'

'We didn't know… He opened fire. I'm sorry. We thought he was with the killers.'

'Nico? No, he was a very kind boy. I would have taken care of him. I don't know where his father is – he and Ma were only together for a short time.'

'Did you find him when you found your mother?'

'No. I feared for him, of course, but I only heard that he'd died when I came back to fetch the children.'

I stepped out into the yard. The sky was a strong, deep, mid-day blue. Birds courted noisily in the woods, periodically scattering as a rumble of artillery fire echoed down the valley. Beside me was the galvanised bin I'd hidden behind while Ollie checked the farmhouse. I thought of how I must have seemed to TJ's men: one of the officer race, ignorant, arrogant, eager. Had they guessed that

the boy I had punched to death was not a member of the Bura
gang? Probably. But they'd tried to protect me from the knowledge
that I'd killed an innocent boy. It's one of the things good soldiers
do for each other, along with covering their arses and avenging
their dead.

* * *

We walked back to the refuge. As we came level with the church, I
said: 'Want me to check?'

He nodded, so I went. Corpse. I beckoned him from the
doorway.

'We could deal with the body, if you like?'

We dragged it out of the church and round the back, then
rolled it over the escarpment. It crashed into a clump of blackthorn
forty feet below. It weighed a ton – a good few hearty meals for the
scavengers hereabouts. *For what you are about to receive,* I said (to
myself, for fear of offending Father Daniel), *the world will be truly
thankful.*

We went indoors and ate, but though Daniel offered beans and
some ancient crackers, all I could manage was tinned fruit. I told
the rest of my story and Father Daniel watched me with those lumi-
nous eyes that had always seemed to invite you to wonder what
it was that made him so sad – and I realised the look had gone.
No, the sadness was still there, but the mysterious entreaty was not.
Something pent up had been released, the shutters pulled aside.
Daniel Cady had stepped clear of the hell Wulfstan made for him.

I came to the moment when I arrived back at Anna's apartment
and found he'd run off.

'I might have killed you that night. The details in Wulfstan's
book were harrowing. Where did you go?'

'Back to the refuge. I'd realised I wasn't going to hunt down

Haclan Adjani and avenge my mother's death. There was nothing more I could tell any of you about Katarina, and I felt that my presence there was just a strange form of torture for Anna. And I was frightened of you, James. I knew there were things I'd done or not done which could be misconstrued, and... Well, you carried about you at that time an air of pure violence.'

He meant it as a compliment, I suppose, the kind of thing to make a soldier puff out his chest, but I was appalled.

'I thought I was ready to face Wulfstan without quailing again. That proved not to be true,' Daniel Cady said ruefully. 'He wasn't here when I arrived, and the children were fending for themselves. They were just about OK, but frightened – and lonely in the way even large groups of children are when they're not being looked after. Six of them were missing – Katarina and the five other girls you rescued from the ship. The Mitsubishi had gone, but I wasn't going to wait for Haclan's men to return. We walked to the border – the weather was mild and we only encountered one Serbian patrol, who turned out to be just ordinary young men not really sure what they were doing and pleased to give the children chocolate and help us on our way. After three days we reached Blace, where I handed them over to the care of the UNHCR – with some misgivings, but at least the case officer's name was not Bryan Harley.'

'It was all recorded in the UNHCR database. A friend of mine went to their HQ in Skopje and checked.'

'So the children are all right? They're all accounted for? You know that for sure?'

'They'd just been transferred to Stankovic Two, we were told. I guess the children from the ship will have joined them by now. Sixteen children like Katarina. What do we know about them?'

'Not much – in one or two cases, nothing at all.'

'None of them are all right, though, Daniel, are they? Not really. And there aren't just sixteen, there are thousands of Katarinas all over the Balkans. Orphans, refugees, slaves, corpses. Not one of them is all right.'

'Will this war do any good, do you think?'

'Nobody knows. Least of all the people who started it. We should get going.'

'I'm not going with you, James. I belong here now. It's the only good work I've ever done, and I am supposed to be a priest, after all.'

'Kosovo is a dangerous place, Daniel – and it's not going to get better any time soon.'

'That's why the refuge must stay open.'

'Why not go back to Northampton first? Someone has to take over the running of the Order. And Father Neil ought to know what's happened.'

I couldn't dissuade him – and in fact I envied the certainty his calling granted him. I collected some food and stood at the door. It was a strange moment. I had spent several weeks of my life believing this timid and unworldly man to be the most evil creature I had ever encountered. Now, the ties of destiny that bound us were permanent and profound. Yet the simple, comfortable quality of friendship itself was entirely absent from our relationship, and we did not quite know how to say goodbye. That would change over the coming years. For the present, we shook hands, and I looked into his eyes and felt that if Daniel Cady had not now earned the right to a benevolent hand from God or fate, then no one ever could.

52

I made slow progress, my jarred back obliging me to walk with soft steps and the throbbing in my throat distracting me from the route. Orienteering was not my strong suit anyway, and it was as well that I was in no hurry to get anywhere.

I kept following paths and tracks heading south, only to find myself looping round the flank of a hill and looking up at a vista of mountains I'd already seen. Meltwater sluiced down ditches and gullies hidden beneath my feet and a scent of damp moss filled the air. The intermittent skirmishes of war still chattered in the distance, but it felt as if I'd been released into a different dimension and permitted to meander through these deep, sheltering forests, sunlight filtered by the canopy of trees splashing my shoulders with a lattice of sinuous gold.

A part of me was distraught at the discovery – or rather the confirmation – that I'd killed an innocent boy; but already I felt a sense of relief, too. I was weary of evading the truth, of twisting away from its insistent light. I could not bring Nico back to life, but I could face up to what I had done. By comparison with the events I had witnessed over the last weeks, the state of my soul seemed a matter of indecent triviality, but it was all I had and it needed the truth. How else could I be sure that I would not make the mistakes I had made with Nico and Katarina all over again, in some other time, some other place?

After three hours, the light began to fade. I left the path and waded through dense undergrowth until I found a place where a ledge of rock protruded from a steep, peaty bank. I eased myself up to the ledge and opened tins of beans and fruit. There was a huge oak tree here, with a deeply riven trunk that had the girth of ten men and lower branches zigzagging out thirty feet and more on all sides. Attracted by the smell of food, a mob of squirrels arrived and started crashing through the boughs. I flung the remnants from the tins away down the slope and they scuttled after them. Then I lay down to sleep.

A few hours later I came hard awake. Aircraft droning overhead, the air vibrating with the weight of their engines. I climbed a few branches of the oak until I got clear of the undergrowth. I could just make out the cross-frames of the bombers, like pale dimples in the blackness of the sky. They skimmed smoothly into the east and started to unload. Flashes of sheetlight popped and flared, low growls stammered over the hills. The fires caught, a corona of sooty orange brimming over the horizon, and the bombers banked away to the north, bay-doors sliding shut.

Our planes, our bombs, I thought, reaching out to kill across the great gulf of the sky.

* * *

I entered Maria's restaurant at midday.

'James, you look so much better. You are tired, but the trouble has gone from your eyes. Well, some of it has, anyway. I thought it never would.'

'Leonard Cohen,' I said. '"Famous Blue Raincoat".'

'See, you learn one thing good in my restaurant!'

'More than one,' I said with feeling. I hugged her hard and told her I was going back to England.

'Not before lunch,' she said.

She fed me without further comment, then sat at my table and said: 'You are sensible to go. But Karela deserves better. You must invite her to stay with you in England. You do not have to marry her.'

'That's good to know.'

'But anyway it will make her happy. You do not have nice memories of Skopje, but you must come back and see me, please, and the children?'

I told her I would always have nice memories of her and the restaurant and her bumptious offspring. Then we hugged again.

* * *

I called Eleni's apartment, and she answered.

'Can I come over? I need to talk to you.'

'James, what has happened? Are you safe? We have worried non-stop—'

'Is Anna there?'

'She has taken Katya for a picnic in Vodno. Come to visit us – at six o'clock?'

'It has to be now,' I said. 'Can you and I meet?'

We agreed a rendezvous, and I was shamefully relieved that Anna and Katarina would not be there. I felt guilty about pitching Katarina into the hands of child traffickers, of course. I still do. And I had kept so much hidden from Anna, and had my subterfuges exposed so often, that I felt I had lost the right to her company. In short, I had estranged myself from her – courageous, trusting, generous-hearted Anna, with her graceful intelligence and humour, and her painful integrity that was such a contrast to my own confused disingenuousness. That estrangement was a heavy part of the burden I bore for the years that followed.

So I met with Eleni and made her the receptacle for a garbled account of my return to the refuge, and she listened and interjected with frequent expressions of horror and sympathy, and then I left the poor woman to bear this awkward sort of ending back to her apartment and pass it on to Anna and Katarina as best she could.

I got a taxi to the airport and took the next flight back to London. I was detained at Heathrow. In the privacy of the interview room, I started a fight with two and eventually five security guards. It ended with me lying in a hospital bed, heavily sedated and with plenty of bruising to keep my mind off other things.

* * *

Andy Hillson came to my rescue. The charges were dropped and I was released into the world on the strict understanding that I reported to him weekly.

'What will you say to me, sir, do you think?'

'Apart from stop being such a bloody prima donna? I haven't the faintest idea. You may as well know that there's a move to get you back into GCHQ.'

'A spell on the naughty step, before I'm let back into the playpen?'

He declined to answer. I went to Lowestoft and rescued the Jack Taylor from the golf club near the harbour, then took it back to the ramshackle garage in Norfolk. On the way, I returned the money I'd stolen from the honesty box. That pretty much completed the task of putting right the wrongs I'd done – or at least, the revocable ones.

* * *

I spent the next year engaged in a low-level war with Iain Strang and Clive Silk. All I sought was to clear my name – not in public (none of this was in public), but in the annals of espionage, where falsehoods accumulate and feed on each other like rats in a dump. Silk was terrified of what might come out, but Strang was made of sterner stuff. He had his video of me in the brothel with an underage girl on the bed beside me, his (well-founded) suspicion that I'd killed two men in the back of a van in a cul-de-sac off Syrna Street, and his inviolable sense that the world must dance to his tune or dance not at all. I won that skirmish eventually… But that's another story. Hillson kept out of it all, sensible man that he is.

In the meantime, I kept in touch with Father Daniel, and Anna, Eleni and Maria. Karela came to stay and was happy and did not require or even want me to marry her. Then I got the email from Eleni about the incident at the bus stop in Pristina, how Katarina had lashed out at a man who groped her and put him in a coma. How she'd been wearing the knuckleduster I had taken from the Bura HQ and left in the playground, where Anna found it and used it to clout the man attacking her brother-in-law Piotr.

I followed Katarina's trial. The defence lawyer made great play of her silence. *The clinical term is elective mute,* he informed the jury, *and each of you should take a moment to consider what kind of hurt might make you elect to say not a single word to anyone for over three years.* The story he proceeded to tell the court was a pallid version of the truth – like a dark tragedy recast as an edifying bedtime fable. During the summing up, he linked Katarina's plight with the fate of Kosovo. *My client is a symbol of the suffering of our young nation, traumatised by war and the crimes of those who profit by it. Who can hear her story and remain unmoved? Who will dare judge her after what she has endured?*

The ploy worked: along with the inevitable guilty verdict, the jury made a plea for clemency. A six-month sentence was apparently the very least she could have expected.

*   *   *

When I'd read through all the trial reports, I took out the manuscript Anna had sent me a year previously, in which she recounted her own experience of what happened. Reading it always made me feel close to her – and then mournful, because we had known each other only during those bleak times. She'd sent me the manuscript partly as a prompt, I guessed: it was her way of asking me to set down my side of the story. I'd never done so, and it wasn't just laziness. I'd concealed the truth more thoroughly than anyone, and I was nervous about how Anna would take it.

Katarina's silence... and mine. She, too frightened to speak of what befell her; I, too ashamed. I dwelt bitterly on this contrast.

Still, I've written it now, and I am glad.

I want to finish by saying how proud I am of you, Katarina. You were clever and determined and brave. You deserve to be back home because you never gave up. It wasn't your fault that you got mixed up with cruel men and a cruel war, but you kicked and fought and ran your way clear of that and if people say you were lucky, they are wrong: all the luck you had you made yourself, and you were stronger than most grown-ups would have been, faced with the things you endured. Wulfstan and his brothers, and the Bura gang who abducted you; and the big men and women at Rambouillet who feasted on wine and cheese and ordered the destruction of Kosovo because they couldn't think of anything better to do; and I, who thought it was more important to prove myself to TJ and his crew than to make sure you were safe... We can hang our heads in shame. But you, Katarina, you can hold yours up high and walk tall into the future.

Epilogue

From: Dr Eleni Asllani [eleni_a@uni-pr.edu]
To: james.palatine@hotmail.com
Sent: 12 November 2002 21:41
Subject: K!

Dear James,

Katarina is talking again! Just last night she suddenly said that she
wished we would stop treating her like a silly little girl, because there
are not many silly little girls who have spent three months in prison.
Since then, it is almost like she is a normal teenager again, which of
course means she does not say much and most of it is complaining.
But to her mother and me they are the sweetest complaints.

Then this morning she suddenly said she didn't know why we
were always pulling long faces and feeling sorry for her, because in
fact she was the lucky one. She was never made to work in Haclan
Adjani's 'bars', as she called them, like the other girls.

Very gently, Anna asked her to say more. It seems Adjani said
she was being saved for someone special and was not to be touched.
They were very frightened of the Boss and would never disobey

him. Anna and I then had the horrible thought that this special man might be his brother Wulfstan, and I am more than ever glad that monster is dead.

It was such a relief to hear this that Anna cried and Katarina got cross and ran to her room and banged the door shut, so that is all we know right now, except that her therapist said that people who are spared while others are abused may suffer terrible guilt. We should not forget what else she has endured, either.

Also, James, she said to tell you that the pasta with tomato sauce you cooked was the most disgusting thing she has ever eaten, and she hopes you will do better next time. So you see, the humorous spirit of the Galicas is strong within her.

Anna asked her if she would like to see you and she said yes, she would. So you must come to Pristina, James. Stop whatever you are doing and come here to be with us and share our joy.

With love,

Eleni

A Note on the War in Kosovo

Say a Little Prayer is set against the backdrop of the struggle for an independent Kosovo, which came to a head with the bombing and subsequent occupation of Serbia by NATO forces in 1999. It was the last of the so-called Yugoslav Wars, which marked the implosion of the former Yugoslavia during the course of the 1990s and led to the creation of independent states in Slovenia, Croatia, Macedonia, Bosnia Herzegovina, Montenegro and Kosovo.

It was a horrible decade, even for a part of Europe accustomed to horrible decades. The Balkans are cursed by their geography. Whenever empires expand, they trample the Balkans, and this has been going on for two millennia. The Romans and then the Ottomans occupied the region entirely. In the thirteenth century, Genghis Khan menaced from the east; in the nineteenth century, the Austro-Hungarian Empire bulged down from the north. In the last century, the Third Reich had its baleful day, followed swiftly by the oppressive yoke of the Soviet Union. Just as the grinding of tectonic plates beneath the Earth's surface causes earthquakes and tsunamis, so the geopolitical ambitions of competing empires cause violence and war. We who enjoy life within settled borders cannot begin to imagine what it must be like to know that the history of one's kinsfolk is one of being repeatedly crushed by marching armies and tyrannical regimes.

The wars of the 1990s were the latest incarnation of this history of conflict. In the power vacuum that followed the death of President Tito and the collapse of the Soviet empire, the Yugoslav state fell apart. The populace quickly redefined itself along ethnic and religious lines – Yugoslavia had only been established at the end of the First World War and commanded little loyalty outside Serbia. As the regional states erupted into civil war, the world watched uneasily. The idea of defining nations by ethnicity was hard to stomach – wasn't that exactly what Hitler tried to do in Germany?

It soon became clear that the various conflicts were being fought out against a backdrop of persecution punctuated by appalling incidents of ethnic cleansing – most notoriously the genocide of 8,000 Bosnian Muslims by Serbian forces at Srebrenica in 1995. Muslims and Christians who had lived as neighbours for centuries became sworn enemies, and pockets of peaceful diversity became focal points for the ugliest fighting. To enshrine these religious and ethnic differences in the redrawn map of the Balkans seemed like a counsel of despair – although this is for the most part what happened.

The empire of the West, represented by its military wing (NATO) and countless civilian bureaucracies, played its own hand in the Yugoslav Wars – animated by a hotchpotch of motives which are hard to disentangle. The Western appetite for capitalising on victory in the Cold War was far from sated, and to this extent, Serbia – under Moscow loyalist Slobodan Milošević – was 'the enemy'. There was also an understandable determination not to allow the conflict in this dangerous area of Europe to fester. And given the humanitarian crisis, the justification for intervention could be couched in moral terms, which suited everyone – especially the self-styled moralist British Prime Minister Tony Blair, who described the wars as 'a battle between good and evil'.

However, the role of the Western powers was badly tainted by a child-trafficking scandal, which is referred to several times in *Say a Little Prayer*. A private security company called DynCorp had been hired to provide peacekeeping services for the UN-sponsored International Police Task Force (IPTF) in Bosnia. A DynCorp employee called Kathryn Bolkovac discovered that IPTF and DynCorp personnel – including some of the most senior and powerful men in the organisations – were regular customers of brothels selling trafficked women and children. Furthermore, the worst offenders were complicit in the trafficking itself, buying women and supplying forged documents to make it easier to move them around Europe. Rescuers by day, clients by night, is Bolkovac's bitter assessment. The extent of the corruption was such that it took years of vigorous whistleblowing before the brave and resourceful Bolkovac got her story heard, and to this day efforts to bring the culprits to book have been half-hearted at best.

This scandal was the tip of an iceberg. It has been estimated that more than 200,000 women and children from Eastern bloc countries were being trafficked annually. Bolkovac notes in her book *The Whistleblower* that nothing in Bosnia at the time worked as smoothly or efficiently as the people-trafficking business. In *Say a Little Prayer*, it is fear of a similar disgrace in Kosovo – and its potential to derail the Rambouillet peace talks – that the UK intelligence services believe justifies taking such radical steps to cover up the scandal of the Vegas Lounge – though of course this is all fiction.

* * *

The Dayton Accords of 1995 brought the worst of the fighting to a close, but the agreement ignored the situation in Kosovo, which was trapped in a cycle of increasingly violent protest and increasingly cruel oppression.

The population of Kosovo is over ninety per cent Albanian and Muslim (Kosovar), but to Serbs it is their historical heartland, which they defended to the last man against the advancing Ottomans in the Battle of Kosovo in 1389. Both armies were annihilated and the Ottomans soon took over the territory anyway, but nothing inspires nationalistic folklore like a heroic defeat.

The territory was under the formal government of Belgrade, but for much of the 1990s, the situation was kept calm by the wisdom and skill of Ibrahim Rugova, who established a parallel Kosovar regime which, although lacking real power, commanded widespread support. Rugova preached peaceful protest, but towards the end of the decade the Kosovo Liberation Army (KLA) became increasingly active. Kosovo was descending into war, and the Kosovar population reacted the way peaceful civilians do when they see their livelihoods and communities destroyed and sense that worse is to follow: they left.

The Western powers called the Serbian and Kosovar leadership to the negotiating table (though Milošević refused to attend), and in February 1999 they met at Rambouillet outside Paris, where Anna's narrative in *Say a Little Prayer* is partly set. This may be the only peace conference in history that was conducted under the threat of war – not from the parties to the negotiation but from its organisers: the NATO Activation Order that authorised the use of military force in Kosovo had been in place since October. Despite the seriousness of its objectives, the conference was somewhat farcical – many of the details I have used to describe it are based on fact, and there are plenty more to choose from. The negotiations never really advanced beyond the tautologous statement with which they began, which proposed granting autonomy to Kosovo while respecting the territorial integrity of the Federal Republic of Yugoslavia.

The conference stumbled to an end, and reconvened in Paris a few weeks later, where the Kosovar leadership signed the

Rambouillet Accords. The Serbs did not – and their refusal paved the way for the NATO bombing campaign, called Operation Allied Force, which began on 24 March.

In *Say a Little* Prayer, Anna and James come to believe that the powerful men and women who preside over Rambouillet actually want to bomb the Serbs into submission, or at least regard it as an acceptable solution. This was the view of many at the time. Ex-US Secretary of State Henry Kissinger wrote: 'The Rambouillet text, which called on Serbia to admit NATO troops throughout Yugoslavia, was a provocation, an excuse to start bombing.' And State Department adviser Strobe Talbott thought that 'it was Yugoslavia's resistance to the broader trends of political and economic reform – not the plight of the Kosovar-Albanians – that best explains NATO's war'.

What is not in doubt is that the NATO bombing campaign, far from averting the humanitarian crisis, turned it into a catastrophe. As the bombers appeared in the skies over Kosovo, people were leaving at a rate of 20,000 per day. An inquiry by the Organization for Security and Co-operation in Europe noted 'the vast increase in lootings, killings, rape, kidnappings and pillage once the NATO air war began on March 24'.

These were feverish, chaotic and terrifying times for the people of Kosovo, and it was not until ground troops invaded in early June that the flood of refugees abated. By then, more than a third of the region's 1.6 million population had been driven from their homes.

I tried not to be partisan about all this, because being Serbian or Albanian or Muslim or Christian does not make people intrinsically right or wrong, whatever the interlocking creeds of religion and nationalism may declare. However it originates, violence begets violence. And whether inflicted by soldiers at the behest of emperors and ministers of state, or by robbers and rapists on their own account, it takes the very best of humanity to bring the cycle to an end.

* * *

For the purposes of the story, I have truncated the timeframe in which these events occurred; and most of the characters and events in *Say a Little Prayer* are fictional and not based on real people. The only exceptions are the Kosovar leaders Ibrahim Rugova, Rexhep Qosja and Hashim Thaçi, who appear briefly in the Rambouillet section, along with the British Foreign Secretary, who some may recognise as Robin Cook. Their words and actions are entirely fictitious, of course, and all my own invention.

Kosovars refer to their country as Kosova, not Kosovo, but for the sake of clarity I have stuck with Kosovo throughout.

Acknowledgements

My thanks to my wife Emma for her generous and thoughtful advice on an early draft of *Say a Little Prayer*, and to Wynn Wheldon, who gave me an invaluable commentary on the Rambouillet section.

I owe a debt of gratitude to a number of books and their authors. *The Balkans* by Mark Mazower is a dazzling overview of this complex region – a mere 176 pages, but rich in both broad insights and illuminating detail. Tim Judah is a journalist who covered the conflict from start to finish, and his book *Kosovo: War and Revenge* has the pace and power to shock of the best thrillers. Marc Weller's *Contested Statehood: Kosovo's Struggle for Independence* is a fascinating and judicious account of the formal negotiations over the future of Kosovo, by a man who acted as legal adviser at the Rambouillet Conference. Kathryn Bolkovac's *The Whistleblower* tells the story of her brave campaign to expose the trafficking scandal among military contractors in Bosnia.

The book that affected me most deeply is *On Killing* by Lt. Col. Dave Grossman, which explores the psychological cost of training soldiers to overcome their instinctive aversion to killing their fellow human beings. Some have criticised his research, but it doesn't matter: Grossman has first-hand knowledge of his subject and his compassion and integrity shine from every page. Read it, and find out what we are really doing when we send young men and women to war.

About the Author

Giles O'Bryen is married with three children and lives in London.